COUNTDOWN TO

MIDNIGHT

BY

RODNEY TAYLOR

ISBN-13: 9781468053227
ISBN-10: 1468053221

DEDICATION

This book is dedicated to the men and women of the legal profession who recognize, acknowledge, and act on their high calling to render unselfish service to a public whose rights have been guaranteed by the Constitution of the United States.

ACKNOWLEDGMENTS

No book is ever produced in a vacuum. And neither was this book. While I shall claim the credit for the original idea and the words contained herein, numerous others have touched its development. For their help and encouragement, I offer sincere thanks.

First, I must express a special thanks to a friend who persuaded me to quit thinking about the project and actually to get started on it. Buddy Macon, Deputy Director of the National Museum of Naval Aviation, whose creative genius I respect and admire, provided the final motivation to me to tackle this project. He continues to be a source of inspiration and encouragement.

I am also grateful to my daughters, Leigh Ann Cates and Julie Wilson, and to my son, Brian, who read the manuscript more than once with a critical eye. Who will be more honest than one's own children? Their personal enjoyment of reading mystery novels resulted in suggestions and insights that made this book a profoundly better work.

I also thank B. B. Boles III, Attorney at Law, for the unselfish contribution of his time to providing me legal advice necessary to developing the trial defense strategy. To Paula Sauer, fiber analyst in the Tallahassee office of the Florida Department of Law Enforcement, I offer an immense thank you for her advice and counsel on the scientific details of fiber analysis and its contribution to the resolution of this crime. To Dr. Steve Havard, I am grateful for providing me an experiential education in forensic pathology, and to Dr. Walter Maestri of Louisiana who served as my personal trainer in understanding the Cajun dialect, I tender my gratitude.

Others who deserve acknowledgement include Stephen Trombley, whose book The Execution Protocol offered a sober understanding of both the history and the process of capital punishment; Charles Bodiford, former warden at Holman

Correctional Facility in Atmore, Alabama, and his staff for the tour of Death Row and the death chamber; three judges who both provided the resources to enlighten me on criminal court trial procedure in the State of Florida and read the drafts, offering special insights from the perspective of the sitting judiciary.

How can I ever adequately thank Sandy Young for her part in reading, editing and offering suggestions with respect to plot and storyline? A gifted English teacher and longtime friend, her talents have been recognized by educational publishers who have enlisted her assistance over the years. I can never thank her enough for her perseverance in reading this manuscript and providing such high quality editorial recommendations to make it better. Thanks, Sandy.

To Becky Clark and Craig Granger I express my appreciation for their creative and artistic genius in designing a book cover that tells the story so graphically. Thanks, guys.

And finally to my wife, Patty, English teacher and editor extraordinaire, who sacrificed nights and even some days to watch me struggle with words and phrases and who edited the initial manuscript for content and grammar. For her advocacy, support, encouragement, and recommendations, I am grateful.

Justice is truth in action.

Joseph Joubert, Pensee

THE CRIME

CHAPTER 1

The cool, crisp air of the early December evening seemed to penetrate even the lightest wrap. Clouds hung heavy in the eastern sky, and the humidity increased to uncharacteristically high levels. A misty, thick sea fog had rolled in during the late afternoon from the Gulf of Mexico, reducing visibility and making driving hazardous—a typical fall evening in the Florida Panhandle.

Thanks to reduced lighting in the parking lot, a lone figure, attired in a black jumpsuit, was almost invisible as he crouched low in the shadows of the apartment building. He was not there to cause trouble for anyone. He just wanted to talk with her.

Several hours earlier he had observed her leaving home, appearing to be dressed for a night on the town. Assuming she would be away at least three or four hours, he had returned at 11:30 to find her car still gone.

So he waited. Patiently.

Careful to move about as little as possible so as not to draw attention to himself, he strolled casually to the corner of Building B. Due to the angle of the light from the sidewalk lamppost and the thickness of the fog, the building cast a dim, oblique shadow out toward the parking lot. It was a perfect place to avoid detection and yet be able to see the entrances to all of the apartments in Building C, where she lived.

He squatted to present as low a profile as possible, and there he waited. He felt for the plush velvet pouch in the right pocket of his dark jacket. It was still there. In spite of the damp, cool evening, he felt flushed with warmth and excitement, if not a bit nervous.

The lights of a car appeared from out of the gloom around Building C. A foreign car, something like a BMW, wheeled slowly around the corner and parked near the lamppost. As the driver and single occupant emerged into the light of the lamppost, he recognized him as a man in a picture that had appeared in the newspaper only the week before. He was a local hero.

Being the first on the scene of a tragic car accident, the young man had observed the body of a small child in the floor of the back seat. The child had somehow been ejected from his car seat and flung into the floor, where it lay limp. With the car quickly becoming a fiery inferno, the young man had risked his own life to break out the rear window of the sedan and rescue the little boy from certain death. The child's mother was not so fortunate.

The media called him a hero—less concerned about his own well being than that of others. *I doubt that*, thought the figure in the shadows as he remembered the incident. *Probably just an opportunist.*

Voices. At once the furtive figure became keenly alert. He did not so much as move but hugged the building closely, careful to remain in the darkness of the building's shadow. A young couple, obviously in love, was holding hands, laughing, talking, and strolling down the sidewalk. He watched them as they lingered momentarily in the light of the entryway, kissed deeply, and entered apartment C-4. The lights came on in the apartment, and soon the only sounds to be heard through its slightly raised windows were giggling and moaning from the passionate encounter the couple enjoyed.

Another car approached. Its lights became visible from around the corner of Building C. He glanced at his watch. Almost midnight. Suddenly he was alert, aware. It was her car.

After parking in her reserved space, she opened the car door to exit. Before emerging, she reached onto the floor to retrieve the purse that had dropped off the seat beside her. When she lifted her head and turned to disembark from the car, he was standing there, waiting for her. She was startled by his presence.

"Oh! You frightened me. What are you doing here this time of night?" she asked as she stood firmly in her half opened car door.

—

3

"We need to talk," he said, inching closer, closing the gap between them.

With a rising, dreadful sense of fear from the threatening look in his eyes, she tightened her grip on the door. "There's nothing to talk about. I will not change my mind," she said.

"Why?" he asked. "Why would you do this to me and destroy all that I've worked so long and hard to achieve?"

No more than three feet now separated him from her and the car.

"It's a matter of principle," she responded.

"I brought something that might change your mind." Reaching into his pocket, he retrieved a small, dark-colored, velvet pouch and placed it in her hand. Even in the light from the street lamp, the gold, diamond, and emerald brooch was exquisite, the most beautiful piece of jewelry she had ever seen. "I paid a small fortune for this, but it's yours, if you will only keep quiet."

Hesitating, she returned the brooch to the pouch, handed the pouch to him, and said, "No. It's a matter of conscience. I can't keep quiet about this. Too many people are affected by it. I won't keep silent about it."

"We'll see about that," he said, reaching for her with the speed of a taekwondo master, swiftly turning her around, and putting his hand over her mouth before she could utter a sound. She struggled to break his hold. Inhaling the bitter odor, she slowly lost consciousness. Only a low grunt and the muted sounds of a fading struggle could be heard. Her world went dark.

CHAPTER 2

As though some unseen force had shaken her awake, Sharon Farrell's eyes suddenly opened. Glancing at the clock on her antique nightstand, she noticed the time was 2:45 in the morning. As she cleared the cobwebs from her mind, she thought about Lillian, her apartment mate. She did not remember hearing Lillian come home from her date. *Is she home yet? I don't remember hearing her,* she thought.

Sharon Farrell and Lillian Reins shared a modest, two-bedroom, two-bath apartment along the scenic shores of Escambia Bay. Lillian, a thirty-one-year-old statuesque brunette, gymnasium solid, sun bronzed with dancing eyes and personally confident thanks to Dale Carnegie, was five years senior to Sharon. Self-assured, gregarious, and beautiful, Lillian had served a stint in the United States Navy as an aviator. When reenlistment time came around, she had decided against further exploits as a naval aviator and had resolved rather to settle into her chosen profession in Pensacola.

Sharon Farrell probably could best be described as the exact opposite of Lillian. Dishwater blonde hair, slightly heavy, and with a penchant for junk food, Sharon displayed a quiet spirit, shy almost to the point of appearing cold and indifferent. Yet she was highly intelligent and possessed an analytical mind that was the envy of all those who knew her professionally.

A member of MENSA, the national organization of the preeminently intelligent, Sharon was an accountant by profession, working with a local accounting firm which held contracts with the Navy and other governmental agencies. At the moment, she was the senior accounting officer for the X-37B, the first unmanned shuttle mission that was launched in 2010.

2:47 A.M.: I just don't remember hearing Lillian come home, she kept telling herself. *Maybe she tiptoed in, and I just didn't hear her.*

5

Quietly, she slipped from the warmth of her down comforter, put on her favorite, tattered chenille robe, and eased open the bedroom door. "Rats! That squeak." The door squeaked with the sound of a hundred-year-old, rusty hinge, as it seemed to echo throughout the apartment. She hesitated, waiting for Lillian to call out or emerge from her room in search of the foreign sound.

Nothing.

I'm going to oil that thing tomorrow, she promised herself. Slowly opening the door so as to prevent it from squeaking so loudly, she stepped softly into the narrow hallway between the two bedrooms.

As she moved stealthily along the soft carpet, she halfway expected to run into someone. Approaching Lillian's bedroom, she noticed a dim, flickering light beneath the door. She remembered that Lillian had watched the early evening news while she dressed for her date. And it was her custom to watch the late news on television, turning the set off before retiring completely.

"Lillian," she spoke softly through the door. No answer.

"Lillian, are you awake?" she repeated. Still no answer.

Silently she pushed on the door that was slightly ajar, and it eased open. She looked toward the corner and noticed that the television set, indeed, was on, but muted. *No wonder I couldn't hear the thing,* she sighed, somewhat relieved.

She stepped toward the queen-sized bed, squinted in the low light of the television screen, and saw that the bed was still neatly made. The handmade wedding ring quilt that Lillian's grandmother had given her as a birthday present lay undisturbed across the bed. The bed had not been slept in at all.

As though stunned by fear, she gasped aloud, "Where is Lillian? It's almost 3:00 in the morning, and she's not even here. Something's wrong."

Sharon Farrell turned on her bare heels and headed for the telephone resting on the oak roll top desk in her bedroom. She dialed 911. Her pulse raced as her mind ran through a litany of bad things that could have happened.

*   *   *   *   *   *   *

At precisely two minutes after three in the morning, Sheriff's Deputy Antoine Boudreaux rang the doorbell at the apartment of Sharon Farrell and Lillian Reins. With a ruddy complexion and fly-away hair he sometimes slicked down with hair gel, Boudreaux was a native of the Delta country of Louisiana, and he had always wanted to be a police officer. His characteristic vice was chomping on cigars that he never lit.

Boudreaux was raised the son of a fisherman, and at age nineteen, he hitched a ride to New Orleans to pursue his dream. His young age prevented him from succeeding.

For three years, he worked at odd jobs in New Orleans before traveling east. He stopped in at Pensacola and, using wages earned while working as a stevedore at the seaport, he funded three years of his criminal justice studies at the local junior college. He attempted to lose his deeply ingrained Cajun accent but never succeeded because remnants of the flowing cultural dialect often punctuated his speech.

Finally deciding the time was right, he applied for a job as an Escambia County deputy. He was appointed two months later.

"Come on in," Sharon offered politely.

Boudreaux beheld a look of worry on Sharon's face, her eyes puffy from sleep. Her hair appeared disheveled, and the chenille robe seemed to be at least a size too small. The room was cold as though the heat had not been turned on, and she wrapped her arms around herself for warmth. "What's your problem?" he asked. "The dispatcher said something about a missing friend."

"Yes," Sharon replied. "It's my roommate. She hasn't been home tonight."

"Why you worry about that?" Boudreaux pressed.

"Because it's not like her; she wouldn't do something like this without calling me," Sharon retorted, rather exasperated at his

7

tone. "You see, she left a message for me on our answering machine saying she was going out tonight, but didn't expect to be out later than midnight. I know something's happened," Sharon said.

"Maybe she decided to pass the night with her date," Boudreaux suggested, searching for a plausible explanation.

"Never," Sharon responded, almost shouting, her eyes beginning to fill with tears. "She's not that kind of girl. She would never consider spending the night with a man until she was married. Besides, she would have called me if she weren't going to make it on time."

"We had this deal. If either of us was going to be out later than agreed, the one being late would call and notify the other so she wouldn't worry," Sharon explained.

"Did she go with her date in her car or his?" Boudreaux asked, seeking as many facts as possible.

"They went in her car. She said her date's car was in the shop."

"Did she tell you the name of her date?"

"Yes, it was Jeff," Sharon said. "She's engaged to him."

"Do you know his phone number?"

"Yeah."

"Have you called Jeff to see if he's home yet?" Boudreaux inquired.

"No, I haven't."

"But *cher*, that would be a good place to start, no?"

"Yes. But I hate to bother him at this hour of the morning.'"

"Go ahead, make the call. It may put your mind at ease."

Sharon walked quickly to the phone. With Deputy Boudreaux standing nearby, she dialed Jeff's number, which Lillian had written inside the front cover of the telephone book.

One ring. Two rings. Three rings. Four rings. Five rings. Six. . . . Just as she was about to hang up the phone, a confused male voice answered, "Hel—lo." Sharon had never spoken with Jeffrey

Mitchell so early and had no idea what his morning voice sounded like.

"Jeff?"

"Yes." His voice was shaky as though he were still trying to figure out where he was.

"Jeffrey, this is Sharon, Sharon Farrell."

"Sharon!" Jeff glanced at the digital clock on the nightstand. "Why are you calling me so early in the morning?" he inquired.

"Just checking to see if you're home. Lillian has not been home all night, and I'm beginning to get worried."

"She brought me home about fifteen minutes before midnight. I remember the time because we were joking about me turning into a pumpkin at midnight. And I glanced at my watch to check the time."

"Do you have any idea where she might be at this hour of the morning? When she dropped you off, did she tell you she was going somewhere other than home?"

"No. In fact, she said she had a big day tomorrow, and she wanted to get a good night's rest."

Her voice quaking from a dreadful fear rising from deep inside, she said, "Thanks, Jeff. I'll call you later when I find her."

"Okay, do that." Sharon placed the receiver in its cradle and rested her head in the palms of her hands.

Shaking her head, she said, "This is not like her. I'm worried."

"Now don't jump to no conclusions, *cher*. Give us time. We'll find her. I'm sure she probably had a change of plans and decided to stay over with somebody else."

In spite of the attempt to calm Sharon's fears, Boudreaux himself had an uneasy feeling in the pit of his stomach. These situations were not unusual, but this one seemed to have a sense of foreboding attached to it. A fairly set routine had been broken. This *was* unusual.

"I want to file a missing persons report," Sharon said.

"You do know," Boudreaux responded, "that we can't file the official report 'til she's been missin' for twenty-four hours."

"Why?"

"Procedure."

"To hell with your procedure. She could be out there in a car accident or even worse. And you let procedure stand in the way of doing something?" Sharon's voice became loud and high pitched. She was not only irritated about the problem, but she was also angry with the police for lack of concern for a girl obviously in some kind of trouble.

"You just don't know her like I do," Sharon insisted.

Reading Sharon's emotional state as a sign of genuine apprehension, Boudreaux said,

"Let me tell you what. I'll report it unofficially to the other officers to be on the lookout for her car. What's it look like?"

"It's a teal green, 2009 Ford Mustang. Sorry, I don't know the license number. She just got it four weeks ago from CarMart."

"That's okay. I can get the number. And I'll alert all the officers on duty to be on the lookout for the car. Until twenty-four hours have gone by, I really can't do any more than that."

"Thanks," Sharon said.

Sharon watched through the living room window as Boudreaux walked to his cruiser, wrote something down in a little black book, and spoke into the microphone of his radio. With the interior light still on, Boudreaux dropped the car into gear and slowly moved out of the parking lot and onto Scenic Highway.

10

CHAPTER 3

By now it was almost 4:00. Sharon wondered whether she would be able to sleep. Deciding that it was impossible, she went to the kitchen and prepared a cup of hot chocolate—extra sweet. She tossed in even more artificial sweetener and then emptied twenty miniature marshmallows into her hand and dropped them into the dark mixture. Holding the mug between her cupped hands, Sharon could feel the radiating heat from the hot chocolate. Maybe that same warmth would help her go back to sleep. After all, it was Saturday morning, the only morning all week that she could sleep late.

She drank the smooth, sweet liquid and picked up a book by her favorite writer. After ten pages of the book, she sipped the last savory drops from the cup and felt drowsy. She went to her bedroom, slipped between the covers, and slept fitfully and troubled until 9:00.

*   *   *   *   *   *

It was almost time for Boudreaux to go off duty. On patrol since 7:00 Friday night, he had almost completed his ten-hour shift. He was so looking forward to his three days off from chasing the villainous low-life that comprised the criminal element. He would spend the next three days with his wife and twin boys relaxing and getting ready for the next round of four ten-hour days.

Just seventeen minutes before the shift change, a fellow deputy, Matt Tisdale, reported to the department dispatcher that he had found an abandoned and heavily damaged automobile. Boudreaux's heart skipped a beat, and he quickly picked up the radio microphone and asked Tisdale to meet him on channel seven. After changing channels and making sure Tisdale was on the radio, Boudreaux asked him for a description of the car he had found.

"Teal green Ford Mustang," Tisdale responded. "I think it's a 2009."

"You run the tag?" Boudreaux asked.

"Yep. It belongs to a Lillian McRae Reins."

"Where's this car?"

"North part of the county off Greenleaf Lane."

"Stay there, my man. I'll be there in two shakes of a gator tail," said Boudreaux.

Slowly driving west on Greenleaf Lane, Boudreaux aimed his search light down each little winding trail and dirt road. On the third try, his light fell on the reflectors of a car about a hundred yards off Greenleaf Lane. He turned into the narrow trail and spotted Tisdale standing beside his cruiser, headlights illuminating the teal green Ford Mustang. From the looks of skid marks, it appeared to have left the road and slammed into a tree. It still rested against the tree, as if waiting to tell its story.

"Have you looked to see who's in there?"

"Yeah. There ain't nobody in it. I didn't check any further than that before calling it in. That's when you contacted me."

"You sure there's nobody in there?"

"Yeah. I'm sure. At least as far as the inside of the car is concerned. I didn't check the trunk."

"How'd this car get here?" Boudreaux wondered aloud.

"How am I supposed to know?" Tisdale quipped.

"Let's check it out, *cher*."

Together Boudreaux and Tisdale walked toward the car. Each expressed to the other a sense of apprehension. Tisdale pointed out heavy damage to the right front quarter panel and bumper. Perhaps the driver had become momentarily distracted, causing the car to veer to the right. The tracks indicated that it careened across a shallow swale and into the tree line, glancing off a medium-sized pine tree there and crashing head on into a huge, moss-laden water oak tree. The force of the crash was sufficient to demolish the right front of the car, and the frame was seemingly bent beyond repair.

Boudreaux peered through the right passenger side window and noticed a dark stained sweater in the back seat. He opened the door, carefully removed the sweater with two fingers, and laid it on the hood of the car. He turned once more to the inside of the car and thought, *That cologne smells like somethin' I've smelled before.*

Tisdale opened the driver's side door. "Somebody's been smoking cigarettes in this car and right recently." Tisdale happened to be a former smoker who had quit three years before and was a zealous anti-smoking advocate. His sensitive nose could detect cigarette smoke across the grand ballroom of any major hotel.

"I wonder if the owner smoked," Boudreaux said.

"I don't know, but there is certainly the smell of smoke here."

"Check the ashtray," Boudreaux directed Tisdale.

Opening the ashtray, Tisdale said, "There's ash and a couple of butts."

"You kiddin' me," Boudreaux wisecracked. "Maybe we can get something from them, mes amis."

"Agree," said Tisdale.

The sun was breaking the eastern horizon and beginning its inexorable daylong journey across the southern sky. Boudreaux and Tisdale walked around the car looking for something that might indicate what had happened here and more important to whom it happened.

Then, footprints. Two sets. One set smaller than the other. The first set of prints appeared to be those of a man, with heavy heel indentations, showing that the maker of the prints was either carrying or dragging something heavy. The other set of prints was interrupted periodically with drag marks. The few clear prints from the second set seemed to be made by a woman's casual shoe, possibly with a flat heel. The prints and the drag marks appeared to continue down the dirt trail and then turn markedly in a southwesterly direction toward a heavily wooded area. Boudreaux, trained by his father to be a hunter, knew how to follow tracks, animal or human. And follow these he did.

Close to a hundred and fifty yards down the trail and another twenty-five yards into the forest, the drag marks and footprints abruptly ended. Nothing to indicate that anything had been dragged any farther. A mystery.

Perhaps not. Near the base of a loblolly pine, the ground appeared to have been disturbed. Some of the needles from the loblolly pine and leaves that had recently fallen from the surrounding trees were dry while others nearby were damp from the humid night air and heavy dewfall. Scattered in awkward patterns, the needles and leaves did not appear to have simply fallen from a tree. They appeared to have been disturbed by someone or something.

Boudreaux cautiously walked around the area of disturbed leaves, his heart beating a little faster and his senses quickening. Walking in concentric circles, about five feet apart, he paced slowly, steadily, carefully looking before he stepped ahead. On his third circular pass, he spotted a large water oak tree stood. He moved right to avoid the tree and was stunned by what he saw. A grisly scene. Blood was everywhere. *Looks almost like a deer's been gutted here,* he thought. *But where are the guts?* The fallen leaves and limbs were scattered in disarray like a heap in which children had played. This was no field dressing site; it was obvious some kind of struggle had occurred here.

Blood was spattered all over the northern side of the tree trunk. The pattern indicated that the blood had spurted from its source. A pool of blood had collected at the base of the tree, and the trunk was heavily marked with scratches, either from the antlers of a rutting deer or possibly the desperate clawing of a yet undiscovered victim.

14

From the looks of the area, whoever it was musta put up a pretty good fight. Struggled hard. From the north side of the tree, Boudreaux followed a path of jumbled vegetation, possibly a body being dragged, until it led to a thicket of dense underbrush. Along the path, spattered red droplets of what appeared to be blood could be seen on the tops of the fallen brown leaves. Then suddenly the trail stopped.

Using a small tree limb he had found nearby, Boudreaux cautiously moved the underbrush aside. Deeper. Deeper. The brush was almost a foot thick at this point, and he did not wish to contaminate whatever he found. Then he saw it.

A bright red piece of cloth with a buttonhole. It looked like the top of a shirt. Pulling aside more brush, he exposed the top of a sleeve; he continued until the entire sleeve, including a human hand came into view. Covered with blood, it was doubtless the victim of this crime. This was now a crime scene.

Returning to where Tisdale was communicating with the radio dispatcher about what had been found, Boudreaux walked in a wide turn so as not to retrace the path he had originally followed from the car.

"What'd you find? Anything important?" Tisdale asked curiously.

"Yeah. And it don't look pretty. We got a body underneath some underbrush. Please, *mes amis*, call the crime scene boys."

*　　*　　*　　*　　*　　*

An hour went by; Tisdale and Boudreaux passed the time discussing what had been their plans for a great three-day respite with their families.

"No time off now," Boudreaux lamented. "My wife'll probably make me pass the time on the sofa for a week. I'd like to wrap this one up quickly, but there's really no tellin' how long it'll take."

"Yeah. I don't envy you at all. Just work fast and get it over with as quickly as you can. Maybe the chief will thank you by giving you some extra time off."

"Fat chance," Boudreaux said caustically.

Finally, the crime scene team appeared. Stepping out of the van, Stephen Sasser, head of the team asked, "What do we have here?"

"Found a body. No doubt it's a homicide," Boudreaux said. "Come on this way, and I'll show you what I found."

Following close behind Boudreaux, Sasser and his two associates, Paul Pinkston and Randel Lamont, listened and observed as Boudreaux first pointed out the area of disturbed leaves. He walked toward the tree and showed them the bloodied and scarred tree trunk with the pool of blood at its base. And then he led them to the area of underbrush where he had exposed the red sleeve and the bloodied human hand.

"That's all I got," he said. "Time for you to do your thing."

"That's enough," Sasser retorted. "Looks pretty brutal to me. Must have put up a helluva fight. We just need to find the bastard who did it. Pinkston, start at the trail and stretch the crime scene tape from the trail and out in a circle a hundred yards from the body. Then start on the car; Randel and I will wait until you have the tape up and will start searching the woods."

Sasser, Pinkston, and Lamont retreated to their van to retrieve cases containing the tools of the trade. Pinkston tied one end of the crime scene tape to a tree near the trail. He walked toward the location of the body then out a hundred yards and around in a circle, wrapping the tape around trees as he went. Returning to the trail, he tied the final end of the tape to the same tree where he had started. In the meantime, Sasser and Lamont started searching within the perimeter.

With case in hand, Pinkston walked to the car. Donning a pair of rubber gloves, he began to collect and preserve, according to established protocol, the evidence that hopefully would lead them to the killer. Boudreaux followed.

"You gonna find a sweater on the hood. I found it in the back seat on top of some magazines, newspapers, a beach bag, and a foldin' chair. She probably used that stuff at the beach during the summer and just hadn't cleaned it out yet. From the blood on the magazines, that sweater was likely underneath the pile and got pulled out by the perp. Two cigarette butts are still in the ashtray and what looks like pieces of fingernails are scattered on the floor of the front passenger's side," he informed Pinkston. Boudreaux was careful to stay away from the car so as not to contaminate the scene.

"Thanks. I'll get to that later. Right now I'm more interested in this purse under the driver's seat."

"Purse? I didn't see a purse."

"You weren't looking for it. Sometimes the best place to find evidence is under the seats. So that's where I usually begin. Besides, it was pushed pretty far under the seat. You wouldn't have seen it unless you stuck your hand underneath."

Pinkston extracted the purse with metal tongs and dusted it for fingerprints. The patent leather material made the job easier because oily substances like fingerprints adhere quite well to patent leather. The dust revealed two clear and distinguishable latent prints. After collecting the prints on tape and preserving them for analysis, Pinkston opened the purse, careful to maintain the integrity of any additional evidence.

No unusual contents, he thought.

Pinkston slowly removed each item, one by one, laying it on the hood of the wrecked car. Lipstick, comb, breath mints, hair barrette, fingernail clippers, two gasoline credit card receipts, six pennies, three nickels, a quarter, a checkbook, and a case for eye glasses. Nothing out of the ordinary, he confirmed, as he dropped each of the items into a clear plastic bag, sealed the bag with red evidence tape, and marked and numbered it.

Her wallet was the last item he removed from the purse. It still contained her American Express Gold Card, two Visa cards, her driver's license, social security card, photos, a blood donor card, other assorted articles, and $226.00 in cash. "Robbery won't the motive," Boudreaux offered. Pinkston left the items in the wallet, and it, too, was placed in a plastic evidence bag and sealed.

Boudreaux looked at the gasoline receipts through the clear bag, but the print was too light to read. Obviously a poor printer ribbon. Then he viewed the open checkbook and read the name imprinted there. LILLIAN MCRAE REINS. The address shown was the apartment shared with Sharon Farrell. Sharon had been right.

*   *   *   *   *   *

After several hours of collecting evidence, Lamont and Sasser, now joined by Pinkston, were ready to investigate the body itself. First, they photographed the sleeve and hand just as Boudreaux had uncovered them. They then used special tools to remove the top layer of vegetation, being careful not to disturb the body or its clothing any more than necessary. Brambles and iron weed were plentiful and covered the area. Dull probes and machetes were used to clear away the iron weed and thorny brambles from over and around the body. Slowly and cautiously, they uncovered the blood-encrusted body of a young woman. Her skin had already taken on a blue pallor. Appearing to be between twenty-five and thirty-five years old, slender build, brunette, and sun tanned, she would have been the envy of any South Florida sun worshiper.

The loose fitting, red silk, long sleeved blouse was fastened by white floral buttons and accented by a one-inch, hand-embroidered lace stand up collar at the neck. The buttons on the blouse were opened, fully exposing both breasts. The buttonholes appeared to have been torn as though someone may have angrily grabbed the blouse with both hands and ripped it open.

The open blouse also revealed sharp trauma to the right side of the victim's neck. Her neck appeared to have been cut from the center of the throat upwards to the left ear. With so much blood, it was hard at this point to determine exactly what happened. An autopsy, hopefully, would provide much more information.

Wrapping up their inspection of the body, Sasser and Lamont returned to searching the area for whatever clues might be uncovered. The murderer had been careful not to provide another path to follow, but had apparently exited the woods by the path along which he dragged Lillian. They slowly walked that path, stopping periodically to inspect something that caught their eyes. As they walked, they observed Boudreaux leaning against a hollow tree chewing on an unlit cigar.

Sasser found a small piece of cloth, obviously ripped from clothing by the thorny brambles. Inspecting it carefully in the sunlight, he could not find a match to any of Lillian's clothing. *Must have been from the killer*, Sasser thought.

Lamont called to Sasser, and he walked to where Lamont was standing. Lamont stood with a small blue velvet pouch, the drawstrings hanging loosely. "I found this among a pile of leaves near the bloody tree. Must have fallen out of the pocket of the perp," Lamont said.

"Open it," said Sasser.

Carefully, Lamont opened the blue pouch and retrieved its contents, a gold, rose-shaped brooch encrusted with what looked to the naked eye like diamonds and emeralds. "That's gorgeous," said Lamont. "Yeah, certainly unique," responded Sasser. "Looks like it might be custom made." Lamont returned the brooch to the pouch, placed both in a plastic bag and marked it. With most of the crime scene scoured, Sasser left Lamont to wrap up.

After several hours of working with the crime scene team, Boudreaux returned to headquarters, where Sheriff Jonathan Williams was in his office occupying himself with busy work and anxiously awaiting any additional word about the victim and the murder. Stephen Sasser had called him as soon as the body was confirmed found. "What's the latest, Boudreaux?" Williams asked.

"I confirmed who she is. It *is* Lillian Reins. I found a checkbook with her name on it in her purse as well as other identifying papers: driver's license, social security card, and blood donor card," Boudreaux informed the Sheriff.

"Tony, I'm going to ask you to take the lead on this for the time being. Patrick Monaghan and Raymond Pearce of the homicide division are both away for the weekend. I hate to involve anyone else at this point, so you get on with the investigation. I'll bring Monaghan and Pearce in on it next week. You can brief them on the investigation at that point."

This turn of events pleased Boudreaux considerably. He had always wanted to work in the detectives' division anyway and had, on several occasions, requested a transfer. Now was his chance to prove that he could handle the job. "Thanks, *mes amis*," he said, his Cajun gratitude slipping into his speech. "I won't let you down."

Boudreaux was overwhelmed by the dreadful task he knew he faced—breaking the news of Lillian's death to her roommate. He arranged for Sasser to accompany him and asked Deputy Tisdale to follow him to the apartment. While Boudreaux broke the news to Sharon, Sasser would search the apartment and especially Lillian's room.

By now it was early afternoon, and Sharon would be confident beyond all doubt that Lillian had been in an accident or met with some kind of foul play. Those had been her thoughts throughout the morning; there would be no reason for her to change her mind by this time in the day. In spite of this, Boudreaux dreaded revealing the cold hard truth.

While driving from the Sheriff's Department headquarters to Sharon's apartment on Scenic Highway, he concentrated on how he might appropriately inform her. He decided that it would be best to be direct.

Boudreaux parked in front of her door. Tisdale parked two spaces farther up the driveway. With Sasser following close behind, they approached her door. Boudreaux rang the doorbell. A minute passed before Sharon Farrell answered. As she opened the door, she saw the look on Boudreaux's face and began to weep. Waves of grief overcame her as she lamented, "You found her, didn't you?"

"Can we come in?" Boudreaux asked.

"Yes. Come on in. You found her, didn't you?" she asked again.

Boudreaux could not evade so direct a question. "Yeah. We found her early this morning. You were right, cher, it's not good."

"With tears beginning to make tracks down her face, Sharon said, "Tell me what you know. Was she in an accident or something? Did something terrible happen? Did she meet with foul play? Just tell me about her."

"She was not in an accident, Sharon, we think. . . she was . . . murdered."

More tears even more intense than before overtook Sharon as her body shook and heaved beneath the weight of sorrow. *Why Lillian?* she thought.

"Sharon, this is Stephen Sasser, one of our crime scene investigators. He will be around the apartment for a while to see if there is anythin' here that might be helpful to the investigation.

"OK," she responded, still weeping. Sasser retired toward Lillian's bedroom.

"And this is Officer Tisdale. He actually found the car and is assisting me with the investigation. We'll be around the apartment for a little while as well. Do you mind?"

"Of course not." Sharon retreated to the privacy of her own bedroom while Boudreaux and Tisdale searched the desk, shelves, and trash cans. At the same time, Sasser inspected Lillian's room.

Boudreaux left Tisdale with Sasser in Lillian's room while he went to seek information from Sharon. Going into Farrell's room and finding her sprawled across her bed, Boudreaux asked, "Do you know of her family?"

"I met her mother and father last year when they came during the Easter season. Lillian was from St. Joseph, Missouri. Her father's name is Ernest; I think her mother's name is Norma. They are simple, ordinary people, living and working on a large farm. They had high hopes for their only daughter and did everything within their power to make her dreams come true. I'm sure I can find their phone number here somewhere. Would you like to have it?"

"For sure," Boudreaux replied. "We need to get in touch with them as soon as possible." Probably more difficult than notifying Sharon Farrell, he cringed at the thought of having to inform Lillian's parents about their daughter's death and especially how she died.

Sharon searched the roll top desk for a small, red address/phone book, which Lillian kept in the second drawer. Removing the book, she found the number for Lillian's parents, scribbled it on a small scrap of paper, and handed it to Boudreaux.

"Miss Farrell, we're going to need you to come and provide a positive identification of the body," Tisdale interrupted.

"Yeah," added Boudreaux. "We really do hate to ask you to do this for us, but it'll help speed up the investigation. Can you help us, *cher*?"

"I guess so."

*   *   *   *   *   *

It was now late in the day, and Pinkston and Lamont had finally completed the crime scene investigation off Greenleaf Drive. The body had been removed from its crude burial site and transported to the morgue to await autopsy. After checking and rechecking the boxes containing the evidence bags, they left the crime scene just as a truck arrived to tow Lillian Reins's vehicle to the impound lot for safe keeping until the investigation was complete.

Driving directly to the headquarters building of the Florida Department of Law Enforcement, referred to more commonly as the FDLE, the two investigators delivered the large, plastic crime scene carry-alls to the department's intake office. There Nancy Manning, Intake Coordinator, met them. Manning was responsible for receiving all evidence, assigning a case number, and recording an inventory. The carry-alls were placed on a table as the intake secretary recorded notations of the time of transfer in the intake log.

"Got another one for me?" Manning asked as she noticed and acknowledged the cases.

"Yeah, quite bad one this time, too," said Pinkston.

Manning quickly glanced at the contents of the cases and resealed the boxes with crime scene tape. "Well, I'll take care of it from here. You guys can call it a day and go home to your wives."

"After a day like this, I feel like a brewsky is in order," said Pinkston. "Maybe I'll be a little late for dinner tonight." Pinkston and Lamont left the FDLE office, headed toward their favorite watering hole.

Manning remained long enough to label and number each item and transfer them to the vault. Later she would prepare the paperwork required to get the laboratory analyses of the investigation started.

CHAPTER 4

Sharon Farrell's eyes were red and swollen as she drove to the headquarters of the county sheriff. Boudreaux was to meet her there and escort her to the morgue where she would identify the body that had been found earlier in the day.

Tired from grief, scared by what she was about to do, and in no real hurry, Sharon drove well within the speed limit. A light mist was falling from the dusky, late fall sky. It was one of those aggravating, misty rains—not hard enough really to need the windshield wipers but too hard simply to leave them turned off. She despised weather like this, but it certainly did fit her mood. *The next car I buy will have intermittent wipers*, she thought.

When she arrived at the Sheriff's Department headquarters, she parked her car in a visitor parking space, exited, careful not to fall on the slippery pavement, and walked toward the front of the building. Before opening the door, she removed a tissue from her purse and blew her nose, trying to give the appearance of being "all together." She took a long, deep breath and walked through the revolving door.

A uniformed female officer met Sharon at the front desk. She told the officer that she was there to see Deputy Boudreaux. Myra, the officer on duty, looked at a list of visitors, found Sharon's name, gave her a prepared pass, and directed her to Boudreaux's office.

"Deputy Boudreaux?" she half asked as she lightly knocked on his door. "May I come in?"

"Oh, yes, Miss Farrell," Boudreaux said, "do come in and please call me Tony. We don't need to be formal. You think you can do this?"

"I guess so. If it has to be done, it has to be done."

"Then let's get on with it."

Together, Boudreaux and Farrell retraced her steps to the front of the building. Boudreaux handed Farrell's pass back to Myra and, being the southern gentleman that he was, he motioned for Farrell to go out ahead of him. Outside the door under the protection of the overhang, Boudreaux opened an umbrella that looked large enough for four people.

"My golf umbrella," he said. "It'll be good 'nuff to get us across the street without gettin' wet, maybe."

Entering the county hospital across the street from the sheriff's headquarters, Boudreaux led them through a series of passageways, down the elevator one floor, and through a maze of corridors at right angles to each other, forcing them to make numerous right turns. Finally, he stopped in front of a door with a sign that, in large, bold letters, read MORGUE. He opened the door and asked Sharon to step inside. The door silently closed behind them.

The room was dimly lit with a single low-watt bulb. She noticed that it also had double fluorescent bulbs, which, she assumed, were turned on during regular hours when "viewings" were not being held.

Suddenly she felt cold. The viewing room exuded an obvious, macabre chill, as though the air from the adjacent room were filtering in from where the bodies were stored. It reeked of death. Although the blinds on the viewing room window were closed, it was apparent that the adjacent room, brightly lit with fluorescent bulbs, belied its dark and foreboding purpose.

Boudreaux broke the silence. "The light in the room is dimmed so that you might see the body a little better. We don't like to make mistakes. The body has been brought close to the viewin' window. You let me know when you want to have the sheet turned back. I'll knock on the window, and the attendant'll open the blinds. You can take a look when you're ready," he explained. "You understand, *cher*?"

"Yes."

25

Farrell looked up into the dark ceiling of the viewing room as though offering a silent prayer, drew a deep breath and said, "Go ahead. I'm as ready as I'll ever be."

Boudreaux knocked on the window. The attendant, as instructed by Boudreaux earlier, raised the blind and drew the sheet back only to the base of the Lillian's chin not revealing the severe trauma which was evident around the neck of the victim.

"Oh, my God," Farrell gasped. "It *is* her. My God. What happened? Oh, Lillian, who could have done this to you?"

"You goin' to be all right?"

"No, I feel faint."

Boudreaux promptly knocked on the window again, and the blinds were instantly closed.

*   *   *   *   *   *

Coming to, Sharon Farrell found herself reclining on a sofa just outside the morgue. Boudreaux offered her a soda, which she accepted with gratitude.

"You all right now?" Boudreaux inquired.

"I think so," Farrell responded.

"I need a little help here for just a while, *cher*. You think you can stick with me for a few minutes?" Boudreaux asked.

"What kind of help?"

"Well, now that you positively IDd the body, later today we gonna notify Lillian's family in Missouri. You gave us their phone number, and Officer Tisdale discovered their names and home address from some letters he found in her room at your apartment. So we have all the contact information on them. Can you think of anybody else we oughta notify?"

"Absolutely. We must let Jeffrey know. He must be worried sick just from my call early this morning."

"And who is this Jeffrey?"

"Jeffrey Mitchell. He's Lillian's steady."

"Anybody else?"

———

26

"You probably should notify her supervisor at Goodall and Dohr. His name is Mark Bradley. He and her co-workers will be curious when she doesn't show up for work on Monday. I can't think right now of anyone else who should be notified personally about her."

"*Merci*, Sharon. You been a great help. Do I need to take you home or do you feel like driving?"

"Give me a minute or two. I think then I can make it by myself."

After walking Farrell back to her car, Boudreaux said, "Take care of yourself, *cher*. Call us if you got any questions or remember anything else you think we oughta know about."

She responded with a sorrowful nod.

CHAPTER 5

On Sunday morning, Boudreaux drove to the home of Jeffrey Mitchell, a quaint little dwelling on a quiet suburban street. Mitchell lived alone. An accountant, he lived comfortably from earnings and bonuses at Andrews, Eisen & Tutt, the same accounting firm for which Sharon Farrell worked. In fact, he had met Lillian through Sharon who had worked jointly with him on several accounts.

It was obvious that Jeffrey Mitchell was not a morning person. Wiping sleep from his eyes, he appeared to have been in some kind of sleep-induced stupor. Boudreaux felt bad that he had awakened him.

"I hate to bust in on you like this, but can I come in?" Boudreaux asked politely, showing his deputy's badge.

"Why, yes. I'm sorry. My work is often so hectic that I try to sleep in as frequently as I can on Saturdays and Sundays."

"You a friend of Lillian Reins?"

"Yes. Some people even say she and I were an item."

"When was the last time you saw her?"

"We went out on a date on Friday night. I saw her then."

"No, exactly when did you last see her?"

"When she brought me home and let me out."

"You mean you didn't go on the date in your car?"

"No. We took her car because mine is in the shop for repairs. Why are you asking these questions? Does it have anything to do with that call I got yesterday morning from Sharon Farrell?" Mitchell inquired, puzzled.

"Yeah, it does," Boudreaux said. "I don't really know how to tell you, but Lillian Reins was found murdered yesterday morning."

Jeffrey Mitchell's mouth fell open in disbelief. His eyes flared open, and he finally put his head in his hands and said, "No. Tell me you are mistaken. You are, aren't you?"

"No, *mes amis*."

"I guess you wouldn't joke about somebody being murdered. How did it happen? Do you know who did it?" he asked.

"No details right now. We're investigating. But there's plenty of evidence, and I think we'll have the perp who did this soon," he informed Mitchell.

"How long you know Lillian?" Boudreaux queried.

"I have known her for about nineteen months," Mitchell answered.

"And how well did you know her?"

"Very well. We were serious about our relationship. We had even talked about marriage."

"Are you engaged?"

"Uh, well yes. . . no. . . I guess you would say so. I had given her an engagement ring. But Friday night we talked and agreed to call it off, and she gave me back my ring," he explained. "Are you sure you can't tell me something, anything?"

"No, not right now. But make sure you don't take off without telling me first. We may need to talk with you again."

"Am I a suspect?" Jeffrey asked hesitantly.

Boudreaux handed Mitchell a business card. "Right now anybody who knew her is a suspect. Just stay in town in case we need to talk to you some more. If you have to go out of town, check with me first. Can I count on you to do that, *amis*?"

"Yes, of course," Mitchell replied.

Boudreaux's next stop was Lillian's employer—at least her supervisor. Dialing the home phone number for Mark Bradley, Boudreaux waited for an answer.

"Hello, this is the Bradley residence," came the young voice.

"Can I talk to your father, *cher*?" Boudreaux asked.

Boudreaux could hear the child cover the phone as she yelled, "Dad, some strange sounding man wants you on the phone."

Then the silence was broken: "Yes, this is Mark Bradley."

"Mr. Bradley, this is Tony Boudreaux of the Sheriff's Department. I was wondering if you could meet me at your office in about an hour?"

"What's this all about?" Bradley asked curiously.

"I don't want to discuss it on the phone. Just meet me, *mes amis*."

"Sure. You said an hour?"

"Right. About 11:00?"

"Okay. I'll see you then," Bradley said, puzzled.

*   *   *   *   *   *

Located in a prime downtown high rise, the offices of Goodall and Dohr were resplendent in decor. The firm occupied the top three floors of the twenty-five story building, with the highest level executives situated in the luxurious penthouse offices, while the mid and lower-level executives and their departments occupied the twenty-fourth and twenty-third floors.

Since it was Sunday, the doors to the high-rise office building were closed and tightly secured. Boudreaux waited outside for Bradley to arrive.

At five minutes after eleven, Bradley drove up, parked his car in his private parking space, and walked to the front door, where Boudreaux was waiting. "What's this all about?" he inquired.

"I don't want to talk here. Let's go upstairs." Boudreaux responded. Without another word between them, the two took the elevator to the twenty-fourth floor where Bradley's office was located.

Boudreaux was led through a maze of offices occupied by account executives and their supervisors, typically associate vice presidents. The decor could be described only as gaudy and pretentious. Surrounded by mahogany wainscoting, the upper portion of the walls was painted a rich antique white accented by three-inch dentil crown molding at the ceiling. The offices of the associate vice presidents were lined around the outside walls with ample windows and splendid views overlooking the bay and its scenic beauty. Throughout the interior, ornate, hand-crafted, moveable wall sections separated the offices of the account executives. One of these interior offices belonged to Lillian Reins.

Not unlike most of the others, Bradley's office radiated an air of elegance and excess, bespeaking his importance to the firm and his status in the "pecking order." His desk was large, made from the finest, close-grained cherry wood, carved, and topped with a six-foot by six-foot work surface. Behind him was a matching credenza with grand bookcases accented with leaded, beveled stained glass. On the shelves were individual pictures of his wife and three children. One photo showed the family together at what appeared to be a lakeside picnic.

Boudreaux broke the silence. "Mr. Bradley, did Lillian Reins work for you?"

"Yes. She is an excellent account executive, successful, valuable to this firm, and a fine example of a quality person. I wish I had more like Lillian. Why do you ask and why use the word 'did'?"

"Miss Reins was found murdered early yesterday morning in the north end of the county."

"Do you know what happened?" Bradley asked with a look of astonishment.

"The murder's bein' investigated. We got lotta evidence that's being processed by the crime scene technicians."

"Does her boyfriend know?"

"Yeah, I told him earlier today."

"Good, he and I are close friends. In fact, he and Lillian met through me and Lillian's roommate, Sharon Farrell. I can't believe that something so dreadful has happened to her. Especially this. Are you sure she was a murder victim? She was everybody's friend, quiet, not vicious or mean-spirited. I've never known her to be rude to anyone, even when she probably should have been."

—

31

"Yeah, we're absolutely sure. How well do you know Jeffrey Mitchell?" Boudreaux queried.

"As I mentioned, he is probably the best friend I have in this town. Successful in his own right, I don't know a better 'bean counter' around. He and Lillian made the perfect couple."

"Did you know they had talked marriage?"

"I can't say that I actually knew about it, but it certainly doesn't surprise me," Bradley offered. "They had been dating for some time."

"Can you done show me Lillian's work area?"

"Sure, it's right outside my office."

Boudreaux noticed that there were pictures on her desk. One of the pictures, taken at the entrance to Disney World, showed Jeffrey with his arms around the shoulders of Sharon on his left and Lillian on his right. Another picture appeared to be that of her mother and father. A single picture of Jeffrey, framed in hearts, graced the center of her desk facing toward her chair.

Boudreaux looked through the desk drawers and found nothing of obvious significance to the investigation. Her calendar book lay to one side. He picked it up, thumbed through it, and decided to take it with him. Small tidbits of paper with names, phone numbers, and in a few cases, instructions to herself could be found scattered across the desk. Bundling them, Boudreaux took them also. All else appeared to be associated with work and clients and would likely be of little use to the investigation.

After going through Lillian's work space, Boudreaux re-entered Bradley's office. "Thanks for your time, Mr. Bradley," Boudreaux said appreciatively. "You done been helpful. Stay close to town so that we can talk with you again if we must need to."

"If my plans call for travel, I'll first call you." Bradley asked.

"Good."

Bradley and Boudreaux retraced their steps to the front door. Bradley turned the thumb lock, and the two stepped outside into the brisk, cool wind that blew from off the bay. Using his key, Bradley locked the door behind them, and they parted.

CHAPTER 6

Returning to his Mercedes 480, Bradley drove directly home. His heart was pounding from the tragic news about Lillian. He wondered how Jeffrey was taking it.

Bradley altered his usual route home in order to drive by Jeffrey Mitchell's house. His car was in the garage and the door was up. He decided to stop.

Jeffrey was slow to respond to the ringing of the doorbell.

"Hi, Jeff," Bradley said, trying to sound cheerful.

"Why are you here on a Sunday afternoon?" Jeffrey asked.

"I just heard about Lillian. I felt I needed to come by and see how you were doing. You must be devastated." Bradley was trying to soothe Jeffrey's feelings of loss.

"You will never know. But the worst part is that I'm experiencing a double loss."

"What do you mean?"

"Lillian and I went out Friday night. On that date, we had a long conversation about our future."

"And?"

"And we ended our engagement. It was kind of a mutual thing. Neither one of us felt that the time was right, and even though we have been seeing each other steadily for nine months, the relationship didn't quite seem to be cementing. The mutual support just was not there. We decided to remain friends and would see what the future holds. But now. . ." His voiced trailed off.

"I'm sorry to hear that," Mark said. "You both seemed so devoted to each other. Were there any ill feelings?"

"Like I said, it was a mutual decision. But, Mark, I genuinely loved her. Deep down I didn't want to break it off, but I knew she did, so I went along with it."

"I'm really sorry about all this. Is there anything I can do for you?" Bradley offered.

"I don't think so. I'm so shocked at the moment I don't really know what to do. Just give me some time. And by the way, thanks for dropping by."

CHAPTER 7

Boudreaux decided he had done all he could for a Sunday. He knew he could get back on track early on Monday. He drove home and joined his family for an afternoon picnic at a seaside park. Later in the evening he settled in for his favorite television show. These diversions were refreshing, after his active morning.

* * * * * *

Dawn broke on Monday once again with heavy, dark clouds rolling in from the northwest. The weather seemed to mirror the mood he was in—depressed and grim. The rain was falling in sheets. Boudreaux had planned to meet with the coroner's office to review the autopsy report on Lillian Reins. The autopsy had been scheduled for Sunday evening, and he hoped the report would be ready by this morning.

When he arrived at the department for his shift to begin, Sergeant Barnhart handed Boudreaux a note. It was from the Sheriff asking him to drop by his office for a conference. Concerned about this turn of events, Boudreaux thanked Sergeant Barnhart and strode immediately to the office of Sheriff Jonathan Williams.

Boudreaux knocked lightly on the closed door. "Come in," he heard from the inside. He entered slowly but confidently.

"Good morning, Tony. How are you this fine Monday morning?" Sheriff Williams asked pleasantly.

"Good, except for the Lillian Reins murder over the weekend," Boudreaux replied.

"That's what I want to talk about. Tony, for some time now you've been asking me about the possibility of moving over into the homicide division to work as a detective."

"Yeah. I enjoy the investigative work, and I thought it might give me more time and flexibility with my wife and kids."

"Well, your time has come. Deputy Tisdale told me about the outstanding way you conducted the on-site investigation of the

Reins murder, and Monaghan was impressed with the way you initiated questioning of potential suspects. That kind of initiative impresses me. There is currently an opening in the homicide division—it's small, you know—and I'm going to let you have that position. Are you willing to accept the position?"

A little stunned, but very happy, Boudreaux said, "I done be glad to take the job. This Reins murder stands a good chance of bein' solved pretty quick, so I need to know if you gonna keep me on it," Boudreaux remarked, wondering if he would be placed on another case or sent out to review unsolved cases.

"Yes. You will continue to be the investigator of record on this one. I expect you to do your best and wrap it up with evidence for a strong case as soon as you can. There is an overload of cases in this division, and I can use you on them. But I'm going to let you remain on this one for the time being."

"Thanks, Sheriff. My wife and family'll be happy as I am about this promotion, I'm sure. When do I start?"

"Normally, I would wait about two weeks to make the transfer official, allowing you to work out your shifts, but I want you to get on it today. Lieutenant Stone, head of the division, will give you your duty schedule. As you know, you have to be quite flexible in that division, but work schedules are maintained as closely as possible to original plans. You can check in with Lieutenant Stone this morning and proceed with your investigation."

"I appreciate this chance. You won't be disappointed," promised Boudreaux.

Smiling to himself, Boudreaux left the Sheriff's office and, while checking in with Lieutenant Stone, received his schedule for the week.

What a surprise, Boudreaux thought. *I gotta phone Maggie and let her in on the good news. . . No, it can wait'll I get off this afternoon.*

37

Boudreaux proceeded on with his plans to meet with the county medical examiner at her office.

Entering the administrative wing of the coroner's office, he tried to be as pleasant as possible. "A good mornin', *mon cher*," he said to Cynthia, the receptionist.

"Good morning to you, Deputy Boudreaux," she responded in like manner. She could sense a distinct hint of exhilaration yet despondency in his voice. "Did you have a hard weekend?" she asked, trying to feel him out.

"First of all, it's now Detective Boudreaux. I got promoted this mornin'," Boudreaux said.

"Great. Congratulations. You deserve it," Cynthia noted, thinking that it probably accounted for the exhilaration in his voice.

"As for my weekend, hard won't begin to describe it. What with this murder and all, my time is just not my own. Is Sheila in yet?"

"Not yet, but she is due any minute. Care to wait for her?"

"Yeah. I need to talk wit' her before I done get on with this investigation. By the way, do you know whether she got around to the autopsy on the Reins victim?" Boudreaux inquired.

"She sure did. I have the tape of her report right here."

"You didn't write it up yet?"

"No. I'm doing it the first thing this morning. Should be ready by early afternoon. I'm making it a priority. That's what's on the note from Sheila." Cynthia placed the cassette into her transcribing machine. "Oh, here is Sheila now."

A forty-two year old beauty, Doctor Sheila Josephson, was in her sixth year as the county medical examiner. At six feet one inch, she exhibited the hard body of a trained athlete. She went to the health club four days a week and maintained her weight and body fat at ideal levels. Her shoulder length brunette hair and medium brown eyes accented her athletic build. She was, what Boudreaux often described, as a "head turner."

Not only was Sheila Josephson beautiful but also keenly intelligent. A cum laude graduate of Florida State University, she had obtained her medical degree in pathology from Tulane University Medical School. During her undergraduate years, she had been selected as Miss Florida State and had competed in the Miss Florida pageant.

Sheila appeared in the doorway. Looking stunningly attired, Boudreaux thought, *If I passed her on the street I'd never guess what she did for a living.*

"Good morning, Deputy Boudreaux," Sheila said as she finally walked through the door. "How are you doing this morning?"

"Couldn't be better, *cher*, with this promotion under my belt. You can now call me *Detective* Boudreaux. And thanks for asking—just tryin' to keep the pirogue straight in the bayou, I guess. I'm here to look at the autopsy report on Reins, but Cynthia done tol' me it won't be ready 'til this afternoon. Can you spare me a few minutes and just tell me what you found. I can get the written report when it's ready."

"Well, congratulations on your promotion. Deserved I'm sure. Come on in." Boudreaux followed Sheila Josephson into her office. Simply decorated, like everything else associated with the coroner's office, her desk was piled high with paper. *It'd probably qualify as winner of the messy desk contest,* Boudreaux thought.

"What'd you find?" he asked pointedly.

"A mess. It was a brutal killing. She was stabbed beneath the left arm in what appears to be an upward motion. The killer was probably holding her around the neck with his right arm and used his left hand to stab her. But that was not the wound that ultimately killed her. She was also stabbed in the larynx with the knife drawn toward the left, severing her windpipe and internal and external carotid arteries. The knife also nicked the internal jugular vein. She primarily bled out."

"Any other trauma to the body."

"It appeared she had been slapped around a good bit before the fatal wounds were inflicted. She exhibited heavy bruising on the right side of her face as though having been slapped from the front by a left-handed person. Her hair had been pulled violently because the top portion of her scalp revealed severe root exposure and in a few cases completely separated from the scalp. She had been shot once in the upper chest with a large caliber gun."

"Shot? I don't think the crime scene team found any gun; I will check with them, though. Had she been raped?" Boudreaux asked, seeking at least a potential motive for the crime.

"Certainly possible. Her clothing was in considerable disarray, including her underpants being down near her knees. And there was the presence of semen in the vaginal canal but not deep inside."

"Is there anythin' else you can tell me?" Boudreaux asked, even though he knew he had enough to go on for right now.

"Nothing of investigative significance. The details, blood work, potential DNA evidence, stomach contents, and so forth will be in the written report. I would suggest you give Cynthia until tomorrow morning to finish it. I want to review it before releasing it in final form."

"Okay. I can respect that. I'll be back tomorrow mornin'. Please ask Cynthia to have me a copy ready."

*   *   *   *   *   *

A polished black hearse appeared at the transfer entrance to the morgue. Within a few minutes, two well-dressed mortuary employees emerged from the building carrying a white bag containing the body of Lillian McRae Reins. They carefully and respectfully loaded the bag into the rear of the hearse. The body would be transported to the Elmhurst Funeral Home. There the body would be prepared for shipment back to St. Joseph, Missouri.

The next stop for Boudreaux was the crime lab. He hoped the investigation team had uncovered enough evidence for him to have some kind of trail leading to the killer. Returning to the department, he entered along the outside ramp and into the foul-smelling confines of the crime lab. The place reeked of formaldehyde and God knows what else. Seeing Mike Sasser, he commented, "How do you done stand working down here with this awful smell?"

Amused at the observation, Sasser retorted, "Ever hear the term 'selective olfactory sensitivity'? Well, that's what we got here. You won't find a one of us who can distinguish one odor from another. We've just gotten accustomed to it. It's only you fellas who seldom come here that seem to be bothered by the effluvium and smell. Guess you want to find out what we know about the Reins killing."

"Yeah! Sure do," Boudreaux replied assuredly.

Sasser explained, "I won't go into any detail because my report will provide you all you really need to know. I will say, however, that there is certainly no lack of evidence in this case. Should be a pushover to solve."

"Sheila Josephson told me that Miss Reins was also shot, probably after she died. Was a gun found anywhere in the area of the murder scene?" Boudreaux asked.

"No. The crime scene team searched for any kind of murder weapon and none was found. Even the knife used to stab her was not found."

"Was there any evidence on the body itself?"

"Not that we could tell. No identifiable fingerprints could be detected on the body; perp probably used gloves."

One rather bizarre piece was the gold brooch with diamonds and emeralds found in woods apparently among leaves on the path along which she was dragged. Where it came from I don't know. I can only suspect it was intended to be a gift to the victim. But, perhaps not; only speculation."

Sasser reached to the left corner of a desk that would have given Sheila Josephson's desk a run for its money in the messy desk contest. He picked up a copy of his report and handed it to Boudreaux.

"Tony, you might be interested to know that we found some fairly distinct footprints near the car and on the soft ground at the point where the leaves first were disturbed. The prints have been identified as being made by a Rockport XCS hiking boot."

"You sure on the ID of the boot?"

"No doubt about it. We have a plaster cast of it and will confirm it with the Rockport people, but all three of us crime scene guys are sure of the type because we all do a lot of hiking. We've also shopped quite a bit for our share of hiking boots. We feel certain that the boots were relatively new."

"You weren't wrong when you said we done gotta lot to go on. I think I'll start by talking to Sharon Farrell again."

Back at headquarters, Boudreaux reviewed his handwritten notes. Flipping through his notepad, he found Sharon Farrell's telephone number and punched the numbers in on his touch- tone phone.

"Hi. You've reached the home of Sharon and Lillian..." the answering machine began. Boudreaux hung up the phone. He felt a little stupid not realizing that Sharon would be at work.

Searching through the notepad again, he found her number at Andrews, Eisen & Tutt. After Boudreaux dialed the number, Sharon picked up on the third ring. "Hello, Sharon Farrell speaking," she said.

Boudreaux recognized a weakness in her voice that he had not detected earlier. "Hey, *mon cher*, this is Detective Boudreaux. I was wondering if I could meet with you sometime after work today. I done got a few questions I want to ask. The answers just might help me in this investigation."

She hesitated. "I guess I could meet with you. I was planning on going to the fitness center, but I suppose I can do that tomorrow night."

"I'll see you at 6:30 tonight then at your apartment. Is that all right?"

"Yes."

"Until then," Boudreaux closed.

*　*　*　*　*　*

Just before the agreed-to time, Boudreaux drove into the parking lot of the apartment complex where Sharon Farrell lived. He waited only a few seconds after ringing the doorbell before Miss Farrell opened the door. With a gentle, "Hey, come on in," Farrell invited the detective to enter her apartment.

Sharon Farrell was still dressed in the tweed wool suit she had worn to work that day. Her outfit was highlighted by a long-sleeved fuchsia blouse. Boudreaux couldn't help thinking that although she is quite attractive, she did not possess the stunning beauty of Lillian Reins.

"Miss Farrell, a lot has been done since finding your roommate on Saturday. I'm not at liberty to tell you anything we know right now, but I'd like to ask you a few questions. For starters, how well do you done know Jeff Mitchell?"

"I know him quite well. He has been in a romantic relationship with Lillian for almost a year. I know Lillian loved him very much, but there were some barriers to her marrying him. She was never quite specific about what they were, but she did say to me the night before her last date with Jeff that she planned to cut off their relationship. I think she planned to do it that very night." Small tears, which she struggled to hold back, filled Farrell's eyes as she remembered her roommate.

"You tellin' me that Lillian told you she planned to break off her engagement to Jeff Mitchell? Is that right?" Boudreaux asked.

"Yes," Farrell replied.

"Had he done given her an engagement ring?"

"Yes, as a matter of fact, he had. It was a beautiful one and a half carat emerald cut solitaire. Probably cost him six or seven thousand dollars. And she was very proud of it."

"Yet, she was willing to give it up and stop her relationship with him?"

"Yes. That's my understanding from what she told me. As I said, she was not specific, but she said that there were matters in his background that she could not ignore."

"What other friends did she get with and how often?" Boudreaux was hoping to uncover someone else that might be a potential suspect in the murder.

"Lillian was a loner in many ways, especially when it came to friends. She and I were about as close as two people could be. I really don't know of others whom she would have regarded as close friends. Jeff Mitchell and I were probably the closest to her."

"What about her boss, Mark Bradley? Did he spend time with her after hours that you know of?"

"No. He has a family—a wife and a couple of children—and would have had no reason to associate with Lillian, except on a business basis."

"Did she ever speak about him, good or bad?"

"No. In fact she talked very little about her work. I knew next to nothing about what she did, especially the projects she worked on. I only had a passing acquaintance with some of her closest colleagues. She was a very private person, Detective. Do you have any suspects in the case?"

"We really not far enough along to answer that question. Thanks for talking with me. You've been helpful. We'll stay in touch with you as the investigation goes on. And feel free to call me whenever you done feel like it." Boudreaux was trying to be conciliatory to her and sympathetic to her loss, but he was not sure he was accomplishing that purpose.

*　　*　　*　　*　　*　　*

With at least two and a half more hours of daylight remaining, Boudreaux drove once more to the murder scene off Greenleaf Lane. He retraced his original steps on the morning he found the body. The entire area looked pretty well gone over by the crime scene team, but he was determined to search for the knife and especially the gun that might have been used in the murder.

With a branch from a tree, he constantly moved the fallen leaves about as he walked, looking under brush, around bushes, and in gopher holes. He walked to a nearby stream and ran the tree branch along the bottom of the creek bed trying to locate something hard which might indicate a gun. Nothing. For almost two hours, he searched, all in vain. No gun or knife was to be found anywhere. As darkness descended on the thicket, Boudreaux returned to his car and went home.

CHAPTER 8

What a difference a day makes, Boudreaux thought. Tuesday morning broke brightly with the sun inexorably inching its way across a cloudless southern sky. The deep blue above and the chill in the air were testimony to the passage of a cold front that had moved through the night before. *Typical Florida panhandle weather*, he thought. *Just wait a minute and it'll change. It always does.*

Sitting at his desk in headquarters, Boudreaux noticed that a copy of the autopsy report had been placed in the center where he could not miss seeing it. *Pretty thick*, he thought. Then he began to read. As he read, he made notes. At one point he opened the crime lab report that Mike Sasser had given to him the previous afternoon and made notes in the margin. Line by line the identity of the prime suspect in the case was becoming more obvious to him.

He had finished reading both reports and jotting down notes in his little notepad. He would go see Jeff Mitchell again.

Boudreaux drove to the offices of Andrews, Eisen and Tutt. He entered the front door and was welcomed by an attractive, sun-bleached blond with a distinctively New Jersey accent, "Good morning, sir. And how are you today? How may we help you?" Listening to her talk, Boudreaux was reminded of the melting pot of cultures West Florida had become over the last decade.

"I'd like to see Jeffrey Mitchell, *cher*," Boudreaux asked politely.

"Ooo, like your accent. Just one moment, please." The receptionist punched in several numbers, waited a few seconds, and then responded, "Mr. Mitchell, there's somebody here to see you...Just a minute." She turned to Boudreaux, "What is your name, please?"

"Boudreaux, Detective Boudreaux," he replied.

46

"He says he's Detective Boudreaux...Okay. Thanks." The conversation was concluded. She looked at Boudreaux and said, "It'll be just a minute, sir. He'll come and meet you himself." Boudreaux smiled.

After being seated in the comfortable vinyl chairs of the reception room, Boudreaux waited only a brief time. He noticed that the office was unlike that of Goodall and Dohr, much plainer and less opulently decorated. It appeared to be considerably more functional. *I guess that's accountants for you,* he thought as he looked around.

Jeff Mitchell appeared and invited Boudreaux back to his office. Mitchell exhibited the dress and demeanor considered typical of an accountant, minus the green eye shade. Attired somewhat plainly, Boudreaux noticed that he would not qualify as a candidate for the cover of GQ magazine.

As they walked through the maze of offices, he noticed an empty office. He recognized it as Sharon Farrell's from the wooden and brass nameplate on the desk. He asked Mitchell, "Where's Miss Farrell today?"

"She had to make a sudden unscheduled business trip to the Cape this morning."

"The Cape?" Boudreaux looked puzzled.

"Cape Canaveral. We oversee contracts down there."

Mitchell's work space was much like the remainder of the office, functional, simple, and most certainly busy. "What can I do for you, Detective?" Mitchell asked. "I'm surprised to see you again so soon."

"I got just a few routine questions. You told me you had been with Lillian on the night she was killed, didn't you?"

"Yes."

"Tell me about that date. How late were you coming home? What time did she bring you home? What was she like that night? Did she seem to be worried about anything? What all did you talk about? Just kinda give me a rundown on the date."

Mitchell began, "She picked me up about 6:30. We had dinner at Charley Dee's, a favorite restaurant of ours. I told you that we went in her car because my heater was not working properly, a recurring problem I've been having. It was in the shop for repairs; they had to keep it overnight. Ended up they kept it all weekend. After dinner, we took in a movie and decided to go somewhere to talk. The safest place we knew about was the "chimney park" on Scenic Highway near the bay. We knew that few, if any, cars would be there, and danger didn't appear likely."

"What'd you talk about?" Boudreaux asked showing a more serious face.

"Us. I mentioned to you earlier that we were engaged to be married. We talked about our future together, you know, how many children, what kind of house, those kinds of things. We discussed a little about our jobs, became romantic for while—you know, kissing and making out—and then she took me home."

"Did you have sex that night?"

"That's kind of a personal question, don't you think?"

"Not when you investigating a murder. I need you to tell me, did you two make love that night?"

"Are you saying I'm a suspect?"

"Right now everyone who had contact with her that day or night is a suspect. Now, did you two have sex that night?"

"Yes."

"You smoke, Jeff?"

"Yes, as a matter of fact, that was one thing Lillian wanted me to do that I was having a hard time accomplishing, kicking the cigarettes."

"What kinda cigarettes do you smoke?"

"Camels, filtered."

Boudreaux looked at Mitchell's hands and noticed that he bit his fingernails. He glimpsed a strip bandage on the third finger of his left hand. "Did you hurt your finger?" he inquired.

"Yeah. Bit my fingernail into the quick. It bled profusely. I wish I could stop that habit, too, but I've done it so long, and my job is so high pressure that it's impossible for me to quit."

"I know," replied the detective. "I used to bite mine. Finally used pepper spray on them, and it cured me real fast. You oughta try it."

"I hope you find whoever did this to Lillian," Mitchell said. "She was the love of my life. I don't know what I'll do without her."

"Before I go, could you write down the names of any friends that Lillian had other than you and Miss Farrell. And also write down the name, model, year, and tag number of your car, if you would."

"Why is all this necessary?" Mitchell asked.

"Just getting' routine information," Boudreaux responded.

Nervously Mitchell said, "Lillian was very much a loner and was not close to many people. Sharon and I were her only close friends as far as I know. But I will be happy to provide you the automobile information." He withdrew a pen from his desk drawer, reached for a piece of memo pad paper which he kept near his telephone, and wrote down the information Boudreaux requested. Boudreaux observed that Mitchell was left handed.

"Thanks for your time, Mr. Mitchell. We'll tell you as much as we can as the investigation goes along."

"Please do that. I want to see this creep have to pay with his life for what he did to my Lillian."

Mitchell and Boudreaux arose in unison. Mitchell exited the office first with Boudreaux close behind. As they approached the front door, Boudreaux said, "I got one last question. That's an interesting cologne you are wearing. What is it?"

"Aspen," Mitchell replied.

*   *   *   *   *   *

Back at headquarters, Boudreaux reviewed his notes on the case. He made every effort not to overlook any detail that might lead him to the killer or killers. He silently reminded himself that he had spoken with Sharon Farrell on at least two occasions and could not imagine either a circumstance in which she might have killed her roommate or a motive to do so. For the time being, he would not focus the investigation on Farrell as an active suspect. Three other possibilities, however, loomed high on Boudreaux's list. Jeff Mitchell may have had a motive, and he certainly had the opportunity. Mark Bradley, her supervisor at Goodall and Dohr, could not be dismissed as a suspect. But there was no physical or circumstantial evidence that pointed to him. Furthermore, he was a married man with a family and also did not appear to have a real motive.

The third possibility that had crossed Boudreaux's mind more than once was that the killer may simply have been an unknown stalker or even a drifter coming through town, one who saw Lillian Reins as an opportunity and had assaulted her. She may have resisted his advances, and he killed her for it. The only problem with that theory was the presence of such a large amount of cash in her wallet. And what about the brooch? What role did it play in this murder? A drifter likely would have gone through her purse and taken whatever money was there after he had killed her. While Boudreaux did not discard this theory, he did not place much importance on it.

As he looked at the evidence report from the crime lab, Boudreaux pulled a Polaroid photograph from a large manila envelope. The photo was a copy of the laundry tag that was attached to the bloody sweater found in the back seat of Lillian Reins's automobile. He studied the tag for a moment and decided that he should attempt to track down the owner of the sweater. The easiest way to do that was to trace the laundry tag. He picked up the telephone book and thumbed through the Yellow Pages to the Laundry and Dry Cleaners section. There he found twenty-two retail establishments that processed laundry and dry cleaning.

Starting with the one nearest where Lillian Reins lived, he embarked on his quest to find the owner of the sweater. At the first store, the alpha-numeric form of the tag did not match the system used by the cleaners. At the second, only numbers were used in the tagging system. The sweater tag clearly showed both numbers and letters. The third business used an alpha-numeric system, however, the system employed numbers first and then letters. The tag in question displayed letters first, then numbers.

On the fourth try, Boudreaux hit pay dirt. The clerk recognized the form of the tag and stated that it matched the alpha-numeric data system that the establishment utilized in its identification system. Tracing the number on the tag, a match could not be found.

I may be barkin' up the wrong tree, Boudreaux thought. *This tag could be so old that it might not show up on any computer system.*

"Do you know of any other cleaners in the area that use the same computer program you do for identifyin' the stuff brought in for cleaning?" Boudreaux asked the clerk kindly.

"This system is kind of old and out of date," replied the clerk, "but there are two others that use the same system we do. Quality Cleaners over on Ninth Street and Wet and Dry Laundry and Cleaners on Ambrose Avenue."

"Appreciate it, *cher*" Boudreaux said as he departed.

Driving directly to Quality Cleaners, he repeated the procedure he had followed with the previous clerk. After showing the photograph of the tag, the clerk said, "Yeah. We use that same ID system. What do you need?"

"See if you can find and connect this tag to somebody and tell me who it was registered to."

The clerk took the photograph and walked to the computerized register. After what seemed to be an eternity, he said, "According to these records, the garment was a sweater, specially treated and dry cleaned. It belonged to a J. Mitchell. Would you like for me to print out this record for you?"

"For sure." Boudreaux asked, pleased that the clerk had read his mind.

Taking the printout from the clerk, Boudreaux said, "Great. You been most helpful."

According to the report from the crime lab, the sweater was a Coogi cardigan which retailed for probably $400.00. Certainly not a garment that could be afforded by every Tom, Dick or Harry, but one that's the rage, especially among the yuppies.

Beginning to put the evidence together, Boudreaux decided it was time to pay Mr. Mitchell yet another visit. For the better part of the afternoon, his investigative efforts added to the growing dossier of information on the case. All the while he was thinking about the ways Mitchell's name, along with so much physical evidence relating to him, constantly arose in connection with the case. First, the date with Reins on the very night she was killed. A broken engagement. Last, the left-handed dexterity of the killer— Mitchell wrote the note earlier with his left hand indicating a distinct proclivity toward left-handedness. *If he is the murderer, he sure wasn't a very smart one*, Boudreaux thought.

*   *   *   *   *   *

Boudreaux felt he had enough, but he wanted one more possible piece of evidence. He called Lamont to join him at Mitchell's home and to bring his crime scene case with him. Lamont agreed to meet him there within the hour.

It was getting on into the early evening, and he needed to let his wife, Maggie, know he would be running a little late. He stopped at a phone booth and called. As always, she understood what it meant to be married to a police officer, and now especially a detective. Time was precious in an investigation like this lest the trail of a killer become cold. She may not like it but she did accept his often strange schedule with patience and tolerance.

"I'll be home soon as I finish with this one interview. It ought not to take very long," Boudreaux promised.

"See you in a little while, sweetheart," answered his wife lovingly.

Boudreaux pulled up to Mitchell's home; he saw Lamont's car parked along the street. He pulled into the driveway and Lamont followed him.

Not seeing Mitchell's car in the driveway, he could not determine whether he actually was at home. Nevertheless, he was determined to try to talk with him.

Ringing the bell, he and Lamont waited for the door to open. Nothing. He rang the bell once more. Nothing. Impatiently Boudreaux knocked on the door with his knuckles as loudly as he could. After a second, he heard someone say from the inside, "Hold your horses. I'm on my way." Relieved, Boudreaux drew a deep breath and waited for Mitchell to come to the door. He waited only a half minute, and the door swung open.

Dressed in shorts and a college sweat shirt, Mitchell fittingly presented himself as a man who couldn't quite decide whether the weather was cold or warm. He probably dressed for comfort more than for the weather, especially since he remained inside his house.

"Mr. Mitchell." Boudreaux attempted to be as friendly as he could be. He did not wish to provoke a sense of suspicion that Mitchell was now his strongest suspect.

"Hey, Detective, how are you this evening?" Mitchell replied with the same friendly air.

"Can I come in for a little while?" Boudreaux asked.

"Sure, come in and have a seat. You needing more information? I've given you about all I know. What can I do to help you, Detective?"

"Jeff, do you own an off white sweater?"

"As a matter of act I own several sweaters. I have a Bill Blass red crew neck, a white V-neck Hilfiger, and a blue LL Bean hand knitted wool pullover. I have several other less expensive pullovers that I typically wear over a dress shirt. It's my way of looking and being informal and comfortable at the same time."

"Do you own a cardigan of any kind?"

"No, I don't."

"You ever own a cardigan?"

"Not that I can remember."

"Well, Jeff, that puts me in sort of a bad situation. You see, I got evidence that you own a Coogi cardigan sweater that was dry cleaned a while back."

"Oh, yeah. I remember that sweater. I lost that thing several weeks ago. Just couldn't remember where I left it, and I still don't know where it is."

"So you now saying that you do . . . or did own a Coogi cardigan sweater?"

"Yes. But I am also saying that I lost it and don't know where it is." Anxiety punctuated Mitchell's speech now, and it became obvious to Boudreaux. He decided to let his other questions remain unasked. He already had all he felt he needed to get an indictment.

"Jeff, I need you to do one more thing for me. Do you mind?" Boudreaux asked politely, not wanting to arouse suspicion in Mitchell.

"If I can, sure. What is it?" Mitchell replied.

"I need a DNA sample for you. Lamont here'll take it. It'll only take a sec."

"Why would you need that from me if I'm not a suspect?" Mitchell asked quizzically.

"I told you earlier that everybody who met Lillian that day is a suspect. Sometimes we solve crimes like this by eliminating suspects. At this time, we are tryin' to shut out as many as possible of those who knew Miss Reins. Since you were her boyfriend, it's necessary that we clear you as we will others. The

DNA test will help us eliminate you. You understand?" Boudreaux continued.

"Do you mind?" Boudreaux asked again hoping for an affirmative answer.

"No, I don't want to do that. If you suspect me in any way of having a part in this murder, you're out of your mind. I'm not going to help you pin this thing on me." Mitchell's anger was beginning to rise. His face became red, the veins in his neck became prominent, and he was visibly shaken.

Remaining calm, Boudreaux said, "Like I said, you don't have to do it if you don't want to," Boudreaux said as he opened the front door to leave.

As he and Lamont exited the door, Boudreaux stood at the front door for a moment contemplating his next move. He knew what he had to do, and the sooner it was done, the sooner this case would be resolved.

"I'll see you in the office tomorrow," Boudreaux said to Lamont.

"Back atcha," Lamont responded.

CHAPTER 9

After a night of fitful sleep, Boudreaux opened his eyes, as though on automatic, at 5:00. His wife and children remained asleep.

He always hated when he could not sleep until he felt completely rested. His body seemed to be going on fast forward, especially since the murder of Lillian Reins.

Getting out of bed, Boudreaux dragged himself down to the kitchen, inserted a couple of Egg-O waffles into the toaster and put on some coffee. He ambled out to the street, where he gathered the morning's newspaper and picked up a beer can that had been discarded from a passing car the night before. *Those teenagers got no respect,* he thought. He returned to the warmth of his kitchen. His waffles were ready, and the coffee was almost brewed. Spreading a generous amount of butter on his waffles, he poured on his favorite topping, Alamis Corn Syrup. He then poured up a cup of black coffee and walked to the breakfast room to eat and to read the morning paper.

For almost an hour he went through the same morning routine he had followed for more than fifteen years. After reading the news of the day, he shuffled to the bathroom, where he looked in the mirror. *Getting old and lookin' like it,* he thought. *I'm overweight, always on the go, and constantly tired. Maybe I need to hang it all up and do somethin' less stressful.*

Reality finally hit him. He enjoyed nothing better than the challenge of police work and especially now being a detective. He knew retirement was out of the question. *Just get ready and get on with it,* he thought, finally resigned to his fate.

Arriving at his office, the time was only 7:10. Nobody else had yet arrived in the homicide division.

Always the friend, he started the coffee pot for the others in the division, then sat and waited for it to brew. On the table in front of him, he set the coroner's file, the crime lab file, and the notebook in which he had jotted down information as it was accumulated. He just knew a detailed study of these sources would confirm for him the identity of the killer. He would spend this day reviewing the case and consulting with the team, including the State Attorney's office. In his own mind, he had already determined the murderer's identity. Before the day was over, he hoped to make sure that he had enough evidence to secure a conviction.

*　　*　　*　　*　　*　　*

Deputy Matt Tisdale and Detective Patrick Monaghan arrived and finished their first cup of coffee for the day. "How's it looking?" Tisdale inquired. He knew that Boudreaux had eaten and slept with the Reins case since it happened. Boudreaux looked tired, like he was not getting enough rest. And it was obvious he had come to the office early to get a head start on the day.

"Good, but not good. I read and studied all the reports and I got a hunch who did it. But I got a lingerin' doubt." Boudreaux liked Jeff Mitchell, and it was difficult for him to think that Mitchell could have so viciously killed his fiancé. Yet, he acknowledged the fact that other men had killed their girlfriends or wives in a rage of passion, so he supposed Mitchell could have done the same.

"There're times I'm sure I know who the perp is, but then a hint of a doubt comes, and I question my own conclusions. I need somethin' to convince me without a doubt. I got the evidence reports and my notes right here.

"Monaghan, have you reviewed the evidence in detail?" Boudreaux asked. "You had more experience than me, and I'd like to know what you think." Boudreaux handed him the file.

"I have studied it and will do so once more. Can I get back to you later today?" Monaghan asked.

"Sure. I'll come to your office, and we can talk," said Boudreaux.

57

Sheriff Williams called Boudreaux and Monaghan, asking them to come to his office. Within a few short minutes all three were seated in the sheriff's office.

"Tony, you seem to be doing a great job on the Reins case," said Sheriff Williams. "But, admittedly, you do have limited experience as a detective. I'm going to ask you to work directly with Monaghan here until we solve this case."

"I understand sir and will be glad to work with him. I already gave him the file, and we are meetin' this afternoon to review the case.

"Do you want him to take the lead from here?" Boudreaux asked.

"Let's just make the two of you equals, partners on the case. You can work together, can't you?"

"For sure."

"Just keep me informed," said Sheriff Williams.

As they exited the sheriff's office, Boudreaux said, "See you at three."

*   *   *   *   *   *

At precisely 3:00, Boudreaux walked through Monaghan's open door. "Come on in, Tony," Monaghan said. "I've read the file. The lead suspect appears obvious. But we need to go one step farther before we actually make an arrest."

"What do we need to do?" Boudreaux asked.

"We should get an opinion from the State Attorney and get his reading on it. I want to see if he thinks we got enough evidence to get an indictment and especially a conviction." Feeling deep in his heart that if the State Attorney pegged Mitchell as the killer, then his suspicions would be confirmed, Boudreaux said, "Absolutely, *mes amis*. Let's do it."

Gathering the files and the eight small, pocket spiral notebooks Boudreaux had personally compiled, the two of them turned to head downtown to visit with the State Attorney. *Better call first,* Monaghan thought.

Tapping in the number on his cell phone, he was greeted with a lively "Good morning. How may I direct your call?" The distinctive soft midwestern charm of the phone receptionist dripped from every word.

"I want to talk with Pete Pettis, please," Monaghan responded. "One moment," came the reply.

After a brief moment, Eunice Etheridge, Pettis's secretary answered the phone with a characteristic southern drawl. "Good mawnin', Mr. Pettis's office. Eunice speaking."

"Hey, Eunice, this is Detective Patrick Monaghan at the Sheriff's Department. Is Pete in yet?"

"No, Detective, he's expected in about 10:30 this mawnin'. Is there anything I can do for you?" she asked politely.

"Yes, please. I have a case I want his office to review and offer an opinion on. You got his schedule for the day handy?"

"Sure do. And you are one lucky gent. In spite of all his commitments faw the week, today is completely free. In fact, I think he wuz plannin' on goin' to the golf course this afternoon. Would you like faw me to check with him when he comes in and call you?"

"That would be good. You've got my number. Call me as soon as you know something, and I can come to his office immediately."

"Will do, Detective," Eunice said.

*   *   *   *   *   *

Jeff Mitchell woke up with a severe headache. Downing two aspirins had not helped. He wondered whether the headache was caused by something genuinely physically wrong with him or by the stress he seemed to be experiencing. He decided that he was in no condition to go to the office today.

There was no doubt he was concerned about the numerous visits he had received from the Sheriff's Department. And the request for a sample of his DNA could only mean one thing—they suspected him of playing some role in Lillian's murder. How

59

could they suspect him of murdering Lillian? *Am I losing my mind or what?* he thought. *Certainly they can't really believe that I had anything to do with it; that would be outrageous. . .a crock of. . .* He would call his friend, Mark Bradley. . . *I've got to talk with someone I trust.*

He picked up the phone and dialed Mark Bradley's direct number at the office. Bradley picked up after the first ring. "Mark Bradley, can I help you?" he asked in his most gentlemanly tone.

"Hi, Mark. This is Jeff. I need to talk with you. Do you have some time I could just come and unload a little?" Jeff asked.

"Sure. Today is kind of light. Come on over."

Entering Mark's office, Jeff offered the usual greeting between friends. Mitchell felt comfortable, warm. After all, what are friends for?

"Mark, I need you to keep confidential what I am going to talk about. If it got out, especially to my boss, it might cost me my job, and I can't afford to have that happen."

"You have my word on that," Bradley responded.

"I'm a little worried," Mitchell began.

"About what?" Mark inquired.

"The Sheriff's Department has visited and questioned me several times about Lillian's death, and the questions they are asking are rather direct. They tell me that I'm a suspect, and it seems to me I'm probably the prime suspect."

"Like what are they asking?" Bradley asked, interested.

"They wanted to know what kind of cigarettes I smoke and whether I bite my fingernails. They even asked me about the cologne I wear. Questions like that. Nothing like I would expect them to ask if they were just trying to get general information. Could you help me on this? I'm feeling a little squeezed."

"Remember, Jeff, they have a job to do. They have to look at all her close acquaintances, follow leads, and ask questions that sometimes may be personal. After all, in many killings, husbands, boyfriends, or relatives are the killers. You and Lillian *were* engaged, and I suppose you were intimate. They probably know that, and they are going to ask you questions that appear more personal than most. If you haven't done anything wrong, then I don't think you have anything to worry about. Just relax and let them do their job."

"I guess you're right. I just wanted to hear what you would think if you were in my shoes."

"Jeff, I'll be honest with you. If I were in your position, I really wouldn't worry. You know you didn't do it. So let the justice system work for you. Don't work against it."

"But Mark, there is one request from them that bothers me more than all the questions together." Mitchell's countenance changed, the color drained from his face, and his hands visibly shook.

"What's that?" Bradley asked.

"This Detective Boudreaux who's conducting the investigation asked me to provide DNA. I refused to do it. I guess I'm scared that they are working on building a case against me. Even though I had nothing whatsoever to do with it, I'm feeling unlucky."

"But why did you refuse to provide the DNA sample?" Bradley asked.

"Because, if they are trying to build a case against me, I'm not going to help them. They will have to get a court order to get it from me." Mitchell's fury over these recent developments started to surface. "Am I being unreasonable, Mark. What should I do?"

"Probably nothing. What will happen will happen. Just handle the developments as they occur. Don't worry about it. The system will work for you. Just let it. Keep your chin up and know that your friends know you and will not let you down."

"Thanks, Mark. You've been a lot of help like I expected you would be."

"How about playing golf one day next week? Would you be up to it?" Mark asked, hoping that golf might take his mind off of the entire situation.

"Sure, maybe Wednesday. That seems to be my best day. Want to ask Thad to come along?" Bradley asked.

"Why not. He's a good golfer. Maybe he can give me some pointers," Mitchell responded.

"Call me on Tuesday to remind me, would you? Bradley added.

"Sure will. Look forward to it."

* * * * * *

Monaghan and Boudreaux passed the time nervously. Almost simultaneously they glanced at the clock on the wall. Pete Pettis's office had not called yet. Boudreaux's anxiety level increased by the moment. He felt, with reasonable certainty, that he was close to solving this crime. He knew in his heart who the killer was, and he was anxious to get him into custody.

While Boudreaux was deep in thought, the phone rang. It seemed louder than usual and startled Monaghan, causing him to knock over his coffee cup. "Gez," he said quietly to himself before lifting the phone receiver. "Patrick Monaghan here."

"Pat, this is Pete Pettis. Eunice tells me you called this morning wanting to meet with me. What can we do for you?" Pete Pettis was the ideal State Attorney. With a quiet demeanor, he carefully analyzed cases, keenly conscientious to protect the identity of a perpetrator before the evidence revealed him or her beyond a doubt, and concerned always for justice and fairness. He realized more than anyone that cases were often lost because the police or the courts did not carefully guard the rights of the individual to due process.

A native of Eldora, a small community in central Iowa, he spent most of his growing up years in North Carolina. His father moved the family there after securing a better paying job with R. J. Reynolds Tobacco Company.

Early in his life, Pettis exhibited a level of intelligence never before seen in his family. Not really considered to be a "geek," he became the consummate intellectual during his high school years and earned a full scholarship to Oklahoma University. His leisure time was occupied by involvement in the wrestling team; he won individual honors as a member of Oklahoma's National Wrestling Championship team of 1975.

Upon receiving his undergraduate degree, he was offered, and he accepted, a scholarship to attend the Duke University Law School. There, his skill in the courtroom became evident to all who observed his cases in moot court.

In the real world, he made his name and reputation by being the lead prosecuting attorney in the well-known Harker trial. Richard Harker allegedly killed his wife with a shot of Demoral directly into her veins. Since Harker was not a doctor or a chemist, the proof of his guilt was difficult. Pettis worked with the police to uncover the evidence necessary to put him away for life. The public liked what it saw in Pettis so much that he was later elected as the State Attorney for the First Judicial Circuit of Florida.

"Pete, I got a case I need you and one of your assistants to review for possible prosecution. May Tony Boudreaux and I come over, bring the files, and talk about this case with you?" Monaghan asked.

"I'm free for the day, so yeah, come on over. I'll see if I can't get Douglas Rose to break loose and get him to review it with me. That way two of us could get a feel for what you have. Will that be all right?"

"Yeah. That'd be great. Thanks Pete. I'll be there in a few minutes."

*   *   *   *   *   *

The office of the State Attorney was located in a multi-storied, downtown building. It had become known as the "box" because its design is like boxes stacked four high like children's building blocks. Here the offices of the judges of the First Judicial Circuit, the courtrooms, several county offices, and the State Attorney all are housed.

Monaghan and Boudreaux entered the office through the back entrance and noticed the presence of several rather sleazy looking characters, all of them handcuffed. It did not require a stretch of the imagination to know what they were—criminals awaiting their turns in the system.

Walking down a flight of stairs and through a maze of hallways, they finally found their way to the desk of Eunice Etheridge. "Well, don't you look pretty this morning?" Monaghan said, knowing that Eunice enjoyed receiving compliments.

"And a fine good mawnin' to you too, Detective. Mr. Pettis is expectin' you. Go right on in," Eunice said.

Slowly opening the door, Monaghan called his name, "Pete, you here?"

"Yeah, right here, Pat. Come on in."

Monaghan and Boudreaux made their way into the office. "Take a seat, guys," Pettis said. "Give me just a minute and I'll get Doug Rose in here. How long do you think it will take?"

"Probably no more than a half hour," Boudreaux offered.

Dialing Rose's intercom number, Monaghan and Boudreaux could hear Pettis, "Doug, Pat Monaghan and Tony Boudreaux are here. Come to my office. I want you in on this case. Probably won't be more than half an hour."

Within a moment, Rose had entered the office and greeted both detectives. After all had taken seats around the conference table located in one corner of the office, Monaghan started the meeting. "I have been out of town for the weekend, and Boudreaux here has been responsible for this investigation. So, I want him to brief you on the status of the case."

"Thanks, Pat," Boudreaux began. Hearing him talk with such a heavy Cajun accent put smiles on the faces of Pettis and Rose.

"First, I want to tell you about the murder itself." For ten minutes, Boudreaux described the case in as much detail as was necessary at this point. He mentioned Sharon Farrell's phone call, the location of the car by Tisdale, the discovery of the disturbed ground, the bloody tree, and finally, the body itself.

He noted that he had conducted interviews with several individuals who were connected with Lillian Reins in one way or another. And he concluded by saying, "I got three files here for you review. The first file is the report of the crime scene investigation team. I don't think it'll require explanation. The second file is from the coroner's office. Sheila Josephson's been great in this case. She found a lot of evidence. I'm just askin' you to go over it. The final file contains the books where I done wrote down notes from my interviews of witnesses and suspects."

"I got a pretty good idea who the killer is. But obviously before we arrest anybody we need to know if there is enough evidence to get an indictment and a conviction. If so we'd like the go ahead to get a warrant for his arrest. If your conclusion is different from mine, then clearly, more investigation'll be needed. Just let me know if you think we got enough evidence."

"That, we can do," Pettis promised. "If he's there, we'll find him. If he's not, then we will tell you that as well. Give us a day or two, and we'll get back to you."

"For sure, *mes amis*. That's all I can ask," answered Boudreaux. "Thanks for your help. I'll wait for your call."

CHAPTER 10

For two days, Boudreaux busied himself with mundane duties in the division. But his mind just could not venture too far from the Reins case. It was his first big case, and it was important that he resolve it, and quickly.

What could possibly be takin' Pettis and Rose so long to analyze that case? he thought. *Could there be a problem, maybe some mishandlin' of evidence or a procedural error?* He felt a sense of self-doubt rise within him. *With all the mollycoddlin' of criminals these days, it'd only take a minor mistake for a smart lawyer to get him off on a technicality if we tried him and didn't have enough evidence.*

He rewound the events in his mind as he would a video, trying to recall every step of the case. *Unless the crime scene investigators fouled up some way, there ought to be no doubt.*

Boudreaux was confident that he had covered every base and in his own mind believed that Mitchell could be clearly identified from the evidence contained in the files he had supplied to the State Attorney's office. However, he needed confirmation that his suspicions were correct. Furthermore, he needed the authority of the State Attorney's office to affect the arrest based upon probable cause. *I gotta believe this is simply the prosecutor's way of makin' sure that no mistake's been made.*

The phone on his desk rang loudly, rousing him from deep contemplation. Anxiously, Boudreaux lifted the receiver before the first ring was completed; it was Pete Pettis.

"Tony, Pete here," Pettis said. "I need you and Pat to come by the office. Doug Rose and I are ready to discuss the Reins case with you."

"How does it look?" Boudreaux inquired.

"I'd prefer discussing it here with you rather than by phone if you don't mind," Pettis responded. "Could you and Pat come by here this afternoon?"

66

Boudreaux glanced at his Daytimer and said, "Yeah, we can make it. See you later today."

With that, Boudreaux lowered the receiver to the phone, rubbed his weary eyes, and wondered what the outcome of the Reins case would be. He must await the afternoon meeting.

*   *   *   *   *   *

The service was comforting to the Reins family. Reverend Hargrove had delivered a most appropriate eulogy, praising Lillian for her many accomplishments and successes in life, declaring how tragically her brief life had ended. No music had been rendered. She was buried in a grave that had been reserved for her mother.

Christmas would never be the same. This season of peace and joy had become a myriad of sorrowful experiences and sad memories, memories forever etched in the minds and hearts of this quiet mid-western family. In memoriam to Lillian, the family Christmas tree had remained lighted. It would remain so through New Year's Day.

*   *   *   *   *   *

Sheriff Williams had been away from the office for several days at a conference in Las Vegas. He had left word with his secretary, Margaret Malone, that he wanted a briefing from Boudreaux on the Reins case upon his return. Boudreaux had penned that note in his Daytimer and had asked Monaghan to join him.

Monaghan and Boudreaux knocked on the door at the appointed time. They heard the Sheriff invite them in, and after a few minutes of pleasantries and "war stories" from the convention, Boudreaux briefed Williams on the current status of the Reins case. He concluded by saying that he was leaving immediately to meet with Pete Pettis and Doug Rose, one of the Assistant State Attorneys.

"You want to join us at this meeting?" Boudreaux asked. "That way we can avoid havin' to meet again."

67

"I'll meet you at Pettis's office," said Sheriff Williams.

Boudreaux's heart raced as he and Monaghan drove to meet with Pete Pettis and Doug Rose. His mind focused on a pending arrest. "I talked to Pete earlier; but he wouldn't give me a hint about the outcome," he told Monaghan.

"I learned a long time ago," Monaghan said, "not to worry about something I have no control over. That's right where you are now. If they give you the 'high sign', then arrest him. If not, keep on investigating."

"But I'm so certain about his guilt."

"Certain or not, wait for the meeting, and don't give yourself a headache."

They continued on in silence.

Lost in his thoughts, Boudreaux ran a red light and almost collided with a red Toyota van carrying a family, including five children.

"Look out," Monaghan yelled. Boudreaux executed an evasive move, avoiding the accident. "Get your mind on your driving, Tony. Focus on driving safely before something else bad happens."

Finally, the parking garage for the judicial center was in sight. Turning in, he breathed a sigh of relief. There he saw Sheriff Williams standing near parking spaces reserved for the Sheriff's department.

Hurriedly, the three made their way through the labyrinth of offices occupied by assistants and secretaries. Boudreaux opened the double doors to the suite occupied by Pettis, allowing the others to go through first. Then he saw her, the legendary Eunice Etheridge. "Good afternoon, *mon cher*," Boudreaux said, breathing heavily. "I need to get back on my treadmill, and I need a job that doesn't keep me on the run so much," he added, smiling. "But then, I probably wouldn't be as happy and satisfied in my work as I am now."

"You know you wouldn't be happier doin' anything other than what you are doin'." Eunice chided him, having already heard about his promotion. "After all, you finally reached the job that you wanted most, haven't you?"

"Yeah, *cher*, I sure have. But I hope all the cases I work won't be as physically tiring as this one though."

"I assume Pete is in," Sheriff Williams said, questioningly.

"Yeah. He's expecting you. Just a itty bitty minute," Eunice said.

Tapping in Pettis's intercom number, she informed him that Detectives Monaghan and Boudreaux had arrived for the meeting and that Sheriff Williams accompanied them. "Send them in," Pettis said. Eunice motioned for Monaghan, Boudreaux, and Sheriff Williams to go in.

Stepping into Pettis's office, Pete was around his desk quickly, shaking hands with the detectives and the Sheriff, thanking them for being so prompt. "I wasn't expecting you, Sheriff," Pettis said.

"Well, during a briefing this afternoon, Tony informed me that he was meeting with you, so I asked him if I could come along. I hope you don't mind."

"No, no. It's good to see you. Give me a minute to call Doug Rose in."

Walking behind his desk, he dialed Rose's intercom number. "Doug, Pete. Tony, Pat and Sheriff Williams are here. Come in and be sure to bring all the Reins files."

In a minute, Rose had entered Pettis's office. In the meantime, Tony, Pat and Sheriff Williams had taken seats near the head of the conference table. When Rose came in, he took a chair next to Boudreaux, while Pettis sat in the chair at the end of the table adjacent to Williams.

"Tony," Pettis said. "You've done a great job on this case. Admittedly it is not a difficult one, because there seems to be substantial evidence pointing to a specific person. To have been assigned as a detective for so short a period of time, you have conducted this investigation like a pro. You are to be commended."

Boudreaux sat more erect in the chair, pride rising in his throat. "Thanks for the vote of confidence," Boudreaux said.

Feeling considerably more self-assured, Boudreaux was certain that he would be given the go-ahead to arrest Mitchell.

"Doug and I have gone over the case thoroughly. We think you have a strong case against Jeff Mitchell. The evidence is so overwhelming that it's somewhat scary. Almost seems like a slam dunk. Once in a while a case comes along where the perpetrator is completely unaware of the trail that he is leaving behind. This may be such a case," Pettis said.

"I have asked Pete to let me prosecute this one," Rose interjected. "It seems like such an open and shut case, a no-brainer," he added. "I want to be a part of bringing him to justice."

"I thought so, too, but I wanted to make sure. Since you feel we got probable cause, I assume you'll get a warrant for his arrest ASAP," Boudreaux said.

"Yes," replied Rose. "It should be ready for the judge's signature by late this afternoon. You could probably execute the warrant by early evening if that is convenient."

"Just call my office as soon as the warrant is signed," Boudreaux responded, finally relaxing and breathing deeply. "In the meantime, I'll be puttin' together the team that'll actually go with me to make the arrest. Thanks again for confirming my suspicions. You've done more to boost my confidence than you'll ever know," he added. Gathering his belongings, he joined Monaghan and Williams and headed for the door. Before departing, Boudreaux turned and said, "I'll wait for your call and come down personally to pick up the warrant."

"I'll be in touch," said Rose. "Stay close to the phone."

Boudreaux, gratified by the meeting, strode out of the office. *By the book,* he thought.

*   *   *   *   *   *

"It's ready," Boudreaux heard the voice on the other end of the line. It was Eunice Etheridge. "Rather than have you come for it, Mr. Pettis suggested that I send it over by courier."

"We'll be waitin'," Boudreaux said.

The time had come. The warrant would finally be executed. It was 6:15, and the warrant for Mitchell's arrest would soon be in his hands.

Boudreaux had asked his partner, as well as Detective Raymond Pearce, to accompany him as he arrested Mitchell. He also sought and obtained approval for Tisdale and two other teams of deputies to go along for back up. All were now in the office of the homicide division, waiting for the warrant to be delivered. At last the courier entered the room and handed the warrant to Boudreaux. He signed the necessary paperwork, and the courier departed.

"Thanks," he said, as the courier left the room. Then turning to his colleagues, he said, "Are we ready?"

Almost in unison they replied, "Yeah."

Then Monaghan added, "Let's move on out."

*   *   *   *   *   *

Jeff Mitchell was in the mood for Chinese food. He had stopped after work by the China Moon Restaurant to pick up a carryout order. Tonight was a popular TV night. He would change clothes, eat his fare of egg roll, fried rice, and deep fried cashew chicken, and watch his favorite sit-coms. He would enjoy a relaxing evening at home.

After changing into his choice blue jeans and sweatshirt, he placed his food on a lap tray, carried it into the den, and settled in for a night of leisure and amusement. Fifteen minutes into the first segment of "must-see" TV and his second bite of dinner, Mitchell heard several cars outside. They silently pulled up, no emergency lights illuminated, and abruptly stopped near the sidewalk entrance at his house.

—

71

Getting out of his Lazy-Boy, he peeked surreptitiously through the blinds. At the edge of the street he saw several sheriff's cruiser cars.

His mind raced. *Why are they here? Why are there so many of them?*

His thoughts quickly replayed the questioning of previous days, and he was struck with paralyzing fear. He became hysterical. Anger, mingled with fear, now arose within him. *I am not about to be arrested for a crime I did not commit!*

Swiftly, he walked to his bedroom and put on the shoes and socks he had shed before relaxing in the den. He grabbed a jacket from the closet and walked to the door that led from the laundry room to the garage. There he waited.

The doorbell rang loudly. He snatched open the door leading to the garage and, without missing a step, jumped into his car that he had earlier backed into the garage as was his custom. Simultaneously he pushed the button to the remote garage door opener and turned on the ignition. The car roared to life. He sped out of the garage, driving across the grass to narrowly avoid two cruisers that blocked his driveway. He reached the dark pavement of the street and skidded the car in a motion he had learned as a teenager. Pressing the pedal to the floor, he accelerated toward the main thoroughfare.

By the time Boudreaux and his colleagues could reach their cruisers, Mitchell was on his way, speeding north toward the interstate. The detectives took up the chase and found themselves with quite a distance to make up. Mitchell was driving his Jaguar XK, a powerful and fast machine, and he concentrated on putting even more distance between himself and the detectives chasing him.

"Crap," Boudreaux railed. "We done gone and lost him in the traffic."

Although Boudreaux and his colleagues continued to follow what they believed was the route Mitchell might be taking, they could not locate him or his vehicle. This was a turn of events Boudreaux had not expected. He thought the arrest was "in the bag," but Mitchell had successfully evaded them.

*　　*　　*　　*　　*　　*

Thanks to his speedy and maneuverable Jaguar, Mitchell had outrun the pursuing police. Constantly changing directions but maintaining a general course toward Interstate 65, he had avoided the deputies who were second-guessing his route. Tired but alert, he abandoned the main road and backed into a stand of trees. *I may be better off sitting still right now. If I see no police for fifteen or twenty minutes*, he thought, *I can relax, at least for the moment.*

The events of the past hour consumed him for a time. *Why?* he thought. *Why are they after me? If they think I'm going to jail, they have another think coming.*

Mitchell could only picture the horrible tales he had heard and read about prison life. If necessary, he would run as far as he could, take on a new identity, and forget that he ever knew Lillian Reins.

After waiting fifteen minutes, Mitchell headed out once again, driving more slowly and cautiously, not to arouse suspicions. He simply drove with no real destination in mind.

Eight o'clock in the evening. Surely the Sheriff's Department had issued an APB or BOLO on him and his vehicle. Mitchell was vigilant, keeping an eye out for the police, avoiding areas where they might patrol.

His senses were highly keen now. He drove slowly and observed a dirt road off the main route and turned onto it, pulling completely off the highway so as not be detected. He turned his car around so that the front faced the main road just in case he needed to make a hasty retreat. After shutting off the ignition, he turned on his radio to listen to some soothing music. He found a great station airing oldies from the seventies.

73

He laid his head back on the headrest and relaxed, listening to the mellifluous sounds of the radio. *I must think this through,* he thought. *This has happened so suddenly I really don't know what to do. I didn't kill Lillian, but they probably won't believe me; otherwise, they would not have come for me.* "Where can I possibly go from here?" he said aloud to no one.

Reaching into his back pocket, he fearfully realized his wallet was missing. The driver's license didn't really matter, but his credit/debit card and PIN number did. Otherwise he might not be able to get any money. He had $200.00 in his wallet that would help him get away, but it lay on his dresser at home. Could he possibly afford to go back? Would they be watching his house? He decided to lie low for a while, staying put until the police assumed he would certainly be long gone from the area.

With his fear and worry subsiding moderately, he lay back for a short nap. He drifted off slowly. . . consciousness left him. . . peaceful rest.

*   *   *   *   *   *

While six deputies continued to search the north county, Boudreaux and Monaghan returned to Mitchell's house. They would conduct a preliminary search for any evidence pertinent to the case. Tisdale had issued the APB, and Pearce went on home to be with his family; he had the next four days off.

During the search, Boudreaux and Monaghan discovered several cartons of Camel cigarettes, filtered. Mitchell must have been expecting a dramatic rise in tobacco prices. He had stockpiled an entire case of the smokes. On his bathroom counter Boudreaux sighted a half-filled bottle of Aspen cologne. "Aha!! That's what I smelled in the car that night," Boudreaux shouted to Monaghan. Curious at the shouting, Monaghan joined him in the bathroom. "I knew I smelled it before but just couldn't place it the night of the murder. It was Aspen cologne I smelled when I opened the door of Lillian's car." Both the cologne and the cigarettes were marked and removed as evidence.

Monaghan walked through the den area to the bedroom and noticed that the TV set was still on and that several cartons of Chinese food were left untouched on a table beside the recliner rocker. It was pretty obvious Mitchell had been in quite a hurry. Monaghan reached for the remote and turned off the television set.

He searched through Mitchell's closet and located several pairs of shoes, including a relatively new pair of Rockport hiking boots. Turning the shoe over, he noticed the "XCS" pressed into the arch of the sole. He tagged the boots and placed them in a paper bag, depositing them near the front door.

Back in the closet, Monaghan found several items of clothing with the dry cleaning tag still attached. He withdrew all of the items still containing tags and placed them in a paper bag and deposited them with the other evidence.

Meanwhile, Boudreaux searched the dresser, finding Mitchell's wallet, along with spare change and a set of Trim fingernail clippers. Remembering the nail remnants found in the floor of Lillian's wrecked car, Boudreaux thought, *The evidence is mounting*.

After two hours of searching, Boudreaux and Monaghan returned to the department with the evidence bags. In the evidence room, the items taken from Mitchell's house were duly registered. The items removed would be taken to the crime lab tomorrow.

*   *   *   *   *   *

By mid-evening, the Sheriff's Department had issued a statement to the press. The alleged murderer of Lillian Reins had been identified as Jeffrey Mitchell, a local accountant. A picture secured from his home accompanied the press release. The announcement read:

"Earlier this evening, deputies from the Escambia County Sheriff's Department attempted to serve a warrant on Jeffrey Mitchell, a local accountant, for the recent slaying of Lillian Reins. At the time deputies attempted to take Mitchell into custody, he fled the scene in his forest green Jaguar XK. After a lengthy pursuit, he successfully eluded officers and is presently at large. He is not believed to be armed, but anyone who spots him should assume he is dangerous. Anyone having knowledge of the whereabouts of Jeffrey Mitchell is asked to call the Sheriff's Department or Crimestoppers at 1-800-NO CRIME."

Within thirty minutes, most of the radio stations in the area had aired the press release, along with background information about the crime. The attempted arrest headlined the 10:00 newscast on all four local network television affiliates.

The *Coastal Chronicle* featured the story in 72-point headlines in the regional news section of the morning newspaper. The story outlined the key figures of the case including Sharon Farrell, Antoine Boudreaux, and Jeffrey Mitchell. The shocking details of the murder were omitted, but the cause of death, the location of the body, and the circumstances leading to Lillian Reins's death were noted. The story concluded with the press release written as a quote from Sheriff Williams.

*　　*　　*　　*　　*　　*

While it seemed that he had slept only a few minutes, the rising sun in Jeff Mitchell's eyes betrayed that thought. He switched the ignition on for a minute to look at the digital clock. He noticed that the time was approaching 7:00. He looked around and then remembered that he had parked in the woods. He intently watched the road in front of him, observing several cars passing, their occupants hurriedly on their way to work.

Suddenly, he felt the pressure of the night before. He recalled seeing the officers at his door and the urge he felt to run. *Probably was the wrong thing to do,* he thought. He remembered getting into his car and driving as fast as he could in any direction away. . . from the threat of the moment. . . the officers. But what was he to do now?

He turned on his radio to find the local news. To his surprise, he heard the morning account of the announcement released the previous night. The sound of his name startled him at first and then brought chills to his entire body. *They actually believe I killed Lillian.* Tears were near the surface, but fear kept them subdued.

He said aloud to himself. "Without money or identification, any avenue of escape will be difficult."

He looked down at the gas gauge and noticed that he still had slightly more than a half tank of gas. That would take him at least two or three hundred miles. "I'd better put a little more distance between me and the authorities. Then I can have more time to decide what to do," he said again to himself.

Mitchell sensed the ravenous appetite that was now rising in his stomach. He remembered that wonderful Chinese dinner he had so quickly left at home last night. How the uneaten egg roll would satiate the gnawing hunger he felt inside right now!

He had spent the night in the northern part of Escambia County near the Alabama state line. He was not more than sixteen miles from the on-ramp to Interstate 65 where he could drive as far north as his fuel would carry him. Deep in thought and with his hands on the steering wheel, he noticed the onyx and diamond ring on the third finger of his left hand. He also wore a heavy gold identification bracelet that Lillian had given to him on his last birthday. *Pawn them,* he thought. And then he remembered the golf clubs in the trunk of the car.

He pulled the trunk release, opened the door, and walked to the rear of his Jag. Looking into the lighted trunk, he saw one of his most prized possessions, an exquisite set of golf clubs. The set consisted of two Taylor-Made SuperFast 2.0 and one R11 wood drivers with graphite shafts and a full set of Yonex titanium irons with graphite shafts. He housed these clubs in an expensive embossed, leather golf bag enclosed in a custom-made hard-side travel case. The entire package had to be worth almost three thousand dollars. If he could get to a pawn shop without being detected, he might solve his immediate cash flow problem.

Furthermore, he could calm the growing hunger pangs that continued to plague him.

He closed the trunk lid and jumped back into the driver's seat. He dropped the car into forward gear and inched toward the main road. As he approached the intersection, a red Chevy Camaro ZL1 convertible whizzed by at breakneck speed. Mitchell wondered if its driver, too, might be running from the police.

After the Camaro passed, Mitchell drove slowly out into the roadway. Closing rapidly behind him was a white Lexus, obviously a late model. With traffic fairly clear, the Lexus eased smoothly around Mitchell, pulling back into the right lane, and proceeding on. He noticed the Lexus still had a temporary license tag attached.

Mitchell drove from his remote location, very careful not to exceed the speed limit. He drove south along U.S. 29 past Hydes Dairy Road to a small suburban shopping area. The pawn shop occupied a free-standing building on the west side of the highway. As he was about to enter the pawn shop's parking lot, he spotted a county Sheriff's patrol approaching from the south. Instead of parking his car, he turned into a quiet residential subdivision and then onto Pine Street, hoping that the deputy had not seen his vehicle.

Pine Street ended suddenly in a cul-de-sac. He drove to the far end of the cul-de-sac and stopped his car so that he could see cars coming from the direction he had just taken. After several minutes, he moved slowly back along Pine Street, observing the two streets which intersected with Pine. No cars in sight. Once more he felt safe, at least for the moment.

Cautiously approaching Highway 29, he searched intently in both directions for the presence of police. None was apparent.

He turned left and proceeded to the Cash 2 Carry Pawn Shop. With his golf clubs in hand, he walked through the door and straight to the counter. A small, flat-screen television set blared the local, morning news from the corner of the counter. A burly looking gentleman with a deep, resonant voice greeted him. The guy, whose small ID badge read "Norman," looked pleasant and said, "Good morning. What can I do for you today?"

Mitchell hesitated, attempting to determine if the man recognized him. Satisfied that he had not, Mitchell said, "I want to sell this ring, this bracelet, and these golf clubs. What kind of deal can you give me?"

"Well, let me take a close look at them first," Norman responded. Taking the ring from Mitchell's hand, Norman eyed it carefully with a jeweler's glass. "Quality piece of work," Norman said as he lifted his head and made eye contact with Mitchell.

"Should be. Cost me enough," Mitchell said.

Norman then grabbed the bracelet from Mitchell and inspected it in a similar fashion. Carefully inspecting the latch, the links, and the intricate filigree design each link bore, Norman said, "Twenty-four carat, I see. Don't see many of these any more. And the design is unique; I've never seen anything like this before."

"Thanks. Could you speed this up? I'm in kind of a hurry," Mitchell asked, becoming impatient. He was afraid his car might be spotted outside.

"If you want top price, I need time to inspect. If you don't want top price, then I'll just give you fifty dollars for both of them, and you can go on your way," Norman said, annoyed at Mitchell's growing impatience.

"Okay. Okay. And don't forget I have these golf clubs too," Mitchell reminded him.

"Let me take a look at them." Norman opened the bag and noticed that the clubs were quite valuable. The bag was embossed leather. And he saw that the entire set was housed in its custom-made travel case.

"Three hundred for the ring, a hundred and fifty for the bracelet and seven hundred and fifty for the golf clubs. That's the best I can do. I can pay you that much, cash. But remember, pal, a sale is a sale, and once you leave this store, this transaction's final. To get them back, you have to pay for them." Norman handed Mitchell a piece of paper with several hand-written lines. They comprised the terms of the sale.

"Sign it at the bottom, and the money is yours if you want it," Norman said.

"I'll do it," Mitchell responded.

As Norman counted out the money into Mitchell's hands, the newscaster announced that the police were on the lookout for Jeffrey Mitchell, the alleged killer of Lillian Reins. Mitchell reached quickly for the last hundred dollar bill on the counter and made a hasty retreat to his car. At that moment, Norman turned toward the corner counter and glanced at the television set just as the newscast flashed a picture of Jeff Mitchell on the screen. Turning around to record an ID, he saw that Mitchell had exited in haste.

"My gosh," Norman said to himself. "That's the guy they showed last night. It just didn't register with me."

With the face from the television broadcast lingering in his mind, he looked out of his store window and noticed that Mitchell turned north on Highway 29. Turning on his heels Norman went to his phone and dialed 911.

CHAPTER 11

Boudreaux and Monaghan had remained late into the night in the office of the homicide division hoping for a break in finding Jeff Mitchell. No luck. Hunger forced them to order a large pizza, fully loaded, with extra cheese. After the pizza arrived and Boudreaux had generously tipped the prompt and affable delivery man, they spent the next twenty minutes devouring the thin-crust delicacy and savoring the mozzarella cheese, a taste sensation all the detectives often craved.

Fully satiated, Boudreaux lay on an old army cot he had purchased from a surplus store. He had set it up for these long days and nights of working and waiting. *Just a short nap*, he thought; Monaghan reclined in his office chair. They both awoke at 8:00 the next morning.

Boudreaux sat upright, rubbing his eyes. Even though he had slept only a few hours, he still felt tired, almost as though he'd had too much sleep. Within fifteen minutes, he had made a pot of fresh coffee, poured himself and Monaghan a cup, and sat at his desk to catch up on the Jeff Mitchell case.

He thought about his family, picked up the phone, and dialed his wife. "Maggie, Tony. Honey, I'm sorry I didn't make it home last night. We still lookin' for the Reins killer, and I just got to be here."

"Couldn't you wear a beeper or be contacted through your radio at home?" his wife asked, sounding slightly exasperated at the night work for the past few days.

"Yeah, I probably could, but it's really better to be here where I can grab a patrol car real fast if I need to. I promise to try to come home for dinner tonight unless somethin' happens to force me to stay on duty."

By now fully awake and alert, Boudreaux contemplated his next move. Jeff Mitchell was out there, somewhere, and

Boudreaux wanted him apprehended. But his trail was becoming colder and colder as time passed.

Boudreaux recalled the arrest scenario with Monaghan. Over and over they replayed the event, trying to surface some fact or conversation or piece of evidence that might help them determine where Mitchell might have headed. The telephone rang. The emergency operator was transferring a call. "Please stand by for a call, Detective," the operator said. With two quick clicks on the phone line, the caller responded.

"Hello, is this Detective Boudreaux?" the caller asked. "My name is Robert Norman. I own the Cash 2 Carry Pawn Shop out on Highway 29. I just saw a report on TV showing that you're looking for a guy named Jeff Mitchell."

"Yeah. He's still on the run. He's wanted for a local murder," Boudreaux informed the caller.

"Well, he was just in my store," Norman informed the detective. "He's been gone only about two minutes."

"How do you know it was him?" Boudreaux inquired.

"I glanced at the television set in my shop and saw his picture on the report while he was standing right in front of me. He came in to sell some stuff he had. Kinda scared me at first, him being a murderer and all. Left pretty quick. Got into a green Jaguar like the one I saw on TV. I know it was him."

Boudreaux was elated at the prospect that Mitchell might have been sighted, especially in the area. He quickly wrote a note on a small pad and motioned to Patrick Monaghan to take a look at it. The note read, "Caller w/line on Mitch." Boudreaux then asked Norman, "Did you see where he headed?"

"Sure did. He left the store in a big hurry and drove north on Highway 29."

"North on Highway 29. You sure about that, *cher*?" Boudreaux pressed.

"Yes, I watched him until he was out of sight over the viaduct," Norman assured the detective.

"Thanks. We'll alert our deputies in that area, and I'll be seeing you in just a few," Boudreaux told Norman.

*   *   *   *   *   *

Detective Tony Boudreaux, along with Patrick Monaghan, pulled his police cruiser into the parking lot of the Cash 2 Carry Pawn Shop. While it was a stand-alone, rather non-descript building, it did not actually appear sleazy as one might expect. Painted a pale green, it was garish, however, considering the yellow stripes that zig-zagged across the front and along the sides of the building. The front door appeared as though it might have come from a second-hand furniture or materials shop or even an antique store. Containing a beautiful but out-of-place beveled glass window on the upper half, the door was solid wood throughout. Beneath the area where the green paint had been chipped off, was a layer of walnut colored stain, giving one the notion that the door had probably originally been a rather expensive addition to someone's home or shop.

Boudreaux entered the shop, all the while mentally registering the layout. Directly in front was a long counter occupying approximately half the width of the store but centered so that there was equal space on either end of it. The cash register sat in the center. On the right end extending from the counter to the back wall was a glass display case. On the wall end of that case was a small, flat screen television set.

Along the left wall of the shop was another display counter containing cameras, electronic devices, and an assortment of other small pieces of equipment. With approximately fifteen hundred square feet of display space, Norman also had strategically placed three six-foot tables containing his "specials" for the week. These were located in the middle of the floor in order to attract the immediate attention of the customer and increase the prospect of a sale.

Behind the center counter was a man, small in stature, probably five feet nine and weighing no more than a hundred and sixty pounds. Well-dressed in a pair of blue Dockers and a green knit shirt from The Greenbrier, he wore bright white Reeboks trimmed in blue and an FSU Seminole belt. His hair was neatly combed, and he wore a pair of wire-rimmed glasses.

"Good mornin', *mon cher*. You Robert Norman?" Boudreaux inquired.

"Yes, I am," came the response. Norman appeared to possess an assertive personality. He was confident and spoke with assurance. "I called you fellas to let you know that man you are looking for was just in here. The television said his name was Mitchell or something like that. He parked his car in the very same space you're parked in, came in for a transaction, and left not more than fifteen, twenty minutes ago heading north on Highway 29."

"What kinda business did he want to transact, buying or selling?" Boudreaux inquired.

"He was selling," came the response. "He wanted to sell these three items." Norman handed the officers the two pieces of jewelry and continued, "I paid him four hundred and fifty dollars for the two pieces of jewelry." Norman turned his back to the officers and reached through a door in the back wall, returned, and laid a set of golf clubs on the counter. They appeared to be quite expensive. "I also gave him seven hundred and fifty dollars for these. It was the best I could do and make a profit on the deal. These amounts give me a pretty nice profit if I don't have to hold on to them for very long," Norman informed the detectives.

"So you handed him twelve hundred dollars for all three items?" Boudreaux questioned.

"That's right," Norman said.

"Did you require that he show you some kind of identification?" Monaghan had taken up questioning the pawn shop owner. Boudreaux was looking around the store seeking any indication that the man might be putting up a false pretense.

84

"No," Norman replied. "Just as I was about to ask for ID, he quickly ran out of the store. I did have him sign a bill of sale and a disclosure statement before I gave him the money."

"Where is that?"

"Right here. I haven't filed it yet," Norman offered. He reached toward the top of the display counter to his left and fetched the signed bill of sale and the disclosure statement and placed them on the counter in front of Monaghan.

"Do you have a copier?" Monaghan asked.

"Yeah. You want me to make you a copy of these?"

"Yes, so you can keep a copy for yourself. We will need to take the originals," Monaghan answered. Norman turned and walked through the door in the back wall to an office he maintained there. In a minute, Monaghan could hear the hum of machinery. Norman quickly returned and handed the two original documents to Detective Monaghan.

"Thanks," Monaghan said. "These will be helpful."

"I can't imagine how, but I hope so," Norman replied tersely but sincerely.

"You do know we gotta take the items he sold you," Boudreaux said, once again entering the conversation. "But don't worry about them. They'll be brought back to you as soon as our lab is done finished goin' over them."

"Do you have any idea how long that will be?" Norman inquired.

"Probably a few days at most. We gotta test for fingerprints. As soon as that's finished, the items'll be brought back to you," Boudreaux promised. "Thanks for bein' so prompt in callin' us. I wish everybody was as good a citizen as you are. We'll be in touch."

Boudreaux and Monaghan left the pawnshop with the jewelry items tagged and placed in small, individual plastic evidence bags. Monaghan wrapped the golf clubs in a large blanket from his car and deposited them in the trunk of the cruiser. As they drove out of the parking lot, the radio crackled alive with a report from a deputy that he had spotted the green Jaguar belonging to Jeff Mitchell and was now in pursuit. He called for backup, locating his position as proceeding east on Big Bridge Road.

*   *   *   *   *   *

Jeff Mitchell now acknowledged to himself that he had made a mistake in trying to go back nearer to Pensacola to sell his jewelry and golf clubs. But it was too late. He could hear the loud wail of the deputy's siren behind him, and he could feel the rush of adrenalin.

Got to get away, he told himself. *Turn left; go a block, then right. Back toward the main road and then off into the country.* He concentrated, listening to hear if the siren sounds seemed closer. They did not.

Panic set in. He increased his speed, slowing down only to make a right turn on Highway 4. He sped along Highway 4 until it reached the juncture of Old Pottery Plant Road.

Old Pottery Plant Road could best be described as a severely rutted, clay country road which ran from just south of the Alabama line north to Highway 29, where it made a connection with Interstate 65. The road got its name from being the route along which was located the factory site of an early nineteenth-century pottery maker. The pottery plant having long been out of business, the locals persisted in using the road as a shortcut into Alabama—at least when it was navigable. Today's weather continued the pattern of the past two weeks, warm, less humid, and dry. What was normally a temperate and rainy time of the year had been unusually warm and dry. The road remained rutty but passable. And Mitchell hoped that the deputy, now joined by several others, would not find him or wish to follow him along such a rundown byway. Otherwise, he would have to try to make as good time as he could, evading at every opportunity.

Mitchell moved north along Old Pottery Plant Road at a speed that would not completely destroy his car yet would offer him the benefit of avoiding the deputies. He could hear the wail of sirens, but they seemed to be fainter in the distance. He forged on, and within twenty minutes he had reached Highway 29.

Listening intently, he could no longer hear the sirens in the background. He had actually done it! He had again successfully evaded the cops. He would not make the mistake of becoming too public again.

He turned onto Highway 29, careful to observe any oncoming traffic. There was none. Proceeding cautiously, he drove at the speed limit, concerned that he not attract attention. For twenty miles he drove along Highway 29 in Alabama until he approached the interstate on-ramp. North was his choice.

*   *   *   *   *   *

After receiving the phone call from Robert Norman, Boudreaux had updated the APB on Mitchell and his car. Fearing that he might go into Alabama, he also had the communications center notify the Alabama Highway Patrol and the sheriffs of Escambia, Baldwin, and Butler counties in Alabama. The net was about to become tighter.

Soon the radios crackled again with new information. The pursuing deputies had lost him along the maze of narrow roadways. Boudreaux exhibited extreme, almost exaggerated, frustration. He could not believe that these cops, who had been trained so well to pursue suspects successfully and apprehend them, had now lost this man not once but twice. "No doubt, when this man is captured, the procedures for pursuit gotta be reviewed," he said aloud to himself.

*   *   *   *   *   *

Night was falling. Mitchell had been traveling for more than five hours. He was beginning to tire. He also was hungry from not having eaten since two days prior. As darkness approached, he exited the interstate highway to get some nourishment. How great a hamburger would taste about now! Pulling into a Wendy's drive-up, Mitchell ordered a bacon deluxe double, medium fries, and a large Coke. After approaching the window to receive his order and to pay, he added an apple pie. He paid for his meal and drove along a rural gravel lane to hide and to eat. After about two miles, he spotted a narrow dirt road, bounded by tall short leaf pine trees. It appeared to be in good enough condition to try. The sign at the intersection read "Tea Garden Lake" and pointed to the right.

He made a right turn and had driven no more than a mile when he eyed a small clapboard cabin. It obviously was a retreat for someone during the summer months and at other times when they wished to get away. It did not appear to be a permanent home.

Slowly pulling to the front of the house, he stopped, put the gearshift in "park," engaged his emergency brake, and stepped out, leaving the motor running. Reaching for his flashlight in the glove compartment, he walked around to the side of the house; he then proceeded quietly to the back. About 150 yards in the distance, he could see the reflection of moonlight on Tea Garden Lake, a beautiful fresh-water getaway that looked as though it might be a great place to catch bass or bream. Barely visible in the beam of the mag light was a narrow dock extending out from the property no more than thirty feet. A small, metal rowboat was loosely tied to the end of it, the oars hanging over the side.

No one seemed to be at home. He walked to the west side of the house, then looked under the raised floor into the crawl space beneath. Casting the flashlight beam in every corner, he saw nothing. No one. Not even a dog or a rat.

Back at the front of the house, he slowly mounted the steps that creaked beneath his weight. He did not wish to scare anyone if they were present, nor did he wish to be recognized. *They probably wouldn't know about this case this far off the beaten path,* he thought.

Mitchell reached for the front door and tried to turn the knob. Locked. Just as he expected. He really did not want to break down the door or damage the house, but he thought this might be a good place to spend the night. It appeared to offer all the comforts of home.

Quickly, he walked back down the steps and pulled from the trunk of his car the lift handle to the tire jack. He ran to the front door, and used the metal handle to punch a small, jagged hole in the corner of the lower right window of the door. He quickly punched at the glass with the jack handle until the hole was large enough to get his hand through without cutting himself. He reached in and first turned the lock on the door handle; then he released the dead bolt. Pushing on the door, he opened it easily.

Before entering, Mitchell waited for sounds. He knew that the sound of breaking glass would draw attention to the front of the house if someone were there to hear it. *No one.*

He returned to the car, turned off the ignition, picked up his now cold meal, and walked inside. *What a great place,* he thought. *When all this is over, I would love to have a place like this to relax and enjoy life.*

Hunger pangs now gnawed at his insides. The full moon rose slowly in the southeastern sky, casting long shadows around the house. None of the nearby houses was illuminated. *No one seems to be in the other two houses, so I think I'll eat out on that dock. Finally I can relax. And I have space to run if I have to.*

*   *   *   *   *   *

After savoring every morsel of his food, Mitchell lay back on the deck of the pier gazing into the clear night sky. He continued to sip on his Coke and look into the sea of stars. He located the Big Dipper, the Little Dipper, and the Orion constellation. As he stared into the sky, his thoughts returned to the chase earlier in the day. *How could I have been so stupid as to think I might make an appearance in public and get away with it?* he thought. *I can't let that happen again. I must lay low for awhile until the dust settles, the publicity dies down, and the cops are a little less vigilant. I need to find some kind of hideaway for a time.* With the sun down, the night air chilled.

Stirred from his thoughts, he arose and silently walked toward the house, double jumping the steps and landing in three bounds onto the back porch. He entered the house and walked toward the front.

The house was cozy and warm in spite of the cool, crisp, early winter air outside. The floors were wide oak planks that had been sanded to a fine finish but had not been sealed or coated. The walls appeared to be of knotty pine, colored with walnut stain and coated with lacquer. On the north side of the open front room was a stone fireplace. The smooth stones were obviously river rocks that probably had been extracted from nearby streams.

Mitchell decided to build a fire in the fireplace. Stepping outside, he selected several pieces of fat kindling wood from the corner of the back porch. After wadding and stuffing under the fire grate several pieces of newspaper from the magazine rack in the den, he laid the kindling neatly in the fireplace. From a built-in storage bin next to the fireplace, he took two large, split logs, which he placed on top of the paper and kindling. In the kitchen, he searched for and found a box of matches. Lighting one and touching it to the paper in several places, he watched the kindling ignite. Soon a warm, glowing fire was blazing.

Confident that he had found at least momentary utopia, he turned on the television set and settled into a cushioned rocking chair. Soon he was fast asleep.

*　　*　　*　　*　　*　　*

Henry and Rosa Bosarge had enjoyed their North Alabama hideaway for ten years. They never tired of going there at least every other weekend. During the summer, they even closed down their Walton County, Florida, home for three months and retreated to Tea Garden Lake. "You know, honey, it's been more than a month since we went up to the lake house," Henry mentioned in passing.

Not wishing to appear too eager, Rosa responded longingly, "Actually it *has* been a while since we were there, especially

90

alone. Being Christmas time and all, why don't we take a leisurely drive up this afternoon and spend a few relaxing days? We might could even go into Cullman and see the Christmas lights."

"I hoped that would be your answer," Henry smiled. Then putting his arms around his wife of more than thirty years, they embraced, kissed each other, and he followed her to their bedroom to pack a few things.

By early afternoon, Rosa and Henry had left their North Florida home behind. Driving a special back-roads route, they drove north to Interstate 65 somewhat more quickly than they would have on the public, better-known routes. After intercepting the interstate, they proceeded north for their weekend rendezvous at their lakeside getaway.

Passing through Birmingham, Henry and Rosa drove through the northern suburbs and on into Cullman County. There they exited the interstate and drove along State Road 97 toward Tea Garden Lake. As they drove along the dirt road approaching the driveway, Henry suddenly stepped on the brakes, bringing the car to an abrupt halt. "Rosa, what's that car doing in our driveway? And why would there be lights on in the house and obviously a fire burning in the fireplace?" he asked.

Rosa looked up from bracing herself against the sudden stop. Henry allowed the car to proceed at a crawl. Concerned over this turn of events, Rosa all but shouted to Henry, "Don't go up there. Something is really not right here. I think we should call the police."

"Yeah, so do I," he agreed.

Retrieving his cell phone from the console of his car, he quickly dialed 911. "Cullman County 911," came the answer from the operator on the other end of the line.

Henry tried to explain the situation, "Yes, my name is Henry Bosarge, and I own a house on Tea Garden Lake. I came up to spend the weekend at the house. As I was driving up to my house, I noticed a dark car sitting in the driveway and lights on in the grand living room and the kitchen-breakfast room and a fire in the fireplace. Nobody has been authorized to use that house, so before I get into a situation I couldn't handle, I thought I'd better call the police and have it checked out."

Seeking clarification the operator asked, "You're asking me to dispatch a cruiser to your house on Tea Garden Lake?"

"Yes," Henry responded.

"One moment, please." The 911 operator went off the line. Henry waited. What seemed like an eternity was probably no more than half a minute.

"Mr. Bosarge, I have a Cullman County officer on his way to your house right now. Where would you like for him to meet you?"

"Have him drive down Tea Garden Lake Road off State Road 97 for about a mile. I will be in a white Chevrolet Blazer parked alongside the roadway. I can point out the house to him," Henry explained.

"Thanks, Mr. Bosarge. The officer should be there in a few minutes."

The ten minutes that Henry and Rosa Bosarge waited seemed like forever. Looking in his rearview mirror, Henry saw the headlights of an automobile approaching. Since there was so little traffic along the lake road, he was fairly certain that it was the deputy. "This looks like him," Henry commented to Rosa. Rosa turned just as the deputy pulled his cruiser alongside the Bosarge vehicle.

"Good evening, sir. You Mr. Bosarge?" the deputy asked.

"Yes, I am," Henry responded.

"Could you step out of the car, Mr. Bosarge, and tell me what's going on?"

Emerging from his car, Henry Bosarge met the deputy at the front of his cruiser. Together they stood in the light of the headlamps. "My name is Homer Tate," said the deputy, all the time shaking Henry's hand. "I'm with the Cullman County

Sheriff's Department. What kind of emergency are you having here?"

"I own the house at the top of the hill on Tea Garden Lake. You can see from here that there is a car sitting in the driveway. It's not a car that either my wife or I recognize. Also, you can see lights on in the house, and the smoke from the chimney shows there has to be a fire in the fireplace. No one has a key to that house but me and my wife. There is no reason for anybody to be there. Suspicious situation and I thought it would be a good idea to have you check it out."

"You did the right thing calling us," replied Deputy Tate. "I'll go take a closer look at the house and see what I can learn. Might even just knock on the door to see if anyone is actually in there or if you might have left lights on from the last time you were here."

"It's been more than a month since Rosa and I have been here. I would think one of the neighbors would have called me to let me know that the lights had been left on if that was the case," Henry rebutted. "We're kind of a close-knit group of neighbors even though we don't stay around for long except during the summer months. We all have each other's telephone numbers and have a kind of neighborhood watch."

"Wait right here, and let me see what I can find out," said Deputy Tate.

Bosarge and the deputy had parked their cars approximately two blocks from the house. Quietly, Deputy Tate approached the house. First, he looked inside the car. It was a dark colored foreign make. Without looking at the insignia, he could not readily identify it. He decided to approach the house and knock on the door to see if there was anybody inside.

Tate then walked up the seven wooden steps that led to the front porch. The steps squeaked beneath his feet. Striding across the front porch, he was about to knock on the door when he noticed the broken pane of glass in the lower right corner of the top half of the door. Instead of knocking, he peered inside.

Someone was occupying the house even though that person was not visible. He decided that maybe he should call for backup just in case the situation heated up.

Tate returned to his cruiser, picked up the microphone to his radio and said, "Unit 15 to headquarters."

"Go ahead, 15," came the response from the dispatcher.

"I'm out at Tea Garden Lake. I need a backup unit to join me here."

"Is there a problem, 15?" the dispatcher asked.

"Not right now. I'm trying to avoid one. Make it snappy," Tate said softly.

"Unit 10 is on his way."

Inside #3, Tea Garden Lake, Mitchell thought he heard noises outside. He had been jumpy ever since the near miss at the pawnshop. He had to be alert to any unusual sound or distraction. *The noise seemed to have come from the front side of the house,* he thought. He walked toward the front and entered the bedroom. He turned on the light. Nothing there.

He walked to the living room. Nothing there. He turned off the lamp that was lighted in the corner. *Probably just an animal or some tree limbs swaying against the house.* But then he looked out a corner window and noticed two cars parked alongside the roadway a couple of blocks away. He observed a deputy walking toward the cars. Looking more carefully, he saw that one of the cars was a police cruiser.

Fear gripped his entire body. He was so tired of running, but he just could not settle for being captured and having to defend himself against a murder he did not commit. No, he would not be their scapegoat. He had to get away. He gathered his car keys and prepared to make a run for it.

*   *   *   *   *   *

Deputy Homer Tate decided to run the license plate on the automobile as he waited for his backup to arrive. He called in the Florida license plate number AZZ 333 as he drummed his fingers on the seat. Within three minutes, the dispatcher responded. "Unit 15, this is headquarters. The Florida plate AZZ 333 belongs to a Jeffrey Mitchell from Pensacola. His DOB is 1/24/69. He currently is being sought on a fugitive warrant for murder in Escambia County. Approach with caution. He could be armed and dangerous."

By now, Tate had been joined by Deputy Lester Keys. Together they walked swiftly but quietly toward the house. Keys was to take the back door, and Tate would approach from the front.

As Keys broke from Tate to take up a position on the back porch, he saw a tall, lean figure run from the back door of the house toward the south end of the lake where a stand of trees would serve to block the deputies' vision of his getaway.

"He's headed toward the woods," shouted Keys to Tate. Keys had a head start on Tate, but Tate's younger age permitted him to catch up with Keys quickly. With flashlights in hand, they followed Mitchell as he entered the thicket of trees. Fearful that he might be armed and unsure of his next move, they did not immediately enter the woods after him.

"Why don't you call in more backup and the K-9 unit for us?" Tate told Keys.

"Okay. Good idea. We can track him with the dogs."

Tate remained in place listening to the now slowed pace of Mitchell as he ran through the darkened woods. Soon the sound of breaking twigs and rustling leaves ceased entirely.

*　　*　　*　　*　　*　　*

Tate stayed put. Within twenty minutes, four more units had arrived in addition to the K-9 unit. Tate flashed his light in the direction of the deputies. They hastily ran around to the south end of the lake where Tate stood watch. The dog barked loudly, eager to take up the chase. "He ran into the woods right here," Tate said, pointing to the trail left by Mitchell. "The dog can pick up the scent."

The K-9 unit from Cullman County consisted of Deputy Gus Pointer and Rex. Rex, a four-year veteran of the force, had been instrumental in the capture of thirty fugitives and the discovery and seizure of more than two tons of drugs. A brown and black German Shepherd, Rex had an hour glass marking across his back which made it easy to identify him. Friendly to his handlers and the Pointer family with whom he stayed, Rex became a ferocious beast when faced with a criminal.

"Get the scent," Pointer commanded Rex. "Get the scent, boy." Rex nosed around the area until he picked up Mitchell's scent and began to pull Deputy Pointer through the trees. Still attached to his leash, Rex led the officers down an embankment toward a creek bed, keeping his nose to the ground. The deputies trained their flashlights on the area immediately ahead of and behind Rex.

Through the creek bed and on to the other side, Rex picked up the scent once again. Following the scent, Rex and the deputies neared an open field of marsh and grass. The ground was mushy under foot, and their shoes sank into the soft earth. Going was slow, but Rex continued on relentlessly, excited by the chase.

By the time they reached the other side of the field, Rex was frenzied with the scent of Mitchell. Then he suddenly slowed almost to a crawl. They were close. Pointer raised his hands indicating that the deputies following him and Rex should stop. Like a bird dog ready and about to point, slowly Rex paced through the underbrush. Abruptly, not fifteen feet ahead, Mitchell raised up from his hiding place and ran, Rex in hot pursuit. "Halt or we'll shoot," Pointer shouted. Mitchell seemed to pick up the pace. "Stop or I'll turn the dog loose on you," Pointer promised.

Mitchell dashed through the brambles and thicket as fast as he could. Pointer released Rex from his leash, Rex suddenly leaping forward like a spring.

Just as he was about to make it into a clearing, Mitchell was jumped by Rex and brought down instantly. Struggling to get back on his feet, Mitchell's arms were being mangled by the dog. Blood flowed, and he felt a sharp, searing pain. Within a minute, the deputies were on him. "No more, Rex," Pointer instructed. Rex turned loose as the deputies rolled Mitchell over on his stomach and handcuffed him behind his back. Breathless, they all waited a few minutes, reliving the chase as their lungs gasped to return to normal.

After reading Mitchell his Miranda rights, he was led to Deputy Tate's waiting squad car. Tate drove him in silence to his rendezvous with the Cullman County Jail.

CHAPTER 12

The nightmare had begun in earnest for Jeffrey Mitchell now. He found himself in the rear seat of a squad car being transported to the local county lockup.

"Why'd you do it?" asked Big Al Horton, the Cullman County deputy, from the front seat of his cruiser.

"Do what?" Mitchell responded.

"Kill your girlfriend?" Big Al asked, his voice harsh with disdain and years of smoking roll-your-own cigarettes.

"I did not kill her. She and I were friends. I had nothing to do with her death," Mitchell replied, his voice dripping with anger and disgust at the whole scene.

"Yeah, yeah. That's what they all say," Big Al said sarcastically.

"Well, I don't know what they *all* say, but I do know I didn't kill her."

"We'll see." That was all Big Al could think of to say.

In silence, Jeffrey Mitchell, the alleged killer of Lillian Reins was taken to the Cullman County Jail where he would remain pending extradition to Florida. After the usual booking procedures were complete, Mitchell was placed in a holding cell. There he would stay until he was transferred into the general population of inmates.

*　　*　　*　　*　　*　　*

Upon notification of the arrest, Cullman County Sheriff Burden Copeland prepared to notify the Florida authorities. "Get the Escambia County Sheriff's Department on the phone for me," he told Rosie, the deputy on desk duty for the evening. "I need to let them know we have their man." Sheriff Copeland spent the next few minutes calling Escambia County and leaving a message for Detective Boudreaux to return his call.

*　　*　　*　　*　　*　　*

Jeff Mitchell cowered in the corner of the holding cell. No more than eight feet square, it consisted of a rear wall of solid concrete and three walls of steel bars one inch in diameter. The door was latched at the top and bottom with secured slide locks in addition to the keyed lock at the center of the door.

Weary and with his head resting on his forearms, Mitchell pondered his circumstances. He did not know who to turn to. He knew only one lawyer, Fred Roush, a racquetball friend of his who primarily tried civil negligence cases and had never gone near a criminal court in his entire ten-year career. *I assume they will give me at least one phone call,* he thought. I probably should call Fred; at least he will be a place to start. Maybe he can advise me what to do.

Mitchell heard heavy footsteps coming down the corridor. They belonged to Big Al. "C'mon, Mr. Mitchell. Time to go," he said.

"Where are you taking me?" Mitchell asked.

"To the jail. Where else?" replied Big Al.

After cuffing Mitchell, Big Al grabbed him by the collar of his shirt and led him roughly toward the jail area. Down the corridor, up a flight of stairs, through an interrogation room, and along another corridor, Mitchell and Al walked until they came to an area that had the appearance of a control tower at an airport. Surrounded by glass and television monitors, the three corrections officers inside the "tower" maintained a constant vigil over the more than thirty prisoners who were being held at the Cullman County Jail. Mitchell looked around and wondered, *How could such a small Alabama county afford a state-of-the-art jail like this one?*

As they approached the barred door, it slid open as if by magic. Mitchell and Al passed through, and the door closed behind them. They approached another door, this one leading into the lower tier of jail cells. Three tiers of five cells each filled

Mitchell's vision. Every cell seemed to have more than one or two prisoners.

They walked halfway through the jail concourse, up a flight of noisy metal stairs, turning right at the top. In front of cell number B-4, Al ordered Mitchell to stop. Automatically the door slid open, and Al lightly pushed Mitchell into the waiting cell. There he met, for the first time, his new cellmates, Frank, better known as "Squinty," and Tino, known on the streets as "Catcher."

*　　*　　*　　*　　*　　*

Dialing the number he had been given, Boudreaux waited for someone to answer. "Good evening," came the voice from the other end. "This is the Cullman County Sheriff's Department. How may I help you?"

"This is Detective Tony Boudreaux of the Escambia County, Florida Sheriff's Department. I'm returnin' Sheriff Copeland's call."

Shortly, Sheriff Copeland could be heard. "Detective Boudreaux, this is Sheriff Copeland. I think we have someone here you might be interested in," he said smiling into the telephone.

"And who might that be?" Boudreaux replied, as if playing some kind of guessing game.

"A man named Jeffrey Mitchell," Copeland replied.

"Mitchell, huh. For sure we want him. Tell me little bit about how you found him," Boudreaux inquired.

"He apparently holed up in a house on a lake near here and had the misfortune to be there with lights on when the couple who owns the house decided to come up for the weekend. Knowing no one should be in the house, they called us when they saw the lights. After a chase and a brief scuffle, the deputies and a dog subdued him, and he is now here in my jail," Copeland said.

"We'll start extradition immediately," Boudreaux responded. "I'll be there before the night is out."

———
100

"He is maintaining his innocence, and I wouldn't be at all surprised if he fights you on taking him back. He's been making all kinds of racket about how you're pickin' on him," Copeland said.

"Pickin' on 'im?" Boudreaux said. "Wait till he sees how much evidence we got on him far as this murder is concerned. I'll see you by mornin', and we'll start the proceedings to bring him back to Escambia County. Thanks for calling Sheriff. I'll done see you soon."

After talking with Copeland, Boudreaux placed a call to Patrick Monaghan. "We got him!" he began.

"Got who?" Monaghan asked.

"Got Mitchell," Boudreaux said.

"You mean he's in jail?" Monaghan asked, wondering why he had not been notified of the arrest.

"Yeah, he's in jail, just not here. He was found and arrested in Cullman County, Alabama. I just got called about it. We got to go get him, though," Boudreaux informed his detective friend.

"Good. I assume you want me to go with you," Monaghan hinted, feeling the excitement of success.

"For sure. How quickly you get ready?"

"Before you can get here," Monaghan said.

"Then I'll see you in a few."

Boudreaux lifted himself from his favorite chair in the den and walked to his bedroom where Maggie, his wife, had already retired for the evening. Tiptoeing around the room, he quietly threw a few clothes into a battered old duffle bag along with selected toiletries. Before leaving, he stopped at the bedside, lovingly kissed his wife on her cheek and whispered, "I'm leaving, but I'll be back late tomorrow night sometime." She reached up, put her arms around his thick neck, and returned his kiss.

After double checking what he had packed, he walked to his cruiser car. On the way out of town, he stopped and picked up Monaghan, and they headed to Cullman County, Alabama.

*   *   *   *   *   *

Mitchell seemed to draw the attention of Tino right away. Before Mitchell could get his bearings, Tino, who was Italian by birth, was up close, too up close. In his face, Tino asked, "What you in here for, man?"

Backing away from Tino, Mitchell replied disinterested, "They think I killed somebody." Then he quickly added, "But I really didn't."

"Yeah, man," Frank interjected. "None of us in here did nothing. Don't none of us understand why we in here."

"You one of those purty boys," Tino said to Mitchell. "You queer or somethin'?" he asked.

"Nope, none of that for me," Mitchell said, his face turning red from fear. "Just leave me alone and let me be."

"Hey, man, don't be so uppity. You in jail now, don't you know that? I suggest you be nice to the rest of us and don't think you better than us. Understand?" Tino said, his anger at Mitchell's attitude beginning to show. "We don't cotton to your kind making us look bad. Know what I mean?"

"Yeah," said Mitchell. "But I'm tired; been on the run for two days, and I need time to think." Lying down on the cot in the corner, Mitchell fell into a fitful, often interrupted sleep.

Tino and Frank retired to their cots as well. "Tomorrow, we'll try him," Tino whispered to Frank. "I gonna make him mine for while he's here."

*   *   *   *   *   *

Early the next morning, Detectives Tony Boudreaux and Patrick Monaghan drove into the parking lot in front of the Cullman County Sheriff's Department. Entering the front door, they encountered Rita, a tall, attractive black deputy who had

102

drawn receptionist and security duty for the day. Politely Rita greeted them.

"I'm Detective Tony Boudreaux, Escambia County Florida Sheriff's Department. This is Detective Patrick Monaghan. We here to see Sheriff Copeland. He supposed to be expectin' us."

Smiling at hearing Boudreaux talk, Rita said, "I've been expecting your arrival." She looked over a stack of notes and found the one from Sheriff Copeland advising her to contact him immediately upon the arrival of Boudreaux.

After buzzing Copeland on the intercom, Rita said, "You may go see Sheriff Copeland now. Just go down the hall straight ahead, turn left at the first corridor and go to the end. His office is the big one on the right. There's a sign on it," directed Rita.

"Thanks," Boudreaux replied. He and Monaghan proceeded toward the office, where he knocked lightly.

Copeland said, "C'mon in."

The office was spacious, probably twenty feet square. Trophies accumulated by the Sheriff in a variety of bowling activities lined the walls. One wall was exclusively reserved for his awards for valor and "dedicated service." Statute books were numerous, and among them were scattered manuals of procedure for the department. His desk, measuring approximately eight by six, was of typical heavy duty metal with a rubberized top for those late night Coke cans and Waffle House coffee cups. Behind him was a metal credenza containing personal memorabilia, pictures of his family, and a computer terminal.

"Good mornin', how you doin' sir?" Boudreaux offered, extending his hand toward Copeland. "I'm Tony Boudreaux and this is Detective Patrick Monaghan."

"Good morning to both of you, Detectives. Is that a slight French accent I heard?" Copeland asked, rising from his chair first to take Boudreaux's hand and then to vigorously shake the hand of Detective Monaghan.

"Cajun," replied Boudreaux. "Sometimes I just can't shake the habit, you know."

As Copeland arose from his chair, Boudreaux noticed that he obviously had some kind of weight problem. At probably 350 pounds, the Sheriff was short in stature, rotund in appearance, and personable in comportment. "I know you are anxious to interrogate Mitchell," said Copeland, "so I won't keep you from it. I'll have one of my deputies take you to the jail and offer you a room to meet with him. Will that be okay?"

"For sure." Boudreaux said.

In a moment a Cullman County deputy led Boudreaux and Monaghan to the jail facility across the street from the Sheriff's office. Once in an interrogation room and after several minutes of waiting, Jeffrey Mitchell entered the room in handcuffs accompanied by a female corrections officer. "You want me to leave the cuffs on him?" she asked. "Or take them off?"

"Go ahead and take 'em off for now," Boudreaux answered. "I don't think he's goin' anywhere for awhile."

"I won't bother to introduce either of us since we seem to have met several times before now," Boudreaux began. "I have to tell you, first, you made a gator-sized mistake by runnin' like you did. It don't look good for you."

"Probably not, but you can't know how it feels to be accused of a crime you didn't commit," Mitchell said fervently.

"How do you even know that we goin' to accuse you of a crime?" Boudreaux asked.

"It's all over radio and TV. You don't have to be an Einstein to know why you appeared at my door with so many cruiser cars. Every time you talked with me, you asked questions that made me believe I was your prime suspect. When y'all drove up the other night, I didn't know what to do but run."

"You right about one thing. You *are* our suspect. And with what we got on you, your best bet is to own up to the crime and make a deal with the State Attorney. Otherwise, you can expect your butt to be strapped on a gurney and be pumped fulla poison."

"Never," said Mitchell. "I haven't done anything to be charged with, and I will not make a deal for something I didn't do."

"You're only going to make it harder on yourself," Monaghan interjected, trying to convince Mitchell.

"Don't I get a phone call or something?" Mitchell asked. "If you are going to insist on charging me with a crime, then I want a lawyer."

"Have it your way." Boudreaux was becoming annoyed that he had spent so much time on this case to have Mitchell declaring his innocence with such sincerity. "If you are so convinced that you're innocent, are you willin' to go back voluntarily and face the charges?"

"I don't know right now. I need to talk with a lawyer first," Mitchell said.

Bringing the phone from the corner, Boudreaux placed it on the table in front of Mitchell. "You done got a few minutes to make your call. I'll be back in a little while to find out what you done decided." Boudreaux and Monaghan then left the room.

*　*　*　*　*　*

"Fred, this is Jeff Mitchell," he began. Roush could hear the trembling in his usually strong voice.

Hardly had he gotten these words out than Fred Roush interrupted, "Jeff, where are you?"

"I'm in jail in Cullman County, Alabama."

"Why are you there?" Roush asked.

"Because this was as far as I got before the police found me," Mitchell responded.

"Jeff. . . ," Roush did not finish the statement before Mitchell cut him off.

"Fred, I'm in a whole lot of trouble I don't deserve, and I need advice. You're the only attorney I know that I really do trust. Could you help me, please?" Mitchell pleaded.

"Jeff, you know I don't do criminal cases. I'm afraid I might hurt you more than help you," Roush said, trying to suggest that Mitchell seek out someone more experienced at criminal law.

"You may not do this kind of law, but I know you, and I think you know I couldn't have killed Lillian. Just please come up here and advise me."

"What kind of advice do you need?" Roush inquired.

"Right now, I need to know whether to fight this extradition thing or not. Does it make me look guilty if I don't go back and face the music? Or do I duke it out with the state and make them prove that I need to go back?"

"Before I answer that, I've got one question for you, Jeff. And don't be offended, but I have to know. Did you have anything to do with Lillian's death?"

"NO!" Mitchell shouted into the phone. "As God is my witness, I had nothing to do with it."

"Then speaking as a friend and not as a lawyer, I would think it makes you look bad if you didn't go back and prove your innocence. Playing hardball probably won't win you any points, and the state will likely get you back anyway."

"Okay. But if I come back, will you represent me?" Mitchell asked, his voice breaking once more.

"Only as long as you understand that you don't have an experienced criminal lawyer on your case," Roush said.

"Believing me is more important than experience right now," Mitchell said. "Your friendship means a lot to me, and your persistence in other cases shows me that you'll do your best no matter what. Now what do I do about this extradition stuff?"

"Go ahead and waive extradition," Roush advised. "I'll see you as soon after you arrive as possible. We can start defending your case then."

*   *   *   *   *   *

Boudreaux was pleased that Mitchell had decided to waive extradition. After explaining about his cellmates, Mitchell asked that he be removed from B-4 and placed in a cell by himself until time to leave for Florida. Boudreaux explained the situation to Sheriff Copeland, the arrangement was set up with the corrections officers, and Mitchell was placed in the only empty cell in the jail, C-5, a third tier cell.

It would take the better part of the day to get the appropriate extradition papers drawn up and to obtain the authorizing signatures. Boudreaux and Monaghan passed the day in an office the Sheriff provided for them. Boudreaux made calls back to Florida in preparation for receiving Mitchell and placing him in jail there. He hoped to depart Cullman County before nightfall.

After eating a family style lunch of fried chicken, mashed potatoes and gravy, and turnip greens followed by tasty pecan pie at the local family-style eatery, Boudreaux and Monaghan returned to the Sheriff's Department. During the afternoon, to pass the time, they played Hearts. After two games, Boudreaux excused himself and called the State Attorney's office back in Florida to inform Pete Pettis that he would be taking Mitchell back. The proper papers were to be filed and a first appearance time set for the following day.

By late afternoon the extradition papers were prepared, signed, and delivered to an extremely impatient Tony Boudreaux. Collecting the papers, he and Monaghan walked across the street to the jail.

Boudreaux showed the papers to the supervisor on duty and said, "I'm here to take Mr. Mitchell."

"Okay. Just a minute, and we'll get him for you. What security are you using to transport him?" the supervisor asked.

"I gotta set of handcuffs and ankle bracelets," replied Boudreaux. "That oughta be enough. I also got Detective Monaghan here to accompany me back with the prisoner. I don't think we gonna have any security problems." Boudreaux was confident that he and Monaghan could handle any situation that might arise. After all, this was not the kind of conspiracy case where somebody might be trying to "spring" the prisoner.

As Boudreaux was wrapping up the official paperwork, Mitchell appeared in the doorway under the watchful eyes and strong security of two beefy corrections officers. "Thank you, *mon amis*," Boudreaux said as Monaghan placed a chain around Mitchell's waist with handcuffs attached. He then affixed ankle bracelets that were connected to the handcuffs by chains. Slowly, they walked toward the prisoner entrance area, a large room with garage doors at both ends, which, upon command, opened and closed independently. With the doors in a closed position, they placed Mitchell in the rear seat of the cruiser and secured him for the trip back.

After getting in his cruiser with his friend and colleague, Boudreaux ordered the big garage door to be opened. The time was 6:15. They were on their way home.

THE TRIAL

CHAPTER 13

Boudreaux decided to sleep a little later than usual because Mitchell's first appearance had been set for two o'clock in the afternoon. After six hours on the road and an extra hour getting Mitchell situated in the local jail, it was two o'clock the next morning by the time he could lay down his bone-weary body. Sleep came quickly.

*   *   *   *   *   *

Mitchell was not excited at all about his new surroundings. A much older facility than the Cullman County Jail, the Escambia County lockup accommodated more than three hundred prisoners. The current population numbered more than four hundred. And in spite of Mitchell's notoriety and his desire to be alone, he shared a cell with six other men.

He had slept part of the trip back to Florida and was not really tired when he arrived. Sleep did not come easily, and his mind seemed relentlessly to chase one subject after another. As he lay awake, he thought about what might happen at his first appearance. He would call Fred Roush first thing in the morning. He decided he'd better not make any statements or allow himself to be questioned until he had his lawyer present. He hoped that the matter could be resolved at the arraignment. Not completely aware of the judicial process, he hoped to convince the judge of his innocence. By just before daybreak, his mind had settled down; he slept lightly.

*   *   *   *   *   *

Boudreaux finally dragged himself out of bed. With cobwebs still in his head, he slowly made his way to the kitchen for a cup of strong coffee. Prepared before he retired to bed, the coffee had automatically perked at the time at which he had set the timer. As he prepared and poured a steaming cup of coffee, he tuned into his favorite country station in time to hear the local newscast. The lead story was the capture and return of Jeff Mitchell.

As he listened to the newscast, Boudreaux felt a sense of satisfaction, a real sense of pride and accomplishment. He had solved his first serious crime as a new detective in the division. *I can be proud,* he thought, as he savored a three-day-old cheese Danish that he had warmed in the microwave. *It'll feel real good to sit in the courtroom and see that guy squirm when he's convicted of this crime. And I solved it.*

*   *   *   *   *   *

The sun peeked over the eastern horizon and began its steady, bright journey through the daytime sky. Jeff Mitchell awoke, startled from an uneasy sleep. Sitting upright, he cleared the drowsiness from his mind and realized where he was. Not pleasant surroundings.

Even though he knew Fred Roush would not be in his office, Mitchell yelled to the officer on duty, "I need to use the telephone."

"Quiet down, Mitchell," the officer replied. "We'll get to you after a while. You can get that phone call in due time," he said. "Until then, stay quiet."

A few hours later, Duty Officer Mullins stopped in front of Mitchell's cell. "Come on, Mitchell," he said. "It's time for you to make your call."

Walking to an interrogation room, Mitchell was directed to a phone on the wall. "Make your call over there," Mullins said. "I'll be waiting right outside the door. Just knock when you're ready. You have fifteen minutes, no more."

Mitchell quickly dialed the office number of his friend, Fred Roush. Instead of a congenial female voice, he heard that of Roush himself. "Fred? Is that you?" Mitchell asked.

"Yeah. Jeff?" Roush inquired.

"It's me. I need your help in getting me out of this mess," Mitchell said, acknowledging his tough circumstance. "My first appearance has been set for early this afternoon. I assume you want to meet with me before that."

"I can't make an early afternoon appearance, Jeff. I have a previous personal appointment I must keep. Who is the judge in the case?"

"I understand the judge is Paul Reid," Mitchell informed him.

"That's good," Roush replied. "I will call him and make arrangements to delay the appearance until another time when I can be there. He's known for being understanding and accommodating. I'll call him and get back to you."

"I only have fifteen minutes at this phone. I'll try to stretch that time, but don't count on my being able to do so."

"If I miss you, I'll leave a message at the desk and ask them to deliver it to you," Roush said, trying to ease Mitchell's anxiety.

After hanging up with Mitchell, Roush called the office of the Honorable Paul Reid. His secretary, Sarah, answered, "He's not in at the moment, but I expect him any time now. I can have him call you." As she was taking Roush's message, Judge Reid walked in. She put Roush on hold and asked the judge if he could talk with Roush. Reid nodded and walked to his office, picked up the phone, and said, "Good morning, Mr. Roush. What can I do for you today?"

Roush explained his predicament to the judge. Judge Reid advised that the first appearance for Jeff Mitchell be reset. Late afternoon, perhaps 4:00. "Thanks, Judge," Roush agreed, even though his preparation time might be inadequate.

Roush then called Mitchell. Mitchell answered on the first ring. "I have talked with Judge Reid, and he agreed to change the appearance time for later," Roush advised Mitchell.

"Is that going to be enough time to prepare?" Jeff asked, apprehension in his voice.

"It'll have to do," Roush said. "Give me a few minutes to get things in order here at the office, prepare a note to my secretary, and I'll be right over to the jail to talk with you."

Mitchell replied with a smile of assurance in his voice, "I'll be sure not to go anywhere."

*   *   *   *   *   *

As Boudreaux quietly enjoyed the satisfaction of the moment, the incessant ringing of his phone startled him. It was Raymond Pearce, the third detective working the case, advising him that Mitchell's appearance was moved to late afternoon.

"His lawyer had a previous commitment that he couldn't get out of," Pearce said, obviously annoyed at the change.

"All right," Boudreaux answered. "I was plannin' to be in the office before noon anyhow. I won't change those plans, since I still oughtta have enough time to prepare any materials the prosecution team might need. See you in a while."

Going through his morning ritual, Boudreaux prepared to go to work. After looking at himself in the mirror, he smiled cynically and declared himself ready to meet the day.

*   *   *   *   *   *

Roush was escorted to a large room in the jail in which a single three by six table sat in the center. Two chairs on either side of the table allowed up to four people to meet. Roush walked to the table, set his valise on it, and removed a legal file folder marked "State of Florida v. Jeffrey Mitchell." He waited.

Shortly, Mitchell, in handcuffs, was escorted to the room. When the cuffs were removed, Roush tried to shake hands with him. Mitchell refused. Instead he put his arms around Roush's shoulders, hugged him tightly, and said, "Thanks for helping me."

Roush reminded him. "First, I want you to remember that I am not a criminal lawyer, so I'll be playing this thing more by ear than anything. However, I'll do the best I can for you. At least I can protect your rights even if I can't get you off. Can you live with that?"

"I would rather have one genuine friend who believes in me representing me than all the criminal lawyers in town who don't know me and might be suspicious that I really did it," Mitchell said. "You are my friend as well as my lawyer, and I know you won't let me down."

113

"You also must realize," Roush said, "that you likely will not be released from jail before your trial."

"Why?" asked Mitchell, loudly.

"Because the crime you have been accused of is a capital crime. Suspects in capital crimes seldom are released before trial. Remember O.J.? Even he had to stay in jail prior to his trial. Furthermore, you took off when the authorities came to get you, and the judge is going to view you as a flight risk."

"I'm not going anywhere. I want to face this thing, now," Mitchell said.

"Maybe so, but your actions didn't show that," Roush responded. "Then there's the problem of bail. Even if the judge decides to release you pending trial, the bail is probably going to be so high that you can't afford it."

"What do you call high?" Mitchell asked.

"Minimally a half million dollars, probably more," Roush replied. "That means you would have to come up with at least fifty thousand dollars. Could you do that?"

"No way," Mitchell said. "Out of the question."

"We can argue for reasonable bail, but don't expect the judge to cut you any slack on that issue," Roush said. "Do you have any idea what evidence they have against you?"

"No idea whatsoever. I really don't see how they can have any. Since I didn't do it what evidence could there possibly be?"

"At this point the prosecution is not required to inform you of the evidence. We'll have to wait and see what they present in discovery. The appearance will give us some idea," Roush said. Then he added, "Is there anyone you want me to call?"

"Not yet. Eventually, I will want you to set up a conference call with my parents. And I would like to notify my friend Mark Bradley. But wait until after the appearance this afternoon. The notifications might not be necessary."

For the next thirty minutes, Roush questioned Jeff Mitchell about his relationship with Lillian Reins, the broken engagement,

114

the date on the night prior to her death, and why he made a run for it once the police tried to apprehend him. Mitchell offered the most intimate and minute details of each issue, assuring Roush that he had never been anywhere near where Lillian was found dead. By shortly after noon, the meeting was concluded.

"I'll see you in court later," Roush said to Mitchell.

*   *   *   *   *   *

The courtroom of Judge Paul Reid appeared spartan in decor but was ornate in style. Light walnut stained walls were accented with panel moldings, giving it the appearance of wainscoting. On the wall at the front of the courtroom was the seal of the Great State of Florida, and below it was the judge's bench, approximately ten feet in length, complete with a computer terminal, a leather-covered, high-backed chair in burgundy, a wooden gavel, and reams of case files. The judge sat about three feet above the courtroom floor and behind the massive bench so that his height forced those who approached the bench to look up at him.

To the left of the judge's bench was the empty witness stand. The gallery was typical Americana courtroom with oak benches resembling church pews lining both sides of the room. Stained glass windows lined the courtroom on the east side, allowing varying tones of colored sunlight to filter into the room during the daytime.

The clock on the rear wall read 4:00 sharp. Shortly, Larry Boxer, affectionately known to his friends and coworkers as "Butch," announced the arrival of Judge Paul Reid, "All rise. Court is now in session, the Honorable Paul Reid presiding."

Judge Reid made his appearance through a well-camouflaged doorway at the front of the courtroom. Dressed in a black robe, only his collar and the top of his necktie were visible. Taking the four steps in two strides, Judge Reid sat with the dignified demeanor one expects of a judge.

Boxer barked loudly, "Be seated."

The judge then removed a file from the top of the pile and said to the Clerk, "Please announce the first case."

"The State of Florida versus Jeffrey Mitchell," the Court Clerk stated loudly and clearly.

"Is Mr. Mitchell present?" Judge Reid asked, peering over his half glasses toward the defense table.

"He is, Your Honor, and he is represented by counsel," said Fred Roush, standing as he spoke. He nodded toward Mitchell to stand also.

"Mr. Mitchell, do you understand the charges against you?" asked the judge.

"Yes, I do, Your Honor. But I don't understand why I have to be charged. I had nothing..."

Interrupting Mitchell in mid-sentence, Judge Reid said, "This hearing is not to present your defense, Mr. Mitchell, but only to determine whether the case against you is sufficient to present to a grand jury." As he said this, Judge Reid began to twirl a pencil through his fingers, a habit he had formed in law school and had failed to break throughout his years as an attorney and now as a judge.

"Let's take this one step at a time, Mr. Roush. I know you don't do criminal work, so I shall grant you some leeway. Let me explain. Our sole purpose today is to determine whether there is probable cause to hold Mr. Mitchell.

Turning toward Douglas Rose of the State Attorney's office, Judge Reid asked, "Mr. Rose, are you prepared to go forward?"

"Yes, I am, Your Honor," Rose responded. Roush and Mitchell took their seats.

"Then let's proceed with this hearing."

For the next forty-five minutes, Prosecuting Attorney Douglas Rose presented the probable cause elements of the case. As he expounded on the details of the murder, the case seemed to take on overwhelming proportions. Rose revealed the probable cause evidence against Jeffrey Mitchell, but presented only as much as he felt he must to get the case bound over to the grand jury. Since analysis of evidence would take days or weeks, the most damning evidence, that requiring laboratory study, would be saved for trial.

When Rose had concluded his presentation, Roush arose from his seat and said, "Your Honor, the evidence presented by the prosecutor is entirely circumstantial. They have nothing to place my client at the scene of the crime, nor do they have a motive for him to have committed such a heinous crime."

"Mr. Roush," Judge Reid began. "As I told you before, this hearing is to determine whether there is sufficient evidence to take this case to the grand jury. It is my judgment that the evidence, however strong or weak and for whatever circumstances it indicates, is sufficient to bind this case over to the grand jury."

"Your Honor, what about bail?" Roush asked, likely anticipating the answer.

"Mr. Roush, this is a capital murder case. In the State of Florida, a defendant is not entitled to bail when the evidence of guilt is great. Furthermore, your client made a run for it when he saw the police at his door and was subsequently apprehended in the State of Alabama. I consider him a flight risk and, therefore, bail is denied. Let the record show that this case is to be bound over to the grand jury. Call the next case, Madam Clerk."

With those words, Mitchell's nightmare began.

CHAPTER 14

The day following Mitchell's first court appearance, Roush contacted the Sheriff's Department to arrange a meeting with his client.

Roush entered the jail's receiving area. He was escorted to the jail's conference room, where he awaited Mitchell's arrival.

The conference room was a ten-by-twelve-foot rectangle painted institutional green. The windows with imbedded mesh wire were frosted opaque, and the door was heavy metal with a keyed lock that could only be unlocked from the outside. Beside the door was an intercom through which the duty officer could be notified that the visitor was ready to leave.

In the middle of the room was a six-foot table with a Formica top and metal folding legs. Around the table were six gray metal chairs. Roush made himself comfortable in one of the end chairs.

His wait was not long. A corrections officer escorted the handcuffed Mitchell to the room. The door was closed, the handcuffs were removed, and then the accompanying officer departed.

"Hi, Jeff," Roush began. "I had hoped. . ."

Interrupting, Mitchell said, "He did exactly what you said he would do, deny bail. But I just can't believe it."

"Pretty standard stuff, Jeff, in a case this serious."

"Do you have any idea how long it might be before the Grand Jury meets?" Mitchell asked.

"No, not really. Certainly until after the grand jury meets," Roush said.

"Have you been advised as to when that might be?"

"No, I haven't, but I know it meets weekly, so sometime this week it will probably be considering your case."

For the next hour, Fred Roush collected information. He inquired once more about his family, his relationship with Lillian Reins, his work, even his leisure time. He asked for a list of his closest friends who could be called as character witnesses. Among the friends Mitchell listed were Sharon Farrell, Lillian's roommate' Mark Bradley, his closest friend and hiking buddy; and Joe Blankenship, a fellow scuba diver from his high school days with whom he continued to maintain a close friendship.

Roush also asked him about his lifestyle, his hobbies, his away-from-work activities. Nothing that Mitchell revealed about himself portrayed him as a potential murderer. Roush now entertained genuine misgivings that Jeff Mitchell could be the killer of Lillian Reins.

*   *   *   *   *   *

The grand jury met on Thursday after Mitchell's first appearance. Two cases were being presented, including that of Jeff Mitchell. Prosecutor Douglas Rose waited impatiently outside the jury room to be called to present his case. After two cups of coffee, the bailiff finally stepped into the hallway and called for Mr. Rose.

As Rose entered the room, he observed the usual eighteen member panel. The foreman of the jury arose and addressed his colleagues, "The case to be considered momentarily is that of the State versus Jeffrey Mitchell. Each of you has a summary of the case. The Prosecuting Attorney for this case, Mr. Douglas Rose, is here to present the evidence for our consideration. After he has presented the evidence, we shall weigh the merits of the case and determine whether an indictment is warranted. Mr. Rose, the floor is yours."

Doug Rose stepped to the podium, which stood at the head of a fifteen-foot, wooden conference table. Each juror, serving a ninety-day term, sat in a heavily padded leather swivel chair that partially reclined. In addition to the case file, each juror was provided a legal pad and writing implements for taking notes.

Rose arranged his file notes in order. He began his presentation dramatically. "Ladies and gentlemen, this is one of the most brutal murders that I have prosecuted in my ten years as an Assistant State Attorney. A charge of first degree, capital murder has been placed against the prime suspect in this crime, Mr. Jeffrey Mitchell. It is our judgment—and we believe we can prove it—that Mr. Mitchell, the ex-fiancé of Miss Reins, became intensely angry at her over the breakup of their engagement. His anger led to extraordinary rage, and, in a fitful moment, he killed her. The evidence in the case, especially the physical evidence, is overwhelming and points unmistakably to Mr. Mitchell."

For the next hour and a half, Rose introduced witnesses who supported the preliminary findings placed in evidence. Throughout the testimony of Deputy Boudreaux, Rose used a computer and projector to present photographs of the crime scene, a close up photograph of the rose-shaped broach which had been found in the underbrush along the path where the victim had been dragged, and the body at the morgue prior to autopsy. Dr. Sheila Josephson explained the results of the autopsy using computer projections of her notes on an outlined figure of a human body. Stephen Sasser testified that fingerprints found inside the car belonged to Jeff Mitchell and no one else. He also offered information about Mitchell's bloody sweater, which had been found in the back seat of Lillian Reins's car. Each juror took notes.

Rose placed the plaster cast of a shoe print on the table where Sasser identified it as matching a pair of hiking boots that Mitchell owned. Rose concluded the State's case by describing Mitchell's flight from the Escambia jurisdiction, his arrest in Cullman County, Alabama, and his waiving of extradition back to West Florida. The jury had no immediate questions.

After shutting down the computer and projector and collecting the case file, Rose left the room. He would wait outside in case the jury had questions during deliberation.

For more than an hour, the jury deliberated. At half past seven, the door opened and the bailiff stepped into the hallway and asked Rose to come back in. After asking Rose to take a seat at the head of the table, the foreman of the grand jury then said, "Mr. Rose, we have reviewed the evidence you have presented and the testimony of the state's witnesses. We have only one question. What have you learned about the brooch that you discovered along the path? Do you have any evidence at all that Mr. Mitchell purchased the jewelry? Do you know where it might have been purchased?"

"Mr. Foreman," Rose began. Rose never believed the brooch to be an important piece of the evidence puzzle, so he wondered about the questions. "The investigators have surveyed every jewelry store in town and have come up blank. Quite frankly, we believe the other evidence in the case is so overwhelming that the brooch becomes less important, even mundane, to the case and will not be considered seriously or even presented as direct evidence in the case. We present it here only to let you know that additional evidence is available for investigation and analysis if needed."

"Thank you, Mr. Rose. That will be all." Rose stood and again left the room.

For another hour the grand jury deliberated, finally reaching a verdict late in the night. The indictment, which Rose and his staff had prepared, was signed by the foreman of the grand jury for delivery to Judge Reid the next day.

*   *   *   *   *   *

By the next morning, a copy of the signed indictment had been delivered from the office of the Clerk of Court to Douglas Rose. He was pleased with the results of the grand jury deliberations. Picking up the phone, he called Fred Roush.

"Fred, this is Doug Rose at the State Attorney's Office." Rose was tentative in his approach. "The grand jury met yesterday and indicted Jeff Mitchell. I have a copy of the indictment on my desk and will be happy to send you a certified copy of it."

"I'm sorry to hear that, Doug. Although I have not seen the evidence, I had hoped that there would be insufficient evidence to warrant an indictment. I guess there's more evidence than I thought," Roush said.

"It is considerable," Rose said, lowering his voice. "I will be calling Judge Reid shortly to arrange a time for Mitchell's arraignment. I'm sure you and he will be notified. In the meantime, I'll see that a copy of the indictment is on your desk before noon."

"Thanks, Doug. I appreciate your consideration," Roush offered. "When might we begin the discovery?"

"As soon as I can pull everything together, I'll have copies available to provide to you," Rose responded. "Then I'll see you in court."

Before he could dial the judge's number, Rose's phone rang. "Doug Rose here."

"Mr. Rose, this is the Court Clerk. Judge Reid wishes to set the arraignment for Jeff Mitchell for this afternoon. Can you meet that schedule?" she asked.

"Yes. That'll be no problem," Rose said.

"I will be calling Mr. Roush shortly to inform him of the time as well," the Court Clerk said.

*   *   *   *   *   *

By 4:00, all parties were present in Judge Reid's courtroom. Dressed in standard issue green coveralls with "ECCC" stenciled in large white letters in the center of the back, Mitchell entered the courtroom, handcuffed and in leg irons. He was directed to a chair next to Roush at the defense table. Opposite Mitchell and Roush sat Prosecutor Doug Rose and his two associates Kemper Nixon and Samantha Kralick. All sat quietly, patiently waiting for Judge Reid to enter the courtroom.

Representatives from the local media had stationed themselves in the courtroom to get a good look at the infamous man who had allegedly murdered Lillian Reins. One was a sketch artist, who began to sketch his face in chalky hues as soon as Mitchell entered the room. All of the reporters had their writing pads at the ready position. Because of the notoriety of the case, Judge Reid had disallowed any television or still cameras in the courtroom, so the television reporters would have to be creative in reporting this story for the evening news.

The hushed courtroom took on a solemn character as Judge Paul Reid entered and strode to the bench. Drawing the case file toward him, he asked, "Mr. Mitchell, would you please rise?"

Jeff Mitchell, along with his attorney, rose from his chair and stood silently before the court.

"Mr. Mitchell, you have been charged with the crime of murder in the first degree. The grand jury of Escambia County has deliberated and issued an indictment in this case remanding it over for trial. At this time, how do you plead?"

"Not guilty, Your Honor. I'm not guilty," Mitchell said clearly but respectfully.

"Your Honor," interjected Fred Roush. "I would like once more to request bail for my client."

"Mr. Roush, in the case of capital murder, bail simply is not allowed. Bail, therefore, is denied, and Mr. Mitchell is remanded to the custody of the Sheriff until trial. I am setting the date for this trial to begin the second week of May. I expect all parties to be ready to proceed to trial at that time."

Upon adjournment, Mitchell was handcuffed and led away to the county jail for incarceration until his trial.

Noticing Mitchell's reluctance, Roush stated, "I'll talk with you tomorrow."

*   *   *   *   *   *

The next day Fred Roush once again found himself in that dreary institutional conference room at the county jail. When Mitchell entered the room, it was obvious, even to the most casual observer, that he was depressed. "How do you feel?" Roush began.

"Not well at all, thank you. I never expected that this would happen," Mitchell said.

Distress etched deep lines in Mitchell's face, his skin took on a paler color, and he had developed the nervous habit of alternately biting his fingernails and drumming them on the table. His hair was not combed, and he had not shaved from the day before. The experience was wearing on him.

"We need to get down to business, Jeff," Roush said. Mitchell did not seem to listen, his head buried in his hands. Roush continued, "First, let me tell you I don't have the evidence from the State Attorney's office yet. Under the discovery rule, they are required to release that to me as soon as possible. Until then, I'm going to obtain as much information about you, your whereabouts on the night of the murder, your family, your work, and anything else I can think of."

There was a long pause. "Look at me, Jeff," Roush said. "You've told me about your relationship with Lillian, your engagement, and your breakup, but you haven't told where you were the night she was killed. That's probably the best place to start."

Mitchell stared out into space as though in deep thought. "Lillian picked me up at my apartment that night about 7:30," he said. "My car was in the shop for repairs, so we took her car instead. For two hours we enjoyed dinner at Charley Dees, then drove to the chimney on Scenic Highway to spend some time just talking."

"Is there someone at the restaurant who could corroborate that?" Roush asked.

"Yeah. Our waitress was Christina. She could confirm that we were there. I even left her a larger tip than usual." Mitchell drummed his fingers on the table.

"What happened next?"

"We found a secluded spot at the chimney park. There was only one other car there, and its occupant or driver was not in sight. We decided it would be perfectly safe. It always had been. The car could be clearly seen from the road. We talked about our lives and how different our lifestyles were. She was a homebody, enjoyed being with her friends, loved her work, appreciated the classics, and was into physical fitness. However, she didn't like sports or fancy outdoor activities. But the one thing we had in common was a strong sexual appetite. We often made love simply for the stimulating pleasure it brought. But we knew that a life together based principally on sex was not realistic."

"When did you realize you were not compatible?"

"Actually we realized it within weeks after our engagement. But neither of us wanted to be the first to admit it. I think we hoped that it would work out, and we gave it ample time, but it just wasn't in the cards."

"What did you do after you talked that night?"

"We stayed in that car talking for almost two hours. We agreed to remain friends, but we had no future as husband and wife. During the last thirty minutes, we mutually consented to pleasure each other for one last time, no strings attached. The night air was cool and the windows of the car fogged from our body heat. I opened a window slightly to let in some fresh air.

"And after making love, what did the two of you do?"

"Just prior to starting the car, Lillian took off the ring I had given her, reached for my hand, placed the ring in my upturned, open palm, and closed my fingers around it. It was a sad time. While we both knew it had been inevitable, the finality of ending the relationship, I believe, caused us both difficulty. I know it did me. Then, after looking into each other's eyes for a moment, Lillian said, 'Friends?' And I responded to her, 'Friends.' She then turned in her seat, started the car, and took me home."

"You went nowhere else. Nothing else happened in that car. You didn't go out into the woods. You didn't get angry at her. You didn't physically accost her. What you have told me is all that happened that night?"

"That is all that happened that night," Mitchell declared.

125

Roush could not believe he was hearing a description of a simple date that had turned into a nightmare for Jeff Mitchell. If Mitchell was telling the truth, how could there be evidence that so completely implicated him as the killer? He would have to wait for the evidence to come to his office.

"Jeff, I'll do my best to try to keep you in a cell by yourself. I can't promise I'll succeed, but I'll certainly try. Meanwhile, I am completely baffled by the story you have told. I will be getting with the State Attorney's office as soon as possible to obtain the evidence against you. Keep your chin up. I'll check with you in a few days."

Roush shook his head as he left the jail. Emerging into the bright December sunshine, he couldn't help believing that this case was simply one of mistaken identity or over-zealous detective work.

Jeff Mitchell returned to his cell on the fourth floor of the jail. Depressed, despondent, weakened from not eating, he pondered his future. *What future?* he thought. *If it's left up to Escambia County, I won't have a future.* Lowering his head into his hands, he breathed a prayer, asking God to release him from this horrifying experience and to return him to a normal existence.

CHAPTER 15

Fred Roush knew the chances of getting paid for defending Jeff Mitchell were slim. He might receive some modest compensation, possibly from his family, but to be paid for the enormous amount of time it was going to require was likely out of the question. Nevertheless, his conscience would not allow him to abandon his friend, especially since he believed in his heart that Jeff was innocent.

On Monday, after rearranging the scheduled meetings for several cases on which he was working at the time, Roush called the office of Prosecutor Doug Rose. "Doug, I would like to make arrangements to complete discovery on the Jeff Mitchell case. Today, I plan to submit the appropriate papers under the rules of discovery to get those files. You want to help me out here?"

"I see you've done your homework, Fred. You may become a criminal lawyer after all. As soon as I can get it together, you will have all that we have. Give me until noon tomorrow and I'll provide you with everything, including the results of all laboratory tests. I plan to be ready for trial by the May date set by Judge Reid," Rose said. "After reviewing the evidence, you may wish to consider a plea arrangement for your client. You can get back to me on that as soon as you have had a chance to see what we have on him," Rose added.

"I will consider anything that will help Jeff get a fair trial and be acquitted," Roush said. "I will prepare the Notice of Discovery as quickly as possible and get it filed for the paper trail."

After hanging up the phone, Roush decided to spend the afternoon in criminal procedure research. Because of his limited experience in criminal law, he knew he needed to review several procedural rules before continuing with the case, especially those regarding filing under the rules of discovery. Pulling his copy of the most recent issue of *Florida Rules of Court*, he read and took notes for more than two hours.

When he returned to his office, he dictated the information for his secretary, Joanie Foster. Carefully following his research notes, he prepared the Notice of Discovery, expressing the willingness of the defendant to participate in the discovery process and laying claim to all the evidence that the prosecutor's office might have, including a list of potential witnesses who might be called at trial on behalf of the prosecution. After completing the dictation, he advised his secretary to have the completed documents on his desk by that afternoon.

* * * * * *

It had suddenly become clear to Jeff Mitchell that his stay in jail was going to be neither a short one, nor a pleasant one. He needed something to occupy his time. He requested a computer, and his request was denied. Finally, he decided that it might be best that he learn something about the criminal justice system, so he requested several law books. He would spend his time researching not only the law but also other cases that related directly to his. After all, he might even be able to help himself, if worse came to worse.

He decided on two law books that would give him his best introduction to the system and judicial procedure. He asked that copies of the most recent *Florida Statutes* and *Florida Rules of Court* be sent to his cell. Within three hours, the books were there, on loan for the next four days, and renewable, subject to requests by inmates.

* * * * * *

The Notice of Discovery had been prepared and was on Roush's desk, ready for his signature. Checking his notes and reviewing the papers at the same time, he made several corrections in wording, resubmitting each page separately to his secretary as he made the changes. She completed each page by the time he had finished with the next one. Within thirty minutes, the papers were ready.

Roush signed the documents and asked his secretary, Joanie Foster, to make several copies of the paperwork for office and personal use. After the copies were made, he personally delivered an original copy to the office of the Clerk of Court at the courthouse just before it closed for the day.

*　　*　　*　　*　　*　　*

The next day, Fred Roush arose early from bed, dressed, and arrived at the office by quite early. It was going to be a long day. He had to prepare for a civil trial the next day. Most of the work had been done already, but he knew he needed to review the evidence and the depositions that he had taken from both his witnesses and those of the defendants; then he needed to prepare his opening statement. The trial was expected to last only two days.

Before noon, hunger began to grip him. While eating a hamburger from Jimbo's Drive-In down the street from his office, Roush poured over the materials, writing furiously as ideas came into his mind. This was a difficult case, but it was one of merit. His client, a twenty-nine-year-old, unmarried, school teacher, had been assaulted and robbed in his apartment by a man who had broken in through the patio door. Believing that the apartment owner and the management had a responsibility to maintain adequate security, he had discovered that lighting had been very poor, the doors had not been adequately secured, and no night watchman was available to handle emergency situations or to guard the property, especially at night.

More aware now of the incidence of local violence, the young man was frightened, had sought extensive psychological counseling, and continued to have nightmares, now four years later. It should be an open and shut case, but who knows how juries will react. He was asking for two million dollars in damages.

By late evening, Roush felt he had done all he could to prepare for the case. Nevertheless, he decided to sleep on the couch in his office. Being weary from the day's work, he fell asleep quickly and slept uninterrupted until 5:30 the next morning. When he arose, he drove home, showered, changed clothes, and returned to the office. Court would convene at 9:00.

Roush was seated behind the plaintiff's table awaiting the arrival of his client. Ten minutes later, his client had arrived, conservatively attired in a gray and black pin-striped suit, white French-cuffed shirt with gold accenting cufflinks, a button tab underneath a red and gray paisley tie. Looking the epitome of the GQ man, his deep set, dark eyes seemed to reflect uncertainty.

The judge appeared promptly at the appointed hour. After the judge cleared several requests by the defense, the case was ready to present to a jury of four women and two men. Roush opened with a stirring statement, outlining the strategy of his case and how he hoped to prove that the circumstance could have been avoided had the defendants taken a little time and spent a little money to insure adequate security. He spoke of his client's problems and the fear with which he continued to cope. His statement was brilliant and both emotionally and convincingly delivered. In college he had been a master debater. Little wonder that he had now gained a reputation for effective and dramatic oratory.

For the next eight hours, the trial ground on, breaking only an hour for lunch at noon. By 5:00, Roush rested his case. It was now time for the defense to present whatever evidence and witnesses it had prepared. After two hours of defense testimony, it was obvious the trial would be carried over to the next day. The judge adjourned for the evening, advising the jurors not to talk with anyone about the trial or matters pertaining to it.

The next day, the trial resumed. Roush surmised that the defense likely had a weak case. Now that he had seen it actually presented, he considered it to be worse than weak. It was almost non-existent. He felt good about the outcome. Nevertheless, he had to ensure his client's victory with a convincing closing argument.

Time for closing arguments came after the noon lunch break. Roush spoke first, noting how the evidence in the case supported his position and how his client deserved to be compensated for the personal loss that he had experienced. His presentation was brilliantly thought out and articulately delivered.

After the defense presented its closing statement, the jury was charged, and deliberations began. The jury took only three hours to reach a verdict. During those hours, Roush and his client passed the time first by visiting a local art gallery, only a few blocks from the courthouse. After an hour there, they strolled to a corner sports bar, each ordering a hot dog, fries, and a chocolate milkshake. While eating, they never discussed the case. They talked about each other's families, favorite hobbies, and his client's future marriage. The client had planned a March wedding and was excited to offer details of the plans, so he spent the better part of forty-five minutes sharing those details along with his hopes and dreams for the future.

While finishing his milkshake, Roush's cellular phone rang. His secretary, Joanie Foster, was on the other end. "Mr. Roush," she said, "the jury has reached a verdict. You should get back to the courthouse as soon as possible."

Quickly, he took in the last of the milkshake, and the two of them walked briskly to the courthouse, only two blocks away.

Entering the courtroom, Roush noticed that the defense attorneys had already returned for the reading of the verdict. After about five minutes, the presiding judge appeared and asked the bailiff to bring the jury into the courtroom. Each juror filed in quietly, exhibiting no expression that would reflect the results of the verdict.

The judge asked the jury to be seated and called on the foreperson of the jury, a woman about sixty years old. She arose as the judge asked, "Have you reached a verdict?"

"Yes, we have, Your Honor," she replied respectfully.

"Would you please read the verdict?"

"We, the jury in the above entitlement, do find for the plaintiff, and that . . . guilty of negligence . . . award damages of one million two hundred and fifty thousand dollars. So says one, so say all. Dated this twenty-second day of December." After reading the verdict, she sat down.

It was over. He had succeeded. With this kind of award, his fee would be substantial. He could now afford to focus more time on the Mitchell case without having to seek other cases.

*   *   *   *   *   *

With a fee of more than four hundred thousand dollars from the trial just concluded, Fred Roush took some time off during the Christmas holidays. Returning to the office on December 28th, he now considered more seriously than before the possibility of adding an attorney to his staff. Although he had been pondering the addition of an associate with civil trial experience, the Mitchell case had altered his thinking. If he hired a lawyer with criminal experience, he could expand the bounds of his practice and possibly get some assistance on the Mitchell case as well.

For two days, he contemplated the pros and cons of the move, deliberating and arguing with himself. Finally feeling that his decision was a wise one, he initiated a search for a lawyer with criminal trial experience.

For more than three weeks, Roush conducted an intensive search, narrowing the field to two candidates. After interviewing the younger of the two, Roush was certain that he would hire him. But to be fair, he scheduled an interview with the second candidate.

That second candidate was Blayne Simmons, a tall, gangly, and somewhat clumsy individual. A graduate of Memphis State, he was the first of his family to attend college. His father, a southern sharecropper in Mississippi, worked hard to help put Blayne through college.

Growing up black in rural Mississippi did not lend itself to great achievement without persistence and perseverance. Blayne learned that lesson at an early age when one of his teachers, seeing immense potential in him, took him aside one day and encouraged him to work hard and make something of himself. He promised to do that, and do it he did.

Graduating from high school second in a class of fifty students, Blayne was offered and accepted a scholarship to study the liberal arts at Memphis State University. He majored in English and graduated with a minor in political science.

During his tenure at Memphis State, Simmons studied hard, earned excellent grades, and initiated the pursuit of his lifelong ambition, to become a lawyer. His academic accomplishments as an undergraduate student earned him a scholarship to Stetson Law School, where he excelled academically, eclipsing all of his peers at moot court. With a little help from the outside world, he would become a great lawyer.

After law school, Simmons accepted a clerkship with a federal judge in Tallahassee, Florida. There he learned the intricacies of the law, legal procedure, grounds for and processes associated with appeals, and the analysis of details of testimony at a trial. After two years as a law clerk, he settled into a practice with the firm of Maples, Gentry & Spellman in central Florida.

For seven years, he practiced successfully with Maples, Gentry & Spellman, trying more than two dozen criminal cases. He had prevailed at three "high profile" cases and won more than half of the others he defended. In spite of his record, he had not been invited to become a partner, and partnership was one of his career goals. He had begun to look for possibilities with other firms where a potential partnership might be in the cards.

Contacted by a mutual friend, Simmons learned that Fred Roush, the principal in a one-man firm was seeking a lawyer with criminal experience. Thus began a career journey for Blayne Simmons that would inevitably change his life.

* * * * * *

Fred Roush waited in his office to be notified that Blayne Simmons had arrived. When Joanie announced Simmons's arrival, Roush immediately invited him in. For more than three hours, they discussed the opening that Roush had created. Roush was impressed with the demeanor, capability, and experience of this young, black lawyer from Mississippi.

Changing his mind from earlier, he offered Simmons the position on the spot surprised both Simmons and Roush. Simmons appreciated the opportunity to join a small firm, offering him the real chance to become a partner and opening new doors of experience. After all, his final goal in life was to become a Supreme Court justice. He accepted the job almost before Roush finished offering it.

* * * * * *

Mid-January. It was time to concentrate on the Jeff Mitchell case. Since he had spent so much time at the law library earlier in the week, Roush was keenly aware of the need to conduct significantly more research into the criminal law process. He was good at civil cases, but a criminal case often has much more at stake, and it would be more than three weeks before Blayne Simmons joined him. He determined to spend the next two days at the law library where he would not be interrupted with visits or phone calls.

The days were long and hard. He often appeared at the library promptly at its opening time, often waiting for the attendant to arrive. He took extensive notes, carefully jotting down the source of each entry and the page numbers where the information could be found. He reviewed the trial process, the calling of witnesses, and finally the rules relating to plea bargaining. *I hope I never have to resort to pleading Mitchell's case*, he thought.

His stomach growled loudly; he checked his watch. The time was half past two. He had become so engrossed in what he was doing that he forgot about the time and missed lunch. He opted for a diet soda and would try to make it until dinner.

Research into other criminal cases similar to that of Mitchell's had convinced him that he was even less capable than he thought to accept such a case. But for the benefit of his friend, he would proceed and do the best he could, getting advice from Blayne Simmons and other colleagues who had defended similar cases.

From his notes, he ordered transcripts of similar trials in which the defendant was acquitted. When the transcripts arrived, he would review the language contained in them, the opening arguments, direct and cross examinations of witnesses, and closing arguments. From these he would plan his strategy and the manner, style, and wording he would use. After all, there was no need to re-invent the wheel.

*   *   *   *   *   *

Twenty-five days after accepting Roush's offer, Simmons appeared at the law office of Fred Roush, Esq., ready to begin a new era in his career as an associate.

CHAPTER 16

Robyn Weeks was a beautiful brunette with dancing brown eyes, whose magic entranced everyone who met her. Besides her outward beauty, her gregarious personality endeared her to friend and adversary alike. A graduate of the University of North Carolina at Chapel Hill, she had majored in criminal justice, migrated to Florida, and had accepted a job with the Florida Department of Law Enforcement. She specialized in DNA analysis.

Robyn Weeks loved her work. Each day brought yet another challenge which she met head on with unabashed enthusiasm. Today she arrived at work at mid morning and went directly to her office, where she arranged her plans for the day. Next to her desk she discovered a small FDLE evidence case containing items that required her immediate attention. Accompanying the evidence case was her department's case folder. She noticed from the label on the folder that the evidence was from the Reins case.

Wishing to get started on the analyses as quickly as possible, she went to the laboratory, put on her white lab coat, curiously read through the evidence inventory list, and began to remove the items from the small container. Excited to work on such an important case, she carefully adhered to approved and accepted procedures and due process under the law.

As she documented each test, she became more and more cognizant that a man's life was at stake. She had never worked on a capital case before with such grave potential consequences. What she discovered could mean life or death for Jeff Mitchell. She took her responsibility quite seriously.

*   *   *   *   *   *

Roush understood that filing the Notice of Discovery would result in requiring his client to participate in the discovery process itself. He had spoken to Jeff Mitchell before he filed the Notice to ensure that he was willing to do whatever it took to defend him. Mitchell had agreed to cooperate.

On Wednesday, seven weeks following the submission of the Notice, Roush arrived at his office to find a formal request from Doug Rose on his desk. It required that a sample of Jeff's DNA be provided to the state no later than four days following receipt of the signed request. Joanie had signed for the Notice when it was served the previous afternoon.

A copy of the Notice had been faxed to Sheriff Jonathan Williams. In a quick call to Roush's office, Sheriff Williams confirmed 4:00 in the afternoon as the time for the DNA sample to be taken. After confirming the time, Williams ordered the County Jail Superintendent to notify the CSI office and to deliver Mitchell to the jail's conference facility. Both Williams and Roush would meet them there.

Sheriff Williams met Fred Roush outside the jail. He accompanied Roush into the conference room to await Mitchell's arrival. Also present was Paul Pinkston from the FDLE, who would actually transport the sample to the lab for comparative analysis. Upon Mitchell's arrival, Williams read the official Notice. "Do you understand what we're doing here?" he asked Mitchell.

"Yes," Mitchell replied. "Let's just get on with it."

Williams nodded to the CSI to proceed. Mitchell opened his mouth, and the CSI swiped a cotton swab inside his cheek. The CSI drew the cotton tip into a plastic cover, snapped a lid on it and placed it in a small paper envelope which was then dropped into a padded sleeve and sealed for Pinkston's transport to the laboratory at the FDLE. Mitchell was returned to his cell.

*   *   *   *   *   *

After parking his car in the intake lot, Pinkston carried the small, brown padded envelope into the intake office and handed it to Nancy Manning. "Another item for the Reins case," Pinkston

137

informed Manning. "This should complete the inventory of items, for our purposes anyway."

"Good. I'll send out an amended inventory list to every department and ask that the original list be shredded and replaced with the new one," Manning told him. Turning, Manning added the case number and item number to the evidence tape securing the envelope.

"Do you need me to take that upstairs to Robyn?" Pinkston offered.

"No, I think I'll just put it in the vault for the night and deliver it to her tomorrow morning," she replied.

"In that case, I think I'll call it a day and go home. See you tomorrow," Pinkston promised.

"Yeah. Have a good evening, Paul," Manning said.

* * * * * *

Although it was late in the day, Roush returned to his office. Darkness seemed to have overtaken him. For an unexplainable reason, he felt a foreboding about the case that he had not experienced before. While the burden of proof lay with the state as it always does in a criminal case, he was determined to make every effort to establish the innocence of his client.

"Mr. Roush, a package was delivered by courier a short time ago," Joanie informed him before he could get completely inside the door. She handed the envelope to Roush and added, "It's from the State Attorney. It's labeled for your immediate attention."

Curious as to its contents, Roush ripped the package at the top and retrieved the documents inside. "It's the first of the evidence that the state has against Jeff," he said softly but loud enough so that Joanie heard him.

"Evidence?" she inquired. "If he didn't kill Lillian Reins, how can the state have any real evidence against him?"

"According to this paperwork, they have his fingerprints all over the car. In searching the victim's car, they seem to have found a bloody sweater with a laundry tag attached which the investigators traced to Jeff. They also have bootprints that match Jeff's Rockports."

"None of that proves he was at the crime scene. Wouldn't that all just be circumstantial evidence? Besides, he admits he was in her car and with her that night. But it doesn't prove he killed her. Even I know enough law to know that" Joanie said.

"It may be circumstantial, and that evidence alone wouldn't be sufficient to convict him, but remember, we don't have all the evidence yet. Until we can know all that the state knows, we can't do much except corroborate the findings with Jeff's story. I'll plan to meet with him tomorrow to go over these first pieces of evidence. By the way, where is Blayne?"

"He arrived today and stayed just long enough to get his office in order," Joanie said. "He left early to try to make his apartment livable. He said he expects to be here early tomorrow morning to officially start work."

"Good," Roush replied. "I'll go over the Mitchell case with him, bring him up to speed, and get his advice on how we should proceed. I'll want him to go with me to meet with Jeff tomorrow. Would you please make arrangements for that meeting? Sometime during the afternoon would be best."

"Sure. I'll call right now," Joanie replied.

*　　*　　*　　*　　*　　*

Robyn Weeks had already initiated testing on the items delivered to her. Those to be tested consisted of a semen swab taken from the victim, the butts from cigarettes, remnants of numerous fingernail clippings, nail clippers found at Mitchell's home, and a tissue containing several absorbed droplets of blood. Weeks went about her work efficiently.

Near noon, Nancy Manning entered the lab. "Good morning, Robyn. Looking for some more work?" Manning asked facetiously.

"I'm up to my ears right now, with all this Reins evidence," Weeks responded.

139

"Get ready for some more. You probably expected to get more DNA requests, and here is at least one of them," Manning said, handing Weeks the envelope which contained the Jeff Mitchell DNA sample. "The request is fairly self-explanatory. This is a DNA sample from Mitchell to compare with your other DNA findings. I have included a copy of the request as well as an amended copy of the evidence inventory."

*   *   *   *   *   *

When Roush arrived at the office the next morning, Blayne Simmons had already begun the process of getting settled. Shelving the final set of books in his office and upon hearing the door open, Simmons turned to meet his new colleague. "It's great to see you again, Blayne," Roush said. "This Mitchell case is turning sour, and I really need your assistance. You're going to be a quality addition to our legal team here."

"What seems to be the problem with the Mitchell case?" Simmons quizzed.

"Rather than get into it here, why don't we plan to meet about in about a half hour and go over it in detail. I can bring you up to date, and you can have some time to think about strategy. Also, I have arranged to meet with Mitchell this afternoon. I would like for you to go with me. You can meet him and maybe begin to form your own judgment about the case."

Blayne Simmons entered the conference room where Fred Roush already had spread the Mitchell file out on the conference table. On top of the file was the report that he had received from the State Attorney's office notifying him of the evidence gathered so far connecting Mitchell to the homicide. Reading the top page, Simmons picked up the papers and began to scan them. "Looks bad for him on first sight, doesn't it," Roush said, not really expecting an answer.

"What you have here is only preliminary, and it is highly circumstantial," replied Simmons. "We must wait until the entire package is known before we can determine the potential consequences of a trial or whether it would be better for him to cooperate and plea bargain."

"I can tell you now that he will not plea bargain. That is a chip Jeff will not play. He has made it inordinately clear to me."

"If he has the choice of facing a limited sentence of time in prison vis-à-vis the death penalty, he would be a fool, in the face of overwhelming evidence, to choose the latter," Simmons opined.

"You are right, of course, but he has clearly indicated that regardless of the evidence, his conscience will not permit him to plead anything other than 'not guilty'," Roush said. "After having read the file, do you think this is something that we should approach him about today when we meet with him?"

"No."

"Why not?"

"The evidence is too preliminary. Who knows but that another piece of vital evidence may point away from him. In such a case, we will have upset him for nothing."

"I'm sure you're right. For right now, let's leave it where it is and discuss only what we know," Roush agreed.

"I really think this is a better approach at the present time," Simmons replied. "Do you want to go together or have me just meet you there?"

"Depends on what your plans are for later."

Simmons thought a minute. "As a matter of fact, I have no plans for later. Want to go for dinner after we meet with Mitchell?" Simmons asked.

"Sounds great. Let's plan to meet at the jail and then we can travel separately to a restaurant for dinner, your choice, my treat."

"Wow! What a reception. I look forward to our getting to know each other better," Simmons said, satisfied that his decision to join Roush had been right.

*   *   *   *   *   *

Simultaneously, both Roush and Simmons arrived at the parking lot of the jail. Seeing each other, they met and entered the jail together. They were directed to the conference room where they waited for ten minutes before Jeff Mitchell was brought in.

"Good afternoon, Jeff," Roush said. "How are you doing?"

"Not very well," Mitchell responded. "I'm frustrated not knowing what's going on in the case. I keep spending most of my time learning what I can about the law and how it might affect my case. What can you tell me?"

"First, let me introduce you to Blayne Simmons, my new associate."

"I'm glad to meet you," Simmons said, shaking Mitchell's hand vigorously.

"Blayne has been practicing criminal law down in South Florida for several years. He has a fantastic track record and knows Florida criminal law quite well. I feel very fortunate to have him on my team. He's going to be the lead attorney on your case, and I plan on fulfilling a supporting role. I hope this meets with your approval."

"Whatever you think is in my best interest," Mitchell said.

In an attempt to be upbeat, Roush told Mitchell about the evidence revealed so far through the discovery process by the State Attorney. "I know it's only fingerprints, a tagged bloody sweater, and a boot print, but together they are important pieces of a puzzle that we have to try to defend."

"Defend!" Mitchell shouted angrily. "I was with Lillian that night, in her car, and all over her. How could I help but have my prints everywhere. I didn't even remember where I left the sweater; I didn't see it in her car. And as for the blood, I have no idea how it got on the sweater. I do own a pair of boots, but I didn't have them on that night. I was nowhere near the place she was found, so how could *my* boot print be there?" The veins in Mitchell's neck pulsed with anger.

"I can't explain the boot print, Jeff. But I want you to think where you might have last worn the boots," Simmons interjected.

"I remember specifically where I wore them. Three of us, myself, Mark Bradley, and Jonathan Rapier, a buddy from the hiking club we belong to, went hiking in the northern end of the county about a month before the murder. We followed a trail not far from the place where they found Lillian's body. We stayed mainly on trails but did venture off into the woods a time or two."

"That would account for the dirt that was found on your boot," Simmons questioned.

"I would certainly think so," Mitchell said.

"Jeff, you've been helpful," Simmons said, trying to be cheerful. "I know you're miserable here in jail, but try to be positive and remember that this is only the opening salvo of a case that has a long way to go."

"We won't stop until we've cleared your name," Roush said. "I believe in you. You've got to believe in us. Okay?"

"Okay."

"We'll see you again soon," Roush said as Mitchell arose and spoke into the intercom alerting the guard to escort him back to his cell.

*   *   *   *   *   *

The two lawyers sat quietly at a corner table in the Boars Head Restaurant, both intently studying the menu. Simmons broke the silence, "What do you recommend?"

"Steak's great."

"Then I'll have a T-bone. Haven't had a good steak in a long time. And since you're paying, now's a good time to enjoy one," Simmons replied, humor accenting every tone.

Vivian, the vivacious waitress with a tendency for small talk, took their orders. "Be back in a jiff with your drinks," she said.

"Fred." Simmons hesitated, then continued. "I studied Mitchell's complete file today. I don't think we ought to leave any possible stone unturned here. If you and I believe him, we may have to go to extremes to prove his innocence."

"What exactly do you mean?" Roush asked, furrows forming on his brow.

"Let's pretend we are casting a play. Begin by listing the characters in the play. In our play, we will want to depose all of the characters for whatever positive contribution each can make to the case. Boudreaux will be a good start. There are significant gaps in his investigation. And because he was new at the job, he has made some rather questionable judgments I think we can challenge."

"You see, that's why I wanted you to join me," Roush said. "You have insight into criminal cases that I just don't have."

"Anybody and everybody associated with the victim or with Mitchell should be deposed and questioned as a witness."

"Good idea," Roush agreed.

"I think it would be another good idea to check out the victim's apartment complex for any signs of suspicious characters that may have been seen loitering around prior to the murder. You know how these places are—there always seems to be one busybody who makes it a point to know everything that goes on. Find that person, and we may dig up some helpful information."

"Good. Anything else?"

"Yes, one more thing. Let's start the whole process by visiting the murder scene. The police never found the gun or the murder weapon. They didn't find any bloody clothes the killer might have worn. The only items they found were those connected with Jeff. Maybe we can luck up."

"I'll be glad to join you. When would you like to go?"

"How about tomorrow morning?"

"I'll meet you at the office, and we can go together," Roush said.

"What about having Mitchell take a polygraph test?" Roush asked. "I know it's not admissible, but would it help the looks of the case?"

"Maybe. If he passes, it won't hurt. If he fails, it would add an unwanted dimension to the prosecution's determination to prove him guilty. It's probably worth a try, though," Simmons said.

Vivian appeared with the steaks. Simmons dived in with a vengeance. "This is the best piece of meat I've ever eaten," he said. "Looks like its been broiled with butter."

"It has. Enjoy it, pal. It may be the last one on me for a while," Roush said, smiling.

*   *   *   *   *   *

On Thursday morning, Roush and Simmons met in the parking lot of the law office as planned. Together they drove to the North County area where Lillian Reins's car had been wrecked and her body found. Remnants of discarded crime scene tape littered a portion of the area.

Using a hiking stick from his apartment, Blayne Simmons probed around the place where Lillian's body had been buried. Nothing out of the ordinary could be found. It appeared that the crime scene investigators had been quite thorough in their search of the area.

CHAPTER 17
SIX WEEKS LATER

For weeks, Roush and Simmons planned strategy for the case. They had spent hours in depositions, and Roush had embarked on a new experience, criminal investigation. It had been informative; he hoped the information would be helpful in the courtroom.

The prosecution had presented more evidence, and each time they received it, they discussed it with Jeff Mitchell in the jail conference room. Mitchell always seemed to have a reasonable explanation.

Simmons had stopped by the law library to review several matters relating to procedure, and he didn't get to the office until mid morning. Upon his arrival, Joanie notified him that he had received yet another notification from the State Attorney's office. Opening the envelope as quickly as he could, he discovered the most damning evidence yet, the DNA analysis. His heart sank. It was the final nail in the coffin of a case that he thought he could win but which was appearing bleaker and bleaker.

Walking into Fred Roush's office, he broke the news. "Fred, the DNA from Jeff matches the key evidence from the crime scene except for some epithelials found on the sweater. Even if Jeff is innocent, his case is so fraught with suspicion of guilt that a not guilty verdict is highly unlikely."

"I admire your judgment, Blayne, but don't shortchange yourself. Don't give up. Treat this case like you have so many others. You can win it even if you have to do so based on emotion rather than fact. You only have to create reasonable doubt. Just do what you have to do to get him off."

"Obviously, I will," Simmons said. "But realistically I can't be optimistic. I think now is the time to lay the cards on the table for Jeff. We must let him know just where we stand in the case and the options that are open to him, especially the option to plea bargain."

Roush thought silently for a moment. "He probably won't go for it, but we owe it to him to let him know how the odds fall right now. Let's plan to go see him tomorrow."

Simmons left the room, saddened but determined to put his best effort into the trial.

*   *   *   *   *   *

The handcuffed Jeff Mitchell was brought once more to the conference room to meet with his attorneys. As he walked into the room he could tell from the looks on their faces that the news was not good.

"You guys look like you lost your last friend," Mitchell said, trying to break the ice and hoping for the best.

Roush started, "Jeff, we have some bad news."

"Can't be any worse than all that other evidence news you've told me about," Mitchell said sarcastically. "Get on with it."

"Well, it probably is. The prosecutor reported the last piece of evidence to us yesterday. The DNA sample that was taken from you at the jail matched the primary evidence samples taken at the crime."

The room was silent!

After what seemed hours, Simmons broke the silence, "Do you understand the gravity of this evidence, Jeff?"

"I guess I don't," Mitchell said. "You tell me."

"It means they think they can pretty well put you at the scene of the crime," Simmons offered.

"But I wasn't there. I know they can put me in her car, but that doesn't prove I killed her"

"The evidence is all quite circumstantial but if viewed in the right light can be quite convincing. The only option remaining that might help your case would be for you to take a polygraph test. Would you be willing to do that?"

"What other option would there be?" Mitchell asked.

"Fred and I have discussed the pros and cons of a lie detector test. If you fail, it would simply be additional motivation for the prosecution to pursue the case as vigorously as possible. If you pass, it might cause the prosecution at least to consider the possibility of your innocence. There's no guarantee. Otherwise, the only option available to ensure no death penalty is for you to consider a plea bargain. It would . . ."

Mitchell broke Simmons off in mid-sentence. "No go! Do you understand me? I will *not* let you do that."

Simmons continued, "Jeff, in the end it's your call, but wouldn't you rather face a minimum of time in prison with a chance of parole than to face the potential for the death penalty? That's exactly what you're facing right now. I know it's your decision and not ours to make, but don't be foolish with your life."

"My decision has been made for a long time. Kill me if they must. I will die for something I did not do before I will announce voluntarily to the world that I am guilty of a crime I did not commit. I am willing to take the lie detector test. Set it up and get on with it. Then, let's go to trial. Okay?"

"You're sure this is your final word in the matter?" Simmons asked.

"Absolutely. Trial, live or die."

*　　*　　*　　*　　*　　*

Upon return to the office, Roush asked Joanie to arrange a polygraph test for Mitchell during the next week. Within ten minutes, Joanie informed Roush that the test was set for the following Wednesday. Roush wrote the time in his Daytimer and wrote a note to Simmons informing him of the test.

CHAPTER 18
MAY 15

Roush and Simmons had worked diligently for the past few months in preparation for the Mitchell/Reins case. Yet, deep down, they did not feel confident of the outcome. In spite of their firm belief that Jeff Mitchell was an innocent victim in this case, they were hardly ready to face a prosecution that was as well prepared with documented, albeit circumstantial, evidence as this case seemed to be. Both men had read the evidence dossier and the list of witnesses that the prosecution intended to put on the witness stand. Mutually, they had decided that only one strategy could possibly save Jeff Mitchell from a guilty verdict, even with the variety of possible outcomes that strategy presented. He must personally take the stand, as risky as that might be.

Entering the courthouse that unusually chilly May morning, Roush felt ill-prepared for the trial by fire on which he were about to embark. It was the first time he had ever been involved in a criminal case, and certainly not one for a crime with such a devastating potential result—death. He was visibly nervous, and he ached as though he might be taking the flu.

Simmons, always the confident defender of truth, strode the steps of the courthouse and entered with an air of assurance seldom seen in a man whose defense was as weak as the one he was about to present. Yet, he would not allow anybody to see him sweat.

Once again, they entered the courtroom of the Honorable Paul Reid. The ever-vigilant bailiff, Larry Boxer, was in his rightful position, near the door of the judge's chambers.

Even though the schedule for the day included only jury selection, the public seating area was crowded with the curious, the interested, and the bored, who had nothing better to do. The news reporters, pads and pens in hand, sat in a group in the first four rows on the left of the courtroom. Jeff's friends, Mark

Bradley and Joe Blankenship, joined Mitchell's family, his mom and dad, sister, Andrea, and brother, Jaimie. They sat together in the second row on the right side of the courtroom. The court session was due to begin at 9:00.

Shortly after the appointed hour, Bailiff Boxer announced the appearance of Judge Reid. "All rise. This court is now in session," he began. "The Honorable Paul Reid, presiding. You may be seated." As Judge Reid was announced, he walked to the familiar bench over which he had presided for more than fifteen years.

Paul Reid had been appointed a Circuit Court Judge after the death of Judge Robert Macon. Judge Macon had occupied this same bench for more than forty years. Although he and his wife, Ruby, had made special plans for his retirement and enjoyment of their sunset years, those plans were cut short by his untimely death, only two months prior to his retirement.

Reid, a handsome man of fifty-five years, wore his mantel of power with dignity. His distinguished white hair provided for him a judicial air, and he simply radiated the authority that he wielded.

Standing more than six feet tall, Reid was the only child of a poor, but hard-working family from agricultural south Alabama. From before he could remember, he had moved from place to place with a mother and father who seemed almost itinerant. Finally settling in Mobile, Alabama, Reid attended the local schools. His intellectual accomplishments in high school earned him an academic scholarship to Louisiana State University from which he graduated Phi Beta Kappa. As an undergraduate, he was a member of the Debate Club and the track team. He attended Tulane Law School, where he often mesmerized his fellow students with his knowledge and handling of complex legal issues. He went on to become *Law Review* editor and to graduate with honors.

Following law school and passing both the Louisiana and Florida bar examinations, Reid was recruited by Berkowitz and Taylor Attorneys, in West Palm Beach, Florida, which specialized in criminal defense. After getting his feet wet with numerous small cases, he was introduced to Max "The Man" Fagenheim, a notorious mobster well known for the rackets he controlled on the East Coast of Florida. When Reid met Fagenheim, he was imprisoned on a charge of hiring a hit man to kill his closest rival, Buddy "The Face" Scalone. Fagenheim proclaimed his innocence and called on Berkowitz and Taylor to get him off. Reid was assigned the case.

For more than three months, Reid toiled laboriously on the case. Filing motion after motion, Reid swamped the court with paper. He was unsuccessful at every turn. At trial, Reid used his brilliance at debate to persuade a jury of six men and six women to acquit Max Fagenheim. His star as a master of criminal defense immediately began to rise.

Reid practiced criminal law in West Palm Beach for five years before moving to the more placid and laissez-faire lifestyle in West Florida. He settled in Navarre, a small community in Santa Rosa County, about halfway between Pensacola and Fort Walton Beach. There he established a successful general law practice before appointment to the bench seven years later.

At the death of Judge Robert Macon, five names were submitted by the local Bar Association to replace him. One of those names, and the one subsequently chosen, was Paul Reid. After serving out the balance of Macon's term, Reid faced the public in a general election and won handily. Now in his third term on the bench, Judge Paul Reid was one of the most respected jurists in the entire state.

"Good morning, ladies and gentlemen," Reid began politely. "Let the record show that counsel for the prosecution and the defense are present in the courtroom. Also let the record reflect that the defendant is also present," Reid noted. With that introduction, Rose, along with his two assistants Kemper Nixon and Samantha Kralick, and the defense team, Fred Roush and

Blayne Simmons, began the delicate task of selecting a jury that would hear the case against Jeff Mitchell.

*　　*　　*　　*　　*　　*

For two days, both sides conducted a *voir dire* examination of potential jurors. One after another, those called for jury duty paraded into the courtroom, and each was questioned by the court, then examined by each side. Except for those challenged by the court or excused for cause, each person returned to the jury room adjacent to the courtroom, where the jury pool had been convened.

By the end of the second day, a jury of five men and seven women was selected. One male and one female were selected as alternates. During the course of the selection process, the defense had used all ten peremptory challenges; the prosecution used only eight. The final jury was not what Simmons had hoped for, but he knew he had to play the hand that he was dealt. He would do his best. Simmons was daydreaming as he heard only the final words of the jurors' oath, ". . . a true verdict according to the law and the evidence, so help you God?"

After the jury was selected and seated in the courtroom, Judge Reid announced, "Ladies and gentlemen of the jury and members of the defense and prosecution, this trial will be held with unquestionable decorum, deferential dignity, and utmost regard for the law. Your cases will be heard fairly, and no preferential consideration shall be assumed. I expect you to maintain the propriety of this court and to uphold the constitutional rights of the man being tried. This trial will resume promptly at 9:00 tomorrow morning." With that brief statement, Judge Reid hammered his gavel once on the bench and departed to his chambers.

For a moment Fred Roush remained transfixed in his seat. He stared at the black and gold seal on the wall thinking only about how well he and Blayne Simmons had performed in selecting this jury. As he stared blankly at the wall, he wondered silently whether he and Simmons had checked out each potential juror carefully enough. Not to have done so could be disastrous.

CHAPTER 19
MAY 17

Fred Roush's eyes slowly blinked open before daybreak. His mind raced with the prospects of the impending trial, and he could not sleep. Never had a trial preyed on his mind like this one. He assumed that it was because the stakes were so high.

Arising from the warmth of a down comforter, he walked wide-eyed to the small library that he maintained in his home. There, behind the large, dark oak, roll top desk that his great grandfather had used during his tenure as a judge in Alabama, he laid out one of the files on Mitchell. He leaned back in his blue leather executive chair and scanned several handwritten notes he had jotted down during his investigation, and he pondered the case, reviewing in his mind the evidence the prosecution was about to present and how he could possibly defend or at least reasonably explain the connection of each piece of evidence to Jeff Mitchell. The truth was, he was going to let Blayne Simmons do most of the questioning. He himself would use the case to learn as much as he could about the intricacies of criminal law practice.

After preparing a cup of hot chocolate, he reread the autopsy report and could be repulsed only by the detailed description of how Lillian Reins had died. As he was about to doze off from the effects of the hot chocolate, the ringing phone summoned him back to reality and the waking world.

Picking up the receiver, he heard, "Fred, this is Blayne. I couldn't sleep, so I thought I might call you and get an early start on the day. Want to meet me at the Coffee Urn for breakfast a little later?" Simmons asked.

"Yeah, sure," Roush responded. "Give me an hour to get my thoughts together; then we'll meet for a good breakfast before heading to the courthouse."

"Okay. I'll see you in an hour," Simmons said. The connection was broken.

*   *   *   *   *   *

The dawn broke dreary with heavy, dark clouds lingering close to the ground. The morning fog quickly dissipated with the increasing warmth of the day, but the clouds stubbornly remained. As Fred Roush left home, he hoped that the day's dark pall was not an omen for the trial.

No better breakfast could be found in the entire city than the Coffee Urn. Quaint and noisy, the Coffee Urn had been the gathering place for governors, businessmen, and politicos for more than fifty years. On a typical day, a potential customer might wait for nearly a half hour before being led to an available booth, table, or stool. But today, at this hour, business was light.

When Roush arrived, he noticed that Simmons was already waiting for him at the front door. They immediately were led to a corner booth set up for four. The sixty year old, perky, red-haired waitress, came by with a coffee pot and poured two steaming cups of black coffee. Each savored the special roasted blend with particular enjoyment.

Simmons started the conversation, "Since you answered the phone so quickly, I guess you couldn't sleep either."

"Sure couldn't. It's been a long time since I woke up so early in the morning," Roush offered, taking a long pull on his coffee, cherishing the bittersweet flavor.

"I've tried my share of big cases, but this one has a hold on me that I can't shake," Simmons said. "I've got this feeling deep down that the outcome of the trial will not be good. Have you ever started a trial feeling that way?"

"No, can't say I have," Roush responded. "In most of my cases, I have a pretty good idea how they will fall. Maybe it's because I've tended to take cases that were somewhat open and shut. Regardless, civil trials are certainly not like criminal trials. I think when this is over, I'm going to stick with the civil cases and let you handle the criminal trials."

155

While the two were conversing, Roush ordered and consumed a hearty breakfast of two scrambled eggs, a slice of cured Tennessee ham, and southern-style grits smothered in red eye gravy. He topped off his meal with two buttermilk biscuits generously covered with smooth, creamy butter and immersed under thick, dark, sweet corn syrup.

Trying to keep his waistline trim, Simmons ordered a small plate of Southern pancakes, generously seasoned with butter and soaked in real New England maple syrup. On the side, he added two pieces of crisp bacon.

"Do you have your opening statement prepared?" Simmons asked.

"Yeah. I'm going to try to convince the jury that the evidence of the prosecution is nothing but smoke and mirrors—not really what it appears to be. I just hope they'll buy it," Roush said.

"I'll take notes as you present it. We can review the results of the day's proceedings and our notes on those proceedings after court each day."

"Guess we need to get to the courthouse," Roush said. Each consumed the last bits of food, walked to the counter and paid his check, and retreated to his car for the ride to the courthouse.

*   *   *   *   *   *

As trial time approached, a light drizzle developed.

For the fourth time in five months, Fred Roush entered the courtroom of Judge Paul Reid. No less impressed than at any time before, he moved toward the defense table with an air of confidence, however muted it may have been. Doug Rose and his team of prosecutors also took notice. With Blayne Simmons at his side, they greeted each member of the prosecution, shaking hands, and exchanging morning pleasantries. After the amenities, Roush and Simmons retired to the defense table.

Simmons noted that the prosecution had brought six boxes of files on the Mitchell case, and he wondered silently how so much paper could have been generated on this case. Together, he and

Fred Roush brought only one cardboard file case, and it was only two-thirds filled.

Within five minutes of Roush's arrival, two county deputies escorted Jeff Mitchell into the courtroom. Tasseled burgundy loafers accenting a blue pin-stripped suit, tab collared blue cotton twill dress shirt, and a colorful Rush Limbaugh "No Nonsense" tie, Mitchell looked like anything but the killer he was accused of being.

Jeff Mitchell, until recently a successful accountant, had experienced the "magic touch" in almost every endeavor. Regardless of how well or how badly he performed on projects, they always seemed to achieve the desired goal. The youngest of three children, Jeff felt the pressure to succeed early in life. His parents, William and Patricia Mitchell, were typical, middle class, working people, yet there were no lengths to which they would not go to provide what they considered best for their children. Jeff's sister, Andrea, had been married when she was nineteen to an airlines pilot, successfully completed four years in nursing school and currently worked as a surgical nurse at St. Simeon's Hospital in Omaha.

His brother, Jaimie, who qualified as a National Merit Scholar and earned a degree in computer science at Rennselaer Polytechnic Institute, decided to try putting his degree to work. After three years of developing medical laser technology, he attended graduate school and earned a Ph.D. degree. Upon completion of these graduate studies, Rennselaer offered him an Associate Professorship, which he turned down in favor of a computer programming position with a major software company in Seattle, a position he held at the time of Lillian's murder.

The family was devastated by the turn of events in Jeff's life. None of them believed that Jeff was guilty. They were equally determined to display their unity as a family and their unquestioned belief in his innocence.

157

Frayed nerves and abject fear coursing through every vessel in his body, Fred Roush suddenly experienced a feeling of unexplained anxiety. Concerned at how thin the defense files appeared to be, Roush was as unsure of himself as a first year quarterback who had never taken a snap in a real game.

Once again, Mitchell's family was present. They had taken their usual places on the second row on the left side of the courtroom. This time, however, Mark Bradley had not joined them. Now officially listed as a defense witness in the case, he could no longer sit among the public spectators. He was limited to the witness room.

Besides Mitchell's family, the courtroom was filled once more with members of the press, the family of the victim, and curious citizens interested in seeing justice prevail. All witnesses were gathered appropriately in an anteroom adjacent to the courtroom. They, like Bradley, would not be permitted to observe the trial in progress.

At a minute after 9:00, Larry Boxer announced the arrival of Judge Paul Reid. "All rise," he said. "This court is now in session. The Honorable Paul Reid presiding." As he walked to the bench, Reid glanced, out of habit, toward the courtroom and said, "You may be seated." As though under the direction of a maestro, everyone was seated in unison.

"Is the prosecution ready, Mr. Rose?" Reid asked as though he were following a written agenda.

"Yes, Your Honor," Rose replied as he had done so many times before. "The prosecution is prepared to proceed."

Looking at Roush and Simmons, Reid said, "Is the defense ready?"

"Yes, Your Honor. The defense is ready," Roush said, feeling like a weightlifter with an impossible challenge before him.

The trial seemed to proceed with programmed precision. Reid called for the jury. Larry Boxer opened the door to the jury room, motioned for the jury to enter the courtroom, and led them into the jury box where they were seated to hear the case against Jeff Mitchell. As the members of the jury walked to their seats, Roush noticed the somber and serious expressions on their faces. *In their hands,* he thought, *rests the life of Jeff Mitchell. God have mercy on all of us.*

*   *   *   *   *   *

As Judge Reid paused for a moment to review a sheaf of papers that he had prepared with respect to the trial procedures, Mitchell leaned, unnoticed by most in the courtroom, toward Roush, "What do you think our chances are?" he asked.

"On the surface, doesn't look good, but we are going to do our best. Count on it," Roush whispered.

Once again the courtroom resounded with the voice of Paul Reid. "Mr. Rose, you may begin your opening statement at this time," he announced.

"Thank you, Your Honor," Rose replied.

Accepting a notepad from his associate, Kemper Nixon, Rose dramatically arose from his chair. He strode to the lectern located at the center of the courtroom and gently laid the pad on it. He leaned over to read the notes he had prepared.

Lifting a solemn, somewhat funereal face toward the jury, Rose gripped the sides of the lectern. He stood staring at the jury, allowing a moment of affected silence to linger.

Rose, still silent, then stepped from behind the lectern. "Ladies and gentlemen, that notepad contains numerous notes about this trial and several poignant remarks about what I planned to say in this opening statement." He walked closer to the jury and leaned against the far support panel at a corner of the jury box. "But, the fact is," he continued, "this case could be tried without the benefit of counsel on either side. The evidence is that convincing. Frankly, only the absence of a video camera filming the event makes this trial even necessary, because, in spite of the fact that we can directly connect this young man with the crime and the victim and have evidence of his hasty departure at the time of his

159

pending arrest, he insists on his innocence. We will construct a case showing that Jeff Mitchell, angry over the breakup of his relationship with Lillian Reins, took her to the woods of north Escambia County and brutally slaughtered her." Rose paused for dramatic effect. "There will be no doubt."

Rose walked from the corner of the jury box toward the defense table where Mitchell sat with his hands clasped in his lap. "We can prove that the defendant was with Miss Reins the night of the murder and that Miss Reins intended to break off a year-long intimate relationship with him. Motive for murder!" Rose, master of the dramatic pause, did so once more.

"We can place him in her car, which was found at the murder scene; we can prove that Mr. Mitchell had sexual intercourse with Miss Reins that night, in fact raped her upon learning of the breakup; and we can place him at the scene of the crime. Mission of murder." He paused.

"And we can show that, once he was implicated in this murder, he ran. Guilty of murder!"

For the next thirty minutes, Rose offered more details on each aspect of the evidence which he and his team planned to introduce to the jury. At the close of each point, he punctuated his presentation with, "Murderer, plain and simple!"

"Ladies and gentlemen," Rose said, "Mr. Jeffrey Mitchell is guilty of this most heinous crime. And yet you have the rare opportunity to be a part of seeing that justice prevails and that the memory of Lillian McRae Reins is not forever relegated to the dusty shelves of a newspaper morgue."

Another pause. Rose could sense that he had the jury in his hands. He then leaned toward the jury, his deep green eyes reflecting the resolve with which he intended to try this case, and concluded, with his voice deepening, "All any honorable and self-respecting citizen would ask is that you weigh the evidence which we are about to present in this case and fairly judge the defendant solely on the basis of that evidence. Our job is to prove beyond a reasonable doubt that Mr. Mitchell is guilty. We will do just that. Count on it."

Raising his voice and pointing toward the defendant, Rose said with somewhat vitriol, "This man deserves no less than to pay the ultimate price for taking the life of Lillian McRae Reins."

Rose stood silent a moment to allow his emotion-inducing words to sink in. Slowly he walked from the far side of the defense table to the lectern, where he retrieved his pad of notes to which he had never referred, and seated himself once again with his team of prosecutors.

"Mr. Roush," Judge Reid spoke.

Engrossed in his notes on strategy, exchanging notes with Blayne Simmons and Jeff Mitchell, and reviewing his written opening statement, Roush was completely unaware that Rose had stopped speaking or that he was being addressed by Judge Reid.

Somewhat more loudly Judge Reid repeated, "Mr. Roush."

Looking up, Roush spoke apologetically, "Sir?

"I'm sorry. Yes."

"Are you prepared with your opening statement?" Reid asked.

"Yes, sir. The defense is ready," Roush said.

"Then please proceed," Reid ordered.

The plan was for Roush to deliver the opening statement and for Simmons to question the State witnesses, present defense evidence, question defense witnesses, and then try to clinch the case with a moving and articulate closing argument. Roush arose from his chair, glanced at the Reins family seated on the third row of the right side of the courtroom, and then toward the jury.

"Ladies and gentlemen, I want to ask each of you a question. You are not asked to answer it aloud, only to ponder it silently. Have any of you ever visited Disney World?" Roush hesitated a moment to allow the question to sink in.

Each juror seemed to have a quizzical look on his face.

Continuing, "There is, at this wonderful park, a ride known as the Haunted Mansion. As you travel through the house in a

161

tracked vehicle, you observe all kinds of spirits, dancing and frolicking in the grand hall of this old haunted mansion. You can even observe a friendly ghost over your shoulder, accompanying you in your vehicle. Yet, as real as these ghosts and spirits appear to your eyes, they actually do not exist at all. In short, they are not as they appear."

Roush walked toward the prosecution table. Pointing to the six boxes of files and evidence, he said, "You see here all that the prosecution claims is evidence linking Mr. Mitchell to this crime. And we will not deny that there is evidence of Mr. Mitchell's relationship with the deceased."

Roush stepped back a moment, then pointing to the files on the defense table, he spoke again, "We don't have much to present because each piece of evidence the prosecution will present can be explained rationally. And while they say they can put him at the crime scene, the facts simply do not support such a supposition. You will see that nothing presented by the prosecution puts Mr. Mitchell physically at the scene of the crime. The evidence is completely and totally circumstantial. Mr. Mitchell is innocent of this crime, and, like those ghosts at the Haunted Mansion, the prosecution's case is not what it appears to be."

Roush stepped toward the jury box. Making direct eye contact with juror number five, Rochelle Carlyn, he said, "You hold this innocent man's life in your hands. Handle it with care. Thank you."

CHAPTER 20

It was near the noon hour. Judge Reid decided that witnesses and evidence would best be introduced after lunch without any potential interruption. After announcing that court would resume at 1:30 in the afternoon, Judge Reid left the bench for his chambers. At the same time, Mitchell was escorted back to a holding cell while the attorneys and spectators streamed from the courtroom. "Keep smiling," Roush said to Mitchell, winking at him as he was taken away. "Be positive. We've got a long way to go." Mitchell managed a forced smile as he walked weakened and broken through the courtroom door.

Turning to Simmons, Roush asked, "Where would you like to go for lunch? We both probably need the nourishment. I suspect the afternoon will be a long one."

"How about The Chowder House?" Simmons answered without hesitating. "They have some excellent conch chowder. I could stand a big bowl with a nice salad. Besides, I need to watch my fat intake."

"Sounds good to me," Roush said. Gathering their papers, they left the courtroom together.

*   *   *   *   *   *

At 1:40, Judge Reid was announced. "I'm sorry for the delay, but it was unavoidable," he stated; then he added, "You may proceed with your first witness, Mr. Rose."

Rose stood, adjusted his trousers and wide burgundy suspenders, and declared with a moderate tone, "The state calls as its first witness Escambia County Detective Antoine Boudreaux."

Larry Boxer escorted Boudreaux from the anteroom to the witness chair. After the oath was administered, he lowered his 278 pounds of well-toned muscle and brawn into the large chair, shifted in the seat to make himself comfortable, took off his glasses and rubbed his eyes a moment, and waited for Rose to begin the questioning.

* * * * * *

Robyn Weeks had worked almost fifteen hours a day for the past month to complete the DNA analysis for the Mitchell case before trial. The trial was to start today, but she knew that she would not be called as a witness until at least the end of the week. She decided to take the day off.

Since it was still somewhat cool outside, the beach was out of the question. Shopping was more to her liking. Checking to make sure she had her credit cards, she took to her recently acquired red Mitsubishi Eclipse and headed toward Alabama. Her special state tag, which read "SHOPPER 1," denoted her keen interest in the activity upon which she was about to embark. Just across the state line in Alabama was a shopping mecca, the Cross Roads Center, an outlet mall containing almost two hundred stores. A shopper's paradise, indeed.

Driving through the countryside removed her mind from the crushing pressure under which she had been for the past few months. Fewer and fewer technicians to perform an increasing number of lab procedures produced burnout quickly. Today would be a stress reliever. The beautiful trees, the pastures of cattle and freshly turned farmland, and the obvious slow-paced life of the rural South jumped out at her like a specter from the darkness as she drove these back roads. *What a great way to live!* she thought.

Arriving at her destination, she decided that, although there were almost a thousand parking spaces, rather than drive repeatedly around the parking lot in search of a convenient one, she would go to the north parking lot where she was sure she would find a spot. She parked her car, mapped out her plan, and started toward her first objective.

* * * * * *

Boudreaux waited, along with everyone else in the courtroom, for Rose to ask his first question. "Mr. Boudreaux, please tell us what your responsibilities were on the night Miss Reins was murdered," Rose said.

"I was on street patrol, just gettin' ready to go home at the end of my shift," Boudreaux answered.

"And are you on street patrol at the present time?" Rose asked.

"No. I been up for promotion to detective for some time now, and it came through about the same time as this murder took place," Boudreaux proudly proclaimed. Smiles creased the faces of many of the spectators as he peppered his speech with that part of his Cajun accent he had not managed to lose.

"Is it not true that, as a result of your promotion, you were assigned as the chief investigator on this murder?"

"Not really as a *result* of the promotion, but I *was* promoted couple of days after the murder, and Sheriff Williams said since I was so familiar with the case, he would lemme take the lead in the investigation."

Looking at his notes, Rose said, "Tell this court about the call and the subsequent finding of Miss Reins."

"May I refer to my notes?" Boudreaux asked, looking at Rose and then glancing toward the judge.

Reid interjected, "If the defense has no objection, you may refer to your notes."

Roush responded, "No objection, Your Honor."

Rose reached into one of the boxes he had brought into the courtroom and retrieved the notebook that Boudreaux had turned over to the State Attorney's office during the course of the investigation. Handing it to Boudreaux, Rose said, "Please feel free."

Boudreaux glanced at the notes he had made as a part of the investigation then explained how Reins's roommate, Sharon Farrell, called him. Concerned that Lillian had not come home, she was afraid that something might have happened to her. Boudreaux detailed how he took the information, reported it to the dispatcher, and had the dispatcher broadcast it to all the police units. Then later, in the hours just before daylight, her car was found.

165

Gruesome would best describe the testimony given by Boudreaux regarding finding the body of Lillian Reins. He spared no details. Explaining that she had been found beneath carefully placed underbrush, she appeared to have been sexually assaulted. Her throat looked like it had been cut almost from ear to ear and her clothes were askew, her skirt above her thighs.

For more than five hours Boudreaux testified as to his role in the case and the chain of evidence that led him to suspect Jeff Mitchell. He mentioned finding the bloody Kleenex and the fingernail clippings. Neither Roush nor Simmons objected to any line of questioning or the answers provided.

"Detective Boudreaux, did you find an item of clothing near Miss Reins's car?"

"Yeah. An off-white Coogi cardigan sweater with smears of blood on the inside left sleeve. It was actually in the back seat of the car on top of a pile of magazines and stuff she had left in there."

Rose walked to the evidence table and reached for a sweater on which were large brown stains. "Is this the sweater you found?"

"Yeah. That's my mark right there."

"And did you learn how the blood came to be on the sweater?"

"No. Not exactly. It's like the guy who killed her probably used the sweater to wipe blood from . . ."

"Objection, Your Honor," said Simmons. "His answer is completely speculative."

"Sustained," ruled Judge Reid.

Rose continued his questioning, "Were you able to determine whose blood was on the sweater?"

"Yes. The crime lab tested the blood on the sweater and matched it to the victim."

"Were you able to trace the sweater to its owner?"

"Yeah."

"How?"

Boudreaux glanced briefly at Mitchell. "The sweater had a laundry tag stuck to it. We use the laundry tag to identify and find its owner, Mr. Mitchell."

"What other items were discovered on the interior of the car?"

"The ashtray had a couple cigarette butts in it, from filter cigarettes."

Rose, satisfied that Boudreaux had contributed all he could at this point, said, "Your witness."

Simmons rose from his chair and began his cross-examination of Boudreaux. "Detective Boudreaux, is it not true that you suspected Mr. Mitchell even before you had any hard evidence in hand?"

"As a matter of fact, yeah."

"And when might that have been?" Simmons asked.

"When I found out that Miss Reins was going to break off the engagement, I considered Mr. Mitchell a fairly strong suspect. He had motive, opportunity..." Simmons cut him off.

"And why might you have considered him a strong suspect rather than simply one suspect among others?"

"Because my experience has done led me to that conclusion. Typically, in any kind of relationship . . ."

Simmons cut him off again. "Your experience, Detective. How much experience could you have if this was the first case you had worked on as a detective?"

Boudreaux seemed a little shaken by the line of questioning. "It is true, this is the first case where I led the investigation, but I certainly been involved as a deputy in my share of murders. And more than once I've observed that in cases like this one, a mad boyfriend'll often take out his mad on the one he supposedly loves because he's afraid of losing her."

"Are you aware that Mr. Mitchell knew of the pending broken engagement and had agreed to it prior to the date with Miss Reins?"

"No, I wasn't aware of that," Boudreaux replied.

"Are you aware that Mr. Mitchell and Miss Reins had mutually consented to have intercourse on the night in question, and . . ."

Rose interrupted, "Objection, Your Honor, the question calls for speculation on the part of this witness. There is no way he could have been aware of so intimate an arrangement," Rose said sardonically.

"Objection sustained," said Judge Reid.

"Do you know why Miss Reins intended to cut off her engagement to Mr. Mitchell?" Simmons asked.

"Objection, Your Honor, more speculation."

"Objection sustained," said Judge Reid.

"Is it not true, Detective, that you were anxious to solve this case quickly?"

"For sure. But I never let my want to solve the case get in the way of doin' my job and doin' it well," Boudreaux insisted.

"Is it not true, Detective Boudreaux, that at every critical decision point in this investigation you *assumed* facts that would point to the defendant's guilt rather than letting the evidence lead you to the perpetrator of this crime? Isn't that true, Detective?"

"No," Boudreaux said, his anger rising. Boudreaux took a deep breath in an attempt to maintain his composure.

"Isn't it true that you ignored other evidence or even lack of evidence that would have pointed away from my client? Isn't that true?" Simmons began to press the issue harder.

"No, and I don't like your insinuation. . ."

Simmons interrupted Boudreaux. "Just answer with a *yes* or *no*, please, sir." Taking a moment to reassure himself, Simmons continued, "Well, is it not true?"

"No, it is not true."

"Detective Boudreaux, did you search the home of the defendant for evidence which might have been there or have CSI personnel do it?

"Yeah, I did it personally."

168

"And what did you find?"

Boudreaux responded sarcastically, "We found cigarettes matching those found in the ashtray of the car, a bottle of Aspen cologne, boots like the ones the perp wore, clothing with cleaning tags like the one on the sweater, a wallet and fingernail clippers. Quite a bit to tie him to this crime."

"Your Honor, I would ask that the last statement of Mr. Boudreaux be struck from the record. It is only his opinion."

"So ordered," said Judge Reid. "Please strike the last statement from the record."

"That's all nice and good but did you find something that physically put him at the scene of the crime?" asked Simmons.

"Nothing directly related to this crime." Simmons displayed his most cynical face. "You are saying you went to the home of the defendant, searched it carefully, and found nothing? Not even a shred of bloody clothing? Not a bloodstain that might have inadvertently soaked into a piece of clothing? No weapon? No nothing?"

"Yeah, that's right."

"Did you do the same with the defendant's car?"

"Yeah."

"And the result?"

"The same. No physical evidence was turned up, only the smell of cologne."

"Now, Detective, you are telling this court that no bloody clothes or other physical evidence was discovered either in the defendant's house or his car?"

"Yeah. That's right."

"Does it not seem strange to you that no bloody clothes or that blood evidence of any type could be found in the two places where the defendant spent so much time?"

"No. He probably destroyed or somehow got rid of the clothing and it simply. . ."

169

Simmons interrupted Boudreaux again. "Your Honor, I ask that the last part of that answer following the "no" be stricken from the record."

"So ordered," responded Judge Reid.

"You told this court that you extracted a sweater from the rear seat of the victim's car on the morning the car was found. Is that true?"

"Yeah. That's true. It was on top of a pile of magazines, newspapers, and assorted other personal belongings, which Miss Reins look like she kept in the back seat of her car."

"And how exactly did you extract that sweater? With your hands? With a set of tongs? How?"

"I release the back of the front seat, reach across the rear seat to behind the driver's seat, and pick it up with my fingers."

"You did not use a set of tongs or some other such device?"

"No."

"Did you have gloves on at the time?"

"No."

"Why not? Isn't that standard procedure, to use gloves or some artificial means of handling evidence until it has been properly examined?" Simmons felt good. He had hit a weak spot in the investigation.

"Yeah, that's standard procedure, but I didn't think about it at the time." Boudreaux lowered his head. He had been afraid that his handling of the sweater might put its value as evidence in jeopardy.

"You didn't think about it at the time. Is that your response?"

"Yeah. That's my explanation."

"That explanation is not good enough." Simmons hesitated a moment to consider his next line of questioning.

"In how much detail were the footprints investigated at the crime scene?" Simmons continued.

"A plaster cast was made and compared to the sole of the defendant's shoe. That was enough for me."

"That was enough for you. Then you are telling me that the boots underwent no microscopic examination for pits or unique characteristics that would have set them apart from any other seldom used Rockport XCS boot? Or any residue on them was never collected and analyzed?"

"Yeah. There was no microscopic examination of the boots or residue that I know of."

"Why not. Isn't that standard procedure?"

"I didn't see a need for it, frankly. His boots matched the print. With all the other evidence available, that seemed enough."

"Did your inspection of the boots turn up any traces of blood. Surely, if my client killed Miss Reins so viciously while wearing those boots, there would have been bloodstains on them, bloodstains that with any amount of effort would never be erased. In the cracks and crevices or even in the grain of the leather."

"The boots were not analyzed."

"I have nothing further to ask this witness, Your Honor. Obviously anything I need from him will be speculation because his investigation . . ."

Reid interrupted Simmons. "Mr. Simmons, your questioning of a witness is subject always to my approval, but your testifying from your position as a defense attorney will not be tolerated. Are you finished with this witness?"

"Yes, Your Honor, no more questions," Simmons said.

Reid responded, "Mr. Boudreaux, you may step down."

As Boudreaux left the courtroom, Kemper Nixon stood, "The prosecution calls Deputy Matt Tisdale."

Larry Boxer accompanied Tisdale into the courtroom and toward the witness stand. After being sworn in, Deputy Tisdale testified about how he found Reins's car, its location and condition, his call to Boudreaux, and his version of how the body was discovered. He explained how he had been on routine patrol in the northern part of the county throughout the night and how he had happened upon this car that appeared to have crashed into a pine tree along the edge of the rural dirt road.

Rose smiled, aware that he would soon elicit testimony that would seal this case. "Officer Tisdale, did you or Detective Boudreaux find the weapon used in this murder?"

"We did not find the knife that was used to actually murder the victim. The gun that the killer used to shoot her after she apparently was already dead was also never found."

"I have no further questions of this witness."

"Mr. Simmons, do you wish to question Officer Tisdale?" Judge Reid asked.

Simmons rose from his seat, "No, your Honor. I have no questions for him at this time."

Now approaching 7:00 in the evening, Judge Reid dismissed the jury with the admonition not to speak with anyone about the trial. "The trial will begin again at 9:00 tomorrow morning," he exclaimed. With a final rap of the gavel, he said, "Court is adjourned until tomorrow morning."

*   *   *   *   *   *

Jeff Mitchell's family had continued to pay the payment on his house in the hope that he would be acquitted and would return to as normal a life as possible under the circumstances. Since Jeff's arrest, his mother and father had lived in his house, maintaining it in the same meticulous fashion as Jeff had done. They now gathered after this first full day of trial and discussed it.

Jeffrey Mitchell came from a loving and close family. His father, William, originally from Alabama, had moved in the early 1950s to Minneapolis where he worked as a plumber for a construction company. His mother, Patricia, had never worked outside the home.

"I really think the case looks bad for Jeff," Mrs. Mitchell said, tears welling in her eyes.

Trying to console his mother, Jaimie put his arms around her and said with emotion in his voice, "This is just the first day. I

172

really think Blayne did a great job of discounting the evidence presented today, especially with that Boudreaux guy. We have to keep believing in Jeff's innocence and that justice will prevail."

Jaimie Mitchell was aware of the magnitude of the case against his brother. He requested to use his personal and sick leave time with the computer company for which he worked to be with his parents during Jeff's trial. Because of his professional value to the company, his request had been granted.

"The most important consideration to remember is that Jeff could not have committed this crime. If we honestly feel that the system of justice in our country works, then we also must believe that it will work in his case," Jaimie said. By now emotions were running high.

"Do any of you know whether Fred Roush employed a private investigator on behalf of Jeff?" asked Andrea, Jeff's younger sister.

"I don't think he did," said Mr. Mitchell. "He probably did his own investigating and then depended on the information from the state. Besides, it's a little late to be hiring somebody to help the case."

"It would seem to me that we just need to wait this one out," said Mrs. Mitchell. "It has already gone too far."

"Right," said Jaimie. "We can certainly hire someone if it becomes necessary. The outcome of the trial will dictate whether a private investigator is needed. There's no reason to get embroiled in something which might be unnecessary."

"We will all do better if we get some much-needed rest," said Andrea. Ever the nurse, she thought first of everyone's health.

*　　*　　*　　*　　*　　*

Having spent the day in the back of the courtroom listening to the testimony, Thad Whetstone felt relieved that neither the prosecution nor the defense had approached him about the Lillian Reins case. After all, he had been engaged to Lillian three years before, and they, too, had mutually agreed to end the relationship.

173

Yet, not one single investigator from the Sheriff's Department ever met with him, questioned him, or indicated any serious interest in what he might have to add to the investigation. He assumed no one knew of his involvement with her.

Whetstone remembered Lillian as an aggressive and ambitious woman, with definite career plans. She was not the kind of woman to be tied to a man with old-fashioned ideas about marriage. She was passionate and loving and could make a man feel every bit the man he wished to feel.

Their relationship had lasted eighteen months. During that time, he came to know her intimately. He understood why her relationship with Jeff Mitchell might not have worked out—after all Jeff was an "old-fashioned guy," from a family with conventional values, which included the traditional roles of wife and mother.

Sitting now in the den of his small, rented house, Whetstone reflected on the fact that he had not been questioned. He knew that an alibi was out of the realm of possibility. No one could corroborate his whereabouts because no one knew where he was at the time of the murder. He felt he had dodged a bullet.

*   *   *   *   *   *

The night was long for Jeff Mitchell. Having observed so many trials on Court TV and network shows, he was not unaware of the gravity of his present situation, especially after the testimony of the day. The seeds of his guilt had been planted well by the prosecution; he only hoped that Fred Roush and Blayne Simmons could, in some way, mollify the harm that had already been done in just twenty-four hours.

After being transported back to jail, Jeff was offered a late meal of a ham sandwich, potato chips, dill pickle, and Coca-Cola. After taking a couple of bites from the sandwich, he washed it down with a small bit of Coke, and lay on his bed, staring at the ceiling and wondering what tomorrow might bring.

Morning came too soon for Jeff Mitchell.

"Good morning, Mr. Mitchell." He heard a cheery voice through the fog of a sleepy mind but could not quite recognize whether it was real or whether he was dreaming. "Rise and shine; Breakfast is here," said Theresa Mullins.

Breakfast consisted of two eggs, scrambled, grits, buttered toast with grape jam, and coffee. "You know I don't like coffee. How many more times am I going to have to tell you people not to bring me coffee?" Mitchell said, exasperated.

"Okay. Give me a few minutes. What would you like instead?" asked Mullins.

"Hot tea," Mitchell responded. "Hot tea and artificial sweetener, thank you very much!" The rise in inflection at the end of the sentence betrayed his irritation.

"I'll be right back with it," Mullins responded.

Mullins arrived with his cup of steaming hot tea. She recognized the deep depressive state into which Mitchell had gone.

"Want to talk about it?" she asked.

"No. There's really nothing you could do anyway," Mitchell said.

When Mullins returned to pick up his tray, Mitchell seemed to have regained his composure and appeared more resolute. "Look at this as another day to prove your innocence, Jeff. Have confidence and don't let circumstances or setbacks get to you. The innocent win in the end. Just remember that."

*   *   *   *   *   *

The tableau inside the courtroom was as though some invisible hand was directing a drama scene. Everyone seemed to be in the exact same spot as the day before, the only change—the clothes being worn.

Both Mitchell's mother and sister seemed to reflect the more serious, even depressive, mood of Mitchell in the clothes they were wearing. During jury selection and the first day, they wore very stylish, colorful garb that expressed a sanguine attitude, a positive and hopeful outlook on the trial's result. Today, long sleeves, long hemlines, and dark colors characterized the clothes these two women had chosen.

Mitchell approached the railing and met his family. The change in apparel was not lost on Mitchell. He thought, *Maybe some unseen force has influenced this change in attire. Is this a portent of the trial's outcome?* At that moment, his thoughts were interrupted by the sound of Larry Boxer announcing the arrival of Judge Reid.

"Let the record show that the prosecution is present and the defendant is present in court with counsel," Judge Reid said. "This court is now prepared to hear the arguments of the day. Gentlemen, I wish not to protract these proceedings more than is necessary. Be certain that unnecessary activities, unwarranted witnesses, and superfluous questioning do not become the order of the day. Mr. Rose, you may continue with your case."

"The prosecution calls Nancy Manning," Rose announced so that the entire courtroom could hear.

Manning was ushered in from the adjacent witness room. Once on the stand and sworn in, she settled in her seat. She identified herself as the Intake Coordinator at the FDLE.

"Ms. Manning," Rose said, "would you tell this court about the process which you use in the intake process at the FDLE? Be specific about how you handled this case, please."

"Sure. It's pretty simple. The investigators bring in the evidence they have collected at a crime scene. In this case, it was quite late in the day when they arrived. Because of that, I sealed the boxes with crime scene tape and stored the evidence in the vault overnight. The next day I retrieved the boxes from the vault, broke the seals on the boxes and initiated the paperwork required before analysis could be authorized. I prepared an inventory form on which all items are catalogued for analysis. Each item was carefully noted with an identification number and a case number that I assigned. The items and the accompanying requests for analysis were separated and placed in small plastic containers, sealed for delivery to the appropriate department. Once all that was completed, the packages were delivered. In this particular case, I asked my assistant to deliver each container and a copy of the case folder to each department."

"You are saying that the procedure which you just described is precisely the same as the one you followed in this case?"

"Yes," Manning replied.

"No further questions, Your Honor," Rose said.

"Do you wish to question this witness, Mr. Simmons?" Judge Reid asked.

"No, Your Honor. I have no questions for this witness."

"Call your next witness, Mr. Rose," said Judge Reid.

"The prosecution calls Dr. Sheila Josephson to the stand."

After being sworn in, Dr. Josephson was seated, staring blankly out into the courtroom. Having performed this ritual many times, she patiently awaited the first question.

Samantha Kralick took up the questioning. "Dr. Josephson, would you please describe the findings from your autopsy of the body of Lillian Reins?" The questioning of the coroner by a female prosecutor was no accident. The prosecution strategized that a female prosecutor asking the questions about a female victim might draw more dramatic attention to the responses. Only time would tell.

"The body of Miss Reins was somewhat mutilated," Dr. Josephson began. "The fatal wound was the one inflicted to the medial portion of the neck, slightly above the larynx. It was a severe wound, two to three inches deep, which extended from near the base of the right ear lateral toward the left to approximately an inch and a half to the left of the larynx. The

177

windpipe had been severed. The actual cause of death, however, was profuse and unabated bleeding from the right anterior carotid artery."

Dr. Josephson paused. Mrs. Norma Reins leaned her head on the left shoulder of her husband and wept uncontrollably. For the first time in her career, Dr. Sheila Josephson was witnessing a family in profound emotional distress. She could not go on. She waited what seemed like an eternity, not only to allow the Reinses to leave the courtroom but also to compose herself. She had been moved by this display of emotion.

Mrs. Reins and her husband quietly exited the courtroom.

"Please continue, Dr. Josephson," Samantha Kralick said.

Swallowing hard and determined to appear to be the objective medical examiner that she was, Dr. Josephson detailed the brutality of the crime. Using charts to illustrate the nature and location of the wounds, she described the bruises which appeared on Lillian Reins's face and body; she offered additional details regarding the neck wound; she identified and described the stab wounds to the torso; she pointed out the gunshot wound to the chest but added that Lillian Reins was probably already dead when the shot was fired."

"Did you collect anything from under her fingernails?"

"Residue from under her nails was never collected," Dr. Josephson testified. "Actually I asked my assistant to collect it, and I thought he had done so, only to find out after the body was released that he had been called away from the autopsy room for an emergency and had failed to collect it."

"Did you find samples of body fluids that did not belong to Miss Reins?" Kralick asked.

"Yes," Dr. Josephson answered. "She had been vaginally penetrated recently, and there were excellent samples of semen. Those were extracted and taken to the lab for DNA analysis," Dr. Josephson stated.

"No further questions, Your Honor," Kralick said as she seated herself.

"Mr. Simmons, do you wish to question the coroner?" Judge Reid asked.

"Yes, Your Honor, I would," Simmons responded.

Simmons referred briefly to his notes. "Doctor, could you tell the court the specific cause of death?"

"Yes. The cause of death was exsanguination. She simply bled out from the right anterior carotid artery."

"And how long would it have taken the victim to die from such a wound?"

"Probably only a very few minutes. The blood loss would have been rapid, and unconsciousness would have occurred rather quickly."

"Is it your opinion that the other injuries on the victim were inflicted post-mortem?"

"Yes, most likely."

"Including the gunshot wound."

"Yes."

"Your Honor, I have no further questions for this witness."

Rose announced his next witness. For the next five hours, Rose entered into the record the testimony of four witnesses from the state laboratory at the FDLE. Crucial testimony included the positive identification of Jeff Mitchell's fingerprints inside Lillian Reins's automobile; the bloody Coogi sweater that belonged to Mitchell found in her car; a comparison of the Rockport boot print made at the scene with boots owned by the defendant. In spite of his efforts to the contrary, Blayne Simmons could not alter the material and scientific facts to which these witnesses testified. Even though Simmons thought he had made headway in creating some doubt in his questioning of Boudreaux the day before, by late afternoon, the case had turned ominous, and Jeff Mitchell, as well as his family, knew the results of the day's testimony did not bode well for the young man.

179

"The day has been a long and tiring one," said Judge Reid. "I think it would be best to adjourn and continue with the prosecution's case tomorrow." Having announced adjournment, he slapped the desk with his gavel and left the bench.

* * * * * *

The sandwich for lunch had lost its effects by mid-afternoon. Nevertheless, Jeff Mitchell experienced no feelings of hunger. Upon returning to his cell at the county lockup, he advised the deputies to forget bringing him anything to eat.

Mitchell lay back on his bunk, pondering the events of yet another trial day. The prosecution had successfully tied him to the major evidence in the case. What else could possibly remain to link him to it?

* * * * * *

Jeff Mitchell awoke to a morning that looked exactly like he felt. The sky hung heavy with dark, swirling clouds. The thunderstorms, with their bright lightning and loud, deadly thunderbolts, intermittently passed through the area. Mitchell could remember the sound well from the days of his youth on the Kansas plain before his family moved to Minneapolis. And, in spite of his age, he still dreadfully feared thunderstorms.

Still reeling from the testimony of the day before, Mitchell refused breakfast.

* * * * * *

The courtroom smelled of wet hair. Upon entering, Mitchell got a whiff of the odor; it reminded him of his elementary school days when the girls would come into class after a rain. Their hair had that same distinctive, rancid odor he smelled today.

The jury filed in and each juror took his assigned seat. Their faces, especially that of Rochelle Carlyn, exhibited somber expressions. A retired school teacher, she had nearly been excluded from the jury by a peremptory challenge. At last, Roush and Simmons decided that her teacher qualities made her an ideal juror. White, divorced and remarried, and with two grown children, Carlyn had the time to focus on the evidence in the case, the intelligence and objectivity to analyze the circumstances of the case, and the insight to see that Jeff Mitchell did not kill Lillian Reins. Today, her face indicated otherwise.

Everyone seemed to be in his place, almost as though the seats were reserved or assigned. Judge Reid ascended the steps, simultaneously speaking to the prosecutor, "Are you ready, Mr. Rose?"

"Yes, Your, Honor," Rose responded.

"Proceed then."

Confidence now characterized Rose's every facial expression and body movement. The trial was going his way. "The state calls Mr. Paul Pinkston."

Pinkston mounted the witness stand and was sworn by the clerk. After he was seated, Rose said, "Please describe your job, Mr. Pinkston."

"I am a crime scene investigator for the FDLE. I am responsible for collecting evidence at crime scenes, for preserving the evidence according to established procedures, and for transporting that evidence to the lab for study."

"Can you assure this court that every established procedure was followed in the gathering, preservation, and transportation of the evidence in this case?"

"Yes, I can."

"Your witness, Mr. Simmons."

"Mr. Pinkston, during the course of collecting evidence at the scene of this crime, did you find the butts of cigarettes?"

"Yes."

"Please tell the court where, precisely, the cigarette butts were found."

"Two butts had been snuffed out in the ashtray of the victim's car and left there. Another half-smoked remnant was found on the ground near her body."

Rousch and Simmons looked at each other in astonishment. They had been aware of the finding of the cigarettes in the car but not any near her body.

"How far from the body?" Simmons pressed.

"Maybe eight feet."

"Thank you, Mr. Pinkston. That's all I have."

Standing, Simmons said, "Your Honor, the defense was never advised of the finding of such evidence near her body."

Doug Rose, irritated at being accused of withholding vital information answered, "It's in our report. You just didn't read it."

Without allowing Simmons to respond, Judge Reid asked, "Do you wish to question this witness?"

"Not at this time, but I respectfully ask that he remain available for recall later, Your Honor."

"The state calls Robyn Weeks to the stand," Rose said as though commanding a military platoon.

Robyn Weeks entered the courtroom from the witness anteroom. The statuesque brunette drew considerable attention from both the male attorneys trying the case and the males in the public section of the courtroom.

After being sworn in, she was seated in the witness chair. "Miss Weeks," Kemper Nixon said, smiling and addressing her politely, "would you describe your position with the Florida Department of Law Enforcement?"

"I am principally a DNA analyst," she responded.

"Exactly what does a DNA analyst do?" he asked.

"We take samples of body fluids and analyze them for DNA matches."

"Could you explain, for the court, what DNA is and why it is important to a case like this."

"DNA is the basic molecular structure of the human body, and it is different for every individual. By using analytical techniques, we can take samples from a crime scene and samples from suspects and determine a match to a probability of better than ninety-nine percent."

Nixon continued his questioning of Robyn Weeks for the better part of the morning. He asked her about the semen found in Lillian Reins, the fingernail pieces found on the floor of Reins's automobile, and the small blood droplets soaked into the tissues that had been found on the floor of the car beside the passenger door. In each case, Weeks described the techniques used to analyze the samples and concluded that the matches were within a range of 99.95 to 99.98 % probability that they matched the DNA sample taken from Jeff Mitchell at the jail.

Roush laid his head on his arms in relief. He could not believe what he was hearing. Lifting his head, he leaned toward Blayne Simmons and whispered so that Mitchell could not hear him, "What do you think?"

Before Simmons could answer, Roush heard the judge say, "Your witness, Mr. Simmons."

Stunned by the testimony of the prosecution's most believable witness, Simmons asked the only question he could think of. "Miss Weeks," he said, "are you telling this court that you analyzed all of the DNA evidence and it points to Mr. Mitchell?"

"That is not entirely true, sir."

"What do you mean?" Simmons pressed.

"While analyzing the blood on the sweater, a second DNA profile appeared," said Miss Weeks. "It's almost as though the person who committed this crime wiped the blood from his hands on the sweater and left a small sample of epithelial cells embedded in the blood."

"Were you able to match this profile with anyone?"

"No, sir. There was no match in the database."

With a glimmer of hope, Simmons said with a sense of gratitude, "Thank you, Miss Weeks."

Robyn Weeks, fatigued from her extended time on the witness stand, stepped down and left the courtroom.

183

Doug Rose stood before the court, waiting to be acknowledged by the judge. "Mr. Rose."

"Your Honor, the state rests."

*   *   *   *   *   *

Juror number two, Artie Hodges, had made his decision. For the remainder of the trial, his mind would be closed to any other evidence. A white male who worked as a plumber, he did not need any more information to convince him that this guy was a murderer and deserved the worst of punishment. Married and the father of one son from a previous marriage, Hodges really did not care what the defense had to say. What could the defense say to change the overwhelming amount of evidence that had already been presented?

CHAPTER 22

The trial of Jeff Mitchell had been recessed immediately after the testimony of Robyn Weeks. Because of an important personal matter, Judge Reid was unable to continue the trial in the afternoon, so he announced that the proceedings would continue on Tuesday. Prior to leaving the courtroom, Roush and Simmons told Jeff Mitchell that they would visit him later in the afternoon to discuss strategy. Neither man wished to tell him the real reason for the meeting.

After lunch, Roush and Simmons met in the conference room of their offices. For a moment each stared at the other blankly, stunned by the fact that the evidence seemed to be mounting against Jeff Mitchell and not knowing what to say.

Roush broke the silence, "Where do you think this is going?"

"I think we may very well be 'down the drain' on this one already. I want very much to be optimistic, but . . . ." Simmons could not bring himself to complete the sentence. "I think we need to stick with our strategy and it's simple—if we don't convince the jury that Jeff is telling the truth about where he was and what he did that night, the case will be lost."

"Agreed," said Roush. "But we have no witnesses to put on the stand who can corroborate Jeff's whereabouts that evening. Jeff can deny being with Lillian, but who is really going to believe the defendant? Naturally, he would be expected to deny having killed her. Most of the evidence is circumstantial. Our only chance to at least save him from the needle is to refute the evidence based on Jeff's undeniable wholesome character and unquestionable reputation. We simply have no physical evidence to introduce."

"Or don't we?" asked Simmons. "Remember the epithelials on the sweater. That perhaps could be a gift and Robyn Weeks testified that no DNA match could be found. Why don't we get samples from the FDLE and have a private lab test them? Perhaps we can stumble on a match."

"Great idea," said Roush. "That's at least a start."

* * * * * *

Roush and Simmons arrived at the county jail. They were immediately escorted to the same conference room where they had so often met with their client. Sanitized, as was most of the jail, the room fairly shouted "institution." Green walls, vinyl tile floor mopped and polished to a high shine, and metal furniture highlighted the room.

Sitting in chairs around a two-by-six-foot table, Roush and Simmons awaited the arrival of Jeff Mitchell. After about five minutes, Mitchell was escorted in by corrections officer Mullins. The cuffs were removed, and Jeff seated himself between Roush and Simmons.

"Jeff," Roush said. "This is very difficult for both of us, but, due to the testimony so far in the case, we simply must ask you several key questions. And we insist that you be honest with us."

"Do you own a gun?" Roush asked.

"Yes, I do . . . or rather . . . did," said Mitchell.

"Mark Bradley, Thad Whetstone and I went target shooting one Sunday afternoon, but I don't recall leaving it with either of them. I just don't remember.

"When I went to get it out of my closet a week or so later, it was gone, stolen. That was stolen a couple of weeks before Lillian's murder."

"Did you report it stolen?" Simmons asked.

"No, I didn't," Mitchell said.

"Why not?"

"I was afraid I might open myself to civil liability if it were used in a crime and traced to me," Mitchell explained. "I know it's against the law, but that was my thinking at the time I missed it. Will that cause me a problem here?"

"Probably not in this case since the gun was never found and can't be introduced into evidence," Simmons responded.

186

Mitchell then asked Roush, "You never told me the results of the lie detector test."

"That was not by chance but by choice," Roush said. He reached for Mitchell's forearm and gently held it. "Jeff, the fact is, you failed the test. Lie detector tests are not fool proof; that is why their results are not admissible in court. You failed it and the prosecution is aware of the failure. Regardless of the accuracy of lie detection, I'm certain that is why they are pressing this case so hard. We played that card in the hope that it would fall in our favor. It didn't. Realistically, your failure probably cemented the prosecution's resolve to get a conviction and go for a death sentence in this case."

"There is one ray of hope here, Jeff," Simmons began. You may remember from today's testimony that the epithelial cells found on the sweater did not match you. Do you recall anyone, friend or acquaintance, that might have borrowed the sweater at any time?"

Roush added, "If you can think of anyone, however remote, let us know. We are going to have the DNA tested in the hope that we might learn something that the FDLE and the state could not find. But that probably won't happen before the end of the trial."

Simmons laid his arms on the table, his hands clasped in front of him. Lowering his head, he stared down for a few seconds. The silence in the room was deafening. "As much as I would like not to raise this issue, if we can't go somewhere with this evidence, then we probably should at least consider some alternatives. Jeff, their case is strong no matter how circumstantial, and you don't really have a viable, provable alibi. You might be better off considering a plea agreement. Would you do that?"

"Under no circumstances," Mitchell said angrily. "I have told you before, and I have not and will not change my mind. I will not plead guilty to a crime I did not commit, regardless of the outcome."

"Even if it means your life?" Roush asked in a solemn tone.

"Even if it means my life," Mitchell said. "I would rather die an innocent man than to defame my character and dirty a reputation that has taken me years to develop."

"That is your final word?" Roush asked.

"Yes," Mitchell said. "Just do your best, and if that isn't good enough, don't be ashamed at the outcome. It'll only prove that justice is not always served."

*　　*　　*　　*　　*　　*

Roush and Simmons returned to the office, alarmed by their meeting with Mitchell. Roush sat in the chair behind his desk; Simmons sat on the couch across the room near the bookcases. Roush rubbed his temples. His head had begun to pound the way it often did when he developed a migraine headache. Reaching into his desk, he retrieved two Advil tablets, washing them down with a glass of stale water that remained on his desk from the morning.

"Any ideas?" Roush asked.

"Only one," Simmons responded. "Mitchell mentioned the name of Mark Bradley, Lillian's supervisor. Bradley is the person who knew them best both as individuals and as a couple. Perhaps we should focus on his testimony; it could be crucial. It might even make a difference in whether the jury believes Jeff or not."

"That and putting Jeff on the stand are about all that will help his case at this point. And Jeff himself must be very convincing. I don't see how we can rebut the physical evidence. It's there, scientifically provable, and seemingly beyond contestability."

"That's right," said Simmons. "But we still have closing arguments. In a criminal trial, closing statements can be as critical to the outcome as the testimony during the trial. I plan to spend a good deal of time preparing my closing. Maybe it'll give us a ray of hope."

*　　*　　*　　*　　*　　*

Simmons rubbed his tired eyes. Just to be sure he had exhausted all defense possibilities, he had spent the better part of

188

the day researching other cases for clues as to how he might offer a viable defense. Cases seemed to be running together, but he was determined to discover a defense strategy that neither he nor Fred Roush had thought of. He ended the research where he had started—nothing left but to offer witnesses who might create doubt in the minds of the jurors and finally to put Mark Bradley and then Jeff Mitchell on the stand.

CHAPTER 23

Another day. Roush and Simmons had decided to adopt a more positive attitude. The prosecution had completed its case. At least now there would be no more surprises. The case for the defense presented a new beginning.

The courtroom once again filled to capacity. Each player in this drama was in place, awaiting only the appearance of the judge and jury. Shortly, Judge Reid appeared. Soon after, the jury filed in, led in by Larry Boxer.

"Mr. Simmons," Judge Reid began, "you may call your first witness."

"The defense calls Sheriff Jonathan Williams."

Sheriff Williams emerged from the witness room, walked to the witness stand, and waited for the clerk to swear him in. After Sheriff Williams swore to tell the truth, Simmons approached him slowly. "Sheriff Williams, please tell this court why you promoted Deputy Boudreaux to the position of detective."

"Deputy Boudreaux had been with the department for a number of years, had paid his dues, had passed the appropriate examinations for promotion, and deserved due consideration."

"Why, then, did you assign him, the newest, least experienced detective in the division, to one of the highest profile murder cases ever to be investigated in Escambia County?" The tone of the question was purposely sarcastic.

"A vacancy in the detective division made that consideration possible. His record, exam scores, and experience made him the ideal appointee to the vacancy. The move was a good one then, and even now I still think it was a good move."

"What about assigning him to such a case as this one?" Simmons pressed.

"In the beginning, we did not think the case would be so high profile. However, Mr. Boudreaux has worked several murder cases as a deputy . . ."

Simmons interrupted, "You mean to tell this court that he has investigated cases like this one before?"

"Well, no, not as an investigator. Only as a deputy."

"Would you please tell the court the difference?"

"A deputy is essentially a street patrolman who responds to crime scenes or emergency calls. While at a scene, the deputy determines whether other law enforcement officers are required."

"You mean as backup?"

"Well, as backup, or to assist in the investigation of the problem at hand."

"Continue, please," Simmons implored.

"The detective assumes the responsibility of a case, calling in the necessary personnel to investigate—removing evidence from a crime scene, handling of evidence removed from a crime scene, and directing the entire investigation into the crime."

"Doesn't the responsibility of a detective require at least some hands-on experience as a secondary officer before assignment as a primary investigator, especially on a case as important as this one?"

"In retrospect, I probably should've assigned a more experienced detective to lead in the case. I did assign Patrick Monaghan, a very experienced detective to partner with Detective Boudreaux on the case. I was confident that they would conduct this investigation properly and effectively. I remain confident that they did."

"You don't think at any time that Detective Boudreaux took liberties with the evidence in the case or arrived at conclusions without first allowing the evidence to point to such a conclusion?"

"No, I do not."

Simmons questioned Sheriff Williams for an hour, inquiring about others whom he might have promoted in a similar fashion. Williams testified that he had never before taken such action but remained confident about Boudreaux's actions. Williams could not be shaken.

Upon dismissal by Simmons, Rose reckoned that little or no damage had been done by Williams's testimony and chose not to question him further.

Simmons called Rita Maloney to the stand. Mrs. Maloney, a widow of fifteen years, lived alone in the same apartment complex as Lillian Reins.

Red-haired and sporting a heavy layer of makeup, Rita Maloney would be characterized by most people as the quintessential local busybody. "Mrs. Maloney, tell the court where you live."

"At the Spanish Bay Apartments," Maloney replied.

"Is that the same apartment complex where Lillian Reins lived?"

"Yes, it is."

"Mrs. Maloney, have you ever observed any suspicious characters at your complex? Someone you believed might be up to no good?"

"Yeah. There was this one car that parked near Miss Reins's apartment building. I often saw a man watching her apartment."

"How do you know he was watching her apartment?"

"Because I saw him standing at her bedroom window one afternoon trying to look inside."

"Did the police ever question you about this man?"

"No. I wondered why they left me out of all this. I thought I had something that they'd be interested in."

"Could you describe this man and his car?"

"Shoot, I don't have to describe him. I got a picture of him."

Maloney pulled a Polaroid picture from her purse. Taken from a far distance, the picture of the man was somewhat fuzzy, and the tag on the car did not appear in the picture.

"Why didn't you bring this photo to the police?"

"I fig'erd if they needed my help, they'd have come and talk to me. They never did, so I just kept the picture."

Maloney testified that she had seen the man on at least ten occasions prior to the murder, once late in the evening.

"You didn't think looking in somebody's apartment window appeared suspicious?"

"Yeah, but I didn't want to get involved in something that wasn't none of my business."

"Your Honor," Rose stood speaking. "In light of this evidence, I would like to ask the court for a postponement of these proceedings while this new information is investigated more thoroughly."

"Mr. Rose, your motion is noted and acknowledged, but a postponement is unnecessary and is, therefore, denied. Please proceed with questioning this witness, Mr. Simmons."

"Your Honor, I would like to introduce this picture as evidence. I have no further questions for this witness."

"So noted. Would the clerk please notate the picture for inclusion as evidence in this trial?"

Kemper Nixon cross-examined Maloney, ultimately getting her to admit that the man in the car and the man she observed looking in the windows of Reins's apartment were not the same person. Nixon smugly returned to his chair, and Mrs. Maloney was dismissed.

Simmons called Calvin Madsen, a local distributor of Rockport boots. He testified to the fact that more than five hundred pairs of Rockport XCS boots were in stores in Escambia County and in the surrounding area.

He next called Christina Dooley, a waitress at the Charley Dees Restaurant. She testified that she served Jeff and Lillian the evening of the murder. She testified that they left the restaurant around 10:00, as Mitchell said.

Under cross-examination, Dooley could not remember what each of them ate that evening. And when asked how she remembered them so well, she responded, "They are regular customers of mine, and Mr. Mitchell is a great tipper. As to the time, I checked the computer terminal that indicated the time that the food order was placed and the time when the ticket was printed out." Dooley was dismissed.

To bolster the defense, Simmons next called Randolph Tutt. Jeff Mitchell's immediate supervisor and a senior partner in the firm of Andrews, Eisen & Tutt, Randolph Tutt exemplified the epitome of success. Dressed in a blue Armani suit, a white French-cuffed shirt with his initials embroidered on the base of the sleeve, a gold Rolex watch on one arm and a heavy, linked-gold identification bracelet on the other, Tutt's appearance bespoke the obvious prosperity he had achieved.

"Mr. Tutt, tell us what you know about Jeff Mitchell," Simmons asked.

"Jeff Mitchell is one of the kindest, gentlest, most compassionate people I have ever met. He's ever the gentleman with the ladies and wouldn't hurt a soul. There is no way he could have killed Lillian Reins."

"Mr. Tutt, please keep your answers more directly related to the questions," Judge Reid demanded.

"Yes, sir, I'm sorry. Jeff is just such a fine example of manhood, a man whom I would wish my boys to be like."

"How was he as an employee?" Simmons asked.

"One of the best. He knows his work better than most, enjoys a wonderful relationship with his clients, and has constantly worked to improve his skills. He would have been a senior partner one day if all this hadn't happened. And certainly he will be if he is ever cleared in this case. He's a man whose character is unquestioned and remains so with his colleagues at the firm."

During the questioning, Tutt offered examples of Mitchell's personal qualities, and he droned on until Simmons finally cut him off. "Thank you, Mr. Tutt. Your witness, Mr. Rose."

Rose could see no real reason to question Tutt. Character witnesses were almost always presented in a defense as a last resort. "No questions, Your Honor."

Simmons then called Mark Bradley to the witness stand. "Mr. Bradley, describe to this court your relationship with Jeff Mitchell."

Bradley began tentatively, "I consider Jeff my best friend. Before I married, we enjoyed each other's company frequently, often double dating. We both loved the outdoors and became scuba diving partners and hiking buddies."

"What would you say about his character?" Simmons then inquired.

"Jeff is the kind of person who would give you the shirt off his back. He is mild mannered, genteel, vibrant in spirit. I would trust him alone with my wife and any of my children. He is even tempered, not given to outbursts of anger. He is intelligent, well read, skillful and knowledgeable in his field of endeavor, and was quite ambitious about his future potential as a senior partner of his firm. He often shared his hopes and dreams with me. He is anything but the man the prosecution has portrayed in this trial."

"Objection, the last statement was not relevant to our purposes here today, Your Honor," Rose said.

"Sustained," said Judge Reid.

After offering descriptions of several hiking and scuba diving trips he, Mitchell, and Joe Blankenship had taken together, Bradley, addressing the jury, concluded, "I hope that the jury will realize that this man is a person whose character is beyond reproach and whose personality is anything but aggressive. I hope that you will consider the gravity of your decision and at least offer him the hope that one day he will walk away a free man." Secure in the strength of his case for the death penalty, Rose declined to cross-examine Mark Bradley. Having made those final statements without an objection from the prosecution, Bradley stepped down from the witness stand.

"Your Honor," Simmons said, "the defense would like to call Jeff Mitchell."

195

Mitchell arose from his seat at the defense table and slowly walked the fifteen feet to the witness chair. There he settled in for an inquisition that he hoped would convince the jury of his innocence.

After being sworn in, Simmons began the questioning. "Mr. Mitchell, tell this court how you first met Miss Reins."

"I met Lillian at a happy hour one night after work. Seems as though this meeting was not accidental, having been secretly and separately arranged by her roommate and Mark Bradley. She was there alone as I was. We just sort of migrated toward each other and started talking. We seemed to have so much in common at the time, and she was quite attractive. I was so shy I could not bring myself to ask her out. After meeting her several times at the same bar, I finally got the courage to invite her on a real date."

"How long did you date before becoming engaged?" Simmons asked.

Mitchell thought before he spoke. "Probably ten months. We enjoyed each other's company and mutually decided that, when the time was right, we would get married."

"Did you and Miss Reins ever engage in sexual activity during the time prior to your engagement?"

"No."

"When did the two of you initiate sexual intimacy?"

"We had been engaged for about three months. We had already gotten involved physically, but emotions often ran high during those times we were together. One night, she just blurted out all of a sudden, 'I can't stand it. Let's do it.'"

"And where did this first incident of sexual intercourse occur?"

"In the bedroom of my house."

"Tell the court about your most recent relationship with Miss Reins."

"Lillian and I enjoyed becoming involved in mutually rewarding activities. But the longer our engagement extended, the less I desired to be married and the less compatible I thought we actually were. The time for marriage was not right for me. I often felt that the only thing that kept us together was the sex."

"Who made the first move toward ending the relationship?"

"It was actually mutual, although she was the first to verbalize it."

"And when was that?"

"About a week prior to her murder."

"Mr. Mitchell, tell us about your activities the night Miss Reins was murdered."

"My car had been put in the repair shop in the afternoon. Because I had no car, she agreed to take her car on our scheduled date that evening. She picked me up about 7:30, and we drove for about thirty minutes to Charley Dees, one of our favorite restaurants on the outskirts of the city."

"Do you remember what you ate that night?"

"No, I don't."

"Continue, please."

"We enjoyed our meals and the relaxed atmosphere. By 10:00 or shortly thereafter, we left and drove out Scenic Highway to the Chimney Park and pulled into the parking lot. It was dark, and there was only one other car there. We never saw its driver. We talked for about two hours and agreed that we would end our relationship. She handed me the ring, and I put it in my pocket."

"How did the evening end?"

"We had agreed that sex was the only thing that seemed to keep us together. So we decided on one last fling. We made love there in the car. Afterwards, she returned me to my house and left. I never saw her again."

"Do you or have you ever smoked cigarettes?"

"Yes."

"What brand?" Simmons asked.

"Camel filtered," Mitchell responded.

"Can you account for the fingernails and the bloody tissue?"

"Yes. I bite my nails." Mitchell lifted his hands in the air with the outside of his hands facing the jury. "It's a bad habit I've had since childhood. Don't seem to be able to quit. In any case, I bit one of my nails to the quick that night and it bled. I used the tissue to stop the bleeding.

"Mr. Simmons, I am prepared to admit to all of the evidence presented by the prosecution in the case. I was with Miss Reins that night. I was in her car; my fingerprints naturally will be all over it. We had sex, accounting for the semen. But none of this evidence places me at the actual scene of the crime. It only proves that I was with her and in her car sometime during that evening. To that, I admit. But I can say unequivocally she was alive when she dropped me off at my house."

"No further questions."

"You may question the witness, Mr. Rose," Judge Reid said.

Samantha Kralick took up the questioning. "Mr. Mitchell, you told this court that the idea of the breakup was Miss Reins's, correct?"

"No. I said the idea was mutual. She was the first to mention it."

"Isn't it true that she had made it clear to you not long after you were engaged that she thought she might have made a mistake in becoming involved with you?"

"No. She didn't."

"And didn't she actually detest some of your habits so much that she once told you, 'I'd never consider marrying you'?"

"She did not."

"Aren't you really the one who pushed this relationship because of your strong sexual appetite?"

"No. The relationship was mutual."

"Mr. Mitchell, do you not admit to a strong sexual need?"

"Yes. I admit to that. But she . . ."

"Mr. Mitchell, didn't you decide that if Lillian was going to end your relationship, you would see that no one else would have her?"

"Objection, Your Honor," shouted Simmons. "Miss Kralick is badgering this witness and trying to provoke him into saying something that is not true."

"Your objection is duly noted, Mr. Simmons. But Miss Kralick has the right to ask these questions. Mr. Mitchell is only required to answer them truthfully. Please answer the question, Mr. Mitchell."

"Would you please state the question again?" Mitchell asked, his eyes saddened by the direction of the cross examination.

"I asked you if you did not decide that if Lillian was going to end your relationship, then no one else would have her either?"

"No. That is not how it was."

"Mr. Mitchell, didn't you kill Miss Reins because she had actually found someone else she considered to be more compatible with her lifestyle, and you couldn't stand to think about them being together?"

"No. I did not kill her I tell you."

"No further questions, Your Honor."

"Mr. Simmons," Judge Reid said. So stunned by the line of questioning Simmons did not hear the judge address him.

"Mr. Simmons," Judge Reid repeated. "We're trying to have a trial here. Please try to stay alert."

"Yes, Your Honor."

"Please proceed."

"We have no further witnesses, Your Honor. The defense rests."

"So be it," said Judge Reid. "This court is in recess until tomorrow morning. Both sides be prepared for the closing arguments." With a rap of his gavel, the day ended.

*　　*　　*　　*　　*　　*

During the course of the trial, Blayne Simmons had meticulously penned notes about testimony provided by each witness. Now, after devouring a meal of steak and potatoes, he lay down on the couch of his office for a power nap. Soon he was sound asleep. Awakened forty minutes later by his inner alarm clock, Simmons prepared for the long night.

CHAPTER 24

The slamming of the front office door awakened Blayne Simmons. Apparently he had fallen asleep after an exhausting night, reading his notes from the trial, researching closing arguments in several famous trials, and hand writing twenty-five legal pad pages of ideas he wished to offer during the closing argument.

"Blayne, you look like a bum fresh off the street. Didn't you go home last night?" Roush asked.

"No. I thought it best to stay here where my resources were to prepare for the closing argument today," Simmons responded, rubbing his eyes and trying to clear them of sleep-induced blurriness.

"I'm sorry I couldn't stay with you and help out."

"There was no need for that. This is something I had to think through for myself," Simmons said, finally becoming fully awake.

"Are you ready?" Roush asked.

"I really think if we can't convince the jury with this closing statement, it just ain't possible to convince 'em," Simmons retorted. "I'm going on home and take a shower. I'll see you in court."

*   *   *   *   *   *

A sunny day. A packed courtroom. It was all about to be over.

Both Roush and Simmons sat, with Mitchell between them, staring blankly into space. Their gaze was interrupted by Doug Rose and his team huddling at the prosecution table. Even though they were speaking softly, the air was thick with a sense of assurance.

Judge Reid took his place on the bench. A moment later, the jury filed into the courtroom. Reid gaveled the court to order.

"Ladies and gentlemen, we are here today to hear the final arguments in the case of the State of Florida versus Jeffrey Mitchell. No time limits will be placed on either the prosecution or the defense. I would urge that the members of the jury pay close attention."

After hesitating a moment, Judge Reid continued, "Mr. Rose, you may proceed."

Doug Rose, ever the melodramatic advocate, stood, buttoned the front of his blue pin-striped, double-breasted Hart, Shafner & Marx suit, and walked toward the jury. In his left hand, he held several sheets of notations he would use during this summation.

"Ladies and gentlemen of the jury, in my opening statement, I declared to you that the prosecution would provide you with a motive for murder, describe and prove the defendant's mission of murder, and prove beyond a reasonable doubt that he is guilty of murder. The principal motive for Mr. Mitchell taking Miss Reins's life was his anger over their breakup. He testified that he loved her, but that love was returned only through some consensual but perverted act. Unrequited, Mr. Mitchell satisfied his anger in a murderous rage.

"The facts speak for themselves. Modern DNA testing not only can place Mr. Mitchell in Miss Reins's car the night of the murder but also inside her body. A bloody sweater belonging to the defendant had been left at the murder scene. His fingerprints were all over her car. Cigarette butts containing his DNA and the aroma of his cologne remained in the car. All these facts point undeniably to the defendant."

For more than two and half hours, Doug Rose babbled on, detailing the testimony of each prosecution witness in the case. Never once did he refer to any testimony by a defense witness.

Rose ended his summation, "Ladies and gentlemen, the defense would like for you to think that the defendant is a genuinely nice guy. And I'm sure that, in other circumstances, he may very well be a nice guy. But Jeffrey Mitchell is a murderer. The last person to see Miss Reins alive, Jeff Mitchell decided to settle Miss Reins's fate. If he could not have her, no one else would have her.

"I said earlier that the prosecution would prove, beyond a reasonable doubt, that Jeff Mitchell, in a fit of rage, killed Miss Reins and tried to make the crime appear to be one of a sexual assault gone wrong." Accentuating his remarks by hammering his right index finger onto the top of the jury box railing, Rose continued, "The fact is, Mr. Mitchell perpetrated this abhorrent and vicious act in an effort to satisfy his own inadequacies. Do not let the emotions of his words cloud your judgment. You must find Jeffrey Mitchell guilty—guilty of a sin against Miss Reins, guilty of a sin against humanity, guilty of a sin against the very God that created them both."

Rose returned to his seat with an air of self-confidence rarely seen. He had won this case, and he knew it.

Judge Reid asked, "Are you ready for your summation, Mr. Roush?"

"Yes, we are, Your Honor," Roush said, "but first I would like to enter a motion to dismiss all charges against Mr. Mitchell on the grounds that the state has failed to prove its case against Mr. Mitchell and request a directed verdict of acquittal."

"Mr. Roush, your motion is duly noted for the record. This court is not prepared to grant such a request. Motion denied. You may proceed with your summation, Mr. Roush."

"Mr. Simmons will deliver the closing statement," Roush said.

"You may proceed, then, Mr. Simmons."

"Thank you, Your Honor," Simmons said. He walked toward the jury box, notepad in hand.

During the course of the trial, Simmons had carefully observed each juror's reaction to the testimony. Not only did he try to get a sense of what each juror was thinking, but he also sought diligently to identify one juror in particular to whom he might direct his closing statements. He hoped he could convince just one juror of Mitchell's innocence. If so, the trial would, at least, result in a hung jury and a mistrial.

Looking over the jury that sat before him, he hesitated, making cursory eye contact with each one individually. He decided to focus on juror number six, Naomi Rogers.

A black female, Rogers could be described as an advocate for social justice. She was employed by the Florida Department of Children and Families, administering the Family Services Division. A liberal Democrat, she had voted for every candidate in the Democratic Party for the past ten years. Her quiet demeanor never revealed to any except her family and closest friends, the fire she felt with regard to the under-represented. Her husband, himself a social activist, shared her enthusiasm for righting social and political injustice. Together they fought diligently for the rights of abused spouses, the rights of children, and the need for the state to bear its share of the burden for righting social ills. Rogers sat in the middle of the front row.

Simmons stopped directly in front of Naomi Rogers. He placed his notepad on the railing of the jury box and looked directly into her eyes. He smiled. "It's all there is," he said. "What you have heard from the prosecution is all there is to this case, and it's simply not enough to convict a man who is fighting for his very life."

Simmons diverted his eyes away from Rogers. Facing away from the jury, he continued, "Ladies and gentlemen, this case is not just about a murder; it's not about finding justice. It is one man's crusade to make himself look good. Let's begin at the beginning."

Simmons retrieved his notepad and walked to the podium in the center of the front of the courtroom. There he laid it down and turned to the second page. "Ladies and gentlemen of the jury, my client never has denied being with Miss Reins the night she was killed. He does not deny having dinner with her; he does not deny having been in her car that night; he does not deny discussing with her their impossible future together, a decision to which they mutually agreed; he does not deny having engaged in consensual sex with her. All of these things happened; he testified to them in that chair," Simmons said as he pointed to the witness stand.

"But being with her on the night of her murder, talking together alone, and even having sex with her does not constitute murder. The fact is Detective Boudreaux found himself in the enviable position of making himself look good by accusing the person to whom he could connect the greatest volume of the evidence, both scientific and circumstantial. He simply wanted to look good, especially in the eyes of Sheriff Williams. After all, this was his first case as a detective, and a lead detective at that; and it was a high-profile case. What more could a detective ask for? He did not want to disappoint the man who had placed so much faith in him.

"At no time during this investigation did Detective Boudreaux assume anything other than the guilt of Jeff Mitchell. He focused solely on him out of convenience. At every critical decision point in the investigation, he presupposed facts that would point to Mr. Mitchell's guilt, rather than searching for the evidence that would actually put Mr. Mitchell at the scene of the crime. The problem with that approach is that *none*, let me say it again, *none* of the evidence puts him there at the time the crime was committed. And since no eyewitnesses can put him there either, such evidence as a bloody Kleenex can easily be accounted for. The evidence is entirely circumstantial."

Simmons walked toward Mitchell, laid his hand over Mitchell's right forearm and said, "This young man has been tormented by the State of Florida and made to look guilty without any regard for the kind of person he is, the character he possesses, or the exemplary life he has lived."

Simmons walked to the evidence table and picked up the Rockport boots that had been taken from Mitchell's house as evidence. "Take a good look at these boots. We've had testimony in this court that as many as five hundred people in this geographical area could be wearing a pair of boots identical to these. Yet the state is willing to admit them as physical evidence in this case without any microscopic analysis for minute, but unique indentations on the soles, without any analysis of soil residue, or any other forensic analysis that would lend credibility to the State's case. Only the boots. Yet another dubious entry into the ledger of assumed guilt." Simmons returned the boots to the evidence table.

Simmons walked toward the jury box and once again looked directly into the eyes of Naomi Rogers. As though directing a question to her, he said, "Do you recall Detective Boudreaux admitting that neither he nor any of his investigators could find any physical evidence either at the defendant's house or in his car which could connect the defendant to the actual crime scene? Nothing. Let me emphasize, NOTHING. And that seems to characterize this case. It is empty except for the scientific evidence of the defendant's presence in Miss Reins's car that evening, a non-issue with this lawyer and the defendant simply because the timeline cannot be corroborated."

Simmons walked back to the defense table and reached for a law book. As though opening the book to a specific page, he pointed to the page and pretended to read, "In a court of law, a circumstantial case against a defendant must eliminate any reasonable hypothesis of innocence. That means in order for a defendant to be considered guilty beyond a reasonable doubt, there must exist some shred of evidence, however minor, that unquestionably points directly to the defendant as the perpetrator of the crime," he discontinued his pretend reading. Then he continued, "No such evidence exists in this case. No bloody clothes at Mr. Mitchell's house; no blood in his car; not even any apparent blood on these boots that the prosecution would like for you to believe the defendant wore during the commission of this horrible, bloody murder. What reasonable explanation can be proffered for the absence of blood in any location associated with Mr. Mitchell?"

Simmons replaced the book on the table and walked to the jury box once more. This time he made direct eye contact with juror number ten, Nicolas Lentz. A nurse, Lentz prided himself on being a conservative Republican who espoused conservative causes. He considered law and order to be the number one priority of society; it was to be maintained at all costs.

Believing that if he could convince Nicolas Lentz of Jeff's innocence, his apparent strong opinion might sway others. So Simmons focused his attention on Lentz.

"Does Mr. Mitchell look stupid to you?" Simmons directed the question to Lentz, but he did not expect an answer. Simmons turned toward the far wall and allowed not only Lentz but also the entire panel to ponder the question. Then turning again toward Lentz, he emphasized, "Does THIS MAN look stupid to you?" He hesitated again for effect.

"I don't think so. Jeff Mitchell is a well-educated man. Testimony in this trial from those who knew him best reveals that he is a man of keen intellectual ability; his character is above reproach; all who know him testify to and appreciate his abilities as an accountant as well as his sensitivity and insight as an individual. If these witnesses are to be believed, then how could a man of such keen intellect and rare insight be so stupid as to leave so much incriminating evidence that could be linked directly to him?" Simmons almost snarled when he said the word incriminating. He continued, "The two descriptions just don't run parallel."

Simmons turned away from the jury as he began his final remarks. "The fact is, each of these pieces of evidence has a plausible and rational explanation. Only a man who feels his reputation as a detective hinges on a speedy resolution to this crime would even consider this evidence to possess any real credibility, except as a means to identify or eliminate a suspect."

At the last moment Simmons decided to focus on one final juror, number three, Monica Hoehn. He concluded, "Today you will decide whether justice really does prevail in our society, whether justice is blind, whether justice succeeds over ambition. Jeff Mitchell sits before you an innocent man. Return him to his rightful place in society. You will not regret it."

After a delay for dramatic effect, Simmons returned to his seat.

"I would like for us to take a brief recess," declared Judge Reid. "Please return to the courtroom in fifteen minutes, at which time I will charge the jury and provide some time for the jury to deliberate."

CHAPTER 25

Thirty-five minutes later, with all parties to the trial present, Judge Reid appeared from his chambers and mounted the bench.

Judge Reid reached for a loose-leaf notebook in which he retained information regarding charges to the jury. He released a sheaf of notes that obviously he had prepared beforehand. "Ladies and gentlemen of the jury, you have heard the testimony presented in this court by both the prosecution and the defense. The final decision pertaining to Mr. Mitchell's guilt or innocence is now to be determined by you. Let me thank you for your attention during this trial. Please pay close attention to the instructions I am about to give you."

Judge Reid turned several pages, then continued his instructions. For forty minutes he read the instructions outlining the options available to the jury including murder in the first degree, murder in the second degree, murder in the third degree and manslaughter.

Reid stopped reading for a moment, drew himself a small glass of water, and drank it.

Doug Rose squirmed in his seat. He had heard these words so often, he could almost repeat them from memory. He covered a yawn and awaited Reid's resumption of the instructions.

Simmons suddenly experienced an overwhelming feeling of dread. Unexplainable darkness clouded his mind and thoughts. He did not hear the last few sentences of the charge.

As his mind returned to the reality of the moment, he heard Judge Reid, "Reasonable doubt is not a possible doubt, a speculative, imaginary, or forced doubt. If, after carefully considering, comparing, and weighing all the evidence, there is an abiding conviction of guilt, then you must return a verdict of guilty. It is the evidence introduced in this trial, and in it alone, that you are to consider for that proof."

Reid concluded, "In just a few moments you will be directed to the jury room by the bailiff. Your First act should be to elect a foreman. The foreman presides over your deliberations, like a chairman of a meeting. The foreman will bring the verdict back to the courtroom when you return. Either a man or a woman may be foreman of the jury. Remember, your verdict in finding the defendant either guilty or not guilty must be unanimous. The verdict must be that of each juror, as well as the jury as a whole. You will now retire to begin your deliberations."

*　　*　　*　　*　　*　　*

Once settled in the jury room, the group stared silently at one another for a brief time, not really knowing how to begin. The jury sat around a large walnut conference table with chairs for fifteen. The walls were wainscot, and from the center of the ceiling hung a chandelier that dated to the early part of the 20th century. Jurors enjoyed the comfort of high back, black leather chairs, accented with brass hardware.

Monica Hoehn was the first to speak, "I guess we first should elect a foreman." Everyone agreed.

Small pieces of blank paper were distributed. A pencil had been placed on the table at each seat. "Write a number representing the juror number on your paper and pass it to the head of the table. Mrs. Carlyn and Mrs. Rogers can count them and give us the results," Hoehn said.

When the votes were tallied, juror number seven, Ernest Guest, had been selected to be foreman. He garnered six votes. The balance of the votes had gone to jurors number nine, Clayton Collins; number eleven, Lee Lei Chiu; and number one, Alexander Fields. Reluctantly, Guest took the seat at the head of the table.

"Let's take a first vote to see where we are on guilty or not guilty at this point. We can discuss the case after this vote is taken," the jury foreman said. Paper was once again distributed, votes marked, and the paper passed to Guest. He asked juror

210

number four, Thomas Lewis, to assist in the vote tally. The results were five guilty votes and seven not guilty.

Before anyone else could speak, Artie Hodges wished to be heard. "This man is guilty as sin, and we all know it. How could any of you vote 'not guilty' when there is so much evidence against him?"

"But it's all just circumstantial," said Naomi Rogers. "Nothing the prosecution presented actually proves he was at the crime scene. The evidence only implicates him."

Hodges countered, "I remember seeing on a television show one time that a murder is usually solved by looking for the person with motive, means, and opportunity. Mitchell had all three."

The next two hours were spent in heated discussions, principally between Artie Hodges and Naomi Rogers, with other jurors periodically offering their perspectives on the matter. A second vote resulted in six guilty votes and six not guilty.

"Personally, I think we've done all we can do today," said Clayton Collins. "Maybe a good night's rest will clear our heads." Harris Pettit, who sat nearest the jury room door, knocked on the door to signal the bailiff that they wished to retire for the night.

"Just a minute, let me check first with Judge Reid," Larry Boxer said.

After five minutes, Boxer returned. "The judge will convene court in ten minutes. I'll come back shortly to direct you into the courtroom."

Within a few minutes, Boxer opened the door and led the jury into the courtroom, where each took his seat. "Ladies and gentlemen," Judge Reid said, "you have asked that you continue your deliberations tomorrow. You will be required to be sequestered overnight, and arrangements have been made for you at a local hotel. You will return tomorrow morning. You are reminded not to discuss this case with anyone, including your fellow jurors, until you return." With his gavel, Judge Reid declared the court in recess.

The next morning the jurors were returned to the jury room. With Boxer safely seated outside, the jury resumed its deliberation.

"I want to say something before we get too far into this discussion," said Rochelle Carlyn. "What I'm about to say probably appears like the ramblings of an old lady, but I really think this man is not guilty. I saw no evidence he had a raging temper, no evidence he held a grudge against the victim—even though the prosecution said he did—and no evidence he was actually at the scene of the crime."

"Wait, now," said Collins. "What about the semen and bloody Kleenex?"

"Those things seem to have been explained rationally by the defense. Besides, nothing in this man's background shows me he is capable of committing such a horrible crime."

Though not outspoken, Thomas Lewis spoke up. "I just don't believe him when he said the breakup was both their ideas. It just don't make sense. Somebody had to come up with the idea first. How does he know they thought of it together?"

"And besides that, no other suspects are remotely implicated in the crime," added Monica Hoehn.

"But he seems like such a nice man," Carlyn said.

"That may be true," said Hoehn, "but looks can be deceiving. Gentleness and a likeable personality can mask the jealous rage a man might feel if he is rejected. I remember one time being asked out by a fella who fit the same description as Mr. Mitchell. When I refused to go out with him, he flew into a fit like I never saw before; he even threatened me. I called the police."

Lewis spoke again, "I hate to keep harpin' on it, but it's his word against Lillian's that they both wanted to break up, and she ain't here to say he's tellin' the truth."

Heated deliberations lasted all day and halfway into the next. Finally the light on the outside of the jury room was extinguished, indicating that the jury had reached a verdict.

*　　*　　*　　*　　*　　*

All parties to the trial were notified that a verdict had been reached. With all of the principals in the courtroom, Boxer led the jury into the box. Roush and Simmons looked at the jurors' faces, trying to read a verdict. Every juror's countenance was grave. Not a good sign.

"I understand that the jury has reached a verdict in this matter," Judge Reid said.

"Yes, Your Honor, we have," said the foreman, Ernest Guest.

"Would you please hand the verdict form to the bailiff."

Boxer took the verdict from Guest and handed it to Judge Reid. After reviewing it to ensure its proper form and, after handing it to the Clerk of Court, Reid asked her to announce the verdict.

The Clerk stood and read, "We, the jury, at Escambia County, Florida, this date find the defendant, Jeffrey Mitchell, guilty of the offense of First Degree Premeditated Murder. So say we all."

Gasps of surprise, followed by quiet weeping, could be heard in the gallery of the courtroom as the verdict was read. Mitchell, in a profound display of emotion, pounded his fist on the table, turned his head heavenward, and shouted, "Why? Why? Why?"

THE PENALTY

CHAPTER 26

Incredible hopelessness clouded Jeff Mitchell's mind like an enormous thunderhead on a stormy, mid-summer day. Never would he have thought that the trial he had just been through would result in being falsely convicted of a crime, especially murder. He had believed so strongly in the American system of jurisprudence; that faith had now been shaken to its very foundations.

Yesterday seemed like an endless nightmare, he thought as he paced the sixty square feet of his stark, lonely cell at the Escambia County Jail. Dazed and bewildered, he sat on the cot with his aching head cradled in two cupped, shaking hands, his emotions frayed and at the point of breaking.

"Mitchell." Hearing the sound of his name did not immediately register in his consciousness. The voice seemed far away, as though waking him from a bad dream. "You have a visitor downstairs. You wanna meet him?" Corrections Officer Mullins asked, her noisy keys hanging from an elastic cord dangling from a belt loop.

Clearing his head and regaining a modicum of inner composure, he answered, "Who is it?"

"Mark Bradley."

"Yeah. Mark. I'd like to see him," Mitchell responded. Through the slot in the cell bars Mitchell reached his hands, which were beginning to show the results of not eating adequately. Mullins placed handcuffs on his thinning wrists, then unlocked and opened the door. Mitchell stepped out into the center of the drab hallway. Together they walked to the visitors' area where Mark Bradley waited.

Separated by a screen, Bradley could only speak to, not physically touch, Mitchell. "Hey, buddy," Bradley began. "How you doin' today?"

"How would you expect me to be doing?" he said, sarcasm punctuating each word. "I'm about as low as I could possibly get. Do you have any idea what I've been through? And now in four days I'm going to find out what sentence this screwed up system is going to mete out to me for this mess. How would you feel about that?"

"Not so good, of course. Is there anything I can do for you, any way I can help?" Bradley asked.

"Not unless you can somehow magically turn this runaway train around."

"You can count on me to do anything within my power to help. You know that, don't you?"

"Yeah, I know you will. And I appreciate what you tried to do in your testimony during the trial. You can't imagine how grateful I am that you believed in me enough to take vacation time from your job just to be there every day even when you knew you wouldn't testify until near the end of the trial. That is more than just a friend. That's like family." Moisture glistened in Mitchell's eyes as he briefly reminisced about their friendship. Within moments both were searching for words, trying to console the other.

Bradley broke the silence of the moment. "I brought you some magazines and a few books I thought you might like to read. I was told to give them to the officers. They said they would see that you got them."

"Thanks for being so thoughtful. You and my lawyers and my family appear to be the only people who genuinely believe I'm not guilty." Talking about the crime was becoming progressively more difficult for Mitchell. The more he talked about it, the clearer his current circumstances became, and the deeper into depression he drifted.

"Just because you couldn't convince those twelve people doesn't mean that other people don't believe you. Keep your chin up. Fred and Blayne will appeal the case; they're sure to find some legal ways to get the appeal heard and the conviction overturned."

"Thanks. I sure hope so." Mitchell bit his fingernails nervously.

"If I can do anything for you, don't hesitate to let me know either through the prison staff or through Fred. Okay?"

"Yeah. Thanks. And thanks for taking time to drop by and chat."

*   *   *   *   *   *

The first four days of his post-trial incarceration were days of adjustment. Now, only three hours away, the next phase would begin. He would find out how long he would have to endure the excruciating pain of innocence in the narrow cell of an institution built for the guilty.

Mitchell had dressed and was in court with his attorney, awaiting the arrival of the judge. The large number of spectators, including Mitchell's family, Mark Bradley and Jeff's now former boss, filed into the courtroom. Shortly, Judge Paul Reid, stately in his judicial garb, appeared in the doorway of his chambers and then walked up the two steps to the bench. Appearing to disregard the crowded courtroom, His Honor directed his next statements to the lawyers on both sides of the room. "Gentlemen and lady," lady referring to the presence of Samantha Kralick from the State Attorney's office, "we are here today to consider a sentencing recommendation by the jury and to impose a lawful but fair sentence upon Mr. Jeffrey Mitchell for the murder of Lillian Reins. Please be aware that all witnesses sworn in during the guilt phase of the trial will still be considered to be under oath."

The bailiff stood silent and erect in his corner of the courtroom. As though on cue, he said, "Mr. Mitchell, please stand as the judge addresses you." Mitchell stood in compliance; Fred Roush and Blayne Simmons stood on either side of him.

Addressing Mitchell as though he were the only person in the room, Judge Reid removed his half glasses and said, "You have

217

been lawfully found guilty of murder in the first degree. In a few moments the jury will be directed into this courtroom where each juror will hear evidence before rendering a recommendation regarding the sentence to be imposed." Then turning to Mitchell's attorney, Reid asked, "Mr. Roush, are you prepared to commence with the sentencing phase of these proceedings?"

"Yes, Your Honor," Roush answered almost apologetically.

"Mr. Rose, are you ready?"

"Yes, Your Honor," the nattily dressed Rose responded confidently. "The State is ready."

Then directing his attention to Larry Boxer, Judge Reid said, "Would the bailiff please bring in the jury?"

The twelve jurors filed into the courtroom, each taking his seat in the jury box. The gravity of the occasion was clearly reflected in the faces of all the jurors. One particular juror made direct but only momentary eye contact with Roush as she walked to her assigned seat. Everyone in the courtroom, including the jury, was seated.

Judge Reid spoke to the jury, "Ladies and gentlemen of the jury, you have found the defendant guilty of first degree premeditated murder. The recommended punishment for this crime is either death or life imprisonment without the possibility of parole. The final decision as to what punishment shall be imposed rests solely with the judge of this court; however, the law requires that you, the jury, render to the court an advisory sentence as to what punishment should be imposed upon the defendant."

Turning toward the prosecution and defense tables, Reid continued, "The State and the defendant may now present evidence relative to the nature of the crime and the character of the defendant. You are instructed that this evidence is presented in order that you might determine, first, whether sufficient aggravating circumstances exist that would justify the imposition of the death penalty and, second, whether there are mitigating circumstances sufficient to outweigh the aggravating circumstances, if any such circumstances are found to exist."

Roush tried to read the expression in the face of juror Monica Hoehn. The wife of a successful insurance salesman and mother of three, she had been one of the most attentive jurors throughout the trial. Her sad eyes spoke volumes to Roush. He was confident that her sympathetic facade concealed an opinionated, uninhibited, and independent personality. Roush could only hope to break through to her, appealing to her more compassionate and sensitive side for the recommendation of a lighter sentence.

Roush suddenly realized that he was staring at Hoehn. Quickly he diverted his gaze toward the judge.

The Honorable Paul Reid glanced at the clock on the rear wall of the courtroom, then after whispering something to Larry Boxer, said, "You may proceed, Mr. Rose."

Doug Rose described the murder scene in minute detail. He introduced again the coroner's report and the painful, agonizing death suffered by Lillian Reins. For more than an hour, he presented evidence to support his request for the death penalty, focusing on the heinous nature of the crime and the evident suffering through which the murderer had put Miss Reins. Then he called Mr. Ernest Reins, father of the victim, to the stand.

"State your name and place of residence," Rose requested.

"Ernest E. Reins. St. Joseph, Missouri," Reins replied quietly, almost in a whisper.

"Please speak up, Mr. Reins. It will be hard for the court reporter to hear you," Judge Reid said.

"I'm sorry. Is that better?"

"Yes, sir. Thank you."

Respectfully but dramatically, Rose addressed the father of the victim, whose face reflected the anguish and grief of losing his only daughter. "Mr. Reins," Rose said, "under the laws of the State of Florida, the victim's family has the right to make any statement it might desire at this sentencing hearing. If you would like to say something on behalf of the family, you may do so now."

For the next few minutes, Ernest Reins haltingly and sometimes tearfully described the birth of his daughter, her teenage years, her career ambitions, and her desire to get married and have children. Several times he choked to the point of stopping his testimony to collect himself.

He talked about how proud he and his wife were of her accomplishments as a naval aviator and her subsequent successes in the field of advertising. "In many ways," he said, "Lillian was the ideal daughter. I'm sorry that this man has seen fit to cut her life short. She could have achieved so much had she only had the years to do it. I hope the court will sentence him to the just punishment he deserves." Hands quivering and anger in his voice, tears now streamed from his eyes.

Reins pressed a tissue to the tears that glistened on his cheeks and gathered his thoughts. "Mrs. Reins and I always wanted a houseful of children. Unfortunately, because of complications during her pregnancy with Lillian, we never had another child. In fact, my wife almost miscarried with Lillian. She was very special to us. Her loss will trouble us for the rest of our days, especially the way she died."

Silence penetrated the courtroom as Reins began to weep uncontrollably. The silence lingered as Reins attempted to pull himself together. Once Reins got his tearful emotions under control, the only sound heard in the courtroom was the quiet sobs of Mrs. Reins.

Mr. Reins continued, "The loss of our daughter is tragic, and no punishment can bring her back. We only ask that justice be done."

Neither Roush nor Simmons had questions for Mr. Reins.

After assisting Mr. Reins to his seat, Rose called Sharon Farrell, Lillian's roommate, to the stand. She described their lives together, their friendship, and a few of their most intimate thoughts, which each had shared with the other during special times. "Lillian really wanted to get married, but she was not certain that Jeff was the person she wanted to marry. She had met several other men on some recent business trips, having dinner and going dancing with at least two of them. These experiences seemed to open her to new ideas and expectations. She seemed to come to life. I think that's why she decided to call off the engagement to Jeff. She just wanted more time to consider her options."

"Any questions, Mr. Roush?" asked Judge Reid.

"None, your honor," he replied. Sharon Farrell was dismissed to take a seat in the courtroom near the Reinses.

"That concludes the penalty phase of our case, Your Honor," Rose said.

"Thank you, Mr. Rose," Judge Reid said. "Are you ready, Mr. Simmons?" Judge Reid asked.

"Yes, Your Honor. The defense is ready."

"Please proceed then."

During a twenty-minute introduction, Blayne Simmons described his client as a quiet, almost shy, individual who grew up in a loving home under the strict discipline of two godly parents who were determined that their children would be compliant, productive, and successful citizens. He described Mitchell's Army career, his achievements and his education following his service in the Army, and his career choice as an accountant. He detailed his relationship with Lillian Reins and their mutual decision to call off the engagement. Then he called Randolph Tutt to the witness stand.

After Tutt was comfortably seated in the witness chair, Simmons, standing near the rail of the jury box said, "Mr. Tutt, I have one question to ask you. Please carefully consider your response before answering." Pausing for effect, Simmons sought diligently for the right words. "Your willingness to give testimony in the trial phase of this proceeding indicates a belief in Mr. Mitchell's innocence. Would that assessment be correct?"

"Yes. I do believe him to be innocent."

"Even in spite of the fact that he has already been adjudicated guilty by this jury?"

"Yes."

Simmons continued, "Jeff Mitchell has been found guilty, but if by a miracle, the truth of Jeff Mitchell's innocence were finally and unequivocally ascertained, would you accept him back into your firm?"

Silence.

"Mr. Simmons," Tutt's voice strong with conviction, "nothing would give me greater pleasure than to see Jeff Mitchell, the free man he should be, back at his desk at Andrews, Eisen & Tutt. I would gladly accept him back into the firm, and, as stated before, we still would consider him for a senior partner."

"Thank you, Mr. Tutt," Simmons said. "That's all I have for this witness, Your Honor."

For the next few minutes, Simmons heard none of the questioning by Rose. He could only feel the flush of optimism from the testimony of Tutt. Points had been scored by such a strong vote of confidence. With his faith restored, Simmons would continue to press for a light sentence.

Simmons called for William Mitchell, Jeff's father, to be escorted to the witness stand. Arising slowly from his place in the spectator gallery, William Mitchell made his way to the front of the courtroom. "Please be seated," said the Court Clerk.

Simmons walked toward the witness stand and smiled. "Mr. Mitchell, please state your name and place of residence for the record," said Judge Reid. Mitchell responded softly.

Simmons began, "Mr. Mitchell, tell us about your son."

A shy but imposing gentleman, Mitchell turned his chair toward the jury and spoke confidently. "My son is a disciplined, sensitive, caring, and intelligent man. He was as compliant a child growing up as any parent would want. Oh, he got into his scraps with friends and even once played hooky from school. But after being punished for that escapade, he never skipped school again."

Mr. Mitchell described Jeff's teen years and his struggle to chose a college to attend. He spoke with pride of Jeff's distinguished and heroic career in the Army. He described one incident in which, during a routine training exercise, a fellow soldier nearly drowned in a swamp crossing. Without thinking of his own safety, Jeff returned to the water to save the young man. As a result, Jeff developed hypothermia and almost died.

Mr. Mitchell recounted how Jeff would send money home to his parents to help with some of their financial problems and to avoid losing their farm. Then he told about Jeff's anonymously paying off the family's long-term debt with the bank, a debt that had been incurred just to keep the farm going. It was several years later, Mr. Mitchell declared, that he learned who actually had paid off the loan.

Mitchell concluded his testimony, "I know my son, and he is incapable of such a crime. One day it will be proven beyond doubt. But I plead with you at least to spare his life so that when that day arrives, he will be alive to enjoy the freedom he deserves."

Mitchell started to leave the witness box. "One moment, please, Mr. Mitchell," said Judge Reid.

"Do you have any questions for Mr. Mitchell?" Judge Reid asked. He addressed his question to Doug Rose.

"No, Your Honor. We have no questions."

"You may stand down, now, Mr. Mitchell," Judge Reid said courteously.

"Any further witnesses you wish to present, Mr. Simmons?"

"No, Your Honor, that concludes our case."

Judge Reid once again faced the jury. "It is now your duty, ladies and gentlemen, to advise the court as to what punishment should be imposed upon the defendant for his crime of first degree premeditated murder. Your advisory sentence should be based upon the evidence that you have heard while trying the guilt or innocence of the defendant and evidence that has been presented to you in these proceedings. You may now retire to the jury room to consider your recommendation. When you have done so, please advise the bailiff." The twelve members of the jury orderly vacated the courtroom and entered the jury room to begin their deliberation.

As the jury filed out of the courtroom, Roush could not help noticing the consternation in the face of Naomi Rogers. She had demonstrated no emotion until now. In her job as a caseworker for the Florida Department of Children and Families, she had witnessed many instances of false accusation, especially in child abuse cases. Roush could only hope that the confident testimony of Tutt, accentuated by the positive attributes of his client, and the impassioned plea by his father would, at least, raise a doubt in her mind about his guilt and convince her to plead for a lighter sentence.

*   *   *   *   *   *

Within approximately forty-five minutes, the jury announced to Larry Boxer they had reached a decision. He immediately notified Judge Reid whose secretary, Sarah, contacted Doug Rose and Fred Roush. Thirty minutes later all parties had returned to the courtroom.

In the brief moments before Judge Reid addressed the jury, Roush examined the face of each juror for an indication of the recommendation. No one made eye contact with him, but he looked intently at Judge Reid who was ready to call on the jury foreman for the reading of the jury's recommendation.

From the bench, Judge Reid announced, "I understand that the jury has a sentencing recommendation in the matter of Jeffrey Mitchell versus the State of Florida." Looking at the jury foreperson, he continued, "Is that true?"

"Yes, Your Honor," came the reply.

"Mr. Mitchell would you please rise as the recommendation from the jury is read?" Mitchell, Roush, and Simmons arose in unison. Mitchell's chin was lowered on his chest as he looked at the floor.

"We, the jury," the foreperson began, "by a vote of twelve to zero recommend the sentence of death in the aforementioned entitlement. . ."

Mitchell collapsed in his chair as Fred Roush reached over to prevent him from falling and hurting himself. Mitchell's head now rested on folded arms atop the table.

"Are you all right, Mr. Mitchell?" Judge Reid asked.

"Could you give him just a minute, Your Honor?" Roush asked.

The minute seemed like hours as Roush offered a drink of cold water, which Mitchell eagerly accepted. His head was swimming as though he were at the bottom of a lake, needing air, lungs about to burst from oxygen starvation. His chest heaved, sucking in air as if a boulder were crushing him to death. *I have to be brave and take this like a man,* he thought. *This nightmare can't go on forever.*

With head in hands, Mitchell wept uncontrollably. He could hear the judge polling the jury. "Juror number five, how do you render?"

"Death," was the restrained response.

And on through the jury until the entire panel had responded with the word *death.* Although a unanimous recommendation was not required by law, the people had spoken.

"Please have your client stand," Judge Reid said to Roush. Mitchell complied as Reid leafed through several sheets of paper, made notes, and initialed where required.

Jeff Mitchell haltingly stood, looking straight ahead at the judge whose presence on the bench radiated the power he possessed over life and death. Judge Reid, eyes narrowed by the weight of the decision he was about to hand down, began, "Jeffrey Mitchell, a jury of your peers has found you guilty of murder in the first degree. That same jury recommended that you be put to death for what can only be described as a most heinous crime. It is the sentence of this court that you be remanded to the custody of the Escambia County Sheriff until such time as is convenient for your removal to the state penitentiary near Starke, Florida, where you will be incarcerated until the date of your execution. You are hereby sentenced to death by lethal injection . . . "

Mitchell's ears suddenly went deaf, and he heard no other words that afternoon. Now he was to die for a crime he didn't commit. *What greater tragedy could befall a human being? Now I know how Jesus must have felt when he was unlawfully and illegally put to death.*

He could feel the strong, muscular arms of Fred Roush embracing him as the sentence was pronounced, but he heard nothing. The words of the judge sounded as if he were speaking on a tape whose speed had been slowed to a low, unintelligible mumble. As silence filled the courtroom, he heard the voice of his attorney, "I'm sorry . . . didn't do enough . . . should have gotten someone else . . . I don't know what . . ."

Again Mitchell collapsed in his chair; Roush and Simmons knelt beside him. The cameras, allowed in the courtroom for the first time only for the penalty phase, recorded every word of the sentence and every movement and response of the defendant and his lawyers. To be sure, the sentencing of Jeff Mitchell would be the lead story on the evening news.

Decorum returned to the courtroom. After some concluding remarks about citizen participation in the judicial process, Judge Reid dismissed the jury. With a rap of his gavel on the top of the desk, he declared the trial to be complete and asked that Mitchell be taken into custody and retained in the county jail. With noticeable strain in his sallow cheeks, Mitchell was finger printed, then handcuffed and led from the courtroom to a waiting van for transport to the jail.

Before stepping into the van, Fred Roush put his hand on Mitchell's shoulder and told him, "I will appeal the case. Try not to worry. Keep the faith. We will find a way to get at the truth. I still believe in the system; we simply must let it work *for* you and not *against* you. I'll get back to you in a day or two."

CHAPTER 28

The loss of the Mitchell case weighed heavily on the mind of Fred Roush. It was obvious that the evidence against Mitchell, however circumstantial, was overwhelming, and knowing the public's current state of mind over the increasing incidents of violence did not help. Because of Roush's inexperience in criminal trials and Simmons's lack of time to prepare adequately, the case probably ended the only way it could have under the circumstances. But it was difficult to realize that his client now faced lethal injection and certain death.

Convinced beyond a doubt that Jeff Mitchell was an innocent man, Roush determined to begin a one-man campaign to discover the truth—just one shred of evidence that might eliminate Mitchell as a suspect and provide grounds to reopen the case. But first he would take a few days off and go to the mountains to clear his head before starting out on his crusade. Death cases often took years to carried out; time was on his side.

Now the third week of June, Roush drove to Gatlinburg, Tennessee, where he spent a long weekend at the Mountain Vista Hotel, overlooking the quaint but now crowded scenic village. The nights were pleasantly cool, and the view from the tenth floor offered a scene unparalleled anywhere else in the South. The lights from across the valley gave the appearance of stars in an ink black sky as they twinkled in the shadows of wind-blown trees. The chair lift to the top of the mountain had long since closed for the day, and just before midnight the tourists began their descent from Ober Gatlinburg's ice rink and tourist shops.

Daylight brought the opportunity to visit some antique stores in the area, now a burgeoning tourist mecca with the Dollywood theme park nearby, small shopping centers with curiosity shops advertising cheap T-shirts, and tourist trap entertainment facilities. After lunch at the Apple Barn, Roush drove to several antique shops along the highway, searching for a treasure. Real bargains were nowhere to be found.

Evening led him to Lonnie Miller's Piano Bar Cafe where he downed a rack of delicious pork barbecued ribs and a dinner salad heavily accented with fat-free dressing. He topped the meal off with an ample slice of pecan pie. Roush left the restaurant both satiated and a bit drowsy.

After a short stroll up and down Main Street, he walked the several blocks back up the mountain to the hotel. There he settled in for the night, capping the evening by watching late-night television, but before Letterman could read his "Top Ten List," Roush drifted off into a deep, restful sleep.

*   *   *   *   *   *

On Friday, a gray van drove into the prisoner transit area of the Escambia County Correctional Center. Jeff Mitchell was brought from his cell, where, after signatures were obtained on the required paperwork, he was placed in the van for transport to the state prison. Once in the van, he knew he would not see his beloved home again.

As the van entered the ramp at Interstate 10, Mitchell could see the muddy waters of the bay stretching three miles toward the east. He reminisced momentarily about the times he had spent fishing on that bay with his friends, catching whatever nibbled on his bait. He remembered the crash of the America East Airlines plane in the bay in 1998. He thought about the burning of the train trestle in 2000, and the many times he and his buddies had walked the railroad tracks alongside the bay. The thoughts of the wiener roasts he had enjoyed so much along the shoreline raced through his mind, and the scene of his first kiss on the red clay bluffs—all this he was now leaving behind forever with only the prospects of death facing him.

The trip to the prison was boring. Along the country's most heavily traveled east-west route, for more than a hundred miles he observed nothing but pine trees and pasture land. Mitchell tried to keep his mind active during the trip by performing mathematical calculations of the auto tags on the cars that passed the van.

Passing through Tallahassee, he saw signs advertising Florida State University and its successful football and basketball teams. Then he saw the face of legendary Coach Bobby Bowden, wearing a yellow shirt and pants and donning a yellow hat, looking down from the billboard advertisement of a lumber mill whose branding color was yellow. All too quickly, the exits to the city were left behind.

The next hours passed as though the world were in slow motion. From out of nothingness, the walls of the prison appeared in the van's windshield.

Built in 1961, the Florida State Prison was an impenetrable fortress from which no prisoner had ever escaped. The walls were three feet thick, made of gray limestone, and stacked each one upon the other with only a small seam of cement between the layers. Atop each wall, angled metal stanchions had been erected, attached to which were coils of barbed and razor wire. At the corner of each wall was a tower that permitted guards a 24-hour, 360-degree view of the walls and the prison yard. Outside the prison, the guards' view extended for almost a half mile over cleared land.

The van approached a large gate electrically controlled by the sentry standing alongside it. When the van approached, the guard's scowley features came into focus. With a downturned mouth, furrowed brow and squinty eyes that never seemed to change expression, he would scare any neighborhood kid, his physical appearance that of someone who possessed more brawn than brain.

"Good afternoon, Bull," the driver addressed the burly guard. "We got another one for you."

"Good," replied Bull. "You know where to go and what to do." Reaching back, Bull pressed the large red button on the support panel of the gate. The gate responded, providing an opening just large enough for the van to drive through.

Mitchell looked back as the gate closed behind him. He took a deep breath, reflected on all that had happened in the last six months, and knew that, whatever the outcome, life would never be the same.

*　*　*　*　*　*

Roush returned from his short trip to Tennessee refreshed and ready to tackle new challenges. Reporting to his office early, he checked to make certain that all the file boxes containing the information on the Mitchell case were close at hand. He was determined not to let his client die. He first would file the direct appeal that was mandatory under Florida law in death penalty cases.

Sitting at his desk, he buzzed Blayne Simmons on the intercom and asked him to come immediately to his office for a strategy session. After Simmons was settled into a high-back lounge chair across the desk from Roush, they both picked up legal pads to take notes.

"Let's brainstorm what we need to do to get this verdict reversed," Roush said. "I want us to pursue this case as vigorously as we can, no matter what the cost."

"Do you expect to reap any financial rewards for it?" Simmons asked.

"Doubtful. Whatever we do on it likely will be pro bono. After all, Jeff doesn't have any money, and his family is certainly not in a position to help him very much. I just think we owe it to him. How do you suggest we start?"

"I think we start by reviewing the transcript of the trial to see if there are any grounds for appeal," said Roush. "Let's get a complete copy of that transcript as soon as possible."

*　*　*　*　*　*

Processing for Jeff took about an hour. He was escorted, in handcuffs, to the cell that he would occupy for the next few years.

C-4, an eight-foot-by-ten-foot cell, along one of five corridors on death row was where Mitchell was assigned. The corridors were laid out in the configuration of wheel spokes; each corridor contained twenty cells. Death row could accommodate up to 100 prisoners at any one time. No female inmates scheduled for execution were held in this facility.

The walls of The Row were a bright yellow color, unlike the institutional green of the two previous jails in which he had been held. The floors, vinyl tile, were highly polished and maintained that way at all times by prison labor. Each cell was sparsely furnished, equipped only with a table, a small chair, a bunk attached to the wall, a lavatory and a toilet. It was illuminated by a one hundred watt incandescent bulb at the center of the ceiling.

Each prisoner was allowed books, paper, and a wooden pencil. No pens or metal writing implements of any kind were ever permitted. All approved supplies had been placed in the cell prior to Mitchell being brought to it.

As he entered The Row, Mitchell noticed that it was quiet, almost eerie. None of the rapping, jive talk, and threats that he had seen and heard at the county lockup. In here, life was serious, *dead* serious.

It was early evening by the time Mitchell completed the intake process and was taken to his cell. Just about suppertime. Within ten minutes after arriving, the meal cart could be heard making its rounds of The Row. Tonight was sloppy joe night. Not really very appetizing to one who has just been committed to a short life of detention followed by certain death. "I'm not hungry," he told the steward as he passed the tray into his cell.

"Take it anyway," was the brusque reply. "I have a job to do, and I intend to do it. If you don't want to eat it, that's all right, but you *will* take the tray."

Mitchell accepted the tray of food, stared at it a moment, and set it down on the top of his desk without touching it. Food was the farthest thing from his mind right now.

Jeff Mitchell's first night on The Row was his worst nightmare. He slept only about thirty minutes all night, listening to the sounds of other inmates snoring, the rattle of paper by another, the humming of gospel songs by yet another. And there seemed an almost inaudible hum that constantly droned in the background, ever present, but completely unidentifiable. Underneath it all, he could not help reflecting on his future, if he had any future at all.

He thought about his family and how they must be reacting to the idea of having a con for a son. A condemned con. How disappointed and embarrassed they must be. They had stuck by him throughout the ordeal.

He thought about all the girls he had dated, trying to remember their names in the order in which he had dated them. And then he thought about Lillian.

He often pictured her in his mind—her quick wit, her outgoing personality, the way she crinkled her nose when she smiled or laughed. Now he was sorry that he had ever considered breaking off the engagement. But now was too late. He loved her so much. With the picture of Lillian's mutilated and lifeless body vivid in the deepest recesses of his thoughts, sleep evaded him.

*   *   *   *   *   *

Blayne Simmons gazed intently out the window of his office. Unlike Fred's office that overlooked the bay, the view from Blayne's office included a large city park. The leaves on the trees in the park were now a bright green; renewed life had blossomed in nature the way he longed for hope to blossom in the life of Jeff Mitchell.

Roush's research on the direct appeal was painstaking. He had reviewed the trial transcript at least three times, searching for grounds for an appeal. He was now ready to prepare the appeal. With notes in front of him, Roush considered how to begin, but his mind wandered. He lost his thoughts in a jumble of randomness; he could not concentrate. He thought about the trial;

he thought about the Reins family; he thought about Jeff Mitchell. He never would be able to put out of his mind the picture of Mitchell's face when the verdict was read. Disappointment, fear, panic. The anguished look never could be erased from his memory.

Roush got up from his desk and walked to the window. Although modest in decor, his office was located on the tenth floor of a building situated on the bayfront. Overlooking the bay, Roush took in the scenic beauty of the water and the bright sunlight of a cloudless sky. He longed to be free of work and decided to take an afternoon to enjoy an excursion on his newly acquired thirty-foot sailboat. Maybe an afternoon away from the office would help put him back into a work mode, clear his mind.

Telling Joanie of his plans, Roush went directly home, changed clothes and drove to the marina where his sleek blue and white boat was moored. The boat rocked lazily in the light movement of the water caused by the wakes of other departing and arriving boats. He untied the mooring lines and cranked the little engine that propelled the boat out into the channel. Once out of the marina traffic, he set the sails and headed for the open waters of the bay.

After sailing to the middle of the bay, he lowered the mainsail, leaving only the jib in place, and lay on his air mattress atop the stateroom at the bow. There he lay after saturating himself in suntan lotion, soaking up the sunshine, and trying to get work out of his mind for a while.

After a lengthy nap, Roush awoke feeling tinges of pain, and, knowing that he might be getting more sun than he needed, he set the mainsail and went below decks. The boat moved along slowly in the moderate breeze. At that moment, life was good, and all was well.

In spite of a relaxing afternoon of sailing, Roush was still haunted by Mitchell and his situation. Questions surfaced: Had the coroner looked for fingerprints on the body? How carefully had the car been dusted for prints of others? Could someone other than Jeff Mitchell have been in the car and left evidence not readily discernable? How experienced were the crime scene investigators? What minute evidence might they have overlooked? Where were the knife and the gun? And most important, whose DNA was it that was found on the sweater? Whatever it took to prove Jeff's innocence, Roush was determined to succeed.

The afternoon sun was fast lowering in the west, so, checking the sails once again, Roush headed back to shore. Just before dark, he lowered both the mainsail and the jib, cranked the little engine, and guided the sailboat back to its permanent moorings at the marina. Still perplexed, he tried to raise questions in his own mind about possible overlooked evidence, others with a motive to kill Lillian, and most mystifying of all, why Lillian, who seemed not to have an enemy in the world, could have met with such a tragic end? He soon hoped to have the answers to these questions.

*   *   *   *   *   *

The first full day of Mitchell's incarceration on death row dawned with heavy clouds to the west, moving rapidly toward the prison. The clouds were dark and low, dense with rain, and the source of numerous lightning bolts. What a day to be in a place like this.

Hearing the rattle of the breakfast cart as it emerged into the hallway between the cells and the wall, Mitchell arose from his bed, illuminated the lamp on his desk, and dressed. Anticipating a tasty southern morning meal, what passed for breakfast this day were two bagels with cream cheese and grape jelly and a cup of strong, black coffee. While the food tasted okay, it didn't satisfy his appetite. He now realized that, for some time to come, his hearty appetite would not be satisfied.

Early afternoon, a guard strolled leisurely down the walkway toward Mitchell's cell. "Your family is here to visit. They said they want to see you before they leave to go back home."

"Yeah. I want to see them. Let's go."

Without handcuffing Mitchell, the guard led him to the visitors' area that was near the death row cell concourses. Walking into the visiting room, Mitchell was faced with a frustrating situation. His mom, dad, sister Andrea, and brother Jaimie had driven from Escambia County to visit with him before returning to Minneapolis. Yet because of the way the communication system was set up, he could talk with only one person at a time.

"Hi, Mom," he greeted his mother sadly.

"Hi, Son. Are they treating you well?" It was the only thing she could think of to say. It seemed so lame a greeting.

"All right, I guess."

"You know we are behind you one hundred percent, don't you?" His mother's voice was weak from strain but sympathetic. "All of us know you had nothing to do with this."

"That's important to me," Mitchell replied.

Taking the phone from his wife, William Mitchell told his son, "We are going to do everything we can—everything it takes—to prove your innocence. If we have to mortgage the house, we will do so, Son. Just don't give up."

"Thanks, Dad," Jeff said. "Just work with Fred and Blayne. They are convinced of my innocence, and I'm sure they will work hard to prove it."

Dad handed the phone to Jaimie, who greeted his brother, "Jeff, it's great to see you and talk with you. You know we all love you."

These words caused a choking feeling in Mitchell's throat. He could hardly hold back the tears. Finally a river of emotion streamed down his face as he all but shouted into the phone, "I love all of you. Maybe one day justice will be served, and I'll be out of here. I want the chance to put my arms around you one more time. Just don't forget me."

"Never," came a unison reply from Mitchell's family.

For the first time in many months, Fred Roush felt truly refreshed. Arriving at the office, he started the coffee pot. He retrieved his notepad that contained notes on the appeal and dictated instructions for Joanie to prepare the record that would be forwarded to the trial court along with the official notice of appeal. The record included the trial transcript, the orders from the trial judge, and other miscellaneous paperwork that comprised the completed trial record. As he was dictating into the machine, Joanie entered his office.

"Morning, Fred," she said cheerily.

"Good morning, Joanie. Today's gonna be a busy day, so why don't you put your things away and come on in and let me give these instructions to you personally rather than on tape?"

"Okay. Just a minute. I'll be right in."

After a couple of minutes, Joanie entered his office once more holding Fred's special coffee cup, a black *Phantom of the Opera* mug with a picture of the Phantom's mask which revealed itself when the mug was hot. "I guess I'm ready when you are."

Starting again, Roush instructed her as to the exact way to collate the materials. He also dictated the information required to complete the appeal paperwork. "Get the whole package back to me no later than tomorrow afternoon," he said, "so that I can forward it to the Clerk of Court. It's her responsibility to get it to the State Supreme Court for review. I don't want too much time to elapse before this appeal is reviewed. Do you think you can get it together that fast?"

"I'll try. If not, I'll tell you."

*   *   *   *   *   *

The second full day of Mitchell's stay on death row was a mixture of boredom, exercise, reading, and meals. To relieve his boredom and stimulate his mind, Mitchell requested several books from the prison library. By mid-morning the books had been delivered to his cell.

After lunch, Mitchell settled in to read John Grisham's *The Appeal*. For more than an hour he read until his eyes became heavy, and he fell into a deep sleep.

Startled by noise at the far end of the corridor, he awoke, looked at the clock, and noticed that it was time for exercise. Each prisoner on death row was allowed one hour each day to enter the prison's enclosed yard for a time of exercise. But each prisoner exercised alone.

Not much in the mood for exercise, Mitchell requested to be taken back to his cell after only fifteen minutes in the yard.

After supper he settled in for a night of television viewing. A couple of his favorite programs were scheduled, and he hoped they would take his mind off his problems.

*   *   *   *   *   *

By noon, Joanie had the record ready and the mandatory appeals paperwork prepared to be taken to the Clerk of Court. After noon, Roush returned to the office from an early lunch, to be greeted by his secretary, "The package is ready. The box containing the record is on top of your desk and the appeals paperwork is in a file folder beside it."

"Fantastic. You did that so quickly. You know, Joanie, I'm glad to have you on my team."

"Thanks," she said. "Just win the appeal and get a new trial. It would make all the effort worthwhile."

Roush went to his office, reviewed the contents of the box and carefully read the paperwork. It all seemed in order. He then gathered the box and the file and walked out of his office toward the courthouse.

Arriving at the office of the Clerk of Court, Roush informed the receptionist that he had brought the material for Mitchell's automatic appeal to the Clerk. "Could you wait a few minutes?" she asked Roush. "The Clerk is taking a late lunch, but I know she would wish to receive these in person."

"Sure, I'll wait. I don't mind."

After another twenty minutes or so, Clerk of Court Manley entered the office and saw Fred Roush seated in the waiting room. Mrs. Manley walked toward Roush, her right hand extended. They shook hands and greeted each other like old friends.

"Mrs. Manley," Roush addressed the Clerk formally. "I have brought the Notice of Appeals on the Mitchell case. Would you prepare the appropriate record of appeal and forward everything to the State Supreme Court? I would also like to be notified when the appeal has been officially filed."

"I'll be glad to, Fred," Mrs. Manley said. "And good luck to you."

After shaking hands once more, the two parted.

*   *   *   *   *   *

Death row Guard Max Hickman came to Mitchell's cell to inform him that he had a visitor. "I must be popular," Mitchell retorted comically. "First, my family, now this. At this rate, as the old song says, 'I'll never walk alone'."

"If you don't want to meet with this guy, just let me know," said Hickman. "I can tell him that you are not accepting visitors."

"Who is he?" asked Mitchell.

"Says his name is Bradley, Mark Bradley," Hickman replied.

"Oh, okay. If it's Mark, I'll see him." Again, without placing handcuffs on Mitchell, Hickman led him to the visitors' gallery area. As he entered the gallery and saw his friend, Mitchell broke into a smile. It was the first time he had smiled for a long time.

Lifting the phone, Mitchell was the first to speak, "Hey, Mark. It's great to see you. After just two days, life is already pretty boring in here. It's good to see a familiar face. Mom and Dad came by yesterday before they took the long drive back to Minnesota. I'm really glad you came."

Hesitantly Bradley said, "I didn't like meeting you in the county jail, and I enjoy seeing you in here even less."

"And I don't like being here, especially with what I'm facing," Mitchell replied.

"I'll try to come by to see you as often as I can. It's a long trip over here, but I know you look forward to seeing someone you know. You can count on me to help Fred and Blayne clear your name. If it helps, we'll take some fantasy scuba and hiking trips. Maybe if you can keep your mind off the problems and on more positive things, life will be a little more tolerable. At least until we can spring you from this place."

"Thanks, Mark. You're a real friend," Mitchell said. For another fifteen minutes, Mitchell and Bradley reminisced about some of the good old days during high school and college. Some of the boyish pranks in which they participated seemed rather silly.

Mitchell recalled the time when he and several of his friends captured Bradley from his college dormitory room and took him on a special ride. Blindfolded and clothed only in his boxer shorts, Bradley lay on the back seat of the two-door coupe while he was driven around town. At intervals of about ten minutes, the car would stop, and Mitchell would ask him if wanted to get out. Since it was mid-January with temperatures hovering in the mid-twenties, he would answer, "No."

Finally, Mitchell declared that he would ride no more, took off the blindfold, pulled Bradley unceremoniously out of the car, and sped off. Bradley found his way back to campus in his underwear, wrapped only in an army blanket his friends had left him to keep warm. While crossing the campus, he was stopped by the campus police, questioned, and escorted in a most undignified manner to his dormitory room. As he climbed the stairs to his floor, he could hear the snickers of his fellow students who had pulled off this prank without remorse.

Bradley laughed as Mitchell reminded him of the escapade. But the laughter quickly subsided. Both returned to reality.

After a few minutes of final pleasantries, Bradley said, "Jeff, we are all thinking about you and trying to help in any way we can. Just be confident that all will end well."

CHAPTER 29
EIGHT MONTHS LATER

The months had been exhausting for Fred Roush. While he had continued successfully to practice civil law, his mind periodically turned to the Mitchell case. What was happening to the appeal? Had all the paperwork and the record been in order? Had the Supreme Court actually reviewed the case at all by now? He knew the wheels of justice grind slowly, after all. How long could it possibly take for the Florida Supreme Court to review the appeal and hand down its decision? Since he had never tried a criminal case, especially a capital case, these questions dogged his every thought. One redeeming experience for Roush, in the more than twelve months since Jeff Mitchell's incarceration on death row, was, however, meeting and getting acquainted with Robyn Weeks. Robyn approached the third anniversary of her employment with the FDLE. She was considered gifted with scientific details, and her analytical skills were well above average. She continually updated her knowledge of DNA sampling and analysis through continuing education courses at the criminology department at FSU and by reading all current materials available on the subject.

Fred and Robyn met one evening while each strolled separately at the beach. Slim, tanned, and stunningly gorgeous, she attracted his eye immediately. While somewhat timid and shy with the ladies, Fred stepped out of character, timidly walked toward this goddess, and timorously introduced himself.

"Hi. I'm Fred Roush. You may not remember me, but I certainly do remember you," he said, rather bashfully, initiating the conversation.

"Really? How?" Robyn asked.

"I defended Jeff Mitchell in that murder case last year. You were a witness for the prosecution, right?"

"Yes. I remember you, now. You're right. I was a witness for the prosecution. Didn't your client get convicted?"

"Yeah, he was convicted. And now he's on death row."

"Too bad."

"Why are you out here?" Roush asked, trying not to sound too inquisitive.

"I'm out here probably like you enjoying the night sky and hearing the waves lap on the shore. I wish I had a tape recording of it. It probably would help me go to sleep at night," Roush continued.

"I have a CD that plays these kinds of white noise sounds, but nothing beats the real thing," Robyn said.

Together, they sat on the sand under the glare of the security lights and just talked. Finally, after working up the courage to do so, Fred asked, "I know it's short notice but are you possibly free for dinner tomorrow night?" Even before he asked, he wondered if she were already attached or if he were being too forward.

"Dinner? I'm not sure I know you well enough," she responded curtly. "You don't expect someone to accept a date so quickly, do you?"

"I guess not. It was rather forward of me, wasn't it? Nevertheless, I'd like to get to know you better, and dinner just seemed like a good way to do it. You're not already seeing someone, are you?" Roush had about decided that his move was too hasty and much too aggressive. Toning down, he added, "Don't mind saying 'no' if you feel uncomfortable. I really am a pussycat and rather shy, so I really do understand if you don't wish to go."

"No. I'm not attached, and you seem like a nice person. Sure, I'll have dinner with you tomorrow night as long as it is somewhere public, and I can meet you there." Roush realized this was one smart girl. She wouldn't take chances being private with someone she didn't know well. He appreciated that.

"Great. Meet me at the Angus. Is 7:00 okay for you?"

"That's a little later than I usually eat, but I guess it'll be all right. See you then."

"Yeah. I'm looking forward to it," Roush said as he departed, whistling into the brisk southerly breeze that swept in from the Gulf of Mexico.

*   *   *   *   *   *

At 7:00 sharp, Fred Roush was standing under the portico of the Angus. Although darkness would not fall for yet another hour or so, the sky was heavy with dark cumulus clouds, and the smell of ozone was evident all around, indicating the onset of rain. Roush patiently waited, thinking, *Most women don't always make it a point to be on time.*

By 7:30 Roush became worried. In spite of having met Robyn only the day before, he was concerned that something might have happened to her. He could not help remembering a carjacking that had occurred only two weeks prior when a woman was shot while refusing to give up her car. He wanted to call Robyn at home to check on her, but in his excitement yesterday, he had gotten neither her address nor her phone number. He continued to wait.

*   *   *   *   *   *

At 8:15 Robyn drove into the parking lot of the restaurant. Half expecting Roush to have given up on meeting her, she drove near the portico where he stood waiting, worry lines etched in his face. By the time she had parked her car, Fred was there to help her out.

"Robyn, are you all right? Has something happened?" asked Roush, somewhat concerned about her late arrival.

"Yeah. Car trouble. I couldn't get it started, so I called my neighbor who is a mechanic. He found the trouble pretty quickly, and here I am," said Robyn, a coquettish grin slowly spreading across her face.

"Are you hungry?"

"Actually. I'm starving."

"It's not too late for dinner?"

243

"Heavens no! Let's go get some of those crab claws they're so famous for."

"Sounds delicious. After you." They entered the restaurant and spent the remainder of the evening enjoying a spectacular meal of seafood with the trimmings and getting acquainted with each other.

CHAPTER 30
ONE MONTH LATER

The mandatory appeal filed by Fred Roush on behalf of Jeff Mitchell had been in the hands of the Florida Supreme Court for more than a year. Not a word had been received.

Although Roush and Simmons had successfully procured more and more civil and criminal cases, they tended to be small ones with only modest payoffs. In several instances in which the civil cases involved a pre-determined legal fee rather than a contingency fee, many of the clients had not yet fulfilled their financial obligations to their lawyers, a circumstance not uncommon in the profession.

The accompanying costs of maintaining the law practice continued to creep higher and higher. As a means of increasing potential income, Roush took a courageous step and added yet another lawyer to his now-growing firm. This young man, Edward Cameron, specialized in personal injury cases. He could be invaluable to the financial future of the firm because his successful track record of civil litigation was rapidly becoming legendary throughout the First Judicial Circuit. That record could be put to work on behalf of the firm now recognized as Roush & Simmons.

During the past several months, Blayne Simmons had been made a full partner with Roush in the firm, and he was taking on more and more criminal cases. He also had been assigned to be a court-appointed counsel in several other criminal cases.

It was very early in the day. Roush had been unable to sleep during the night, and, rather than waste the time, he left home and went to the office before daybreak to get a little work done. As the day dawned, Roush peered out of the window, watching the bay's choppy whitecaps form and dissipate repeatedly. The morning was cloudy with the sea fog quickly dissipating. Joanie had advised Roush the day before that numerous bills remained unpaid and asked how to handle them. Early morning, when his mind was clear and fresh, would be the best time to ponder solutions to these problems.

Looking at the growing stack of unpaid invoices, he sensed the building of the financial pressures. Some release would come; in what form, he would not speculate. The continual concern over meeting financial obligations caused worry lines to creep across his brow, and now a tinge of gray hair was making its appearance from beneath the hereditary dark black mane that he neatly brushed into place each morning. With no one special in his life, both successes and problems left him feeling incredibly lonely.

Not really in the mood to look at bills, he sat down at his desk to read; but before he could complete the first page, his mind and body succumbed to the somnolence that slowly overtook him, and he fell fast asleep.

The silence and contentment of sleep were abruptly interrupted by the entrance of Joanie, who had already been to the post office to collect the day's mail before arriving at the office. "You want the bad news or the good news first?" she asked, loudly and excitedly, barging into his office, not realizing that Roush was sound asleep.

Driving the mist of drowsiness from his head, he attempted to grasp the moment. *Where am I?* Finally, wresting himself from his languid condition, he looked up through squinting eyes and recognized Joanie.

"What?" he asked, still sweeping the cobwebs from his consciousness.

"I just asked whether you want the good news or the bad news first," she repeated.

"First give me a second to wake up."

"How long have you been here?" Joanie asked.

"Since about 4:00 a. m. I couldn't sleep at home, so I came in to get some work done. It appears that I didn't get very far, though."

With eyes now somewhat wider open, Roush asked again. "What was it that you wanted, Joanie?"

"I've been to the post office, and I have good news and bad news. I just wondered which you wanted to hear first."

"I'm not really in the mood to play games, Joanie. Just tell me the bad news, and let's get on with it." Roush was still tired, and he needed more sleep.

Feeling like a scolded puppy, Joanie said, "I was just trying to lift your day. I've been to the post office, and several envelopes containing client payments were included. It looks like all of the back bills are covered. I think there is also enough to cover the expenses for the next two months or so."

"That is great news." Roush said, now wide awake, with a smile on his face reflecting a rising mood. "So what's the bad news?"

"The other is a registered package from the Florida Supreme Court. I didn't open it, but I assume it's probably not good news since it's being received by registered mail."

"You're probably right. Let me have it."

Reaching into the stack of mail, Joanie retrieved the package with the green registration edges still attached. The gold seal in the top left corner announced the sender as the Florida Supreme Court.

Roush pulled from the package a thick sheaf of heavy bond paper. The top of the first page indicated that the document outlined the appellate decision of the Florida Supreme Court. It began: "In the case of Jeffrey Mitchell vs. The State of Florida, the judgment and sentence of the Court is affirmed and the request for a Writ of Certiorari is denied." The remaining pages of this lengthy document discussed, in detail, the aggravating and mitigating circumstances surrounding the case and the basis for the Court's decision. The case would now be placed in the hands of the Capital Collateral Representatives, the group that represents death row inmates after the first appeal has been denied.

Roush sank slowly into his chair. He had been so optimistic that the Court would grant a new trial. That optimism now evaporated in the moment. He turned his chair toward the window and felt more discouraged than at any other time in his career. The cheeks of the square-jawed chin, which so handsomely characterized his face, tensed with emotion. Sensing that he wished to be alone, Joanie left the office, quietly closing the door behind her.

*　　*　　*　　*　　*　　*

Blake Evans sat in the sixth floor offices of the Capital Collateral Representatives pondering an appeal in a savage murder case that had dragged on for fifteen years. Even though the Supreme Court Committee on Postconviction Relief in Capital Cases had now limited the number of appeals and abbreviated the time for those appeals, he, for one, was in favor of it. While he remained an opponent of the death penalty, he acknowledged, albeit silently, that the process was entirely too protracted.

Watching summertime tourists roaming the park across from the capital building, Evans's thoughts were interrupted by the rapping on his office door.

"Come on in," he said.

Entering the office was the short, stocky figure of Gregg Ellis, the head of the office of Capital Collateral Representatives. Assigning cases was among his responsibilities. Today, another case had been assigned to the CCR group.

"I've got another case for you," Ellis informed Evans.

"I'm already working six cases. Can't you give it to somebody else?" Evans asked, somewhat exasperated.

"No, I can't! You have a moderate caseload compared with the other attorneys, and you are next in the rotation. Here's the file. Read over it, and when you're ready, let's discuss an appeal strategy."

"Okay. But just for the record, I'm not happy. I'm working day and night now, and I don't think I can take on much more."

248

"Your objection is noted. I'll try to remember that when the next batch of cases is received."

Staring at the thick case file, Evans was not prepared to look at it today. Maybe tomorrow.

Gregg Ellis returned to his office aware of the heavy burden of responsibility that lay on his shoulders. With more than 350 prisoners on death row, many of whose appeals were being handled by his Capital Collateral Representatives, the job seemed almost impossible to accomplish successfully. All he and his staff could do was try.

As he entered his office, he heard his phone ringing. "Yeah!"

"Gregg," said Della, his secretary. "A Fred Roush is on the phone for you."

"Who is he?" Ellis asked. He did not want to be bothered at the moment, especially by somebody he did not even know.

"He's Jeff Mitchell's trial attorney of record. He has been notified of the Supreme Court decision and wants to talk with you," Della answered.

"Okay. Put him through." Ellis waited a moment; then he heard the familiar click as the call rang onto his line.

"This is Gregg Ellis," he said curtly.

"Mr. Ellis, I'm Fred Roush. I represented Jeff Mitchell in a case that, I understand from today's correspondence, has been shared with your office for aid."

"Yes, Mr. Roush, I recognize your name from a file I gave to one of my attorneys a short while ago. Please give me a moment to locate the log on my secretary's desk."

Ellis walked to Della's desk and retrieved the log. He wanted to have it in front of him while he spoke with Roush. The log contained all the cases received by the CCR and the day and time they were received. It also indicated to whom he had assigned the case and any ancillary attorneys in the CCR who might have been assigned. Fingering down the log he located the Mitchell case that he had just given to Blake Evans.

"Mr. Roush, I know the case to which you refer," he said. "That case was received in our office yesterday from the Supreme Court and just this afternoon was assigned to Blake Evans here in our office. No secondary attorneys have been assigned and will not be unless and until Mr. Evans requests them."

"Would it be possible to talk with Mr. Evans?" Roush asked.

"I'm sure he'd be happy to speak with you. Just a moment." Ellis rang Evans's office on the intercom. The sound of the intercom startled Evans. Ellis advised him of the identity of the caller and announced that he was on the phone and wished to speak with him.

"I haven't even opened the file yet, Gregg. How can I knowledgeably discuss with him a case I know nothing about? Could you delay him for a few days at least to give me time to review the file?" Evans asked.

"Let me see what I can do."

"Mr. Roush," Ellis said. "Blake Evans has just received the file this afternoon and has not yet had time to review it. Could you wait a few days, maybe toward the end of the week, and call him? He said he would be pleased to speak with you at that time."

"Sure. I'll call him on Friday."

*   *   *   *   *   *

It had been one month since his evening out with Robyn Weeks. While the enjoyable and alluring memories of that evening frequently captured his mind, he never seemed to have enough time to call her and make another date. Determined to drop everything if necessary, he looked up her phone number at the FDLE and dialed.

"Robyn, this is Fred Roush," he said.

"Hi, Fred. What's up? Long time no see," she replied.

"First, I want to apologize for not calling you for so long. The burden of the work has been heavy, and we added another lawyer to the group. That, along with the case for Jeff Mitchell, have kept me chasing the fees."

"Don't apologize. I assumed you would call when you got a chance. By the way, I really did have a great time getting to know you."

"So did I. That's why I decided to call in spite of my schedule. I just wanted to know if you might like to spend Saturday at the beach, seeing as how we both like it so much."

"Sure. I don't have any plans. I'd like that."

"I'll bring the food and pick you up about 11:00 for a picnic on the beach. Does that work for you?"

"Sounds great. See you then," Robyn said.

*   *   *   *   *   *

Time stood still. Friday had seemed as far away as eternity to Fred Roush. By 10:00 that morning, he decided to make his call to Blake Evans at CCR.

When Evans came on the line, Roush informed him of the great length to which he and Blayne Simmons had gone to represent Mitchell. They had defended him the best way they knew how, given the evidence against him and the lack of preparation time. However, there was one possible grounds for appeal. . . ineffective legal representation.

Wishing to set Evans's mind at ease, Roush initiated the conversation. "Understanding that Simmons was the only one with criminal trial experience and that he was brought into the case rather late, I would expect, even encourage you, to appeal it on the basis of ineffective legal representation. That would at least buy some time."

For a moment, silence lingered. Finally, Evans replied, "That seems like a slap in the face. You sure you wouldn't feel humiliated or embarrassed for us to proceed on that basis?"

"I'm more concerned about my client than I am my feelings. Our legal successes speak for themselves. This one case won't make or break our future. Feel free to use that basis for an appeal if you wish," said Roush. "We will support it."

251

"First, let me ask you if you ever employed an investigator to check behind the police?" Evans asked.

"Actually, we didn't. We did not have the time, financial resources, or reason to disbelieve the police investigation," said Roush.

"Before we go with ineffective counsel, I would like to attach an investigator to this case and find out what we might dig up," said Evans. "It's not unusual for police to overlook valuable clues and evidence. Sometimes investigators inadvertently discover some new twist in the evidence presented."

"Do you have a list of investigators that CCR uses regularly?" asked Roush.

"We do, but we are always open to new investigators if you know of someone," Evans offered. "Do you have somebody in mind that would do it?" Evans asked.

"I don't personally, but my partner, who specializes in criminal cases, might know someone. Could we have a few days to check and get back to you?" Roush asked.

"Sure, there's really no hurry except if your client is innocent, we don't want him there on The Row any longer than he has to be," Evans said.

"How are investigators paid?" Roush asked.

"They are paid a monthly retainer plus expenses."

"Thanks, we'll get back to you in a few days."

*   *   *   *   *   *

Saturday turned out to be one of the most beautiful days of the summer. The July sun rose in a cloudless sky. The heat increased rapidly, but uncommon to the West Florida climate, the humidity was quite low. It would be a good day for a suntan.

True to his word, Fred arrived at Robyn's apartment promptly. He had prepared a cooler of ham and cheese sandwiches, fresh vegetables, and homemade coconut crisp cookies. An assortment of soft drinks was iced down in another cooler.

252

Roush approached her apartment and, before knocking, saw Robyn standing in the open doorway. He could not believe his eyes. She looked sensational. In a lime green tank top and white shorts, she was the perfect Florida beauty. Gathering her beach equipment, they walked to his car, put the beach bag in the trunk, and drove across the three-mile bridge to the beach.

Once on the sugar-white sands of the beach, Robyn shed her tank top and shorts, revealing a well-toned, beautifully maintained, and tanned body. Her small waistline, accenting her full breasts and nicely proportioned hips, made him the envy of every guy on the beach who laid eyes on her. Her stunning beauty was all the more enhanced by her dark hair and the dark brown eyes that squinted in the bright sunlight. She quickly put on her sunglasses to reduce the glare.

"Great day for the beach, don't you think?" she said.

"Yeah. I've been looking forward to this for some time. I've been so busy with my practice that I haven't been to the beach as much as I'd like," Roush replied.

As she turned her back to him, she asked, "Would you help me with the lotion?"

"Sure." Carefully he applied the suntan lotion to her back. He noticed a small scar on her right shoulder.

"How did you get this scar?" Roush asked, thinking perhaps it was the result of a childhood accident.

"I'd rather not talk about it," she answered. He quickly dropped the matter.

To the touch, her skin was soft and, as he added more lotion, he thought of how it felt to touch her smooth, supple body.

"There, finished," he said.

"Would you like me to help you?" she asked.

"Yeah. That would be nice." Roush went off into a dream world. *This is great!* he thought.

Tenderly, she applied the lotion, rubbing it into his skin. After she finished, they sat on a large blue blanket that Roush always took to the beach. Facing the ocean, they listened to the waves slapping the seashore. They heard the voices of beachcombers strolling along the water's edge and the sound of blaring radios in every direction.

After an hour in the sun, Roush sat up and retreated to the emerald waters of the Gulf of Mexico. As he dipped his toes in to check the temperature, he recalled how often he enjoyed coming to the beach and the warmth of its summer waters. It was paradise, indeed! The tourists enjoyed the mid-summer days, frolicking and sunbathing, often returning home red and sunburned. The locals, like Fred and Robyn, had staked their own personal claims to a piece of this most beautiful of God's creations, and they often viewed the tourists solely as a source of revenue.

By the time he was waist-deep in the water, Fred felt someone come up behind him and push him hard, sending him completely under a crashing wave. Surfacing, he found Robyn laughing childishly. "Gotcha, didn't I?" she said.

"Yeah, but you just wait. Your time is coming." Roush marveled at her adolescent folly. Her laughter was infectious.

For more than an hour, they enjoyed the warmth of the water, splashing around, ducking beneath the waves, looking at the fish, and generally enjoying each other's company. Standing five feet away from Robyn, Roush stared at her beauty. Her wet hair was swept back revealing her fine features, as clear as crystal. He slowly walked through the chest deep water toward her, took her in his arms, and passionately kissed her.

Although she was startled by such a display of passion, she smiled; she enjoyed the kiss.

"I'm sorry. I didn't mean to take advantage of you," Roush said.

"You didn't. In fact I kind of liked it," she replied. Then she reciprocated, taking him in her arms and kissing him, this time with their mouths open wide. After holding each other tightly for a few moments, they strolled back to the blanket together, hand in hand.

*   *   *   *   *   *

When Joanie arrived at the office on Monday morning, she found a large envelope attached to the door with masking tape. Ripping the plain brown envelope from the glass window on the door, she walked to her desk, retrieved a letter opener, and cut open the top of the envelope. She pulled out the contents only to discover a sheet of white paper with cutout letters pasted to read:

LEAVE THE MITCHELL CASE ALONE. IT IS NONE OF YOUR BUSINESS. YOUR LIFE WILL DEPEND ON IT.

Dropping the envelope on the desk, she decided not to handle it anymore. Moments later, Fred Roush arrived at the office and immediately noted the look of fear in her eyes.

"What's the matter, Joanie?" Roush asked.

"Look at this, but don't pick it up, and you'll see."

As the letter lay on the desk, Roush turned it with the eraser of a pencil so he could read its contents more easily. Immediately he walked to his desk and called Tony Boudreaux at the Sheriff's Department. Boudreaux agreed to come to the office without delay.

While it seemed a matter of hours, Boudreaux actually arrived within fifteen minutes of Roush's call. "Whatchu got?" Boudreaux asked.

"Something I think you will be interested in seeing," Roush said, pointing to the letter that remained untouched as Roush had read it earlier.

"Why would somebody not want you messin' in this Mitchell murder any more? The murderer is behind bars and waitin' to die," Boudreaux said.

"I've said all along that Mitchell is not the murderer. This note should prove that now. And it won't deter me. I don't scare that easily. I've been bullied before, and this note will not make me change my mind."

255

Carefully, Boudreaux picked up the piece of paper with a tissue and placed it in the envelope out of which it had been extracted. "We'll go over the letter and the envelope for fingerprints, but I doubt there're gonna be any. Since it's pasted together with cutout magazine letters, it'll be just about impossible to trace, but we'll do what we can and get back to you. In the meantime, watch your back."

CHAPTER 31

Fred Roush strolled casually into Simmons's office right after lunch. "Blayne, have you used a private investigator before on any cases you worked," Roush asked.

"Why do you ask?" Simmons inquired.

"I called the CCR last week, and Blake Evans, the attorney assigned Mitchell's case recommended that a PI be brought in."

"That's probably a good idea. We can use all the help we can get. I've got an old friend in Orlando, a rock solid investigator who has successfully investigated numerous cases for me. I might can talk him into doing the job," Simmons said.

"Give him a call and see if he is available."

Blayne Simmons opened his desk drawer to search for information on his PI friend, Bruce Hopper, in Orlando. It had been a couple of years since he had made contact, so he was not sure he could find him. Finally, under a pile of note cards in his desk drawer he found an address card on which he had uncharacteristically taped a business card that contained all the information he needed. Picking up the telephone, he dialed the number shown on card. One ring. Two rings. Then the familiar, pleasant voice of Raquel could be heard.

"Good morning, Delta Investigations." That same sexy voice he remembered still remained. The Spanish accent, once so distinct, was clearly beginning to melt away.

"Hi, Raquel, this is Blayne Simmons."

"Hey, Mr. Simmons, what's new with you?" she asked.

"Nothing I think your boss couldn't help solve. Is he there?"

"Just a minute. It's good to talk with you again." The phone clicked as she put Simmons on hold. For two long minutes he waited patiently listening to the soothing music of Mannheim Steamroller drone in the background. Suddenly silence. The circuit had been broken.

Quickly he hit the redial button on his phone set.

"Good morning, Delta Investigations," Raquel answered.

"Raquel, this is Blayne again. I lost you," Simmons explained.

"Sorry about that. I'll get Bruce for you." The elevator music resumed. This time it was an oldie, a tune Simmons knew, "Fly Me to the Moon." He hummed along.

"Well, what a surprise," Hopper began. "How in the world are you, Blayne?"

"Well. Doing well. Hit the ground running pretty hard here though. And I need some help I think you can provide."

"What's that?" Hopper asked, clearly curious.

Simmons explained how his client had been convicted of murder and that he was now sitting on death row.

"Have you considered the fact that he might actually be guilty?" Hopper asked.

"Yeah. We've weighed it, talked about it, reviewed the evidence, checked his alibi, and we remain convinced that he's innocent. Call it a gut feeling—something far afield from the way lawyers typically feel about cases—but we are convinced."

"What's the deal? How can I help?"

"As you would expect, we are appealing the case. We are working with the CCR and the attorney handling our case has suggested that we engage an investigator for some exhaustive investigative work," Simmons said.

"And you want me to do it."

"Yeah, Bruce, we do. I just think you happen to be the best, and I'm sure that if there's something out there to help us prove his innocence, you can find it."

"Thanks for the vote of confidence, but let's talk money," Hopper insisted.

"Sure." Simmons started. "We are working with the CCR in Tallahassee, and they can put you on a monthly retainer plus expenses. It might also be a chance for your firm to get on the list for work later with the state."

Only the sound of a light hum on the phone indicated that Hopper was still there.

"Bruce! Are you there?"

"Yep. Do you know what you're asking?"

"I think I do. We are asking you to work for a set fee that may be less than what you are accustomed to receiving, but this case is incredibly important to us. If it were not so important to us and our client, I wouldn't ask you to do it. It's a life or death matter, you know."

"I guess I can help," Hopper retorted. "But I will have to work it in as I can."

"I expected as much, and I'm willing to accept that condition. I'll advise Blake Evans at the CCR that you will work with us."

"How soon could you come up here and get started? Need I remind you that this is a death case and we shouldn't waste time?"

"Before I can answer that question, I'll have to check my schedule. I have several important cases right now, so it'll have to wait at least a little while. I'll call you later today and give you an idea when I can come, if you still want me to do so."

"Don't worry about accommodations when you come. CCR will take care of that for you," Simmons promised.

"Good, I'll call you later today to let you know when I can actually come."

* * * * * *

In the afternoon, the buzzer sounded in Simmons's office.

"Yes, Joanie, who is it?" Simmons asked.

"Your friend, Hopper. He said it was important."

"Put him through, Joanie," Simmons said. "It *is* very important."

After a moment, Hopper came on the line. "I've checked my schedule. I told you that several important, active cases are consuming my time. With the current demands and their follow up, I cannot come to work with you for at least three months."

"That's not the best news I've heard all day," Simmons exclaimed. "But I really believe that you are the one to help us. I'm willing to wait. Stay in touch just in case you might slip away for a few days before that time."

"I'll keep in touch monthly," said Hopper, "and bring you up-to-date."

"Okay, but in the meantime, Fred and I will prepare the necessary information on the case and send it to you. That way you can pick up with the investigative work immediately when you arrive," Simmons promised.

Without so much as knocking, Blayne Simmons barged into Roush's office to tell him the news.

"My friend in Orlando, Bruce Hopper, has agreed to help us with the case," Simmons announced.

"Good. That's the first and probably the best step toward getting this case resolved," Roush said. "I hope so anyway."

"The problem is he can't come immediately. His caseload is quite heavy right now, and he will not finish those cases for another three months. I told him we would wait."

"You did impress on him the significance of this case?" Roush asked.

"Yes, I did. But there apparently is no way he can change his schedule for the next three months. I guess we must accept that or try to get somebody else," Simmons said. "He would drop everything if he could, Fred. I trust him that much."

"You say he's the best, so it might be best that we wait. Delays in a case of this magnitude are not good. I only hope, with this one, we can do everything before the appeals run out and before the governor can get an execution order signed," Simmons said. "After all, with the shortened timeframes for appeals now in effect, this thing could get away from us if we don't follow it closely. If not, all is lost."

CHAPTER 32
FOUR MONTHS LATER

Mark Bradley arrived at his office a little later than usual and only five minutes before he was scheduled to meet with his boss, Lawrence Goodall. Only the day before Bradley had received a personal and confidential memorandum about the meeting. He had no idea what the meeting was about or whether anyone else was involved.

At 9:00 sharp, he tapped on Goodall's door.

"Come in, Mark," came the reply from inside.

Bradley walked into a resplendent office, decorated by Martha Magee, a renowned, local interior decorator, whose genius included the Tudor Westwick home in Greenwich, Connecticut, the Vanderbilt home in Tennessee, and the offices of the Durham Tobacco Company in North Carolina. He was almost blinded by the bright sunlight that filtered into the room through the wall of windows across from the door.

"Good morning, Mark," Goodall said, smiling. "Why don't you sit over here," pointing to a chair near a nineteenth-century end table. On the table, stood a small figurine and a twenty-four inch crystal lamp with an ivory-colored brocade shade. Bradley did as he was directed.

"Mark, I brought you in this morning to offer you a promotion. This may come as a surprise, but the business has been doing far better than expected; the advertising business is experiencing a phenomenal surge, and Goodall and Dohr is getting its fair share of the pie. You have performed so well over the last three years that I'm convinced you are the man to head the first of several new divisions we are creating in an organizational adjustment. We hope the changes proposed by our consultant will improve the efficiency of the operation, especially with regard to costs." Goodall hesitated momentarily to let the good news take effect.

Pointing to an organizational flow chart, Goodall continued, "You can see we are creating four divisions over which you will be a vice president who reports directly to me and Mr. Dohr. You are being offered the newly created job of Senior Vice President for Innovation and Strategic Planning. You will receive an increase in pay of fifteen percent with stock options available to you at the end of each year, based upon your performance. How does this sound to you?"

"I'm flattered, of course, Mr. Goodall. But . . ."

"You are hesitating. Are you not interested in the promotion?" Goodall asked, appearing startled at Bradley's response.

"No. No. I guess this has just taken me by surprise. Of course, I'll take the job. Who wouldn't? How soon does the new organization go into effect?" Bradley asked, now hardly holding back his excitement.

"The reorganization will become effective on January 1, but we want to spend what little time we have before January preparing to implement the new organization. Your promotion will be effective the first of next month, and your increase in compensation will commence on January 1. This allows us to initiate the compensation packages at the beginning of a new quarter."

"Sounds good to me. Is an announcement to be made about the reorganization?" Bradley asked. He was anxious to tell somebody, everybody, especially his family.

"We would not want you to tell anyone until an official announcement is released at the end of the month."

"I can't even tell my wife?"

"We would prefer that the information be closely held so that no misunderstanding occurs among the employees."

"All right. I appreciate your vote of confidence. You won't regret this." Bradley exited the office with a smile on his face and optimism about his long-term future with the company.

*   *   *   *   *   *

While a strong opponent of the death penalty, Blake Evans always had trouble getting started on a new case. There always seemed to be an endless river of cases through the offices of the Capital Collateral Representatives.

Although he understood that, under the new rules, he could take up to a year to prepare the 3.850 motions once the Supreme Court denied the automatic appeal, he did not wish to take the full amount of time. After all, these motions were filed primarily but not exclusively for the purpose of appealing on the basis of ineffective assistance of counsel. In his phone conversation with Fred Roush, he remembered that Roush described how he tried to get out of representing Mitchell because of a lack of criminal trial experience. Roush had also mentioned that he brought Blayne Simmons into the firm and onto the case simply to add a measure of criminal trial experience to the team. The time had been short, and Simmons certainly had insufficient time to prepare the case.

Evans spent several days trapped in his office, researching precedents, and preparing the necessary briefs that would accompany the 3.850 motions. Interspersing work on the fourteen other cases for which he was now responsible, the final draft of the briefs and motions in the Mitchell case was finished within three months. He gave the material to his secretary to prepare in final form.

Three days later, Evans's secretary entered his office late in the afternoon to deliver the appeal documents on the Mitchell case. He signed them and authorized her to put them in the Federal Express system for delivery the next morning to Judge Paul Reid.

Although Evans knew that this part of the process could take up to two or three years, he initiated a research project with Jennifer Bryant, one of the three paralegals in the CCR office, to study the potential grounds of filing additional amended 3.850 motions. These motions could be filed at any time during consideration of the current motion by the trial court judge.

Now the waiting game began.

*   *   *   *   *   *

Blayne Simmons sat at his desk, poring over law books in search of case law that would support a motion that he wished to file in a burglary case for which he was preparing. Deep in concentration, he was startled by the buzzer on his intercom.

"Blayne, Bruce Hopper is on the phone for you," Joanie informed him.

"Thanks," he responded.

Pressing the line on the phone, he heard the familiar voice on the other end, "Hey, Blayne, I have some good news. I have finally wrapped up some of the cases that I was involved in here and can now come to help you all if you still need me."

"Absolutely, we still need you," Simmons insisted. "I will contact Blake Evans and have him prepare the necessary contract papers from CCR and fax them to you."

"I will watch for them," Hopper promised.

Simmons then dialed Blake Evans at CCR. After his secretary put him through, Simmons said notified him of Hopper's availability and asked him to send a contract. Evans agreed to fax it in the afternoon.

*   *   *   *   *   *

Bruce Hopper arrived in Pensacola the next day, prepared to do what he could to assist the CCR and Blayne Simmons in their case. After settling into the apartment that the CCR had arranged for him, he called Blake, advising him if his arrival. They made plans to meet with the CCR attorney, Blake Evans, that evening at dinner.

Greeting each other at the entrance, the three attorneys were escorted to a table in the rear dining room of the Angus. Blayne and Bruce enjoyed talking about several fun times they had shared in the past, then explained to Blake how they had met and briefly reminisced about several cases on which they had formerly worked together.

264

Blayne described to Bruce how the Mitchell case had concluded at trial.

"Because of the inexperience of the lead detective, we want to bring you in to investigate on behalf of our client," Blake said. "We can provide you all the evidence given to us by the state both in discovery and at trial. We are hoping that you can review that material and go over it with a fine-toothed comb to see if there is anything that the state might have missed."

"There is one other consideration," said Blayne. "During the investigation, a Coogi sweater was found in the victim's car with blood on it. Embedded in the blood was another DNA profile that could not be identified because there was nothing to compare it with. Do you have an idea how we might learn whose DNA this might be?"

"Nothing comes to mind," said Hopper, "but I'll keep that in mind as I go forward."

CHAPTER 33

Two weeks had gone by since Bruce Hopper had arrived to initiate an investigation on behalf of the CCR. He had collected evidence in several boxes and returned to his home in south Florida to review their contents in a quiet, less pressured environment.

On numerous occasions over the past two weeks, Hopper had reviewed every file in all the boxes scattered across the floor of his living room. He was convinced more than ever that the answer to the Mitchell case lay somewhere either among the people who had appeared to have little obvious motive for killing her or in yet undiscovered evidence. *But what evidence, and where could it be found? I have searched everywhere.*

He had read and reread each file until he had almost memorized every word. He studied the transcript of the trial twice and could easily describe the trial in his sleep. He had compiled an extensive list of potential suspects, including Lillian's roommate, Lillian's ex-boyfriend, Thad Whetstone, even her friend and co-worker Marilyn McGregor. He compiled a list of evidence he wanted to review again, including the car, which he had not yet seen, and the clothing Lillian was wearing when she was killed. He was more determined than ever to conduct this investigation with conscious deliberation, studying every word, every nuance, every conceivable angle.

The next morning, Hopper went outside and retrieved his morning paper. On the first page below the fold he noticed an update article about the Jeff Mitchell case.

"TALLAHASSEE.—On Tuesday, the Florida Supreme Court handed down its ruling on the appeal for a new trial submitted on behalf of Jeff Mitchell by Pensacola attorney Fred Roush. In its ruling, the Court found no legal basis for a new trial and denied the appeal. Mitchell was found guilty and sentenced to death in the murder of Lillian Reins, a Pensacola advertising account executive. Now in the hands of the Capital Collateral Representatives, the office that routinely handles appeals in death sentences, the case is expected to take several more years to run its course through the courts.

Roush said in an interview that he had asked the CCR to hire a private investigator to examine the case thoroughly and to probe any additional possibilities of evidence that might have been overlooked. "No stone will be left unturned," said Roush. "We intend to find evidence that will prove that Jeff Mitchell is not a murderer. We hope, in the process, to discover just who did commit this ruthless crime and will make every effort to bring that person to justice."

*   *   *   *   *   *

Throughout the day, Hopper went carefully through the boxes once more. He thumbed through file after file, hoping that something—anything—would jump off the page and surprise him. As he rifled through the last box of the day, he noticed the frayed corner of a sheet of paper that had apparently lodged itself and become hidden under the lower inside flap of the case. All he could distinguish was that it appeared to be a single sheet of paper. Pulling up the lower tab inside the box, he found several form sheets stapled together. The top of the first page indicated that the forms were an EVIDENCE LIST, a listing of all the evidence gathered at the crime scene. *Why have I not seen this before?* he thought. *Box flap obviously hid it.*

He scanned the first page, reading each line carefully. Every item of evidence had been carefully listed with a detailed description, a case number, an individual identification number, the name of the CSI team member who had found it, the approximate time of discovery and the time it was logged in to the lab at the FDLE. He grabbed a notepad and began to review the list. He noted items that he had studied previously and then wrote special notes about those items from the list about which he knew nothing. The "about which he knew nothing" list generated a

267

feeling of optimism in his heart. He now had several items of evidence to investigate and several ideas to pursue.

Hopper thought, as he looked over his newly compiled lists, *There's a lot of work to be done and time is getting short to do it.* "Damn the torpedoes, full speed ahead."

* * * * * *

One special box had been set aside and labeled "Priority." In this box, he had placed information that he considered to be the most important and from which he would likely reap the greatest benefit. To that case, he added the evidence list with several of the items highlighted in yellow. One item that had especially caught his eye and which he hoped to investigate in detail was the brooch. He wondered, *Why was the brooch never entered into evidence at the trial? Probably because the prosecution could not tie Mitchell to it.*

That evening as he sat in the den of his home waiting for a Braves game to air on television, he reflected on the discoveries of the day. Random thoughts passed through his mind like fleeting light: *Why have I been looking in all the wrong places for leads in this case? I've investigated the obvious people and places, so I must now check out people and places that are not so obvious.*

It's time to go back to the scene of the crime, he mused. *Tomorrow I'll call Fred and Blake and let them know that I am returning to Pensacola to visit the crime scene and begin to assess this case in its totality rather than simply in bits and pieces.*

* * * * * *

Roush & Simmons was fast becoming the premiere law firm of Northwest Florida. Now boasting a stable of twelve lawyers, the firm had won its first major civil case against the G&N Railroad for a derailment that cost two people their lives and injured several others. The $65 million settlement in the case was the largest to date in the country. It would not be their last large settlement.

With their reputation firmly established, Roush & Simmons continued in a successful practice of both criminal law and civil litigation, but with so many lawyers being recruited for the firm, both Roush and Simmons could now select specific cases in which they wished to be involved, all the while coordinating with and providing legal advice to the other lawyers as they represented their clients. But neither was ever very far from the original case that had launched their careers so successfully, the Jeff Mitchell case.

Staring at the white caps on Pensacola Bay, Fred Roush pondered how lucky he was to have come so far so fast. Roused from his musings, the direct line rang to his office. He recognized the number as being from Hopper.

"Good morning, Bruce," Roush said cheerfully. "It's been a while since I've heard from you."

"Yeah, I've been reviewing and reviewing and trying to put the puzzle pieces together," Hopper responded. "And now I'm ready to get back to town and do some on-site work. You ready for me?"

"You got anything new to report?" asked Roush.

"Actually, I do," replied Hopper. "Yesterday, while examining the contents of these boxes for the umpteenth time, I found a list that had gotten caught under the flap of the box. I had never seen it before. It turned out to be the evidence list from the crime lab."

"I thought we had provided that to you some time ago," said Roush, puzzled.

"Perhaps you did, but I am just now finding it," answered Hopper. "Nevertheless, while going through it, I have found several items of evidence that I want to investigate, so I'm planning on coming to Pensacola on Monday to get started. Can you call Blake Evans and advise him of my arrival and also make me a reservation at the Train Station Hotel there?"

"Sure, I'll have Joanie do that for you as soon as we get off the phone. She can e-mail you the confirmation number."

269

Bruce Hopper acted like a June bug in hot ash as he hurriedly put together belongings that he would need while in Pensacola. He had two problems: He didn't know how long he would be there, and he had not packed last night because he was too tired and sleepy. Now, after not setting the alarm clock and therefore getting out of bed late, he had only a little while to pull himself and his gear together and get to the airport.

Since it was winter, he packed warmly even though the weather in Northwest Florida was not usually bitterly cold like more northerly states in the South. Nevertheless, he packed a pair of shorts as was his custom, because he wore shorts at home even during the winter months. He always chose comfort over anything else.

Arriving at the airport just in time to get a boarding pass and to transit security, he sat at the gate waiting to board the flight. As he waited, he reached into his valise and retrieved the priority list he had prepared last night. Gun, brooch, knife. Gun, brooch, knife. The gun and knife had never been introduced as evidence at trial because neither one had been located. And he never knew about the brooch until reading the evidence list. His intuition told him that these items and two people close to Lillian were to become his primary focus of investigation.

"Flight 1561 for Pensacola is now ready for boarding," he heard the gate agent announce. Hopper arose and walked toward the boarding line, where he presented his ticket, walked the length of the jetway, entered the plane, and quickly located his seat. Next stop, Pensacola.

*   *   *   *   *   *

Hopper decided first to interview Sharon Farrell, Lillian's roommate at the time of her death. Late Monday afternoon, he drove to the apartment that she had shared with Lillian to interview her. Sharon answered the door with a dinner plate containing a pimento cheese sandwich and potato chips.

270

"My name is Bruce Hopper, and I am an investigator working with the CCR on the Jeff Mitchell case. Do you mind if I come in and ask a few questions?"

"No, please do come in," Sharon responded.

"I know it has been a while since Lillian's death, but I would like to know about how you came to know Lillian," Hopper queried.

"We actually knew each other right after college when we worked in the same town. We met one night at a bar and became good friends. We often double dated or might go for a weekend to the mountains. At one time she began dating a boy that I had broken up with."

"What was his name?"

"John Blankenship. I'll never forget him. I was so in love with him at the time."

"What happened?"

"I just decided he was not right for me."

"Do you know where he lives now?"

"Not sure, but the last time I searched him on Facebook, he was in Mobile, Alabama."

"Did you and Lillian get along very well?'

"We were the best of friends. That's why when we both accepted jobs here, we decided to be roommates."

"Well, Sharon, I've taken enough of your time and you need to get back to your sandwich. Thanks so much for the information. You've been helpful."

Hopper returned to his hotel room and initiated a search for John Blankenship. A quick search on Facebook located him immediately. After a few more clicks on the computer keyboard, he had his address and phone number.

*　　*　　*　　*　　*　　*

Right after a breakfast at The Coffee Urn, Hopper drove the forty-five miles to Mobile. He called the number he had found for

John Blankenship, and his mother answered the phone. She told him that her son was at work and gave the work number.

He immediately dialed the number, locating Blankenship at a local mortgage broker's office. After introducing himself to Blankenship and the purpose of his visit, he asked to drop by and chat. Blankenship agreed.

Later that morning, Hopper entered the offices where Blankenship was employed. They retired to a conference room.

"I understand you knew Lillian Reins. Is that correct?" Hopper asked.

"Yes, I did. I fact, for several months I dated her regularly."

"I also understand that you knew Sharon Farrell as well."

"Actually, I knew Sharon before Lillian. Sharon and I had a relationship for nearly two years before I met Lillian."

"Did you fall in love with Lillian?"

"Yes, I did."

"And were you still in the relationship with Sharon at the time you fell in love with Lillian?"

"Lillian was so passionate. She made me feel so much like a man that I fell in love rather quickly. As much as I hated the circumstances, I did continue to date Sharon. In fact, I dated both of them at the same time for a brief period. At least until Sharon found out from a mutual friend who had seen Lillian and me making out in the corner booth of a bar one night."

"And what was Lillian's reaction?"

"She was mad . . . very mad. I've never seen a look like that on her face. The smile that I loved so much had turned to an angry snarl. I felt almost like she would've killed me if she had the chance."

"Where'd this take place?"

"In Pensacola quite a few months ago. They were living as roommates."

"Did you ever date Lillian again?"

"No, actually, I never even saw her again. Soon after, I moved to Mobile, found another girlfriend and soon forgot about Lillian. But I will never forget how she made me feel."

"Do you think Sharon was capable of killing someone, especially Lillian?"

"At that moment, yes. She was so angry that her face turned red, she pulled her hair out by the roots, she pounded the car seat, kicked the dashboard and twice smashed her head against the car window."

"Do you remember what she was wearing that night?"

"I think it was a red long-sleeved blouse. The exact style I don't recall, but the color I do remember because it matched her face and eyes."

"John, thank you for your time. I have your number if I need any additional information." Hopper handed him a business card. "If you remember anything that you think might be helpful to me, please call."

CHAPTER 34
THIRTY-THREE MONTHS LATER

Sunday, August 26. What a day for a wedding! Roush's friends had teased him for years about being slow in love, but three years? This was ridiculous! Nevertheless, the day had finally arrived.

It had been more than three years since their first date. During all those months, Fred Roush and Robyn Weeks had frequently enjoyed each other's company. They came to know each other intimately and discovered over time that they shared numerous common interests. She enjoyed country music, and her favorite pastime was shopping in antique stores and browsing flea markets.

Roush, too, loved country music, and when his schedule would allow, he went to every concert he could get tickets for. He also had collected all the recordings ever made by Hank Williams and Merle Haggard. His Saturdays were often filled with sporting activities such as scuba diving or hiking. But frequently the sporting experiences were a postlude to taking in the early morning garage sales that filled the classified columns of the local newspaper.

Roush's apartment was filled with early American antiques and collectibles he had purchased from numerous places he had visited, and his finds at the garage sales filled both the inside of his apartment and the large storage room in his garage. His favorite garage sale bargain was a very special antique music cabinet that he bought for a meager fifteen dollars. It was of European style and had been refinished in the popular sixties paint finish, antique green. Roush engaged a furniture refinisher to strip and restore the piece, discovering that it was made of cherry wood. It was an exquisite piece of furniture that graced his apartment next to his Steinway baby grand piano.

Attending movies and stage plays, playing golf and sunning on the beach, taking museum tours and eating at restaurants had all served to bring Fred Roush and Robyn Weeks to this day. Nervous, Roush entered the church where the ceremony was to be held. Beautifully decorated, the altar area was highlighted by an arch of white flowers. To each side of the platform were plentiful ferns and candelabra in the form of intertwined wedding rings.

Large white columns graced the lowest step on the outer limits of the platform. Above, in the window of the baptistry, a bountiful bouquet of white flowers adorned the wall.

Robyn and her attendants were dressing in the bride's room located off the foyer of the church. Abundant, noisy chatter could be heard from the room as her friends helped with the wedding dress, makeup, and other last minute details.

Time for the ceremony drew near. Roush and the minister stood with the ten groomsmen just outside the sanctuary door. Roush could see the light streaming through the beautiful and colorful stained glass windows as they cast shadows on the late afternoon crowd.

"Showtime," Reverend Blasingame said. "Are you ready, Fred?"

"Ready as I'll ever be," Roush responded. "Let's do it."

They all entered the sanctuary in single file and took their assigned places. Nothing registered with Fred Roush until the playing of the traditional "Wedding March." Seeing his radiant, beautiful bride walking down the aisle brought a huge smile to his handsome face. *I am such a lucky man,* he thought.

Robyn's gown, handmade by her mother, was of white peau de soie, fashioned with short sleeves and a portrait neckline. The front and back bodices were appliqued in hand clipped Alençon lace, which had been embroidered in seed pearls and sequins. A bustle and self-fabric roses accented the back waistline from which fell a full pleat, caught together with four small self-fabric bows. Lace medallions embellished in pearls and sequins adorned

275

the front and side of the gown and extended the full length of the cathedral train.

She also wore a veil of silk illusion cascading from a matching cap of jeweled Alençon lace. Robyn's only ornament was a diamond heart-shaped necklace, a gift from her groom. She carried a bouquet of white roses and lilies of the valley, centered with a white orchid.

The ceremony concluded— it was like a dream come true. Now in the vestibule outside the sanctuary of the church, about all Fred could remember was seeing Robyn walk down the aisle with her father and the pride he felt in having her for his bride. After that, his mind was blank; he did not even remember saying his vows.

The celebration continued at a large, bounteous reception held at the Greenbrier Country Club. Food, music provided by a local band, and spirited dancing filled the time of the revelers. Fred and Robyn were captivated by the grandeur and excitement of the moment. Soon they would leave for their honeymoon in Cancun.

*   *   *   *   *   *

Even though Hopper had been to Pensacola twice during the last three years, the potential results of his interviews with other possible suspects were making him feel positive about the future. He had visited the crime scene once but had found nothing. Admittedly, he had visited the scene during a rainy period, and the ground was soggy. He had, however, discovered a creek bed some 150 yards from the actual crime scene, but the creek was high, flowing rapidly over its banks. Nothing was found along the creek, but he hoped to revisit the scene when the creek had been reduced to a trickle. He planned to return in the summer.

*   *   *   *   *   *

Surprise on the face of Blake Evans gave evidence he had received word that his first 8.50 motion on behalf of Jeff Mitchell had been denied. Hoping for the best but expecting the worst, he had already initiated preparation for yet another motion on the

276

basis of the cruel and unusual nature of chemical death as a means of administering the death penalty. Recent incidents indicated that the procedure could easily be botched. Needles in soft tissue and even chemical burns under the skin have been found during autopsy following an execution. These would be excellent justifications for appeal. Within a week or two, all the necessary documents would be prepared for its submission to the trial judge.

Not to be discouraged, Evans and his paralegal, Jennifer Bryant, continued to research possible grounds for appeal in the Mitchell case. Few errors could be discovered in the trial phase, and the investigation by the police appeared quite thorough and free from contamination. The potential reasons for appealing the sentence were diminishing rapidly. He could only hope that Hopper might soon uncover something that could become grounds for another appeal.

Evans lifted the receiver and dialed Roush's office number. After Roush picked up, Evans said, "Mr. Roush, our first 8.50 appeal in the Mitchell case has been denied. I just thought I'd call and keep you informed about it."

"I'm sorry to hear about that," Roush said hesitantly. "By the way, have you heard anything from Hopper?"

"Actually, I heard from him this morning. He has some interesting results from interviews and is planning on returning to Pensacola in early summer to complete his investigation. For some reason he wants to be here in the dry season."

*   *   *   *   *   *

Blayne Simmons rushed into Roush's office without knocking. "Don't you ever knock before you go into somebody else's office?" Roush asked, exasperated. This was not the first time Simmons's impulsive nature had manifested itself.

"Yeah, and *they* get mad at me, too," Simmons said. "But I am 'stoked' about the Crist case. I had to tell somebody about it."

Wilhelm Crist, a nineteen-year-old plumber with an inclination to overspend, had been charged with robbing a woman at gunpoint on a dark, cloudy evening four months before. He claimed he had been at home getting ready for bed and could not have committed the crime. Nevertheless, the jury believed the testimony of the victim, who identified him as the perpetrator, and found him guilty. He was sentenced to eight years in prison and released on bond pending his appeal of the conviction.

"Crist had forgotten about a long distance call he made from his apartment only five minutes prior to the alleged attack." Simmons became excited about the information. "I've prepared a Writ of *Habeas Corpus* in an attempt to get the judge to set aside the jury verdict and declare him not guilty. I've talked with the person to whom the call was made, and there is no way he could have made the call from that phone, talked for what appears to have been ten minutes, and still committed this crime."

"Looks good. How did you discover the call?" asked Roush.

"Just a hunch I had. I worked on a case in Orlando in which the accused party was found not guilty at trial because of the record of a phone call. I just thought it might at least be appropriate to look at Crist's phone records. Police never even thought of it. Simply a hunch that paid off."

"Great work, Blayne. I know Bill will be indebted to you for thinking of that. He was probably too confused over his situation to think how he might be able to clear himself."

"Probably so. It should only take a couple of weeks to get him cleared."

*   *   *   *   *   *

Working in her lab on a new murder case that had occurred only three days before, Robyn Weeks Roush carefully inspected the material that had been sent to her for analysis. As she reviewed the evidence inventory form, her phone rang. She picked it up before the second ring.

"Hi, Robyn. Bruce Hopper here," he began.

"Oh, hey, Bruce. What can I do for you?" she asked.

278

"When you worked the Reins case, do you remember seeing a brooch that had been discovered at the crime scene?"

"I do remember that brooch. We tested it for DNA and found none. We also checked for fingerprints with no success. I think the investigators simply thought that they had sufficient evidence for a conviction and did not investigate the brooch very thoroughly."

"Do you think it might still be among the material in the evidence locker," he asked.

"Probably so, unless that material has been tampered with," she responded.

"Do you mind looking into this for me?"

"Of course, not. Anything to help Fred and the CCR."

"And if you find it, I would appreciate it if you could photograph it for me from all sides."

"I can do that."

"You're a dear," said Bruce. "Call me back when you have something."

Checking her computer files, she found the number for the Reins murder case. She was excited about the possibility that she might actually assist in her husband's efforts to prove his client innocent. She walked hastily downstairs to the evidence vault area where items of evidence and the paperwork associated with cases were retained in secured archives.

Nathaniel, the security guard on post at the vault, asked for her photo ID. As she showed it to him, he noted the time on the posting form and asked her to fill in her name and signature.

She used the case number she had retrieved from the computer and found the cabinet containing the box of evidence and paperwork archived on the Reins murder. Shuffling through the folders by number, she located the Reins case files. She opened the master case folder and found the case tracking forms as well as the evidence inventory form. There, she located item eighteen. In the description section was written, "gold, diamond and

279

emerald brooch in plush velvet pouch." The listing for item eighteen comprised the sole entry on the last page of the evidence inventory form. The notation next to item eighteen was unmistakable—RUW, returned unworked. The brooch was not in the evidence case in the FDLE vault. *Must be in the evidence room at the Sheriff's Department*, she thought. Undeterred, she returned to her office. There, on a sticky pad note, she wrote a reminder to herself to discuss the brooch with Fred when she got home.

*   *   *   *   *   *

Jeff Mitchell had now been on death row for more than four years. More than once, during periods of despondency and inner turmoil, he had wished for the means to kill himself. His self-esteem had hit rock bottom; his faith in a fair and just judicial system had long since dissipated; his belief that justice would ultimately prevail rested only in his belief in the hereafter.

He sat to write a letter to his parents, who visited him as often as they could afford to. He contemplated the lined paper for a moment and began to write:

Dear Mom and Dad:

Your faith in me is all that keeps me going. In spite of my innocence, the courts have so far rejected all my appeals. I feel the end draws nearer and nearer. Precisely when, I do not know. While I know Fred, Blayne, and the folks at the CCR are working hard to help me, I have no confidence that anything positive will result.

My soul is in anguish, and I wish to discontinue the appeals and get on with the execution. I know you will not agree; and while it may pain you to hear this, I would rather enjoy the glories that await me in the hereafter than to live a day longer in this perpetual hell on earth.

Do not despair. Just support the fact of my innocence. And when the poison flows, know that I loved all of you beyond the mere description of words.

I promise to be the angel who looks after both of you for the rest of your lives as . . .

Your loving and compassionate son,

Jeff

*   *   *   *   *   *

Robyn met Fred at the front door as he arrived home from work. With a passionate embrace, the two of them kissed, the kiss of newlyweds.

"Did you miss me today?" Robyn asked rather coquettishly.

"Yes, I did. In fact, right after lunch, I laid my head back in my chair, caught a brief power nap, and dreamed of you in that revealing camisole I gave you for our wedding night."

"Want me to put it on?"

"Ah. You're reading my mind!" Fred could feel his face suddenly flush as the excitement arose in his body.

Warm, soft French bread and chili were the evening dinner fare. The aroma from the still simmering chili wafted throughout the house. It smelled delightful. Picking up the newspaper, he sat in his favorite recliner to review the day's news. Before he could finish the front page, Robyn stood in the doorway of the bedroom, sexily and scantily attired in the black camisole.

"Are you ready for dinner, now, dear?" she asked in her sultriest voice.

"You must be kidding," he almost shouted. Rising abruptly from his chair, he took her in his arms and physically carried her to the bedroom.

"A little early evening delight, my dear, if you don't mind," he said.

"Mind? This can be the appetizer for both of us."

Slumber came easily. Dinner sat untouched, cooling on the kitchen stove.

CHAPTER 35

The season of joy and peace had arrived. Christmas tree lots abounded, and shoppers scurried about content to fight for that last doll on the shelves or the prized toy in this year's stuffed animal menagerie. Twinkling miniature Christmas lights were everywhere to be seen, and the season already seemed to be an economic boon for merchants.

Joanie knocked on Roush's office door, but came in without being invited.

"What is it, Joanie? You look a little sad."

"Sad is an understatement. We received a letter from Jeff Mitchell this morning. You need to read it."

She handed the letter to Roush and watched for his reaction. Opening the letter, he silently read:

"Dear Fred:

Words can never convey the gratitude in my heart for all that you and Blayne have done on my behalf. You believe in my innocence and have done so all along. You did all you could to prove it, but nothing seemed to work in our favor.

I have endured the pain of being held in this dreadful place for almost five years. One after another, my appeals have been rejected, and my faith in the system has evaporated. I no longer wish to continue the appeals process. While I have not yet notified the CCR of my decision, I plan to do so in a few days. I just wanted you to know first so that you would not be caught by surprise.

While I know you may not agree with this decision, please know that I am satisfied that you did everything you could to keep me from this place. I am resigned to the inevitable; it is preferable to life in here. I only ask that you not interfere; only allow fate to hasten the day of my execution.

Please accept the finality of this decision. Don't let my pain become your pain. Rest assured that I am at peace.

Gratefully,
Jeff

*   *   *   *   *   *

Roush turned his chair toward the window behind him. A lump arose in his throat as he suppressed the intense sorrow he felt at that moment.

With moist eyes, Joanie left the office silently.

Mitchell's letter had made it difficult for Roush to get through the remainder of the day. Fortunately, no court appearances had been scheduled, and no pressing cases required his immediate attention. He spent a little time informing Blayne Simmons about the Mitchell letter and wistfully hoped that Bruce Hopper would soon uncover evidence to exonerate Mitchell.

Pulling into his driveway at home, he noticed that Robyn had not yet arrived from work. Once inside, he shed his clothes, put on some sweats, started a fire in the fireplace, and sat down to meditate on Mitchell's decision.

The warmth from the fire soon made him drowsy, and he fell fast asleep.

*   *   *   *   *   *

Still in a foggy state, Roush was aroused by the sound of the front door being unlocked. Robyn had finally made it home. The grandfather clock in the hall chimed 8:00.

"Problem at the lab?" Roush asked, noticing that Robyn looked somewhat disheveled.

"Problem is not exactly the word for it," she said.

Seeing that she was tired and not in the mood to set out in the kitchen to prepare a meal, Roush suggested, "You don't look like you're in the mood to prepare dinner, and I'm in no mood to help. Why don't we just go out?"

"Sounds good to me," Robyn responded, her spirits lifting at the prospects of not having to spend the next hour over a hot stove.

283

Silently, they drove to one of their favorite haunts. They ordered their favorite salad and held hands across the table.

After a few minutes of silent staring, Robyn's face lit up like the Christmas tree. She broke the silence of the moment. "Fred, even after I wrote myself a note of reminder, I forgot to tell you about something that happened yesterday. While I was working on a case, I received a call from Bruce inquiring about a brooch that was found at the Reins crime scene. He had discovered it on the evidence list. He asked if I would locate it, photograph it and the bag in which it was found, and send the pictures to him. Do you think it will be all right if I do that?"

"I'm sure it will, so long as you do not let it out of your sight or out of the building. But I would first ask a supervisor."

"I'll do that, tomorrow."

Their meals arrived. Now lifted by what could be a new lead in the case, Roush hurriedly devoured the salad. They returned to the warm comfort of their home with a blazing fire. They lay together in front of the fireplace, embracing each other and sharing these moments of intimacy.

*   *   *   *   *   *

Morning could not come soon enough. Roush was wide awake. He arose, went through his morning routine for preparation, and left for the office, first offering his beautiful wife a good-bye kiss.

At 9:00, Roush drove to the office of the State Attorney. He was determined to visit with Doug Rose.

Being announced to Rose, Roush shook hands with him with business-like aplomb. "Doug, I have a question to which I must have an answer. When you prosecuted Jeff Mitchell, didn't the investigators find a piece of jewelry among the items of evidence taken from the site of the murder?"

Rose was surprised to get questions on the Mitchell case now, especially from the defendant's former lawyer. The Supreme Court had copied Rose about the denial of the direct appeal.

Procedure now required that further appeals in the case be placed in the hands of the CCR.

"Yes, there was a piece of jewelry, but it didn't play a role in the prosecution case, and you never brought it up during the trial," Rose answered. "Why do you ask?"

"The CCR investigator is requesting photographs of the jewelry, and I hope you will approve that request. We feel that it might be helpful to Jeff Mitchell's case."

"I'll call the FDLE today and authorize the photographs."

"Thanks. We will all be grateful, especially if this turns out to be the break we have been looking for."

When Roush arrived back at his office, a phone message had been placed in the center of his desk so he would not miss it. It indicated that he should call Bruce Hopper at his home.

"Bruce, this is Fred Roush. Where are you? I thought you were still in the Middle East."

"No," Hopper began. I had just made a quick trip there to wrap up some of the paperwork required to complete the job. I was only there a few days. I'm back now and working feverishly on the Mitchell case. I plan on coming to Pensacola during spring or early summer when it gets dry. I want to do some hiking."

"Do you think you are making headway?" Roush asked.

"I most certainly do. The last time I was in Pensacola, I interviewed several people close to Lillian Reins who may have had some less than satisfactory dealings with her, maybe even to the point of really hard feelings."

"Can you elaborate?" Roush asked, intrigued.

"There was some real jealousy with her roommate, Sharon Farrell. Seems like Sharon and Lillian, at one time, shared a love interest in the same guy. But Lillian was the one who ultimately shared his bed."

"Anything else?"

"Yes. I also learned that she and her ex-boyfriend, Thad Whetstone, had a very stormy relationship. He physically abused her at times, and even threatened her on one occasion."

"How did you learn about these facts?" Roush asked, gaining more and more confidence.

"By interviewing them. They were quite open with the truth, especially about each other. Neither knew that I was interviewing the other. Kinda sneaky, don't you think?"

"Quite, but effective," Roush said.

"Also, when I spoke with Whetstone, he would only state that he was at home alone on the night of the murder. No alibi; his presence at home cannot be verified by any witnesses. Right now, he stands as my number one suspect. We just have to prove it."

"Great work," said Roush.

"I still have not interviewed Marilyn McGregor, one of Lillian's co-workers, but will do so as soon as I return. In fact, if you don't mind and CCR approves, I'll return to Pensacola next week and stay until I have exhausted all interview possibilities. What do you think?"

"I think that would be a great idea. I'll call Blake tomorrow morning and get his approval and then let you know by e-mail."

"Sounds good. I'll wait to hear from you."

*   *   *   *   *   *

Assistant State Attorney Doug Rose placed a call to Roush.

"Fred, I looked into the matter of the jewelry. A piece of jewelry *was* taken among the evidence at the murder scene. It is shown on the last page of the final, amended evidence listing form but is shown also to have been returned to the Sheriff as unworked. It was a brooch, quite elegant, and looked old— possibly an antique of some sort. Its source could not be traced, although an effort was made by the investigators to learn where it was obtained. It obviously was not bought around here. I've called the FDLE and authorized the photographs," Rose said. "I'll have them and a copy of the evidence listing sent to you by the end of the week. I'll send the photographs to Bruce also.

"Thanks, I'm grateful," Fred, responded.

Rose seemed sincere in his effort to help Roush with the case.

*   *   *   *   *   *

The next day, Bruce Hopper appeared in the doorway of Roush & Simmons. "What's up, Fred, my friend."

"I didn't expect you for a few days," Roush said.

"I just didn't want to wait for an answer from Evans and the CCR folks, so I drove up last night. I'm anxious to get this behind us."

"Well, you're in luck because I received an e-mail from Evans overnight approving your plans."

"Good, then let's get crackin' on this," Hopper said with a smile.

"Got some good news, and I want you to look into it even before you continue with the investigation on Thad Whetstone and Sharon Farrell." Roush explained what Doug Rose had said about the brooch. "If we can find the source of that brooch, we may have a lead on the identity of the real killer. As soon as I get the pictures and description of the brooch, I'll get it to you. Get on it ASAP. In the meantime, I'll notify Blake Evans that you are already here."

"Oh, I'm going to investigate the brooch thoroughly. I made that decision when I saw it on the inventory listing. It could be our best lead if we can identify where it came from. You have my word that I won't let go of this one," promised Hopper. "I also plan to follow up on my investigation of the two I mentioned earlier. I still have all the notes on them and the sources of those notes."

"Thanks, Bruce. It really is good to have you back. We're going to make an unbeatable team."

*   *   *   *   *   *

The newspaper headlines shouted the economic reality of the times: MARKET DROPS; ECONOMY DOWN. The previous day, the Dow Jones average had dropped by more than eight hundred points. Inflation was rising, now past double digits; bankruptcies climbed off the charts; interest rates neared nineteen percent. Unemployment rates skyrocketed due to downsizing, an effort on the part of companies to reduce the cost of doing business. Advertising and marketing businesses were in severe decline, and Goodall and Dohr was among them.

As Mark Bradley entered the office to begin his day, Warren Dohr, the senior partner at Goodall and Dohr, met him. "Mark, could I see you in my office in about twenty minutes?" Dohr asked. Bradley noticed the age lines that Dohr had developed in the last two years. He was not smiling; his usual morning form of greeting and the sound of his voice were somber and serious.

"Sure, I'll be there. Anything wrong?"

"Just need to talk with you. See you in twenty minutes."

The time could not pass quickly enough. A sixth sense told Bradley that something was incredibly wrong and that the news or whatever Dohr wanted to talk about was not good. Past experience had taught Bradley to read body language—what was not said and how a person reacted to questions. He noticed that Dohr did not specifically answer his question about whether something was wrong.

When the appointed time arrived, Bradley knocked at Dohr's office and heard Dohr ask him to come in.

"Sit down, Mark," Dohr began. "You've been with this company for quite a few years now, and we have been proud of the job you have done. Your work under the new organization we implemented more than three years ago has been excellent."

But. . . Bradley thought. He could hear it coming, and he knew the news was ominous.

"But as you know from reading reports on the company, its financial stability is rapidly being called into question by industrial analysts. Without some drastic measures, the company will not survive. And we all have worked too hard to allow that to happen."

The conversation could have ended there, and Bradley would have known the outcome.

"Mark, a total restructuring of the company has been necessary. An evaluation of all the divisions and positions within those divisions has occurred, with the most essential ones being retained. Most of the mid-management jobs are being eliminated, and one of those jobs is yours. While I am not pleased to have to inform you of the decision, someone has to do it."

"What you're saying is that I'm out of a job?" Bradley asked.

"The simplest answer would be *yes*," Dohr said. "I hope you will understand that the sacrifice of some is essential to the total survival of the company. We are willing to offer you an excellent severance package that should tide you over for about six months. During that time, you should be able to find another position. We will support you with letters of recommendation and any other paperwork that you might need to find work."

Bradley put his head in his hands. For more years than he could remember, he had been associated with Goodall and Dohr. It was his first really good paying job, and now, in appreciation for his years of service, he was being let go. He shivered in disbelief.

"Mark, because we feel it best that the employees being caught in the downsizing effort not be required to work out a severance period, we are asking that you vacate your office by the close of business tomorrow. Your first check will be available to you at that time."

Standing up, Warren Dohr reached out to shake Bradley's hand. "We do appreciate all you've done over the years. I know this is a shock to you, but be assured that it is not anything you have done or haven't done for that matter. It's reality; the

———
289

company is doing what is necessary to survive. You simply have been caught in the middle. Best of luck to you, Mark."

Bradley slowly arose, chin on his chest, limply shook hands with Dohr and left the office. His termination had come as such a complete surprise; he had made no plans. He always thought he would be at Goodall and Dohr forever. Now all the plans he had made for the future had vanished like smoke from an open fire. He did not know where to go or where to turn. He must tell his wife; she would not be happy.

*   *   *   *   *   *

By afternoon Doug Rose had delivered two copies of the evidence listing and eight closeup photographs of the brooch to Fred Roush's office.

The eight pictures of the brooch showed an elegantly hand-crafted gold rose. Encrusted within the exquisite rose bloom were seven small, faceted diamonds, appearing to be about a quarter carat each, and ten beautifully faceted petite emeralds set in intricately designed leaves. The appearance of the gold surface indicated that the brooch was probably not of recent vintage.

"Joanie," Roush said to his secretary as he stepped to her desk. "Please see that a copy of this inventory form and these pictures are in the hands of Bruce Hopper no later than tomorrow morning."

"I'll take care of it," Joanie promised.

*   *   *   *   *   *

Hopper waited until after work hours that evening to stop by the home of Marilyn McGregor. After being greeted by a friendly face, he was escorted in to take a seat in McGregor's sitting room, decorated with numerous art deco pieces from what appeared to be the thirties and forties.

"Collector, are you?" Hopper asked.

"Yeah. I collect art deco collectibles. Oldest piece I have is from the late twenties. Most of it is from the fifties. May I ask why you've come by?"

"I'm looking into the death of Lillian Reins."

"My, that was so long ago. Jeff Mitchell was convicted of that crime. Why would you be investigating that crime now after so long a time?" McGregor asked.

"His legal representatives believe him to be innocent. We need to prove that before his execution date."

"But he was found guilty. Isn't that enough?"

"No, as a matter of fact, it's not."

"I'll do what I can, then."

"Good. Tell me, Miss McGregor, did you and Lillian Reins get along, being co-workers and all?" Hopper asked.

"Yes. We were quite close friends right up until the end."

"And how well did you know Mark Bradley?"

"He was my supervisor as well as Lillian's. I guess you could say I knew him well."

"Did he treat you any differently than he did Lillian?"

"No. Not that I ever noticed."

"Did he ever show any interest in her outside of work that you know about?"

"No," she responded.

"Did he show any romantic interest in you?" Hopper pressed.

"No. He was happily married with children and never exhibited anything but gentlemanly behavior."

Hopper rose to leave. "That's all I wanted to know. You've been very helpful."

McGregor showed him to the door. He could hear her mumble something under her breath as he walked down from the steps to toward the driveway.

Hopper turned, "Pardon me. Did you say something?"

"No. It was nothing," McGregor said.

*   *   *   *   *   *

Bradley's first order of business was to explain to his wife what had happened at Goodall and Dohr. Her reaction was predictable. Scared, uncertain about the future and especially the

291

twin boys who were about to start college, and personally unwilling to change her style of life, which included not working, she blamed Mark for the "fix" into which he had gotten the family.

"What do you expect to do now?" she asked, sounding angry at this new set of circumstances.

"I'm going to search for another job, of course."

"In the meantime, what are we supposed to do for money? And how do you expect us to handle expenses for Christmas?"

"We have the severance pay promised. It's for six months. That should be sufficient to get us through Christmas. With good management, it should last until I can find something."

"And what if you don't find anything?" her tone biting and vitriolic.

"I don't think we need to be thinking about that until the time comes. Try to be positive. We'll be all right." The tremor in his voice evidenced feelings of uncertainty about the future. He knew that employment in advertising and marketing had been shrinking, and the economic bottom had not yet been reached, according to industry sources. While maintaining an outward appearance of confidence, inside, his self-assurance was shattered.

*   *   *   *   *   *

The next evening, Hopper drove to the home of Mark Bradley. Recognizing Hopper, Bradley invited him inside and offered him a cup of coffee. Hopper declined.

"I need to ask you something, Mark. You were the supervisor for both Marilyn McGregor and Lillian Reins. How was their relationship?"

"Turbulent, unsettling, unfriendly bordering sometimes on disdain."

"How so?"

"Lillian often accused me of showing favoritism to Miss McGregor. I promoted Miss McGregor over Lillian at one time in the past. Lillian never forgave me for that. She only learned to live with it."

"So you're saying that Miss McGregor hated Lillian Reins."

"Yeah. Hatred perhaps is too strong. Tolerate is probably a better way to characterize their relationship. They tolerated each other at work, but they never associated with each other outside the office. Marilyn would have none of that."

"Did you have any relationship with Miss McGregor outside the office?" Hopper pressed.

"No. I'm a married man. Ours was strictly a business relationship."

"Thanks, Mark. You have helped more than you know."

"Hope so."

*   *   *   *   *   *

Thanks to the call from Fred Roush, Blake Evans now had yet another basis for appealing Jeff Mitchell's case. With the discovery of the brooch, the discovery of the inventory listing and the results of interviews conducted by Hopper, he would file another 3.850 motion. It would simply assert that the defense was not furnished all evidence or records in the case, argue that new evidence had been elicited from potential witnesses, and ask the court to set aside the conviction and order a new trial.

At the same time, the first hearing on the previous appeal on the cruel and unusual nature of the death penalty was now set for next week. He was already prepared, although he held little hope, based on past experience, that the court would grant the motion.

Bradley had been unemployed for four months. No reasonable prospects appeared on the horizon. He decided to take a drastic step.

Calling his friend Richard, who owned several Shop-N-Mart convenience stores in the area, he asked to meet with him.

Bradley arrived at the store about five minutes early; Richard was inside checking over the latest financial information from his chain of stores.

"Hi, Richard. How you doin' today?" Bradley was attempting to be friendly and upbeat in spite of his circumstances.

"Hey, Mark. You seemed a little distraught when we talked. What can I do for you?"

"I need a favor. Richard, I lost my job four months ago, and I haven't found anything to replace it. I have severance pay, but I really do have to supplement it. I was wondering if you could let me work in one of your convenience stores. I'll do whatever you can use me to do, and I'll work whatever shift you need."

"Mark, I'm sorry about your job. Sure, I'll do what I can. In fact, I have been looking for somebody to work in this store on the midnight shift anyway. The hours are horrible, 10:00 p.m. to 6:00 a.m. And I can only pay $7.50 an hour. Would you be willing to accept those terms?"

"A desperate man will do whatever it takes, and I'm desperate. I sure will. At least, until I can find something permanent."

"Plan to start tomorrow night. I'll see you when you come in and have you sign the necessary paperwork. I'm really sorry about your job loss, but I hope this helps."

"It'll help more than you can imagine."

*　　*　　*　　*　　*　　*

Blake Evans had not seen the court act as fast as it did on his last two motions. Today's mail had included a letter from the

Appeals Court in which it rejected the last two 8.50 appeals. The letter explained that the cruel and unusual nature of the death penalty lacked substance. Furthermore, the Court denied the motion on ineffective assistance of counsel. The basis for his ruling was that, although Fred Roush lacked sufficient experience in criminal trial law, Blayne Simmons's experience and background more than made up for the deficiency and fulfilled the state's requirements. Preparation became a non-issue.

Time was running out. The hearing on the last motion filed, violation of public records documents, was now scheduled for two months hence. This motion was based on not having been advised of the finding of the brooch.

* * * * * *

Because of what he had learned about Thad Whetstone, Hopper called Roush about a possible DNA sample.

"Fred," he spoke into the telephone with a sense of urgency. " After interviewing Whetstone and Farrell, I would like to get a sample of their DNA from both of them for comparison with any future evidence we might obtain. Do you think we can get a court order to do that?"

"We can try. On what basis?" Roush asked.

"On the basis of new information that has arisen from interviews," Bruce said.

"Can you bring your notes by here this afternoon? We will include them in our request to show the importance of the new information."

"Sure, I'll be there in an hour or so."

* * * * * *

Bruce Hopper had worked diligently on the brooch. With a jeweler's lens, he had carefully scoured every square centimeter of each digital photo of it. A fine, high quality piece of jewelry it was. And it appeared to be an antique of some sort. Patina on the back seemed to indicate that it had some age on it. How much could not be determined simply by looking.

295

He had learned the reason the Sheriff's Office could not track it was that the investigators were looking for it to have been purchased at a jewelry store. Hopper decided, after talking with several reputable jewelers, that the piece had most likely been purchased from a jewelry store somewhere other than in North Florida or at an enterprise other than a commercial business, like a garage or estate sale. Estate sales had become quite popular during the time period of the murder and continued to be so.

Hopper took the pictures of the brooch to a friend, Ben Bush, who specialized in hand- crafted, antique jewelry. Inspecting the brooch with a jeweler's loop, Bush said, "This is a mid-to -late-nineteenth-century piece. The etchings on the blades of the leaves are uneven, indicating that it was hand crafted, and the mountings of the stones are consistent with the craftsmanship of the late part of the nineteenth century. It would be my guess that it was not sold in a jewelry store. Might have been an heirloom passed down to children, or maybe it was bought at an antique store or something like a yard or estate sale. More likely an estate sale, since the workmanship is so exquisite, and the value of the brooch would probably be high. It depends on the quality of the gemstones and the amount of gold in the metal."

"Thanks, Ben. You've been a big help," Hopper said.

Hopper decided to limit the immediate field of inquiry on the brooch to estate sales. He focused on estate sales held just previous to the murder. If he found nothing significant, then he would broaden the search.

*   *   *   *   *   *

Jeff Mitchell had now been on death row for more than five years. New legislation had significantly reduced the length of the appeal time, but he was resigned to the outcome—his execution.

Keeping a diary, Mitchell daily wrote about his experiences in prison and his feelings about being there. He sat down to write the day's entry.

"Today I recall the words of the Apostle James who described life as a 'vapor. It appears for a little while and disappears.' During my brief life, I have climbed some awesome mountains. Their beauty and their challenge drew me to them. But the mountain I now climb is not one of beauty; it is one of personal degradation and deep despair.

In the past, my determination to conquer any mountain has been steadfast because I was confident in my own ability to meet the challenge.

The mountain I now face, and have faced for more than five years, is one which tests my self-confidence, my faith in a system of justice in which I believed for so long, and my firm belief that truth wins out in the end. So much of the outcome of this climb is not in my hands; I feel helpless, and the struggle is so long and hard.

The sights and sounds and smells of this place have frayed my nerves beyond comprehension. I have already witnessed one man meet his death at the hands of the state. I saw the terror in his eyes as he walked past my cell. He, too, claimed to be innocent, but nevertheless he was sacrificed on the altar of justice. He stopped momentarily at my cell on his way to the Death Watch cell. Handing me a small object, he said, "Keep this as a remembrance of me. Maybe it will bring you more luck than it did for me." Looking into the palm of my hand, I found a white rabbit's foot.

I cannot bear to think of the anguish one must experience when he is executed. The thought of going to sleep and never waking up brings stark fear to my heart. Yet, I must be resigned to that fate. Even though I have asked Fred Roush and the CCR to abandon my appeals, I know they continue to work on my behalf. The rejection of the latest appeals only bears out my fundamental belief—the system is determined to execute me, regardless of my innocence.

My thoughts today go to Lillian. What wonderful, fun times we had together. She didn't deserve to die; only her sweet spirit exceeded her beauty. But I don't deserve to be here for killing her. Oh how I wish that things could have been different. As my time draws nearer, the clouds of ultimate release grow darker."

*   *   *   *   *   *

Visiting the newspaper library was a commonplace occurrence for Bruce Hopper. Before researching the classified ads, he read all the articles about the murder that appeared in the newspaper. A picture of the car had been included in one of the articles. It appeared to have been severely damaged in an accident. He wondered if the car were still around. He knew how long it had been since the crime but he still wished to see it and go over it for evidence.

He proceeded to the classifieds. He knew what he was looking for, but so many garage and estate sales appeared during the months prior to the murder that he felt overwhelmed. Since there were fewer of them, he decided to limit his research only to estate sales.

His efforts paid off handsomely. During the three months preceding the murder of Lillian Reins twenty-six estate sales had appeared in the newspaper. He made a note of each one including the company conducting the sale and the telephone number advertised to obtain information about the sale. Now he would truly earn the moniker, gumshoe.

*   *   *   *   *   *

TWO MONTHS LATER

Now with DNA samples from Whetstone and Farrell on file with the FDLE, Hopper placed a call to Robyn Weeks Roush.

"Robyn, do you have the two DNA samples from Farrell and Whetstone yet?" he asked.

"Yes, got them just this morning," Weeks responded.

"How long do you think it will take to get the results?"

"Probably three weeks to get a complete battery of testing complete. Likely another week to complete the comparison testing."

"OK, but if anything comes up before that time, please call me. Will you do that?"

"Absolutely. You will be the first call I make when I have something to report," she promised.

*　　*　　*　　*　　*　　*

Blake Evans made his appearance thirty minutes early in the gallery of the Appeals Court. He sat alone, with court personnel busily preparing for the day's packed agenda. The hearing on the last appeal for Jeff Mitchell had been scheduled for 10:00 a.m.

Within fifteen minutes, Doug Rose appeared on behalf of the state. The hearing began promptly at the appointed hour, Judge Allison Grant presiding.

"Mr. Rose," Grant began, "are you ready to begin?"

"Yes, Your honor," Rose replied.

"And you, Mr. Evans. Are you ready?"

"Yes, I am, Your honor," Evans replied respectfully.

"Then, please proceed with your case, Mr. Evans."

Blake Evans recapped the Jeff Mitchell case and the items listed on the evidence folder that had been prepared by the FDLE. He then announced, "We wish to call Mr. Fred Roush as a witness."

Fred Roush stood and approached the witness chair. After being sworn in, Evans asked, "Mr. Roush, did you at any time during discovery in the Jeff Mitchell case receive from any state agency an inventory list prepared by the Florida Department of Law Enforcement?"

"No, I did not."

"Have you since located a copy of the inventory list?"

"Yes. It had become lodged under the flap of a cardboard box in which the discovery documents had been stored and sent to us. Our investigator found it only a couple of months ago."

"At any time, Mr. Roush, were you furnished a copy of the inventory list that included an entry about a brooch, which was found on the body of the victim?"

299

"As I just said, we did not take possession of the list until a few weeks ago. The first time I was even aware that the brooch existed was when it was brought to my attention by the investigator."

"Were you not suspicious when the inventory list was not included?"

"No. While it is rare that an inventory list is left off, it is not always necessary since one assumes that all evidence is included in the boxes passed down to the defense. In this case, neither the list nor anything relating to the brooch was included."

After excusing Fred Roush, Evans called Robyn Weeks Roush to the stand.

"Ms. Roush, do you recall whether or not any scrapings from beneath the victim's fingernails were submitted to the lab for testing?"

"To my knowledge, no scrapings were submitted," she answered. "They certainly were not on the inventory list."

"I have no more questions of this witness, Your Honor," Evans said.

With no cross-examination from the prosecution, Robyn Roush was released.

Evans then asked if he could call one last witness. After receiving permission from Judge Grant, he called Dr. Sheila Josephson to the stand.

"Dr. Josephson, as chief medical examiner, can you tell this court whether or not scrapings were taken from beneath the fingernails of the victim during autopsy?"

"They were not."

"And the reason for that?"

"My assistant had completed the major elements of the autopsy and was called from the room. While gone, the funeral home arrived and took possession of the body. By the time my assistant returned, the body had been removed to the funeral home and prepared for burial."

"So any evidence that might have been beneath the fingernails of the victim, probably remains there. Would that be an accurate statement?"

"Yes, unless the mortician cleaned them."

With no further questions, the witness was excused.

"Your Honor, we would appeal for a new trial date on the basis that the inventory list has only been in our hands for a short time and our investigation with respect to the brooch is ongoing. Furthermore, we request that the court order a warrant for the exhumation of the victim's body for retrieval of any evidence from the fingernails."

After a thirty-minute recess, court was reconvened for the court's decision.

"Mr. Evans, this court is prepared to issue the requested warrant for the exhumation of the victim's body. We are not prepared to set aside the verdict in this case and order a new trial. There should be plenty of time for you to complete your investigation before Mr. Mitchell's sentence can be carried out." Doug Rose did not object to the court's decision.

*　　*　　*　　*　　*　　*

Bruce Hopper had tracked down more than half of the estate sales and had uncovered nothing of any consequence. As a change of pace, today he would take time off from the estate sales to inquire about the car. During the mid-morning, he drove to the Sheriff's Department. At the reception desk, he asked for Tony Boudreaux. He was directed down a long corridor and to the right. Boudreaux sat behind his desk in the second office on the left.

"Good morning, Detective Boudreaux," he said. "My name is Bruce Hopper, and I am assisting the CCR in investigating the murder of Lillian Reins."

"That case is over and done," Boudreaux said.

"Not as far as the defense is concerned," Hopper replied harshly. "And especially when the defendant is innocent."

301

"That's a matter of opinion," Boudreaux said. "How can I help you, then?"

"Tell me where Lillian's car is."

"Whatchu wanna know about it?" Boudreaux retorted, irritated. He considered this line of investigation to be questioning his ability as an investigator.

"What happened to it?"

"It was totaled in the wreck before Miss Reins was killed. Hit a tree. After the crime scene people finished, it was brought to the impound lot. I think a junk dealer purchased it from the insurance company. All I know is we don't have it."

"Do you know who that dealer was?"

"No, but gimme a minute, and I might can find out."

Boudreaux dialed a number and spoke to the person answering the phone. "Duke, remember the green Ford Mustang in the Reins case from about four or five years ago? The car was totaled in an accident and was brought to the impound yard. The owner had been a murder victim. The guy who killed her was later convicted."

"Yeah, I do remember that case. What about it?"

"Can you tell me what happen to the car?"

"Give me a minute. Let me see if it's still on the computer." Boudreaux could only hear the clicking of computer keys. "The record is still here," Duke said. "I would have thought it would have been filed in the electronic archives by now. It looks like the MIS folks are way behind schedule."

"What'd you find, Duke?" Boudreaux asked.

"The car was sold by the insurance company to Apex Auto Recyclers. It's located north of town."

"Thanks, Duke."

Boudreaux wrote the information on a piece of note paper and handed it to Hopper. "Thanks, Detective. I owe you one."

Before leaving the building, he dropped by the CSI lab and spoke with Paul Pinkston.

"Paul, I need a favor from you," he said. "I have found Lillian Reins's car and would like to do some investigating, but I need to have someone in authority who can attest to the chain of evidence just in case I find something. Would you help me?"

"Let me buzz Stephen Sasser. If he says OK, then I'll be glad to do it. When?"

"Right now if you can."

After getting Sasser's approval, Hopper and Pinkston left the building and drove directly to Apex Auto Recyclers.

*　　*　　*　　*　　*　　*

Driving into the lot at Apex Auto Recyclers was like walking back in time. The company lot looked like a junk dealer's delight, if one enjoyed cars. Every conceivable corner of the five-acre lot was covered with metal. Duke, the colorful owner of the place, met Hopper. Between puffs on a cigar, Duke asked, "What can I do for you, pal?"

"I'm looking for the car that was used in the Reins murder. It is a teal green 1997 Ford Mustang. Do you know where on the lot I might find it?"

"Not right off, but I can tell you in a minute. Is this one Boudreaux called about?"

"Yes," Hopper said, "it's the focus of an investigation."

Duke led Hopper into the small, one-room house on the lot that functioned as the headquarters. After a few keystrokes, Duke said, "It's in A-10."

"I don't know what you mean," Hopper said.

"A-10 is a section in the grid of the lot. You see, the lot is divided kinda like a cemetery." Turning to a grid map behind his desk, Duke pointed to the exact location of the car. "It's right there. I remember it now. You can't miss it."

Duke escorted him outside and pointed him in the right direction.

Duke was right; it could not be missed. Hopper inspected the exterior of the car, noting the severe damage to the right front quarter panel, the hood, and the right passenger side door. The frame appeared out of alignment, and after lifting the hood with some difficulty, he noticed the engine had been sheared from its mounts.

As Pinkston looked on, Hopper opened the front passenger side door. The inside of the car had remained exactly as it had been once the crime scene investigators had finished with it. Since the passenger compartment had not been compromised in the accident, it was completely dry. And no cannibalizing for parts on the interior had occurred since it was placed in the lot.

He carefully scrutinized the obvious places that had likely been gone over by the lab technicians. Remembering a case early in his career that had been solved by evidence found in the carpet fibers of a home, he was most interested in what he might find in or under the carpet.

Retrieving his magnifying glass, he began on the passenger's side. He examined the floor mats and then the base floor carpet; he found nothing unusual. He walked around to the driver's side and slid the seat back as far as it would go. Again he carefully studied the floor mats and then the floor itself. With his flashlight, he probed around on the floor. On the carpet under the back edge of the front floor, his flashlight picked up a shiny glint on the dark carpet.

"Paul, come here just a minute," Hopper said.

As Pinkston observed, Hopper used his magnifying glass to study the strange glint more closely. He discovered a small shock of fiber. He pulled his evidence set from his coat pocket. From it he fetched the tweezers, cautiously recovered the fiber, placed it in a plastic snack bag, sealed it, and handed it to Pinkston for safe keeping. His study of the remainder of the car revealed no other apparent evidence.

Excitement was written all over his face. Finding this one, simple item lifted his spirits. After all, he had seen cases resolved on less evidence. He could hardly wait to tell someone. Sitting in his car, he called Fred Roush to inform him of the finding.

"Fred," he said, "don't get your hopes up, but I just went over Lillian Reins's car with a fine toothed comb and found a small shock of fiber that I think the cops may have missed. It may mean nothing, but then again . . ." His voice kind of trailed off. "Just thought I'd let you know. We'll keep in touch."

*   *   *   *   *   *

At 10:00, the dayshift supervisor of guards in the Death House, accompanied by another guard, walked to Mitchell's cell. "Mr. Mitchell, we need you to come with us."

"What for?" Mitchell asked.

"You'll see," the supervisor replied.

After unlocking the cell door, handcuffs were placed on Mitchell's wrists, and he was led to the conference room in an area off of Corridor C. There, Blayne Simmons, somber-faced and looking like he had lost his best friend, met him.

"Jeff, I have some bad news," Simmons began.

"What kind of bad news?"

"Fred and I were notified late last night that your father died yesterday afternoon." Silence filled the room as Mitchell tried to comprehend the news.

"Seems like he had a heart attack. Doctors think it was stress-related," Simmons continued.

Mitchell broke down in tears as he realized he had lost his best friend. Through the tears, Mitchell said, "My dad believed in me. He did everything he could to prove I was innocent. He was my biggest supporter, and now I've killed him. He's the second victim of this incredible tale."

"I'm sorry, Jeff. That's not true. You are not responsible for your father's death." Simmons walked the step toward Mitchell and took him in his arms. Mitchell's body shook uncontrollably from the sobs.

"I don't think I can go on without my dad. You know, he was more than a dad— he was a friend, my very best friend."

Several moments of silence passed before he spoke again. Mitchell then asked, "How's Mom taking it?"

"She's devastated, but she said to assure you that she would get through it."

"Will I be allowed to go to the funeral?"

"No. Fred and I have already pursued that option, and the prison authorities say that state policy does not allow a death row inmate to be outside the walls of the prison except for legal business associated with his case. But we have made arrangements to videotape the funeral for you. It is scheduled for two days from now. Both of us will be attending the funeral. The day after, I will bring you the tape."

"Thanks, Blayne. I know you and Fred have done all you could for me. Don't think I'm not grateful."

"I know. And we're not done yet."

CHAPTER 37

Blake Evans sat in his sixth floor office watching the trees in the park across the street blow in the hot summer breeze of an August morning. North Florida was experiencing some of its most unusually hot and dry weather in decades. Forty-seven days of temperatures in the high 90s and low 100s with little or no rain had set a record.

Checking his e-mail, he found an entry from Bruce Hopper. In it he said that he was going to spend at least two or three days at the original crime scene just to see exactly how he felt about this case. Evans was skeptical; after all, Hopper had been on the case for some time and, while now awaiting the results of fingernail scrapings from Lillian, he remained cynical as to any possible advances that could be made at this point in the investigation.

He was stirred from his daydreaming by a rap on the door. His secretary, Abigail Nealans, entered. "Mr. Evans, the courier just delivered this package to you. I think it is from Judge Reid. Might be what you've been waiting for."

"Thanks, Abby."

Opening the large brown envelope, Evans pulled a sheaf of papers from inside. The top page was a letter addressed to Jeff Mitchell by way of Blake Evans. On a separate line denoted as "RE:" the subject was clearly indicated—"Denial of Appeal on Violation of Public Records." He needed to read no further. At the moment, his curiosity was not sufficiently aroused.

Turning to the window once again, his heart sank as though mired in quick sand. He had been so certain that the appeal would result in a new trial. It was clear that the violation had occurred. Why the ruling? Then his inquisitiveness got the best of him.

He picked up the papers and continued to read:

"The original copy of the subject inventory list dated on the day of the said criminal offense indicates that the subject evidence was submitted to the FDLE laboratory for analysis. And its subsequent return to the Sheriff's Department evidence room from the FDLE lab is also recorded with the notation "RUW" on the inventory sheet. Since the subject evidence was, in fact, listed on the inventory sheet from the date of receipt by the FDLE, there can be no violation of public records. The inventory having been included in the materials provided to the defense, no violation of public records can have occurred. The later discovery of the inventory list by the defense is not sufficient evidence to uphold a request for a new trial.

Attempts by investigators to identify the source of the subject evidence, while not exhaustive, were well within the bounds of reasonable expectation. Furthermore, since the subject evidence was not introduced as at trial, it did not contribute to the conviction of said appellant. Its absence from trial also does not constitute a violation of public records."

Immediately Blake Evans initiated preparation of a Writ of Certiorari from the Florida Supreme Court based upon all of the 8.50 motions that had previously been filed. Maybe he would have better luck there.

*　　*　　*　　*　　*　　*

Mark Bradley hated the late night hours he worked in the convenience store. But at least it generated some income. His wife returned to work, but they were barely making it financially. By next spring, the twin boys would be attending college. That would pose yet another problem.

Every day Bradley scoured the classifieds in the newspaper for any additional work in the local area. He also subscribed to *Employment Business Daily*, seeking advertising employment in other areas of the country. So far nothing had materialized.

After returning home from work on this particularly bright morning, he prepared a cup of coffee and sat down to read the newspaper. As was his custom, the first section he read was the classifieds. Turning to them, he read the "General Employment" column first. As he read down the list of available jobs, his eye caught an advertisement he had never before seen in any newspaper.

STATE OF FLORIDA

State Executioner

The State of Florida is compiling a list of citizens who wish to participate in the administration of capital punishment.

Compensation: $150.00 one time in cash plus expenses.

If interested write to State Prison Commission, 201 Monroe Street, Tallahassee, FL 32300.

Deadline: September 1

Appearing to be a way to make easy money, Bradley took a few minutes, went to his computer upstairs, and prepared a reply. Upon completion, he drove to the post office and dropped it in the mail.

*   *   *   *   *   *

Bruce Hopper had worked long hours in an effort to locate a private, commercial expert on fibers. He finally contacted a member of the FDLE staff who directed him to the only independent laboratory in the country with expertise in fiber analysis. As he picked up the phone to dial the number, he felt abrupt, severe pain in his abdomen. Reacting to the sudden agony he felt, Hopper cried out.

Joanie Foster was startled by the unexpected noise from the conference room where Hopper worked. She opened the door to the room, and, seeing the anguished look on his face, ran to her desk and called 911. She re-entered the conference room and helped him to the sofa along the front wall, where he collapsed and lay unconscious until paramedics arrived.

Coming to in the emergency room of Heart of Hope Hospital was not the way Hopper wished to spend a morning. The pain in his chest was excruciating. He begged for relief. The doctors and nurses working over him tried to keep him calm, reassuring him that everything would be all right. The pain persisted. Hopper went unconscious again.

Quickly taken to surgery, doctors discovered a severely leaking mitral valve in his heart. Apparently several of the ligaments that anchored the valve had weakened over time. The leakage persisted until the elasticity of the ligaments had been stretched to their limits. Two of the ligaments let go, and the leakage became a steady backflow. Hopper underwent a five-hour surgical procedure to replace the weakened valve.

Roush had been notified of Hopper's surgery but waited until the next day to visit him. Hospitals were not his favorite place; however, Bruce was not only his colleague but also his friend.

Once in intensive care, Roush was impressed by the sterile surroundings. Hopper lay so still that he almost appeared dead. "Bruce," Roush said softly. "It's Fred."

Slowly opening his eyes, Hopper took a moment for Fred's presence to register. "Hey, Fred," he said weakly. "What are you doing here?"

"Checking on my favorite investigator. How you doin'?"

"Okay under the circumstances, I guess. I'm probably going to require some rehabilitation so I'm gonna' have to take it easy for a while. That's going to put a crimp in my investigation. As soon as my family arrives, I'll be making plans to return to Orlando to recuperate. Doctors say it shouldn't take more than six weeks."

"What do you think we should do about the investigation?"

"Just before my attack, I had located an independent lab that could analyze the fiber I found in Miss Reins's car. I can tell you where the fiber is located, and you can see that it gets to the lab. That analysis could be performed while I mend. Maybe by the time I'm back in the saddle, the analysis will be complete."

"Sounds reasonable," Roush said. "I'll come back tomorrow, and you can give me the fiber and lab details. Then I'll take it from there."

*   *   *   *   *   *

Armed with the information from Hopper, Roush called Pamela Schuerer, the fibers analyst for Northern States Labs in Milwaukee, Wisconsin. "Ms. Schuerer, my name is Fred Roush, and I'm an attorney in North Florida. I have a fiber that I'd like to have your lab analyze. The fiber is part of an ongoing investigation into a murder that occurred here more than six years ago. Do you think you could help us?"

"We certainly can try. I'll be glad to have the administrative office fax you a copy of the fee schedule. After reviewing the schedule, you should call the contact person listed and make necessary arrangements to sign the papers. Following the execution of the paperwork, the office will notify me to contact you. Then I will apprise you of the method of transport for the fiber."

"Thank you. Please send me the fee schedule; I don't wish to waste any time on this matter."

By week's end, the paperwork had been executed and Ms. Schuerer notified. By Friday afternoon, Roush, with Pinkston observing, had prepared the fibers for overnight transport to the labs.

*   *   *   *   *   *

TWO MONTHS LATER

Mark Bradley walked to his mailbox and pulled from it a strange-looking envelope. The brown envelope, bordered in black indicated a return address that was a post office box in Tallahassee, Florida. The outside of the envelope gave no evidence of the sender.

Inside was a single piece of stationery printed on white bond paper also bordered in black. The logo at the top of the letter revealed that it was from the State Department of Corrections. The letter stated:

"Dear Mr. Bradley:

In response to your inquiry RE: State Executioner, you are hereby notified that your name has been included on a list of persons to be called on to perform said duty when the judicial process has been exhausted and circumstances warrant your services. As advertised, you will be compensated in the amount of $150.00 plus expenses, to be paid in cash at the time of the performance of your duty. You shall be provided two days' notice requiring your presence at the State Prison in Starke, Florida. As a part of that notification, you will be informed as to the time of the planned execution and the process to be used to maintain your anonymity.

At the bottom of this letter, you will find two spaces. Please mark one of them indicating your willingness or unwillingness to proceed with this assignment. Return a marked and signed copy to the enclosed address within seven days."

The letter was signed by the Commissioner of the Department.

Bradley did not know whether he should be happy or not happy about the appointment. He was having second thoughts about his action. Nevertheless, it was money, so he signed the letter and mailed it the next day.

CHAPTER 38

The struggle had been difficult, draining his emotions to the breaking point and putting a strain on his personal life and his professional self-confidence. Blake Evans had defended the rights of many men who probably deserved to die for their crimes. In several cases he had succeeded in getting the inmate's sentence reduced to life without parole. In several other cases, he had failed, and the inmate met his fate in "Old Sparky," the fabled Florida electric chair. Now the preferred form of execution was lethal injection.

But the Mitchell case was different. The persistence and believability of this condemned "killer" in declaring that he was innocent, along with the fact that only circumstantial evidence, albeit strong, pointed a slim finger at him, were enough to convince Evans that Mitchell was, indeed, innocent. No physical evidence or person could put him at the scene of the crime. His doubt nagged his every waking hour.

"Special delivery for you, Mr. Evans," said Abigail.

The return address indicated that the letter was from the Florida Supreme Court. Anxiously he opened the letter. His heart sank. He had played the appeal process according to the rules. To this point, he had failed.

Today's rejection notice by the Florida Supreme Court seemed to be the final nail in the coffin. It seemed to shout loud and clear, "It's all over. Give it up." He knew that any potential future that Mitchell might have expected now rested in the remaining appeals.

Evans reviewed the case each week to try to discover new angles of appeal, but his efforts always seemed to hit a brick wall. Frustration caused his blood pressure to rise, and the wear was beginning to show. He was pleased that Hopper had discovered a fiber that was being processed, but that evidence was apparently insufficient to get a new trial. He hoped they could find the source of the second DNA evidence on the sweater.

Certainly, this case had presented the greatest challenge throughout his career. He even struck the most casual observer as being obsessed by this case. His colleagues noticed how his appearance had become more and more dowdy. Some days he came to the office looking as though he had slept in his clothes; he seemed much older than his years.

How long will it be before the governor signs a death warrant? he thought. *Now that the final appeal has been rejected, the governor will probably consider issuing a warrant rather quickly.* Depressed and discouraged, he thought out loud, "I give the governor no more than three months."

*   *   *   *   *   *

Hopper had returned to Pensacola after six weeks of recuperation. He appeared refreshed and expressed optimism about the future of the case. Today, he would go to the crime scene.

With the September heat remaining in the 90s and with little rain, Hopper started his search at the point where Lillian Reins had been found. Perspiration poured from his body. From previous searches, he knew about the creek bed located about 150 yards away. He walked in that direction until he reached the creek bed. It was almost completely dry. Only a trickle remained.

He walked both banks of the creek bed for almost 200 yards, stirring the leaves, looking under fallen branches and investigating anything unusual that might catch his eye. Nothing.

Six years had resulted in changes in the forest where Lillian had been killed. Trees had been struck by lightning, brambles had overgrown some of the areas around the crime scene, and at the point where her body was found, no sign of a murder remained.

Over a period of two hours Hopper walked in concentric circles, observing anything out of the ordinary. He found an aluminum soda can, the remnants of a cane fishing pole, and assorted plastic bags hanging from trees. As he stood at the tree where Lillian had been found, he tried to get into the mind of the killer.

If I had committed this murder, what would I have done? he thought.

I would not have retraced my steps to the car; besides, the car was a total wreck and not drivable. I would walk out another way and go home on foot.

Even after considering the amount of time that had passed since the murder, he looked for the best possible escape route and began to walk. He used a metal detector as he walked. Before he could get to the road, he stumbled over a hollow tree that had obviously fallen since the time of the murder. As he stepped over the tree, his detector beeped near what was once the top of the fallen tree. Digging through the leaves, he felt a hard object. It was a knife. Apparently the killer had shinnied up the tree and stuck the knife into the top of the hollow cavity where it would not be found. He had found it only because the tree had fallen in a windstorm sometime during the past years.

The knife was unlike any knife he had ever seen. Carefully he held it by the edges of the protector plate until he reached his car. He then placed it in a plastic evidence bag, several of which he always kept with him. He would give it to Paul Pinkston later in the day.

* * * * * *

After giving the knife to Paul Pinkston for safekeeping, Hopper returned to his office at the CCR. There he called Pamela Schuerer at Northern States Labs. While she admitted to having the fiber for quite some period, the urgency of other more pressing matters had demanded more and more of her time. As a result, she had finally initiated the analysis in the early part of the week; she expected to have it completed by the end of the week.

Hopper pulled his notepad from his inside pocket. He had checked all but two of the estate sales. He planned to complete those last two by the end of the week.

* * * * * *

Blake Evans shouted through the office door, a practice that was totally uncharacteristic of his behavior, and asked Abby to get Fred Roush on the phone. He wanted to share the most recent news.

Upon hearing the intercom buzzer, Evans picked up the phone: "Fred, I have more bad news. The Florida Supreme Court has denied the final appeal. I'm still trying to find a loophole that I might use as grounds for another appeal, but it's eluding me. My concern is that the governor will shortly issue a death warrant in the case, and that will make appealing it even more difficult. I will call Jeff this afternoon to inform him of the latest developments.

"If we can turn up some substantial new evidence," asked Roush, "would that have an influence on stopping the execution process?"

"Yeah, but the evidence will have to be very strong and unquestionable," replied Evans.

"I am expecting a call from Bruce Hopper today about the purchase of the brooch, and he's also expecting an answer in a few days from the lab on the source of the fiber and the fingernail residue. In the meantime, he's found a knife near the scene of the murder that is in the hands of the CSIs now. He expects to have some information on it soon. Please stay close to a phone so I can let you know about any new developments on these issues."

"Do that, but I'm sure he'll call me as well," said Evans.

* * * * * *

Hopper was down to his last two contacts. He now prepared to meet the owner of an estate gallery that had placed an ad in the classifieds only a week prior to the murder. Fischer-Fontaine Gallery of Antiques & Collectibles was a firm that had operated in the area for more than eighty years. Its reputation was unblemished, the quality of its merchandise unequaled. The gallery specialized in seventeenth through early twentieth century antiques, and included in its inventory distinctive jewelry of European extraction, from the mid to late nineteenth century.

Valentino Fontaine now owned the gallery outright; his partner, Walter Fischer, had died five years ago. Fischer's children did not wish to retain the gallery as an asset, so they agreed to sell the Fischer partnership to Fontaine for a reasonable cash offer. Fontaine, who considered the gallery a part of his family, agreed to the amount and took sole ownership of the gallery within one year of the death of his partner. Wishing not to lose the name recognition and good will that had been enhanced over the years, he retained the original name.

The Fischer-Fontaine Gallery was inauspiciously housed in a wooden structure that had formerly been a seafood warehouse. Located near the waterfront, the inventory of the gallery seemed to be a hodge podge of carelessly arranged displays of discarded furniture and household items. But the jewelry collection, so prized by the owners, was housed in beautiful glass cases, luminously displayed and exquisite in presentation. The jewelry, in its display cases, was stored inside a large vault.

"Good afternoon, Mr. Fontaine," Hopper said. "I called you earlier in reference to an estate sale which you advertised more than five years ago. You may not recall it, but I'm hoping you can help."

He handed Fontaine an 8 x 10 photograph of the brooch—it had been enlarged to illustrate the intricate detail—Hopper asked, "Do you remember whether you handled this piece of jewelry?"

Hopper looked at Fontaine as he asked the question. Without Fontaine saying a word, Hopper knew he had hit pay dirt.

"No jeweler in his right mind would ever forget that marvelous piece. It had a royal history. The brooch was the creation of Russian silversmiths, who fashioned the piece for Czar Nicholas II. He had it made as a birthday gift for his German-born wife

317

Czarina Alexandra in 1895. His claim to fame is the fact that he was the last czar of Russia, having been overthrown by the revolution led by the Bolsheviks in 1917. Fontaine's eyes brightened as he offered Hopper a history lesson. It was obvious he enjoyed telling the story.

Well-versed in Eastern European history, Fontaine continued, looking at the pictures of the brooch from every angle, all the while absorbing its unparalleled beauty. "Although the family was reported to have been executed by the Bolsheviks in 1918, stories abound about the escape of his daughter, Anastasia. History records that she smuggled special family pieces out of Russia, one of which was this brooch. Do you actually have the brooch now?"

"No, but I know where it is. What can you tell me about its purchase?"

"Our firm held an estate sale, as you mentioned, at about the time in question. The sale was for a family of Russian descent who apparently knew Anastasia. Anastasia had given the family the brooch for safekeeping more than fifty years ago. Upon the death of the mother, and since the survivors did not know whether Anastasia was even alive, the family suggested that the brooch be put up for sale along with the other items in the estate."

"Do you recall who purchased it?"

"Not precisely. But I probably could find out for you. I've tried to keep very accurate records for more than sixty years, and I'm a packrat, so now every five years, the records are digitized and stored. I'd be happy to research it for you. It may take some time, but I'll do my best."

"That's all I can ask. A man's life could be at stake, so the sooner the better."

"Haste is not characteristic of me, but I'll certainly not put it off. How can I get in touch with you?"

Hopper took out a business card and wrote his local phone number on the back. "Just call me at this number any time."

*　　*　　*　　*　　*　　*

Three days passed. No word from the lab. Just as Hopper had decided to make a call to Northern States Lab, the intercom buzzed notifying him that Pamela Schuerer was on the phone.

"Ms. Schuerer, I hope you have good news for me."

"I don't know whether it is good or not, but I have information which I hope will be helpful. The analyses have been completed, and we have determined the fiber you submitted to be a bullet-shaped polyester fiber manufactured by Morgan Phillips Carpet Mills. The corporate office of the mill is in Dahlonega, Georgia, a small town northeast of Atlanta."

"What can you tell us about the fiber that sets it apart from others," Hopper asked.

"Its diameter is forty microns, large for this particular fiber. It appears that the manufacturing process may have been flawed during extrusion. The carpet contains concentrated amounts of delustrant, and the delustrant appears to have been included in the extrusion mix. The burnt orange color was dyed into the fiber rather than mixed into the slough for extrusion. This coloring process was used for only a brief period of time, about two months, so very little carpet with these kinds of markings actually made it into the marketplace."

"So you're saying, the shape and color of the fiber and the presence of delustrant identify it as a Morgan Philips product?" Hopper asked. He took notes throughout the conversation.

"Yes. But the pitting in the fiber caused by extrusion as well as the length of the fiber also point toward this manufacturer. The color simply pinpoints the time period during which it was manufactured."

"Thanks, Ms. Schuerer. You have been most helpful. I will contact Morgan Philips Mills to determine where they might have delivered some of that carpet in North Florida," Hopper said.

*   *   *   *   *   *

After a meal of chicken and dumplings, Fred and Robyn lay down in front of a blazing fire. Warm from the fire, Robyn removed her blouse, leaving on her tank top. She lay in Fred's arms, lavishing in her feelings of security.

With his wife reclining in his lap, Fred noticed the small scar on her shoulder. "You never told me about the scar," Roush said.

"You never asked except that one time, and I didn't feel like talking about it then."

"Do you feel like talking about it now?"

"Yeah. I'll tell you about it. You see, my father tried to molest me when I was twelve years old. I resisted. It was summertime, and I had on a simple halter-top. In his attempt, I resisted, and his long, unmanicured fingernails gouged my skin. That scar has been a grim reminder of the event, and I've lived with it ever since that day. I always covered it so that my mother would not notice."

"Robyn, I'm so sorry." Reaching down and turning her face toward his, Fred kissed her, then held her firmly to his chest. "I will never let you go, you know that, don't you?"

"Yes, I do. That's why I love you so much. How could I have been so lucky? No woman should be as happy as I am right now."

They lay before the hearth deep in slumber until the fire reduced itself to smoldering embers.

*   *   *   *   *   *

Less than a month!!

Fred Roush could not believe what he was seeing. Someone had gotten to the governor awfully fast to get a death warrant issued so quickly. He called Blake Evans.

"Blake, what's the word on the death warrant?"

"Just got our copy of it this morning. It seems that an execution date has been set for 12:00 midnight on September 29."

"Doesn't give us much time to turn up anything, does it?" Roush asked.

"No, but you can bet we won't give up. In fact, I had already prepared a request for a Writ of Habeas Corpus to the Federal District Court in just such an event. It is being hand delivered to the Court this afternoon. I hope to hear from it within a week."

"Good. Sounds like you are as on top of the process as you could possibly be," Roush said. "For your information, we found the source of the brooch."

"That's great news. What have you learned about it?"

"It's quite a historical piece, and the owner of the gallery that sold it is checking his records even as we speak to determine who he sold it to. Fortunately, he keeps meticulous records, so the chances right now seem real good."

"Anything on the fiber yet?" asked Evans.

"Yes, our analysis has been completed, and we know the type, color, and manufacturer. We are in the process of tracing the distribution markets of the carpet as quickly as we can. We hit pay dirt there, too. It seems that the fiber is part of a limited carpet run that was manufactured by Morgan Philips Mills. As soon as we locate the local distributor and analyze his sales, we should have a better idea about where it came from."

*   *   *   *   *   *

No one could have been more surprised than Mark Bradley at the appearance of the brown envelope similar to the one he had received a year earlier. Brown with a black border, no return address except a post office box in Tallahassee. He knew before he opened it that it contained some information from the State Department of Corrections.

Opening the envelope, he found a black-bordered piece of white paper on which was written "Notice of Appearance." Addressed to him and signed by Warden Howard Moore, it read: "Dear Mr. Bradley:

Please be advised that you are to appear at the main gate of the Florida State Prison near Starke, Florida, no later than 9:00 p.m. on the evening of September 28. The purpose of your appearance will be to serve as the official executioner for an inmate whose execution has been set for midnight.

You are instructed to communicate with no one in regard to this assignment until after said assignment has been carried out.

Your identification will not be revealed, either before or after the completion of the assignment.

You will be paid $150.00 cash upon successful completion of the assignment. This office will also underwrite all expenses for your travel and accommodations. If you wish to be removed from the list of executioners, please advise by written communication (or fax) no later than one week from today."

By the time he finished reading the letter, he realized that he was about to kill a human being. Never had he thought his life would have come to this point. But his urge to survive was too strong. He would do it and not look back.

CHAPTER 39

Sleep did not come easily for Jeff Mitchell. His attorneys with the CCR had notified him two weeks earlier that his appeal to the Florida Supreme Court had been denied and to expect a death warrant to be signed fairly soon. It took less than thirty days for the governor to obtain the necessary paperwork and sign the black-bordered document.

His fate appeared now sealed, and in keeping with his requests, no extraordinary efforts other than the standard appeals to the federal judiciary were being made by the CCR to save him.

He had been awake most of the night, and he sat in the yellow-red light of dawn and read his Bible. He turned to a passage from Hebrews and read:

For God has said, "I will never, never fail you nor forsake you. That is why we can say without any doubt or fear, 'The Lord is my helper and I am not afraid of anything that mere man can do to me'."

A marginal note that he had written years earlier while listening to a sermon by his pastor referred him to the Gospel of Matthew. There he found his most reassuring words from the mouth of Jesus: "Don't be afraid of those who can kill only your bodies—but can't touch your souls! Fear only God who can destroy both body and soul in hell."

Mitchell could see dawn breaking through the frosted glass across from his cell. Although he could not see it clearly, he thought, *How beautiful the sunrise must be. This one seems so special because I probably will not see many more.*

This bright yellow corridor had been home to him for six and a half years. He was tired, and he was incredibly lonesome. His dad had died, and although his dad and everyone else in his family had supported and visited him over the years, this experience was one he must face alone.

It was almost 10:00 p. m. Six members of the death watch team walked slowly down the corridor toward his cell. Mitchell could hear the clacking of shoe taps on the floor as they approached him. The picture that came to his mind was that of Willie-Boy who, only a few months earlier, had given him the rabbit's foot. Apparently the rabbit's foot would provide no more luck for Mitchell than it had for Willie-Boy.

Opening the cell door, the supervisor of the death watch team entered. "Mr. Mitchell, we are here to escort you to the death watch cell. You will be more comfortable there, and you will be able to receive visitors without leaving the area." Without handcuffing him, two team members flanked him on either side. Handcuffs were unnecessary. Besides, where could he run at this late date. Two team members led in front, and two followed close behind.

Together, they walked the forty feet to the death watch cell. With walls painted in a soft blue color, it was located only fifteen feet from the entrance to the death chamber. But it was a spacious area, almost like a barred conference room. The vinyl floor glistened with the same shine as the corridor. After all, this cell was not used very often and got little wear and tear.

As he entered the cell, he noticed that, instead of a prison issue cot, there sat in the far corner an oak bed, fully dressed with colorful linens. A sofa and a recliner with a lamp table between them were situated in the other corner. A table on which he would eat his last meal sat obtrusively in the middle of the room. A desk with lamp, writing paper and pencils, and a dictionary were also a part of the provisions of the death watch cell. *All the comforts of home*, Mitchell thought as he walked over and sat on the edge of the bed. It would be his "home" for the next two weeks. During that time, he would be under twenty-four hour, eye-to-eye surveillance.

*   *   *   *   *   *

In anticipation of this eventuality, Blake Evans had prepared appeal papers to both the Eleventh Circuit Court of Appeals and the United States Supreme Court. Upon receipt today of the denial of his request for habeas corpus by the Federal District Court, he faxed the appeals documents to the Appeals Court before the day ended. Both time and the appeals process were fast running out.

* * * * * *

Blake Evans finally received Word that the Eleventh Circuit Court of Appeals had denied his request for a new trial. One last appeal remained before Jeff Mitchell would meet his fate in Florida's death chamber. Working around the clock, Evans spent the next thirty-seven hours preparing an appeal to the United States Supreme Court. He hoped that the findings of the Supreme Court would warrant the issuance of a Writ of Certiorari and the order for a new trial.

* * * * * *

These last weeks were the loneliest of Jeff Mitchell's life. No contact with the outside world and no visitors had been allowed. At 3:00 p.m., the supervisor of the death watch team stood in front of his cell. "Mr. Mitchell," he said. "I'm here to inform you that your family will be brought in tomorrow before noon. They will be able to stay with you as long as they wish, even up to a couple of hours before time. Is there anyone else you would wish to have here to visit? We shall be happy to call them for you."

"Yes, please contact Fred Roush, my lawyer and ask him to come."

The team left the cell and returned to their appointed duties. Within the next two hours, they would make a final check of the chemicals and delivery apparatus.

* * * * * *

The death watch team gathered in an empty cell on Corridor B, on the side of the death chamber opposite from where Mitchell was being held. The purpose of the meeting was to review the protocol to be employed during the forthcoming execution. One member of the team posed as the "condemned." Each team member was assigned a specific duty.

Two members of the team flanked the "condemned" as he was led to the death chamber. One team member led and two followed behind. As they entered the death chamber, all was quiet. Each member went about his duties methodically, stoically, without emotion. One member was responsible for tightening the straps that would hold the "condemned's" legs and lower torso; another was responsible for his chest and arms. A technician performed a mock insertion of an intravenous cannula in both arms and checked the lines leading into the executioner's booth for kinks, bubbles or foreign matter. Everything appeared to be in order. The apparatus was disassembled and the exercise declared a success.

Outside the death chamber, the warden watched the exercise through a rectangular opening in the wall. Through this same opening, forty-eight inches long by ten inches high, the executioner would perform his duties and a physician would be in attendance to observe the execution.

The warden called in the prison physician to check the system. After several adjustments to the delivery system, the doctor declared the apparatus ready for testing again.

This time no variation, no interruption. The equipment seemed to be in excellent working order. The execution should come off without a hitch.

*　　*　　*　　*　　*　　*

Since his death watch cell was located only fifteen feet from the death chamber, Jeff Mitchell could hear the commotion from the exercise that was occurring. As he heard the clank of metal buckles and clicks from the delivery system, stark fear gripped him, and he clasped his hands over his ears to avoid hearing what was happening. By tomorrow night all that cacophony would escort him to his death.

He crawled onto the bed, longing for sleep to help escape the reality that lay only a few feet away. Sleep would not come. *Oh, if only my family were here.*

*   *   *   *   *   *

EARLY MORNING, SEPTEMBER 28

At 6:00, Bradley arose to the sound of his alarm clock. Disturbed by her husband, Renee asked, "What are you doing?"

"Going somewhere for the day. Got to get an early start. Please don't ask me any more questions about it. Just trust me. I'll be back tomorrow, I promise," Bradley answered. Suddenly, in that moment, he realized how far he had fallen financially and emotionally.

"How can I get in touch with you if I need you? We don't have the cellular phones any more."

"I'll call you. Please don't worry about me. I'll be fine."

For the first time in a long time, Renee recognized the signs of depression and a complete loss of self worth. What a pity for a man who had accomplished so much and who now thought he had nothing to live for.

After dressing and packing a small bag, Bradley kissed his wife, said "Goodbye," and got in his car for the long drive to Starke. Renee felt withdrawn and uncomfortable about her husband's leaving for a destination unknown to her. She decided to call in sick for the day.

The drive for Mark Bradley was boring. He chased various thoughts. *I'd be a wreck, I guess, if I felt I were headed for an appointment with the needle. Just the idea is painful.*

Passing through Tallahassee, Bradley stopped at one of his favorite restaurants, Grindles. It was famous for its fried chicken tenders and the special pink sauce that was unique to this restaurant. The recipe for the sauce was a secret known only to the owners. The food was as good as he remembered it.

Driving on to Starke, he passed through little towns typical of West Florida. Passing Monticello, Madison, Greeneville, and Live

327

Oak, he pressed on toward the intersection with I-75. Proceeding south he drove along Highway 238 to Lake Butler, the state penal facility where prisoners are first admitted to the system. From Lake Butler he took Highway 100 to Starke.

A small town of little more than six thousand people, its primary industry is corrections. Stopping at the first gas station he could find, he asked the proprietor where he might find the Blue Moon Motel. "Just down the street about a half mile," the proprietor replied.

Six-tenths of a mile to be exact, Bradley thought as he pulled into the parking lot. The Blue Moon Motel was a turn of the century clapboard building that looked more like a bed and breakfast house than a real motel. It looked comfortable enough. Bradley walked in and quickly registered, received his key, and took his small bag of belongings to Room 13 at the top of the stairs.

He laid the room keys on the dresser and turned on the television. The time was 1:30 in the afternoon. He had lost an hour when he crossed into the Eastern time zone. Picking up the telephone, he called Renee. She answered on the first ring. "I figured you would call in sick today. Was I right?"

"Yes, you were. Where are you?"

"Sweetheart, I can't tell you right now, maybe later. I just called to let you know I arrived safely. Please don't worry about me. I will plan on spending the night here and will return tomorrow by mid afternoon." Not wishing to carry on an extended conversation, he simply said, "Love you. Bye."

Bradley lay on the bed to rest. He closed his eyes, but the low sounds of the television in the background seemed to keep him awake. He wondered about the unlucky soul he would be executing. Slowly he drifted off to sleep.

*　　*　　*　　*　　*　　*

At 10:30 a.m., Blake Evans received word by fax that the U. S. Supreme Court had denied his request for a new trial. The waiting was over. Nothing else could be done to save Jeff Mitchell from his fate just after midnight.

Evans called Fred Roush who, at the time, was in his car traveling to the prison. Evans informed him of the decision of the U. S. Supreme Court. Roush, bitter and angry, held out hope. The evidence that Hopper continued to investigate became more solid by the hour, but a specific identity had yet to be determined. Roush only hoped that the evidence would be sufficient to halt the execution. Calling up all the courage he could muster, he called Bruce Hopper and reported the action of the Supreme Court then called the prison and had the warden advise Jeff of the court's decision.

*   *   *   *   *   *

Like a whirling dervish, Bruce Hopper pursued all the new evidence he had collected and submitted for analysis.

*   *   *   *   *   *

By 11:00 in the morning, Mitchell's family had arrived. Escorted to the death watch cell, Mitchell's mother broke down in tears, sweeping her son into her arms. "My son, my dear, dear son."

Mitchell's mother held him tightly for what seemed like an eternity. She simply could not let go. Finally, Jaimie, Mitchell's brother, inserted himself between them and offered a brotherly hug of his own. His sister, Andrea, patiently waited her turn to speak with and embrace her brother.

For a long time no one spoke a word. What was there to say at a time like this? Finally, Jeff told his family of the Supreme Court decision. All were stunned and broke down in tears. Silence.

In an attempt to relieve the tension of the moment, Jaimie broke the ice, "Do you remember, Jeff, the time I got mad at you for kissing my girlfriend? We were in the third grade, and I loved Ginny McCormick. I caught you kissing her behind the school one day and got so mad with you I punched you in the face."

329

"I remember," Jeff said, smiling and wiping the tears from his eyes. "I had a black eye for a week. When I came home from school, Mom asked me what happened, and I told her I fell off my bicycle. I didn't want her to know the truth. By the way, did you ever apologize for doing that?"

"You know, I don't think I did. Jeff, I'm sorry for slugging you."

"Oh, think nothing of it." They both smiled. Even Mom and Andrea looked at each other and grinned slightly. But the pain in their faces was difficult to hide.

For the next several hours, Mitchell and his family reminisced. By mid-afternoon silence once more fell across the cell as they came face to face with reality.

With emotion rising in her throat, Mitchell's mom silently remembered when Jeff was born. He was such a beautiful baby. Skin as clear as a bright fall day, dark hair that swirled to a soft curl, and eyes that would melt the winter snows. Her first-born, and he was unforgettable.

*   *   *   *   *   *

Andrea sat in the chair next to the lamp table. Slumped and depressed, she remembered the times her brother had come to her defense. At sixteen, she had begun to date. Not perceptive about boys, Andrea had accepted a date with a guy whose reputation was less than upstanding. On that first date, he had tried to kiss her. She was not ready for that. She told Jeff, and he confronted the boy the next day, punched him out, and told him not to see his sister again.

Jaimie remembered a time when he and Jeff had gone to a local motel to swim. Public swimming pools were not so readily available in those days. In spite of the no horseplay rule, the two brothers chased each other around the sides of the pool, jumping in to avoid being caught, and dunking each other under the water. Near the edge of the pool, Jaimie had pushed Jeff's head to dunk him but accidentally shoved him toward the side of the pool, hitting his face on the edge and cutting a large bloody gash in his mouth. They rushed home, and Mom took Jeff to the hospital. In the emergency room he received ten stitches to close the gaping wound.

*   *   *   *   *   *

Mom recalled the time when, as a five-year-old, Jeff had climbed to the top of an evergreen tree and gotten frightened. The tree must have been at least forty feet high. He was so scared, he could not climb back down. Shouting as loudly as he could, he attracted the attention of a neighbor, who notified his mom. She called the fire department. The firefighters came and retrieved the scared little boy by using a "cherry picker" to get him out of the tree.

She reminisced about his days in little league football. "My, what an aggressive little guy you were," she said. "You played defense and your dad had taught you how to tackle. He was so proud every time you tackled a player in the open field. And you would instinctively glance toward the stands for the approval of Mom and Dad. What days those were."

The reminiscing was interrupted by another visitor. Jeff recognized the sound of Fred's voice and smiled in anticipation. Somber and disheartened, Roush entered, taking Mitchell by the hand and wrapping his other arm around his shoulders. They remained embraced for a long moment.

Whispering to Mitchell, Roush said, "I've told you it's not too late until the final moment. We are still working hard; keep believing."

"Yeah, I know. You've done all you can. I'm resigned to whatever happens."

Mitchell and Roush walked toward the bed and sat on its edge. Roush held Mitchell's face in the palms of his hands and directed Jeff's gaze toward him. "We are working on new evidence that looks very promising. We think we've identified some new suspects, and efforts to tie them to the crime are in high gear.

That's why CCR and the investigator are staying close to home as the tests are conducted on the new evidence. CCR will contact the governor directly if the evidence results are as we think they might be. Please know that there are many of us who believe you are innocent."

"I'm glad to hear that, but it offers little comfort with less than twelve hours to go. I just wish my dad could be here to support me. I feel like I'm the reason he died."

"Jeff, don't ever believe that. Your dad trusted in your innocence as much as the rest of us. If you had committed this crime, you might attribute your dad's death to your circumstances. But you did nothing wrong. Your circumstances are not of your own doing. How can you blame yourself for being in a situation you didn't create?"

"I know. But it's hard not to blame myself. Maybe there was something I could have done differently that might have changed the outcome of all this."

"I don't think there is anything you could have done. The evidence against you, while all circumstantial, was so overwhelming that the average jury could not discount your guilt. It's as simple as that. But we hope we have finally found the keys to proving your innocence. We just hope it won't be too late."

*　　*　　*　　*　　*　　*

At 7:00, one member of the death watch team brought Mitchell his last meal. The day before, Mitchell had put in his request. It consisted of fried shrimp, a broiled rib eye steak, a baked potato, and a green salad with ranch dressing. For dessert he asked for his favorite, apple pie ala mode.

Mitchell sat down to eat, surrounded by his family and Fred Roush. He was not really hungry, and he picked at his food. Eating only shrimp and a few bites of the steak and potato, he pushed the remainder of the meal aside. He did not even look at the pie. Within an hour, a member of the death watch team recovered the leftovers.

*   *   *   *   *   *

At 9:00, Fred Roush said his final "goodbye" to Jeff Mitchell. He would never forget the pathetic look of dread and fear on Mitchell's face. They embraced once more. Holding Mitchell by the shoulders and looking him straight in the eye, Roush tried to offer words of encouragement. Roush smiled and whispered, "Remember, it ain't over till it's over." Mitchell's sad eyes reflected a shattered spirit, a broken man, an unnecessarily wrecked life. *What a waste,* Roush thought as he left the prison. He would be returning to witness the execution.

*   *   *   *   *   *

Bradley had awakened a little later than normal. From the sound of thunder outside, it appeared that the severe weather watch that had been in effect all afternoon had finally developed into a fully developed active thunderstorm. He noticed then that the TV screen indicated the National Weather Service had issued a thunderstorm warning for the area until after midnight.

At the same time that Fred Roush was leaving the death watch cell, Mark Bradley arrived at the outside gate of the prison. By now, the rain was coming down in sheets as the wind swept to the ground at an angle. Across the road from the prison, a group protesting the death penalty huddled under ponchos or whatever else they could find to protect themselves from the rain. The press corps, with its small klieg lights and bulky television cameras, kept watchful eyes on the entrance to the prison, all the while covering their equipment.

Bradley drove up to the guardhouse and passed to the guard a vehicle pass that had been sent to him by Warden Moore. "Just a moment," the guard said. He walked to the phone, where he placed a call to the warden.

After less than a minute, the guard returned to the car, shouting over the pounding of the rain, "Go on in. Please proceed to the visitors area at the far end of the roadway. You will see visitor parking signs there."

333

Bradley drove to the area, found a space, and parked his car. Before he could emerge, Warden Moore was at the door of his car in a raincoat with an umbrella in his hand. "Mr. Bradley, it is necessary that your identity remain anonymous to everyone except those essential to this operation. I'll escort you into the waiting room over there, where you will remain isolated until a few minutes before the execution is to take place. Put your raincoat over your head, and I'll cover us both with the umbrella. That way no one should get sight of you."

Hurriedly, the two of them sloshed across the water-soaked ground to the dull gray building that housed the death chamber. In a drab but brightly lighted room more than fifty feet from the death chamber, Mark Bradley spent almost three hours waiting to fulfill his responsibility. In the room had been placed several small books and a wide variety of magazines. In one corner of the room was a television set. He turned on the television and then picked up a *People* magazine and began to scan it. He found the crossword puzzle in the back and decided to try his luck. After all, what else did he have to do? He had never been good at crossword puzzles.

Because he became entranced by the story on "NCIS Los Angeles," the puzzle took him the better part of an hour. He lacked two entries that he simply could not recall. One of them was a four-letter word that completed the title "Breakfast at

_____," a 1961 Audrey Hepburn film. The other clue was a four-letter word for the name of the off-Broadway theater award.

At the conclusion of "NCIS Los Angeles," he left the TV on the local station to hear the latest news. He had been totally out of touch with what was going on in the world for several days—first due to his work and his efforts to get a job and then because of this trip.

The lead news story was the execution. After the lead-in and a commercial break, the news anchor said, "Today's top story is tonight's scheduled execution at Florida State Prison. Convicted for the murder of Lillian McRae Reins more than seven years ago, Jeffrey Mitchell will meet his appointment with death at the hands of the State of Florida at a minute after midnight."

Bradley heard little else of the newscast. He turned his head upward and, with hands in the air, shouted, "Oh, God, what have I gotten myself into? I didn't know the person to be executed is Jeff Mitchell. I can't come here and kill my best friend? What am I going to do?"

Suddenly, a member of the death watch team, who had heard Bradley's commotion, stepped into the room. "Is there something wrong?"

"Yes. Uh, no." He needed time to think. "But thanks for checking."

Bradley paced the room, thinking, reflecting on the situation. *What can I do?* he thought. *I can't just abruptly tell the warden that I won't do it. That would be embarrassing. I would be the laughing stock of the state; I would forever be the goon without the guts to pull the switch. I can see all the tabloid stories now. And I wouldn't get the money. I need the money.*

For the next hour, Bradley's mind weighed the situation and pondered the thoughts of killing his best friend. He justified the act by reminding himself that Jeff had been convicted by a court of law and so sentenced. He, Bradley, was only a stooge for the state.

The money; always the money. *After all, the only reason I applied to do this in the first place was for the money. I need the money; it will feed our family this week. But I feel like a Judas. No, I just won't think about it. It's just best not to think about it; just do it,* he finally muttered to himself. He then turned off the TV, and, to get his mind off what he was about to do, he picked up another magazine and began to read.

*   *   *   *   *   *

At 10:00, the supervisor of the death watch team came to the death watch cell. "Mrs. Mitchell," he said, "we must ask you and the family to say your goodbyes to Jeff now. We will come back in ten minutes to escort you to the witness waiting area."

Keeping his word, the team returned in ten minutes. Mrs. Mitchell gave her son a final embrace, stoically maintaining a solemn but tearless facade. Jaimie and Andrea could not hold back the tears. Together, the three embraced for a final time. Jaimie departed quietly; Andrea, with her hand covering her mouth, left the cell sobbing.

*　　*　　*　　*　　*　　*

Two hours now stood between Jeff Mitchell and his rendezvous with Florida's death chamber. His hands visibly shook, and he developed a nervous twitch in his left eye. He suddenly felt nauseated and stepped to the sink on the east wall and threw up what little he had retained of his final meal.

CHAPTER 40

The clock on the wall across from the death watch cell read 11:00. Momentarily, the death watch team approached Mitchell's cell, unlocking it, and walking in. Handing him a clean set of white clothing, the team supervisor said, "Mr. Mitchell, we have some clothes here that you need to change into. Take a couple of minutes and change. We will take your other clothes with us." Mitchell retreated to a corner of the cell for some privacy and changed into the new white pants and shirt. No shoes were provided, only white house slippers. The supervisor accepted the old clothes, and the team left the cell. Only forty-five minutes remained of his time on earth.

Mitchell turned on the television set and sat back in the recliner, trying to be as relaxed as possible. At least he could feel comfortable for the last minutes of his life. The movie being shown was his very favorite, *Shenandoah*. Then he thought, *I won't even get to see the end of it.*

Resigned somehow to his fate, Mitchell recalled the letters he had written to Fred Roush and his mom and dad several months back. In them he had hoped that the end would come quickly. He had tired very soon of the monotony and loneliness of prison life. He was now about to receive what he had wished for so diligently. With that realization, his nerves calmed, and he was instantly at peace with himself. He no longer gazed at the clock; he only longed for the experience to be over. Thirty minutes to go.

*   *   *   *   *   *

At fifteen minutes before midnight Warden Moore escorted Mark Bradley to a small cubicle adjacent to the switching room. "Warden," Bradley said. "I need to tell you something."

"Yes, Mr. Bradley."

"Uh. . . I don't think . . .um. Oh, never mind. It's not important."

"Okay, then. Let's get on with this. Mr. Bradley, I would like to familiarize you with the procedure that you will employ tonight." Picking up a plywood sheet no more than twelve inches square, Warden Moore continued. "This is a mockup of the power switch controlling the router to the hypodermics. You will notice that there is one lever. When the signal is given, you will immediately push the lever from its lower position to the highest position. That will activate the router that will initiate the first plunger. The rest is automatic. Do you understand?"

"Yes. But Warden, let me ask you a question. Have you ever had anyone assigned as an executioner to 'chicken out' at the last minute?"

"No, we've never had that happen. Why? Are you having second thoughts?"

"Yes and no," Bradley responded.

"I don't understand. Usually when someone applies to do this job, they are strong supporters of the death penalty and feel that capital punishment is in the best interests of the public. Why would you be having a problem at this late date?"

"The man you are asking me to execute is my best friend," Bradley stammered slightly.

"Your relationship with him makes no difference with respect to the law. And if you refuse to carry out the sentence, then you will have introduced a new problem. State law requires that a civilian, not a member of the prison staff or the warden, do it. So, you see, it's vital to the process that you understand the importance of your role and the legal implications of refusing at this point."

"OK," said Bradley. "I don't want to be the source of a problem that would forever emblazon my name on the pages of history as the only executioner who refused to do his job."

There was now no turning back.

"In a few minutes, you will be fitted with a black hood over your face and led to the control room. The hood has eye openings so that you can observe my signal. You will stand in front of the control and await my signal. No prison personnel, witnesses, or the condemned will see you. There is a bank of telephones at the rear of the chamber. I will be standing at the green phone with a direct line to the governor's office. When I get the 'go-ahead' to proceed, I will simply nod to you to throw the switch. You will then do so as quickly as possible. Do you understand?"

"Yes. But will I have to do it more than once?"

"No, but if I do get a message from the governor, I will raise my hand and drop it quickly as a signal to you to lower the lever to its original position, stopping the execution. So once you have pushed the lever up, be sure to keep your eyes on me in case I hear from the governor."

"I just want to get it over," Bradley said.

"It all will be over before you know it, and you can be on your way home."

The warden withdrew from a wooden case a black hood. Made like a baseball cap, a piece of black denim had been sewn into the underside of the bill of the cap. Two holes were cut for eyes. The cap was adjustable by two plastic flaps in the back.

"Put this on," Warden Moore ordered. Bradley complied.

"Now, let me escort you to the place where you will stand during the procedure."

Together, they walked toward the area behind the ten-inch by forty-eight inch slit in the wall. Bradley now stood directly in front of the control panel. He could see the entire execution chamber from his vantage point. The gurney with its seven leather straps was positioned under surgical lights in the center of the room. It was in full view.

*　*　*　*　*　*

The death watch team, now led by Warden Moore, solemnly but almost ceremoniously stepped the fifteen feet to the death watch cell. Jeff Mitchell still sat in the recliner. The team entered the cell. "It's time," Warden Moore said. Mitchell arose.

As had been practiced, two officers flanked Mitchell, holding him under his arms; the warden led the way, followed by two other members of the team; the last two officers followed behind Mitchell and his escorts. Slowly they walked toward the death chamber.

As they opened the door, Mitchell entered a small area where several prison officials waited. To his right behind a one-way glass, an anonymous figure, whom he could not see, stood with a hood over his face. Mitchell assumed that the executioner was behind that glass. A dark plastic curtain was drawn aside, and Mitchell was startled by the bright light. For some reason he had thought that death would come in a dark corner somewhere deep in the bowels of the prison.

The room was sterile white. Curtains were drawn across the witness windows, obscuring their view until the inmate was securely in place. To the rear of the chamber three phones stood out starkly against the white wall. The green phone, now being held to his ear by the Deputy Warden, was a direct open line to the governor's office. The black and ivory phones were backups in case the green phone failed.

The death watch team went about its duties quietly. No one spoke. They performed their morbid duties exactly as practiced. The only sounds to be heard were those of Mitchell being secured to the gurney and the technician attaching the two intravenous cannulas. Warden Moore took the phone from the Deputy Warden and waited.

As had been practiced, a team member quickly and efficiently attached the straps across the chest of Jeff Mitchell. "Is that too tight?" the team member asked politely.

"No, it's fine," Mitchell replied.

Straps were also secured over each arm just below the elbow; three slightly heavier straps were fastened across his upper and middle chest and lower abdomen. His feet were secured by straps at mid-calf.

After all the leather straps were in place and the intravenous cannulas inserted, the members of the team stepped back from the gurney and took their assigned places along the walls of the death chamber. Warden Moore stood with the green phone to his ear. "Are there any stays, orders, or any other reasons why this execution should not be carried out?" Moore waited for the answer. "Very well."

*   *   *   *   *   *

Bradley had stood for nearly fifteen minutes at the control panel. His only wish was for all this to be over. He had made a gigantic mistake in ever wanting to be a part of this. He could not look at Jeff. He only looked past Mitchell toward the warden.

*   *   *   *   *   *

Warden Moore gave the phone once more to the Deputy Warden. Moore walked to the opposite side of the room, signaled for the curtain covering the witness viewing windows to be pulled aside, detached a microphone from its mounting, and began to speak. "Jeffrey Mitchell, I now must read the orders which are mine to carry out this night." Moore hesitated. State killing was never pleasant, and he disliked it more and more each time he had to do it. Fortunately, mandatory retirement age approached for Moore. Maybe this would be his last.

"Death Warrant, State of Florida," Moore began, reading from the warrant.

"Whereas, Jeffrey Mitchell, did murder Lillian McRae Reins; and

Whereas Jeffrey Mitchell was found guilty of murder in the first degree and was sentenced to death; and

Whereas, the Florida Supreme Court upheld the sentence of death imposed upon Jeffrey Mitchell; and

Whereas, it has been determined that Executive Clemency, as authorized by Article IV, section 8(a), of the Florida Constitution is not appropriate; and

341

Whereas, attached hereto is a certified copy of the record pursuant to Section 922.09, Florida Statutes;

Now, therefore, I, Governor of the State of Florida and pursuant to the authority and responsibility vested by the Constitution and Laws of Florida, do hereby issue this warrant directing the Warden of the Florida State Prison to cause the sentence of death to be executed upon Jeffrey Mitchell. Such shall be carried out during the week beginning at midnight on the 28th day of September, and ending at midnight on the 29th day of September, in accordance with the provisions of the laws of this State of Florida.

"It is signed by the governor and the secretary of state."

Warden Moore stood a moment staring at Mitchell. "Do you have anything you would like to say before the state carries out this sentence?"

"Yes." Mitchell saw the witnesses through the glass partition. Briefly, he paused, silently counting them.

Twenty of them, he counted, his mind momentarily escaping the macabre surroundings.

"I know every person who is in prison claims to be innocent. I just want my family and the citizens of the State of Florida to know that I AM innocent." He emphasized the "am."

"You may put me to death, but by doing so, a stone in the wall of justice has been removed. Remove enough stones, and the wall of justice will crumble. I am not guilty of this crime. I only wish it could be proven. Maybe one day the truth will be known. I forgive you for what you are about to do."

Mitchell slowly closed his eyes as if in prayer. Simultaneously, Warden Moore moved to the green phone once more. The hour had come; all was ready; the execution would proceed.

CHAPTER 41

The eyes of the executioner and the warden met. Warden Moore gave the nod, and Bradley pushed the lever to its highest point as he had been instructed. At the same time Warden Moore hung up the receiver on the green wall phone.

*   *   *   *   *   *

No loud noise emanated from the router, only a low hum indicating that the first chemical, sodium thiopental was flowing. The purpose of this chemical was to render the condemned unconscious. Once the plunger was exhausted, a pause occurred, giving the sodium thiopental a chance to work before introducing the next chemical.

Just as the plunger began to deliver the second chemical, pancuronium, the green phone rang. Warden Moore picked it up immediately.

In response to the voice at the other end, he said, "Yes, sir." And raised his arm and brought it down immediately. Seeing the signal Bradley quickly pulled the lever to the lowest setting.

"Warden Moore, please stop the execution," shouted the governor. "Stop it now. Do not proceed. Do you understand? Check the inmate and tell me his condition."

Moore accompanied the attending physician to the gurney. Mitchell was unconscious. The doctor checked his pulse, heart rate and breathing and discovered Mitchell to be remarkably and incredibly normal except for his unconscious state, meaning that only a very small dose, if any, of the pancuronium had actually entered his system.

Turning to Moore, the physician said, "He appears to be all right. He remains unconscious and will remain so for another two hours. By that time he should be awake, alert, and communicating."

Moore turned again to the phone and advised the governor of Mitchell's condition. "Good. Please remove the inmate from the death chamber and take him to the medical wing until he is fully conscious. Representatives from the local Sheriff's Department and attorneys from the CCR should be arriving momentarily. They will explain why they are there. If any questions arise, please call me. I plan to be in the office for another hour or so."

Mitchell was quickly released from the straps that restrained him and was rolled, on the gurney, to the medical wing where he was secluded from other inmates.

As Warden Moore hung up the telephone, the door to the death chamber opened. Three tall, muscular, local Sheriff's deputies accompanied by two young men dressed in blue pinstriped suits entered the outer room to the death chamber. "Warden Moore?" asked one of the deputies.

"Yes. I am Moore."

"Could you tell us where we would find Mr. Mark Bradley?"

Careful to maintain his anonymity, Bradley had remained firmly in place throughout the duration of the now halted execution. Hearing his name, he turned swiftly, feeling the urge to run. But his feet felt like they were being held to the floor with lead weights. The black denim hood still hid his features.

"That is Mr. Bradley there. But no one is supposed to know who he is," Moore said. "You can't just intrude in here and interrupt an execution procedure."

Two of the deputies took Bradley by the arms. "Mr. Moore, we have a warrant for his arrest, and we are serving that warrant right now."

Moore's face mirrored his utter surprise.

Blake Evans reached toward Bradley and jerked the hood from his head, revealing a man completely astonished by what was happening. "What's this all about?" Bradley asked. "I was assured that no one would know who I am. Let go of me."

Evans said to the deputies, "Let me tell him." Then turning toward Bradley, he said, "You are being arrested for the murder of Lillian Reins. You claimed to be Jeff Mitchell's best friend. How

344

dare you! Willing to throw the switch on your best friend to cover for a crime that you committed is not only reprehensible, it is barbaric and diabolical. Maybe one day you will return to this place, not as the executioner but the executed. Then you will get what you justly deserve."

Warden Moore was numb. He could not believe what he was hearing or what was happening.

*　*　*　*　*　*

As the deputies escorted Bradley to the car, Warden Moore returned to his office, accompanied by the Deputy Warden and Blake Evans. "I need a cup of coffee or something. I'm not sure what just happened."

Evans spoke, "I have only a minute. I want to get to Jeff and tell him the good news."

"You have plenty of time. He still has almost forty-five minutes before he will be fully conscious," Moore advised Blake Evans. "How about taking this time to tell me the story."

"We found conclusive evidence that clearly linked Bradley to the murder. It has taken us so long to get the evidence verified, and with time against us, we cut it awfully close."

"But we had him all but dead," said Moore.

"Good timing, I guess," said Evans.

Moore's faced flushed. "Nothing would have haunted me more than to have put the wrong man to death. At least now, justice can be done."

*　*　*　*　*　*

It had now been an hour and forty-five minutes since Mitchell was removed from the death chamber. As Blake Evans explained some of the circumstances, the warden's phone rang. It was the medical facility reporting tat Mitchell had awakened.

Blake Evans was escorted to the medical wing where Mitchell was being held for observation. "Mr. Evans, what is going on?"

345

"I've got good news for you, Jeff. By this time next week, we expect to have you released and the real murderer indicted. You will be released in a few days.

"We have found evidence that connects Mark Bradley to the crime. After Fred left you, he drove to Tallahassee where he is waiting for Blayne Simmons. Fred had returned that far after visiting with you earlier today when they notified him by cell phone. As soon as Blayne arrives, they will be on their way to the prison. It will probably be midday tomorrow before they can get in to see you. They will tell you what we know. In the meantime, you will be returned to death row and retained there until your release."

"I'm just relieved it's over," Mitchell said.

"Well, the CCR did its part but you can really thank Roush and his investigator friend for believing in you and persisting in this case. They are the reason you're not dead right now."

*   *   *   *   *   *

At 12:30 the next day, a smiling Jeff Mitchell, Fred Roush, Blayne Simmons and Blake Evans joined Mitchell's family around a conference table at Florida State Prison. The kitchen staff had prepared a special meal for the group. The air seemed light and the atmosphere was saturated with joy.

After giving thanks for the food, Jeff Mitchell said, "I can't wait any longer. Please tell me what happened."

Roush started by explaining how Bruce Hopper had been enlisted to investigate the crime. "He discovered the brooch on a lost copy of the inventory list. When the existence of the brooch was known, Bruce spent time researching possible sources of the brooch. It had come from an estate sale and had been purchased with a credit card. Tracking a copy of the credit card receipt pointed to the real killer.

"Bruce also searched Lillian's wrecked car and found a fiber imbedded in the carpeted flooring. Analysis showed that the fiber was part of a rare carpet that was produced by Morgan Philips

Carpet Mills only during one specific two-month period. Bruce simply traced it to the local distributor who had sold only one lot of it. That lot happened to go to Mark Bradley when he built his new home."

Mitchell rubbed his hands together and said, "I like this man already. But there had to be more."

"There was. Bruce learned from the medical examiner that Lillian's body had been processed during autopsy, but scrapings from her fingernails had not been collected. The body had been moved to the funeral home before the nails could be processed. As a result, we were able to get her body exhumed and the scrapings collected."

Mitchell's smile broadened. "I knew there had to be something serious enough to point to the real killer."

"The scrapings contained minute skin fragments traced to Bradley through DNA. She put up a fight, but to no avail."

"With all this indisputable physical evidence, getting a search warrant for his house was easy. That search turned up a pair of Rockport boots exactly like those you own. Roush was beaming from pride over a job well done.

"Hopper worked long hours, sweating gallons at the murder scene. Surprisingly, he discovered a jump suit that Bradley wore at the time of the murder. It had been buried almost two feet deep in a sandy area near the creek bed. Only until the dry season was he able to locate it. The heavy rains over the five-year period washed the soil and ultimately a portion of the garment was sticking out of the dirt. Although somewhat deteriorated, it revealed bloodstains which, through primary testing indicated the presence of blood of the type belonging to Lillian Reins. Subsequent DNA tests will confirm with finality. The clincher was that Bradley had a habit of putting his initials on tags inside his clothing. The jumpsuit had his initials on it."

" But did you ever find the murder weapon?" Mitchell asked.

"Yes, but only by chance," said Roush. "Bradley's wife confirmed that she was with him in an army-navy surplus store one day when he purchased a knife. It actually had a trace of Lillian's blood underneath the pressed leather that covered the metal handle."

"This is nothing less than phenomenal," said Mitchell. "But tell me about the sweater evidence."

Roush smiled. "Because his company had a contract with an agency of the federal government, he and all his employees were required to submit fingerprints and DNA. Once he had been identified potentially as the killer, his corporate DNA profile was sent to be matched with the unknown sample of epithelials on the sweater. And they matched."

Curious, Mitchell asked, "But what could possibly have been his motive?"

Roush answered, "Under questioning last night, he said he was having a torrid affair with another employee at Goodall and Dohr. Lillian knew about it, although apparently no one else did. Lillian threatened to expose him both to Mr. Goodall as well as his wife, Renee, if he didn't cut off the relationship. You see, he had tried to have an affair with Lillian a couple of years before. She had refused him, and he never got over the anger."

"But kill somebody? That's pretty drastic," Mitchell said.

"Yeah, it is," Roush admitted, "but he realized that he would lose his job, his reputation, his family, and his style of living. He enjoyed the high life; to lose that would have been devastating. His cocky attitude led to him actually believing that he could get away with what he did."

"How did the brooch get into the mix?" Mitchell asked.

He had been patient long enough. It was his turn to talk; Simmons quickly jumped into the conversation. "Let me take that one. Last night, he told a detective that he approached Lillian when she returned to her apartment the night of your date and tried to talk her out of telling anyone about the affair. She refused.

His next step was to offer her the brooch as a gift for keeping quiet. She refused again. In his mind he had no alternative but to get rid of the only person who could interfere so harshly with his life."

"How did you know where to find Bradley?"

"His wife, Renee," answered Simmons. "She discovered the memorandum ordering him to go to the prison to perform the execution. Had she not found the memo, we would never have found him, and likely not have stopped the execution from happening."

"But there's more good news, Jeff," Simmons added. "Before we came to the prison today, we got word from the local Sheriff that, within two hours after his arrest, Bradley had confessed to the crime. Seems like it had been preying on his mind for some time, just not preying enough to admit it to authorities and save his 'best friend' from execution."

"How can I ever thank all of you?" Mitchell said. "You didn't give up on me; you believed me. For almost seven long years, you believed in me. For that I am grateful. I guess I'm the only man to come so close to being executed by the state."

They all laughed. Mitchell's descent into hell was finally over.

EPILOGUE

The search warrant that was executed on the home of Mark Bradley subsequently turned up the magazine from which he had cut the letters for the threatening note sent to Fred Roush. The microscopic examination of his boots revealed numerous minute pits caused by rocks and large grains of sand that remained embedded in the sole of the boots. The dried soil along the outer edges of them matched soil taken from the murder scene.

The fear of losing his job, perks, and his family drove him to commit the one act that was not of his nature. As he would have expected had his affair become known, his wife divorced him soon after his arrest, taking his children to an undisclosed location out west. He is now serving a life term without parole in the Florida State Prison. He has not seen nor heard from his ex-wife or children since his imprisonment.

Jeff Mitchell suffered no long-term effects from the execution. Within a few days, he had returned to normal health.

Just as Mr. Tutt promised at trial, Jeff Mitchell returned to his job at Andrews, Eisen & Tutt. After three years, he was made a full partner. He later married; he and his wife have three children. He hopes one day to write a book about his experience.

Fred and Robyn Roush continue to live in Pensacola. The proud parents of four girls, they spend their weekends at the retreat formerly owned by Henry and Rosa Bosarge. It was purchased from the Bosarge estate when Henry and Rosa were tragically killed in an automobile accident on Interstate 65 not far from Tea Garden Lake.

Robyn no longer works for the FDLE; she prefers being a full-time mom. Fred's law practice has exploded with success since the closing of the Mitchell case. While he still practices civil law primarily, he maintains a strong staff of criminal lawyers, a promise he made to Jeff after his release from prison. Today, the single largest damage award in the history of the State of Florida continues to belong to Fred Roush, an $85 million award in a negligence case against a shipping company.

Blayne Simmons no longer works with Roush in the law practice. Simmons achieved his lifelong goal of becoming a judge. Within two years after Mitchell's release, he sought election for and won a seat as a Circuit Court Judge in Escambia County, Florida. He was later appointed by the President as a Federal District Court Judge for the U. S. Fifth Judicial Circuit. He has since married; he and his wife, Amelia, have fraternal triplets.

Repulsed by the way she looked, Sharon Farrell finally decided to do something about her appearance. She contacted a physician, who prescribed a rigorous diet and exercise program. She lost more than sixty pounds. After several cosmetic procedures, she traveled to New York to try the modeling game. She is currently svelte and attractive and works as a Markham model, traveling throughout the world as the spokesperson for a major cosmetic firm. Her runway experience so enthralled one fashion designer that he signed her to an exclusive contract. She remains single but hopes to adopt a child in the near future.

Pete Pettis, the golden-haired State Attorney lost his bid for re-election after the Mitchell debacle was made public. Preferring not to go back to the active practice of law, he retired to a horse farm in Virginia where he now resides with his wife.

Samantha Kralick and Kemper Nixon continue to serve as Assistant State Attorneys in the office in Escambia County. Since the Mitchell trial, both have been successful in prosecuting some high profile cases, several of whose rulings continue today as active case law.

Undaunted by the notoriety of the Mitchell case, Judge Paul Reid remained as a Circuit Court Judge in Escambia County. He continues on the bench and now serves as the senior judge for the circuit.

As soon as Mark Bradley confessed to the crime of murdering Lillian Reins, Antoine Boudreaux's world crumbled. So convinced of Mitchell's guilt, Boudreaux experienced a mental breakdown and was forced to take a leave of absence from the Sheriff's Department and spend several months in a mental health facility. Upon his release, he rejoined his wife, Maggie, who worked for more than eighteen months to nurse him back to health. He never seemed to recover fully.

On the second anniversary of Mitchell's "execution," Maggie left him for no more than an hour to drive to the market. Upon her return, she found him lying on the sofa in the den of their home with a self-inflicted gunshot wound to the head. He had died instantly. While all the others involved in this tragic incident resumed relatively normal lives, ironically, Boudreaux became its victim. So devastated by the turn of events, he could no longer face his colleagues, Sheriff Williams, or even his family. Suicide seemed to be his only option. He chose to take his own life rather than face what he feared most—the dishonor of being wrong.

Thank you for reading this book. I hope you enjoyed it. Please offer feedback at jrodneytaylor.com.

Rodney Taylor

Made in the USA
Columbia, SC
03 September 2023

22432458R00198